T0398895

THE GOLDEN BOY'S GUIDE TO BIPOLAR

THE GOLDEN BOY'S GUIDE TO BIPOLAR

SONORA REYES

HARPER

An Imprint of HarperCollins*Publishers*

HarperCollins Children's Books,
a division of HarperCollins Publishers,
195 Broadway, New York, NY 10007

HarperCollins Publishers, Macken House,
39/40 Mayor Street Upper,
Dublin 1, D01 C9W8, Ireland

Library of Congress Control Number: 2025940655

ISBN 978-0-06-335840-9
Typography by Jessie Gang

25 26 27 28 29 LBC 5 4 3 2 1
FIRST EDITION

For the ones who have to hide,
I see you. I love you. You are not alone.

AUTHOR'S NOTE

Please be aware that the chapter titles in this book are intended as a representation of the specific way mental illness manifests itself in Cesar's personal experience. These stages in Cesar's mental health journey are meant to be read as one way that mental illness and recovery can look, not as universal stages of bipolar disorder for everyone who has it.

Cesar is an unreliable narrator who has a very complicated relationship with both his spirituality and the mental healthcare system. His opinions about medication, therapy, and religion are not meant to be read as healthy, and I hope that the journey and growth he goes through by the end of the book will illustrate that.

That said, I did my best to write this book with the utmost care and sensitivity toward anyone who may relate to the struggle of having severe and/or heavily stigmatized mental illness, including myself.

1

WHEN HE'S A TEN BUT YOU ALREADY DUMPED HIM

lack of foresight

I watch the air leave Jamal's mouth when he lets out a nervous breath—but no, it's not because I was staring at his lips. It has nothing to do with the fact that it's New Year's Eve, and in less than an hour everyone inside will be paired up sharing their midnight kisses. The thought of using the new year as an excuse to kiss my ex-boyfriend/current best friend has absolutely not crossed my mind, and I'm definitely not thinking about it right now.

"Are you sure this is a good idea?" he asks as he crosses his arms and rubs his biceps. I can't tell if he's doing that out of nerves or because he insisted I wear his jacket while we're standing on the curb outside the party.

"It'll be fun," I reassure him. "Besides, I already paid for it; I'm not going back now."

Jamal turns his head when he spots our hookup coming around the corner.

"You have a leaf," I say as I reach out to pluck it from the ripples of his dark hair, careful not to mess up the waves he's been training recently.

"Thanks," he says with an almost-shy smile. That's when I realize I leaned in a little too close to get the leaf, and he didn't back away.

Before I can read too much into it, though, the black Dodge Challenger with tinted windows makes its way to the curb we're waiting at. The window rolls down, and my friend Hunter nods at us from the driver's seat. He was one of my best friends last year, before he graduated. Now that he's in college and free from Catholic school, he's able to get his hands on the kind of stuff us mere minors would have to practically sell our kidneys for.

"You're late," I say as I step closer and lean forward, resting my forearms in the window.

"Well, yeah, this shit wasn't easy to get. I had to go all the way across town!"

Jamal steps up next to me, looking guilty. "Shit, sorry you went out of your way. Do you want to join the party?"

Hunter grins. "Hell yeah. I didn't go out of my way for nothing. No way I'm letting you guys try this shit without me."

"Cesar, what the fuck!" I jump as the gate leading to the backyard slams and a voice shouts from a few paces behind me.

I whirl around to see my sister, Yami, marching angrily over to us. I hadn't heard her open the gate, but it seems like she just overheard some of our conversation with Hunter.

"You better not be in the middle of a fucking drug deal right now. How am I supposed to cover for you if you don't even try to hide your own tracks? Mom and Bo's parents are literally right inside!" Yami yells as she pulls me away from the window and then throws her arms up in exasperation when she sees Hunter inside the car. "You couldn't have pulled up like a block away from Bo's *house*? Our parents are in there!"

I burst out laughing at Hunter's deer-in-headlights look as he stumbles over a frantic denial.

"What? I'm not . . . It's—it's not like that!"

I'm laughing too hard to offer an explanation, so Jamal chimes in. "We bought fireworks for New Year's. It was supposed to be a surprise. Still potentially dangerous, but nothing illegal."

I almost want to be annoyed at Yami for being so overbearing about literally everything I do. Still, the reminder that she has my back if I ever get in trouble is kind of nice.

Just then the front door to Bo's house opens, and Bo walks over to us, followed by our friends David and Amber, who were also invited to Bo's family New Year's Eve party. Hunter parks the car on the curb, and after we explain the situation to everyone, Yami laughs it off and agrees to have some fun with fireworks.

Hunter and David jump at the chance to unpack the fireworks, but Jamal stops them. "Wait, wait! We have to read the instructions!"

"Eh, I feel like fireworks are pretty intuitive," Amber says, without looking away from David's thick black hair as she tries to pull it up into a tiny pigtail. He's been growing it out just enough for it to feel like a rebellion from our Catholic school dress code, but not enough to actually get a violation.

"I respect you for being able to access the intuitive part of your brain, but I'd rather rely on clear instructions than a gut feeling of how not to blow my hands off."

Maybe I'm too protective, but I do a quick scan of the group's reaction. Jamal might have come off a little sarcastic, which doesn't always land well if you're not close enough to the group. Hunter, Bo, Amber, and David met Jamal at Slayton's anti-prom last year, but they probably don't know him well enough to know he's not making a jab at them. Jamal's body language, tone, and general personality all prove to me that he's genuinely trying not to offend anyone right now. Hence the whole I-respect-you thing. Luckily no one looks annoyed.

"I'm with Jamal," Yami says. She's the only other one here who knows Jamal pretty well, since he lived with us for a while after he got kicked out last year. "I'm *so* good at being intuitive. Like, my intuition is talking to me right now. It says we should read the instructions so no one gets blown up."

Yami, on the other hand, is definitely being snarky on purpose. She takes the box and starts reading the instructions out loud. Once she and Jamal are satisfied it's all safe, she holds the box up.

"Who wants to do the honors first?"

David eagerly volunteers, so Yami hands him the box. But before he's able to set off any fireworks, Bo looks worriedly at her phone.

"How long is this gonna take? We only have ten minutes until midnight." She squeezes my sister's hand, and Yami's eyes light up with something eager.

"Hey, Siri, what's my next alarm called?" Yami says with a flirty smile, not taking her eyes off Bo.

Siri responds from Yami's phone. "I found one alarm, 'New Year's kiss,' set for twelve o'clock a.m."

Bo's cheeks go red almost immediately. Considering how shy Yami was about Bo last year, she has clearly been working on her game.

"Aww, I'm getting a New Year's kiss too, right?" Amber looks to David, who pulls his phone out to set his own alarm.

"Of course, babe."

I turn to look at Jamal like muscle memory from when we were together, only to find he was already looking at me. Jamal isn't the type of guy to look away when he gets caught staring, though, so he holds my gaze earnestly. I glance down at his lips and wonder if maybe I should set an alarm of my own. What better time than the new year for a fresh start?

Before either of us can say anything, though, David effortlessly sets off the first firework without warning. Bo lets out a startled scream and hides behind Yami when it goes off. I watch it shoot high into the air before lighting up yellow sparks in the sky.

From the corner of my eye, I can see Yami and Bo holding hands, and David and Amber holding each other. The warmth from Jamal's hand being so close to my own but not quite touching makes my fingers twitch in anticipation. He must notice, because I suddenly feel his gaze on me once again.

His fingers twitch too, and for a tiny fraction of a millisecond, the tips of our fingers make contact. If anyone saw, they'd probably be able to write it off as a firework-induced flinch, but I know better.

Bo and Yami are next to set off a firework. They do it together, since Bo seemed so skittish the first time. Yami pretends to be brave, but the slight tremble in her hands as she holds the firework tells me it's all an act to impress Bo. As if Bo wasn't already completely head over ass cheeks.

As soon as the firework shoots up, Yami's tough-guy look

disappears as she and Bo both hold each other, screaming and laughing.

I watch as the sky crackles again, like really pretty popcorn in an invisible microwave in the sky.

"Question," Jamal says, quiet enough for only me to hear under the sound of exploding lights. He's been prefacing his questions this way ever since his cousin told him his tone doesn't always translate, which I guess makes him sound sarcastic when he's not trying to be. He used to just blurt out questions at random times—anything from a "would you rather" to a deep investigation into your soul. Having the preface of "question" usually does nothing to prepare me for whatever might come out of his mouth next.

"Go ahead," I say, once I realize he's still waiting for me to give him permission.

"What are you thinking?" he asks—one of his go-tos.

"Skycrowave," I blurt out and immediately regret it. A question like "What are you thinking?" while we're watching fireworks and our fingers are almost touching should have been my golden opportunity. The amount of smooth or flirty things you can say to that question are basically infinite. But apparently all the brain cells that got me a photographic memory and a 5.0 GPA don't mean shit when a hot guy's involved. Put Jamal in front of me, and all those brain cells work on overdrive, sifting through all my knowledge and memory files to find the perfect answer, and somehow the best I can come up with is *skycrowave*.

"Skycrowave," he repeats, as if it's a math equation. He pauses for a minute before finally saying, "I understand," which makes me laugh.

"You understand skycrowave?"

"It's the sound, right? Like when you microwave popcorn. That's what this is." He gestures at the sparkling sky. "A sky microwave."

Okay, maybe he does understand. I really can't get enough of how sincere Jamal is about things most people (myself included) would just make a joke about.

Hunter goes to light his firework next, but he must not have been paying much attention when Yami was reading the instructions, because his firework shoots off prematurely, right in Jamal's direction!

Jamal freezes while everyone else runs for it. I must be going off pure adrenaline because I jump right into gear, yanking Jamal out of the way by his hand.

"Sorry, sorry, sorry!!" Hunter shouts as we scatter, screaming and darting in all directions away from the literal explosives headed toward us. Everyone else takes cover behind Bo's car, while I pull Jamal across the street to hide behind his truck.

The street doesn't stop igniting once we're safely crouched and huddled together for cover. I shut my eyes tight, as if not seeing the colorful explosions on the street will keep them from hitting us. It isn't until the metaphorical popcorn kernel-bursting slows down that I finally open my eyes and realize I never let go of Jamal's hand.

He meets my eyes without pulling away. His eyes flicker down to my lips for a moment, not bothering to hide where his gaze lingers before going back to meet mine.

No one can see us. We could kiss right now, and no one would have to know. . . .

The final popcorn kernel bursts, but I don't bother checking on the settling dust on the other side of the truck. The sounds of our panting breaths and beating hearts slow, fading into the background. Maybe I can't hear because of the fireworks having been so loud and so close, or maybe I'm just laser focused on *him*.

Without sound, the only proof that we're both still breathing is the condensed air coming from our mouths in puffs. His shirt slightly tightening and loosening with the rise and fall of his chest. The movement of his shoulder pressing softly against mine.

Then the silence ends as two separate phone alarms go off at the same time, and we're making out before anyone can shut off the sound again.

2

WHEN YOU'RE READY TO GET BACK TOGETHER BUT YOU'RE NOT READY TO GET BACK TOGETHER

trouble making decisions

Yami stays the night at Bo's house, and instead of going home with my mom, I let Jamal give me a ride. If he was anyone else, I'd assume he was offering to take me home as an excuse to hook up within the privacy of his truck. Unfortunately, this is Jamal we're talking about. Which means he wants to talk.

It's one thing to make out at the designated kissing time when everyone else (but Hunter) is also doing it, but it's a wholly different thing to be alone together afterward and *talk* about it. Despite all odds, though, I get in the truck. I'm giving Spartan levels of courage right now. I'm braver than any U.S. Marine. Chuck Norris has nothing on me.

But being brave doesn't make me smart. It doesn't mean I have a single idea about what to say. So the first few minutes of the drive go by wordlessly except for his favorite poet, Saul Williams, playing from the old truck's CD player. Jamal waits for the track to end before stopping the next one from playing. There's a moment of silence before he says anything.

"I still love you," he admits.

"I love you, too." I surprise myself at how quickly I say it back. Like all I needed was to know it wasn't just me, that it wasn't just in my head.

He smiles but doesn't take his eyes off the road. He's a responsible driver like that, even if it's inconvenient for me not to be able to search his eyes for a hint of what he might say next.

"Question," he says, and for once I'm almost certain I know exactly what he'll ask.

"Hmm," I mumble in response, trying to give him the go ahead to ask without sounding too anxious.

"Do you want to get back together?"

Somehow, even though I knew the question was coming, I don't have an answer. I haven't exactly been mentally "well" since last year, and there is one consistent theme of relationship advice every mentally ill person inevitably gets. It's either "You can't love someone else without loving yourself first," or even worse, "You can't expect anyone else to love you if you don't love yourself."

And while I feel like I'm doing better at the moment, I can't lie and say I feel any kind of *love* toward myself. Does that mean I shouldn't be in a relationship? Pretty sure I'll die alone if loving myself is the prerequisite.

"Didn't it kind of suck though?" I find myself asking.

"Not at all." Jamal looks almost hurt. "Did it suck for you?"

"No, I just mean . . . like, you know how my brain is all . . . ?" I do some weird hand gestures around my head to avoid calling myself crazy. "Like, you could never love me into fixing my brain, you know?"

He's quiet for a second as he thoughtfully pushes his glasses up his nose. "Is that why you think I want to be with you?"

I just shrug. The whole I-can-fix-him sentiment is pretty common with people who date people like me, isn't it?

"Well, I don't want to fix you. I mean, I do want you to feel better, but that's not the same thing. I'm a lot more selfish than you think. I *like* being around you. It makes *me* feel better."

I'm glad it's dark in the car so Jamal can't see my cheeks flush. Obviously, he makes me feel better, too. But when we were together before, it was a secret only Yami knew about. And keeping him a secret was like this weird mind game where I had to justify why it was a secret in my head. Like, if we were hiding, we must have been doing something wrong, right? I ended up feeling guilty for keeping the secret, so I told the school's priest about Jamal at confession and got my answer. Definitely a sin. And to get right with God, my penance was to break up with him.

And I did.

Breaking up with Jamal was the hardest thing I've ever done, and if it made God like me any more, I didn't get the memo. I ended up spiraling so hard I wound up in the mental hospital. I've been in therapy and on medication ever since, but honestly, I'm still playing whack-a-mole to keep all The Thoughts buried. The Catholic guilt, internalized prejudice, and mental illness shit keep popping their heads back up, but I'm getting better at whacking them right back down.

As if he's reading my mind, he goes on before I give my answer. "We wouldn't have to tell everyone if you're not ready for that. It can be just between us, for as long as you need . . . if you want to get back together, I mean."

Jamal's hand is resting on the console between us, and I reach for it on instinct. He doesn't take his eyes off the road but does let a little smile crack at the contact. I think on his words for a second, letting his hand in mine be my tether.

Do I want to be with Jamal again? Of course I do. But I don't know if I can be with him again if it's a secret from the rest of the world. Hiding our relationship before mixed all my feelings of shame into our dynamic, and I don't want to do that to him again.

Jamal lives with his cousin now, who knows he's gay. And my extremely traditional Catholic mom is all-in on being an ally now that she knows about both me being bi and Yami being lesbian. Even though I'm still technically in the closet, Bo, David, Amber, and Hunter know I'm bi since I impulsively came out to them at anti-prom last year, so I already know my friends are cool with it. Even if we didn't have to be out to *everyone*, it seems like everyone I actually care about is on board with me being bi now. We *could* tell them and at least be ourselves around some people if we wanted to.

"I don't know, maybe . . ." I trail off and start absent-mindedly tracing the lines on Jamal's palm while I stare out the window.

The only person I haven't heard from since they found out about me and Yami is my dad, but since he hasn't lived with us since I was, like, nine, it's easier to kind of push his existence to the background. Sure, I caved and sent him an email a few months ago, but he never responded, so I sort of just pretend that moment of weakness never happened.

Then there's Father John. It's not that he particularly cares about me or me him, but he's still the closest connection I have to God at the moment. I try to pray and all that, but I'm not one of those lucky people who hears God talking to them or anything. Since Father John is, I guess I do put some stock into what he says.

So, do I believe being with Jamal is sinful? Yeah. I do.

But do I care? Maybe not anymore.

If I don't sin, then Jesus died for nothing, right? Besides, I don't even go to the public high school my old homophobic bullies go to anymore. Though with Jamal still going to Rover, it's almost a shame I'm not there too.

I realize I've been leaving Jamal hanging for a while. He's used to me getting lost in my own head and he's always patient about it, but I do have to give him some kind of answer, even if it's an uncertain one.

"I have to think about it," I finally say. I'm used to acting on my impulses, but this is different. If I get back together with Jamal, I don't want to fuck things up again.

"Okay, that's fair," Jamal says as he pulls the truck into the driveway to my house. "Just let me know what you end up deciding."

"Okay." I want to lean forward and kiss him goodbye, but I hold myself back. That would imply yes, and I want to give myself enough time to be sure. "See you later," I say before hopping out of the truck and heading inside.

When I walk in, I'm not surprised to see my mom still up, cleaning the kitchen. Between her main job, cleaning, cooking, and her side business of making jewelry with Yami, that woman barely ever sleeps.

Ever since my dad got deported, she's been running everything on her own—at least, until Yami started helping with her jewelry business. It's been eight years with just the three of us, but my mom has probably aged a few decades in that time. Wrinkles crease around her mouth and eyes, and the color from her once-black hair has been slowly syphoning into the dark circles under her eyes for years.

Today, though, seems even worse than usual. Her eyes are puffy, and her nose is red. She must have thought I'd be staying the night with Jamal, because she's not wearing her I-was-just-crying sunglasses that she thinks keep me and Yami from being able to see her bloodshot puffy eyes.

"Everything okay, Mami?" I ask.

She smiles and ruffles my hair. "Don't you worry about me, mijo. You have enough going on in your own life."

"Not really," I reassure her, ignoring the hidden meaning behind her words. Ever since I went inpatient, it's like she thinks I'm made of glass and if she lets me carry the tiniest bit of weight from her shoulders, I'll shatter. "Whatever it is, I can handle it, I promise."

"My sweet boy." She puts a tender hand on my cheek and gives me a teary smile, like me asking her what's wrong is worthy of the Nobel Peace Prize or something. "I guess I've been a bit lonely lately. The party tonight was fun and everything, but I'm just too busy to make any time for friends or dating outside of holidays. Too much to do, and when it's done there's always more to do," she admits.

"Maybe I can help?" I offer, knowing I'll probably regret this in the future, but hey, it's the new year. Perfect time to start picking up some slack.

"No, no, no." She waves me off. "You can help by paying for my retirement when you're the next rich and famous inventor or scientist, or whatever brilliant thing you end up doing."

I sigh. "Who knows if I'll even be alive when you retire?" I blurt out, and her pained expression makes me immediately regret it. "I mean, like, anyone can die at any time. Why wait until later when I'm here now, and I can help *now*?"

She shakes her head. "You have school to focus on. I don't want you prioritizing me over your own success."

Sometimes I feel a little bad that she coddles me like this, when she's always been more than happy to accept help from my sister. But I guess I'm the one with "limitless potential" or whatever, according to her. "What about on the weekends? It doesn't take me a whole two days to do my homework. What if I just make dinner or something, like, once a week? You need a break. Like a regular, predictable break. I can start tomorrow for New Year's. It can be our resolution."

She smiles, eyes getting watery again. "I would love that."

"Mami, don't cry . . . ," I say, reaching out and wiping the tear that falls with my thumb.

"It's happy tears, mijo. Now go get some sleep, okay? School is starting again soon, and you need to get your sleep schedule back on track."

"Fine," I say, not bothering to argue that my sleep schedule has *never* been on track. She doesn't need to worry about me any more than she already does.

I pass through what Yami used to call the Hall of Shame on the way to my room. It's where Mami had so many crosses and pictures of Jesus and the Virgin Mary plastered up that you could barely see the paint on the wall. There are still Jesuses and Marys, but now some of the crosses are rainbow and there are Bible passages with uplifting quotes about loving everyone, etc., etc. My mom kind of went a little overboard when Yami and I came out to her last year.

When I get to my room, I pull out my secret poetry notebook that literally no one knows about. Not even Jamal, who does poetry slams and open mics every chance he gets. The thing is, I don't even know if I'm good at poetry. I might be absolute shit.

And that's the entire point.

I'm the family's golden boy. I've always gotten the best grades and picked things up easily and been really good at whatever new thing I tried. But when you're good at everything, that becomes the standard, and then I'm not allowed to just do something because I like it. When everyone is expecting to be impressed, I can't just be good, I have to be the best. And if no one knows I like poetry, then I'm allowed to suck at it. I'm allowed to just have something to myself that no one expects me to be good at. Someone else can be the best at poetry, I don't care.

So, instead of writing a super-deep epic or sonnet or spoken word piece that would make an audience cry, I turn to the Jamal section of my notebook (yes, I have sections, sue me) and write a haiku with a title longer than the poem itself.

A Non-Exhaustive Pros and Cons List of Getting Back Together with Jamal
Pros: I feel like I
Could live forever if he's
There—cons . . . TBD

3

WHEN YOU'RE INCREDIBLY LUCKY AND TALENTED AND SMART AND EVERYTHING ALWAYS GOES YOUR WAY

compartmentalization

I go to the kitchen to start cooking around five, since I want to make sure everything's ready and we're done eating by seven, which is the time Jamal always calls me. Even on weekdays, we're both usually done with all our homework by this time, and it's after dinner for me and before for him. He likes his schedules, so even though we never officially decided on this time, he's always been consistent with it.

Thinking about it now, that does feel like a very couple-y thing to do, even though we haven't been together since junior year. Maybe that'll change soon, though? Who knows.

Yami must hear me getting out the pan and ingredients because she's in the kitchen interrogating me before I can even turn on the comal.

"What are you doing?" she asks, as if me cooking is some miracle of modern science.

"I'm making dinner tonight. And every Sunday, starting now. It's my New Year's resolution, to give Mami a break," I say proudly.

"But you don't cook?" She raises a skeptical eyebrow.

"What are you talking about? I cook like a chef, I'm a five-star Michelin—"

"You can't have more than three Michelin stars," she says smart-assily. "And I don't think you can get a star with only one menu item. Do you know how to make anything besides guisado?" She crosses her arms, all judgy.

"Fuck you, it's a Stray Kids reference! And my guisado is fire, what do you want from me?" She hates when I copy her, so I purposely imitate her crossed arms.

"So, we're gonna eat guisado every Sunday for all time?"

I just shrug, and she pinches the bridge of her nose.

"Ay, ay, ay, let me help. I'll teach you how to make sopa de pan, it's Mami's favorite."

Normally, I'd be annoyed at Yami inserting herself into *my* act of service. But even if I'd never let her know it, cooking with her would be way more fun than doing it on my own. Besides, guisado will probably get old if it's all I ever make.

After a while of swallowing my pride and letting Yami be better than me at something, Mami follows the spreading smell into the kitchen and practically melts, putting a hand over her heart when she sees us working together.

"My kids feeding me, what a treat!" She starts trying to serve herself a bowl, but Yami slaps her hand away.

"Let us serve you, Mami," I say, and she holds her hands up in surrender, then goes to sit patiently at the table with a smile.

Yami ladles the soup into some bowls while I set the table. When I put the napkin and silverware in front of my mom, she beams.

"I'm so proud of you, mijo," she says softly. "You've come so far since last year."

I stiffen at the comment as it hits me why she's so emotional over me making dinner. Why she thinks I need to be coddled and sheltered and why I can basically do no wrong. But I quickly snap into whack-a-mole mode and shoot down all the budding thoughts jumping out at me from where I buried them last year.

My last episode—BAM.

The hospital stay—BAM.

My dad disowning us—BAM.

None of that shit can touch me now. In fact, I'm so unbothered that I scarf down my food and joke my way through dinner with Yami. So unbothered that when Jamal calls afterward, I don't even bring it up. We also don't talk about the lingering question of whether we're getting back together or not. I told him I'd think about it, so I know he's not gonna ask again so soon. Instead, he invites me to an open mic right by his house the Friday after next where he wants to share a new spoken word piece.

"I'm a little nervous," he admits, which isn't really like him. Not when it comes to his poetry.

"Why?"

"This one is . . . uh, well, it's gay."

It takes me a second to register what that means. "You're coming out? Like, publicly?"

"Yeah," he says, sounding more confident now. "But don't worry! The piece isn't about you or anything, I wouldn't do that to you."

I know he means he'd never out me in front of a crowd, but for half a second, I find myself getting a little pouty at not being the subject matter of his gay poem. It doesn't last, though, because I quickly realize I absolutely *don't* want Jamal to write and perform a poem about me in public.

"Thanks," I finally say. "So, are you ready for all that? What about school? Do Nick and all them still go there?" I can't help but worry about Jamal coming out.

When I went to Rover, Nick and a bunch of his little lackeys jumped me pretty much every chance they got. I'd written a note to Jamal back when we were dating, and Nick got ahold of it before I could give it to him. Luckily, he never found out who the note was for, but he still made me his friend group's punching bag until I transferred to Slayton.

"I'll be okay," Jamal says, still sounding cool and confident. "I doubt anyone from school will be at the open mic anyway. So, you want to come?"

"Obviously," I say with a smile.

"Thanks, Cesar. I really appreciate you." I can hear him smiling back, and it makes me blush. Jamal's never said he appreciates something I'm doing or offering. No, he appreciates *me*. I'll take this to my grave, but sometimes he just makes me want to kick my feet and giggle.

After we get off the phone, I lie in bed playing out scenarios in my head. This is usually what I have to do in order to fall asleep, though it's pretty hit-or-miss. Tonight's scenarios all involve Jamal. The first one is me telling him I'm ready to get back together. Who cares if I still don't know if I'm ready in real life? This is my pre-sleep fantasy, fuck off.

Eventually the scenarios go from us getting back together to making out to a full-on sex dream. I'm not really sure which part is my imagination or a real dream, but I must have fallen asleep at some point because by the time I open my eyes again, I've somehow missed my first alarm, and my second one is going off already.

7:00 a.m. take meds

I let out a tired whine as I roll over and force myself out of bed. It seems like even when I do manage to fall asleep at night, my body doesn't get the memo, and I'm still completely exhausted. I quickly throw on my school uniform and make a drive-by trip to the bathroom to swish some mouthwash since I'm too tired to brush my teeth properly.

I'm still swishing it around when I head to the kitchen, where my mom is waiting for me with a plate of fried egg on toast.

I know the deal: meds first, then breakfast. I spit the mouthwash in the sink, then reach for the pill counter and take out the pill for Monday. I make a show of rolling my eyes as I pop it in my mouth.

"Happy? Can I eat now?" I ask.

"Of course." Mami smiles as she hands me the plate, but her eyes look sad. I know I shouldn't give her attitude about taking my meds, but I can't help it. Maybe I just don't like being told what to do or something, but I was never a fan of all the surveillance that came after my inpatient stay. I feel like a fucking zoo animal, being monitored over everything. But since Mami getting sad feels worse than me getting smothered, I push the annoyance down and go along with it like I always do.

Even though I got ready pretty fast today, we still barely make it to school on time, thanks to Yami trying out a new eyeliner look while still insisting on absolute perfection. By the time we get to school, the first bell's already rung, and we have to book it to our classes.

I take my seat in astronomy just before the final bell rings. As soon as the music stops, Mr. Franco doesn't waste a second before getting started, talking in his usual drawn-out monotone that could put even the most caffeinated student to sleep.

"I hope you've all done your reading over the break, because we're having a pop quiz," he says as he picks up a stack of papers off his desk and starts handing them out. Groans echo throughout the room from practically everyone except Jeremy, who sits right in front of me.

"I'm all caught up." Jeremy turns around and smirks at me. "Are you?" he asks with an air of confidence. He's always seen me as his rival in this class, since I consistently set the curve, and he consistently gets the next-highest score.

"I skimmed it," I say honestly, and Jeremy's grin falters, which tells me he may not be as well versed in the material as he's trying to let on. If me just skimming it is enough to make him think I have a leg up, he's probably not much farther ahead than the rest of the class.

Which means I have to recalculate my usual percentage of test answers to purposely get wrong in order to still set the curve without making everyone else fail.

Mr. Franco is one of those teachers who prides himself on being a hard-ass and brags about how impossible his tests are and how many students fail his class. I always make sure to keep my score under a 72 percent, but even that score sets the curve every time, with Jeremy's being the next highest at usually around the high sixties.

When Mr. Franco sets the test down in front of me, I get to work. Setting the curve without screwing everyone else over too bad is an art form, and I've perfected it. Based on the intensity of the groans and Jeremy's feigned bravado, I should probably not score higher than a 65 percent on this one.

Part of me wonders if rigging everyone else's scores like this counts as cheating. Slayton is a zero-tolerance type of school, and people have gotten kicked out for less. If I got caught, I doubt I would get expelled in *this* case. How can it count if my "cheating" doesn't even benefit me? Deciding that I'm probably fine, I finish up the last quiz questions.

Once I'm done, I doodle for a while in the margins to keep from turning it in too early. I know some people get real anxious when other people start turning in their tests if they're not close to finishing yet. I wait until a few people turn theirs in before getting up and handing mine to Mr. Franco.

His eyes catch the doodles, and he gives me an amused smile. "You are something else," he says under his breath, and for a second, I can't tell if he's on to me or not.

After school, Yami and I get a ride home from Bo. She usually only gives us a ride on Wednesdays since our mom works late that day, but lately she's been offering all the time. We don't live anywhere near Slayton, but Bo will take any excuse to spend more time with Yami, which is a development Yami is absolutely thrilled about.

"Wanna hang out at a park or something?" Bo asks once we

start getting close to our side of town. I guess the forty-minute drive wasn't enough quality time.

Yami agrees right away. I kind of assume the invite is just for Yami and that I'll be getting dropped off before they go, but Bo tries coaxing me into it when I don't respond right away.

"We should invite Jamal too!" Bo offers when we start passing his neighborhood, which gives my heart a little tug. I know Bo is Yami's person, but having people in my life who want to be around Jamal makes me happy. I want my friends to like him, almost more than I want them to like me. Actually, definitely more.

"Sure," I say as I shoot Jamal a quick text inviting him.

We end up pulling into the park in Jamal's neighborhood so he can walk over. Just like the one on our block, this one is a little run-down. It's not so much a park as it is an open field with a couple of aluminum park tables at the edge of it and two makeshift soccer goals on either side. Still, we've been coming here since we were kids, so it has that nostalgia appeal. Growing up, this field was our Wembley Stadium, and the park tables were the stands holding the imaginary roaring crowd.

Now, though, it's not Jamal who walks through the field to meet us. I swallow the lump in my throat when I hear a familiar laugh coming from behind me. I turn my head to see Nick and a few of his friends gathering in the field before starting to kick a ball around. I forgot he moved into Jamal's neighborhood last year.

I quickly turn my head forward again so Nick can't see my face. He either doesn't realize I'm here, or they're all ignoring us, so I want to make that option easier for them. Yami sees me tense up and puts a hand on my shoulder.

"Should we leave?" she asks, and I shake my head.

"It's fine. I already told Jamal we were here." I don't mention I also really don't want to give Nick the satisfaction of thinking I'm running away from him. "Let's just talk about something else."

Bo quickly takes the hint. "I can't believe it's already January," she whines, slumping her head on Yami's shoulder.

"Ugh, I know. I still don't know what I'm doing for my senior project," Yami responds, fully committed to distracting me.

"Don't worry, me either. We still got time," I say, trying to sound reassuring, but she just looks even more exasperated.

"You're forgetting I'm the dumb one," Yami says humorlessly, and my chest tightens. Does she really think that? I know I should probably tell her it's not true, but since school is so much easier for me, she'd just think I'm lying.

"Don't say that, babe!" Bo frowns and takes Yami's hand, but Yami keeps going.

"It's true! *You* still have time, Cesar, because you're gonna come up with something brilliant at the last second without even trying, and you'll set the curve like you always do."

"Hey, it's not my fault my brain's so sexy!" I say with a shrug, hoping to lighten the mood. She shoves my shoulder with a laugh.

"You're right, I guess only one of us can be sexy on the out-side."

"Hey!" I shove her back. "Are you calling me ugly?"

"Aww, don't listen to her, Cesar, you're adorable!" Bo says through a laugh.

"Adorable, exactly! Just look at him!" Yami gestures toward me as she goes to pinch my cheek. "Ay, mira que cute!" she says like she's cooing over a baby.

I pretend to gag as I slap her fingers away from my cheek. I swear, I haven't gone a day without her holding the fact that she's a whole ten months older than me over my head.

Finally Jamal walks up and joins us at the table. I'm relieved we can change the subject now, but of course Yami won't miss an opportunity to embarrass me in front of literally anyone.

"I bet he agrees with me, don't you, Jamal?"

"About what?" he asks as he sits next to me, just close enough that it feels like we *should* be touching even though we're not.

"About Cesar being adorable," Bo answers, and Yami goes for my cheeks again, but I snap at her fingers with my teeth, and she pulls her hand back to her chest with a gasp.

Jamal grins. "I can't argue with that."

"That's three against one. Sorry, I don't make the rules," Yami says with a shrug.

I shake my head with a dramatic sigh. "When mere mortals gaze upon the face of an angel, of course they cannot grasp its true nature," I say, trying to sound biblical, which for some reason means I'm using a low voice and a British accent. Basically, I'm channeling Chris Hemsworth's Thor. "Clearly, you're all mistaking sexiness for cuteness."

Yami and Bo burst out laughing, and Jamal looks at me with a small smile. He doesn't break eye contact when he speaks, but his words are quiet enough that Yami and Bo don't seem to hear over their laughing.

"You can be both," he says, and suddenly he's the angel *my* mortal eyes can't bear to look at, so I look away, blushing.

I so badly want to say something back. To flirt with him or tell him he's gorgeous too. His question of whether I want to get back together comes to mind, and the answer is hard to ignore.

I definitely, definitely do.

Despite all the love-yourself-first advice out there, at least right now I don't hate myself more than I love Jamal. That's got to count for something, right?

Before I get a chance to say anything, something whacks the back of my head, hard. I spring to my feet and whirl around as Jamal catches the ball as it bounces from my head. I'm expecting a fight, but Nick and all of them are still on the field. Nick has a smirk on his face like he kicked the ball at me on purpose, but other than that, he doesn't make a move.

"Avery, go get it." He points in my direction. Avery, being Nick's right-hand henchman, obeys without question, jogging right over to us.

I don't know why I grab the ball out of Jamal's hand when Avery approaches. Maybe part of me craves confrontation, or maybe I just want to feel like I have any kind of power over the guys who used to beat the shit out of me.

"He did that on purpose, right?" I ask, and Avery sighs.

"I don't read minds." Avery holds his hand out for the ball, but I don't give it to him just yet.

"Ask nicely," I say, and Avery glances behind his shoulder like he's checking how close by his friends are. Sure, he could call them over if he wanted a fight, but they're far enough away that Avery probably wouldn't want to risk it.

Before I get a chance to milk it too much, Yami plucks the ball from my grip and throws it back to the field. Avery looks weirdly relieved as he runs back over to his friends.

"Do you have a death wish?" she asks me, but I just shrug.

"I don't get what the big deal is. . . . ," I mumble. It's not like Nick would have his friends jump me with Jamal and Yami and Bo right here. He's always been a coward; he only ever picked a fight when he had more than a two-person advantage. Usually when I was by myself.

I don't think I've been truly by myself since before I went inpatient, but I'm not sure if that's a good or a bad thing.

I know Yami was being sarcastic when she said I don't really have to try to do well in life or get what I want, but it's kind of true. It seems like no matter what I do, I have support from Yami, my mom, Jamal, all my friends, all *Yami's* friends . . . the list goes on, but I'm still not really sure how I got here.

Did I earn a single thing in my life? Do I even deserve any of it?

I grab a metaphorical shovel and smack the guilty feeling over the head, then bury it as deep as I can. Sometimes people are lucky, and it's a good thing. I'm lucky, and smart, and talented, and I can do anything I put my mind to. I deserve good things. I'm a good person.

I'm a good person.

I'm a good person.

Maybe if I repeat it enough, I'll actually believe it.

4

WHEN TALKING ABOUT YOUR FEELINGS GIVES YOU HIVES

emotional unavailability

On Tuesday, I barely have enough time to change real quick when I get home from school, grab some Takis for the road, and head to therapy. I'm about to go back out to the car with my mom when there's a knock at the door. Mami and I both ignore it, assuming Yami will answer since she's the only one not about to head out, but she takes one look through the peephole and rushes after me.

"Cesar! Make her go away," Yami whispers, about as loud as you can without it not being a whisper anymore.

I don't have to ask who's at the door. There's only one person who gets under Yami's skin enough to make her want to hide like that.

"I got you," I say as I go to answer the door, and sure enough, I was right.

"Hi," Bianca says shyly. She holds out a Tupperware box full of empanadas, but I don't take them from her.

"What are you doing here?" I ask, making sure to block the doorway so she can't see inside. Yami would not want to be perceived right now, at least not by her.

Bianca sighs. "My mom's making me go around the neighborhood giving these away. She made too many, I guess."

"Thanks, but we're good. I'm sure Doña Violeta would take some, though."

"Okay . . . ," she says, but doesn't move to leave. "So . . . is Yami home?"

"Nope. And I gotta go," I say as I reach to close the door, but she stops it from shutting with her foot.

"Look, I know Yami hates me now, but you don't have to pretend you do too. What happened is between me and her, okay?" She moves the empanadas so they're resting on one hip like a baby. "Don't you even want to know my side of the story?"

"Not really," I say, to keep from drawing out the conversation. "I'm staying out of it." I don't have to know Bianca's side of the story. All I know is that she and my sister used to be best friends, until she outed Yami when we both went to Rover sophomore year. They've hated each other ever since. That's enough story for me.

"Good," Bianca says with a little smile that I can't quite read. It could be genuine, but she could also be pulling some shit right now.

I smile back politely, then go to close the door. But she's talking again before it closes, so to keep from being a dick, I stop it from shutting.

"So, we're good?" she asks, still smiling.

"Uh, sure, whatever," I say, since I know any other answer would start shit, and I really do have to go.

"Okay, good, because I like you." She winks.

"'Kay, bye." I shut the door before she can get another word in. What the hell was that?

I'm not usually one to bring a list of talking points to my therapist, or even know what the hell I'll be talking about in any given session, but today is different. And not because I actually *want* to tell her about anything, but because I need an unbiased opinion here, and asking my mom or Yami would open me up to a swarm of questions that are either none of their business or that I don't even know the answer to myself.

I want to get back together with Jamal. But as much as I hate to admit it, I have some concerns. Which means I could actually use Dr. Lee's help right now. This is only our third session, so she doesn't really know that much about me yet. She's my sixth therapist in as many months, but my mom finally put her foot down and said she's not letting me switch again before giving Dr. Lee a real chance.

Dr. Lee is the first psychotherapist I've seen, though, which means she can therapize me *and* prescribe medication, so I let her go through the meds spiel before getting into the other stuff. She quickly asks if I've noticed any changes or side effects from my medication, and about my recent six-months-on-meds bloodwork I got to make sure the meds weren't giving me any health problems. All clear. Now on to the important shit.

I've learned from experience that a new therapist will ask all kinds of irrelevant questions trying to get to the bottom of things. So, in order to avoid wasting any time, I pull out the list I made on my phone's notes app and start reading immediately after sitting on the couch in her office.

"My mom probably already told you a bunch of shit, and I know you have all my records, so you don't have to pretend to be surprised that I'm bi or that I went inpatient last year or anything else you already know, okay?"

Instead of answering, she just nods and silently writes something down in her little notebook, waiting for me to go on.

"Okay, so here's what you need to know. . . ." I go on to info dump as quickly as I can from the list on my phone. About Jamal, and that we were secretly together for over a year before I broke up with him as part of my penance. About how we stayed friends ever since but ended up kissing the other night. About how we still love each other, but I didn't want to act impulsively like I usually do because I don't want to fuck things up. And about how I don't exactly love myself, and I'm worried that means I can't expect someone else to. Basically, I tell her everything I think might be relevant to the question I came here to ask her.

"So, with that context, do you think I'm ready to be in a relationship again?" I ask her as soon as I finish running through the list.

"Well, I think the fact that you're even asking me shows you're making progress." Dr. Lee's expressions are usually tiny, probably because she doesn't want me to know she has actual feelings or something, but I can still see her mouth's micro smile and happy brown eyes as she answers.

"Okay, but, like . . . what's the answer?" I say, trying not to gag at the unexpected compliment.

"Well, let's talk about it," she says, and I roll my eyes. That's exactly what I'm *trying* to do. "You mentioned not loving yourself as one of the reasons you're having doubts. Do you mind if we dive into that a bit?"

"Um, sure . . ."

"I want you to think about someone else in your life who you care about and love deeply. It doesn't have to be romantic love, just anyone in your life you have love for."

"Okay . . ." I find myself thinking of Yami.

"Now imagine that person is struggling with self-love the way you are. Do you think that would make this person unworthy of your love? Would it make you love them any less?"

"No," I admit, "but don't you think it'd make it easier on Jamal if I'm not . . . you know . . ." I trail off. I don't know how to end that sentence. Sick? Broken? Unlovable?

"No, I don't," she answers without me having to say it. "Working toward self-love is a great goal, but I don't think it's fair to say that those who aren't there yet don't deserve love in their lives."

"So, you're saying I'm ready?" I ask, letting myself feel a tiny bit hopeful.

"Well, I can see you're being careful not to be impulsive about this, which is good. Having healthy boundaries for yourself is a good step. But I'm afraid I can't speak to whether you're ready for a relationship or not. That's a decision only you can make."

I roll my eyes again. I don't ask therapists for advice very often, so she shouldn't take it for granted. But I guess she might not realize that yet, since we're still fresh. I remind myself I can't just ditch her for another therapist this time, so I resist the urge to fire back about how unhelpful that answer is. I let out a measured breath, and an equally measured response. "Then how am I supposed to figure that out?"

"Well, let's unpack that. You said you broke up before because of your penance from confession, correct? Do you still feel that same guilt or shame about your sexuality that led you to want to make amends for it?"

Well, fuck. I hoped to get through this conversation with minimal vulnerability. I hardly know Dr. Lee, so I wanted this to be as simple as me listing off all the relevant information and her diagnosing me with my current amount of relationship readiness.

I shift uncomfortably on the couch at the prospect of a feelings-heavy conversation. Talking about shame and guilt isn't exactly the most clinical topic, but if that's the information she needs for my relationship diagnosis, fine. But if she wants a tragic backstory or to see me cry, she's out of luck.

I don't know how to answer right away, so I grab one of the stress balls in the basket next to the couch and lie down. Something about being horizontal and tossing a ball in the air over and over again makes this whole thing feel more casual. Her question reminds me of a conversation I had with Yami when she visited me in the hospital last year. She asked me then if I was ashamed of her, or of Jamal, or of Bo. And since the answer was an easy no, she reminded me there's no reason to be ashamed of myself.

A fair argument, but it's never been that simple for me. It's hard to explain, but it's like there's this nagging voice in the back of my head that says it's different. That *I'm* different. That I'm special, and uniquely bad.

I told Father John about that guilty voice during the infamous confession, and he explained that it was probably God's way of reaching out to me, trying to save me from the devil's influence. I believed it then, but now I'm not so sure.

"I don't know," I say with another toss of the ball. "If I do, does that mean I shouldn't be with someone?"

"I don't think there's a black-and-white answer here. I suppose it depends on where those feelings are coming from and how you address them. Do your feelings of shame come from within, or is it other people and outside influences that say there's something wrong with you?"

Honestly, I expected her to just tell me I'm not ready if I can't get over that shame, so she gets an unexpected point on my imaginary how-much-I-like-this-therapist scoreboard. "Well, my dad isn't supportive. And I used to get bullied for it at my old school. So I guess some outside influences. And I'm Catholic, too, so there's that. Would religion be an outside or inside influence?"

"That's an interesting question. I'd say your spirituality is your own, but organized religion comes from other humans. So perhaps it's a bit of both."

"Okay, so two and a half points to outside influences, and half a point to myself," I say as I catch the ball in front of my face and toss it up again. People have always described my shame as being internalized, so I never really thought of it as coming from anything but me.

She starts jotting something else down while she answers. "And are those outside influences any threat to you? Is there any fear for your safety or well-being if you were to go against them?"

"I don't go to Rover anymore, and my dad lives in Mexico, so I'm not in any danger or anything, but . . ." I hesitate before tossing the ball again or saying the next thing. Going against God doesn't threaten my physical safety, at least not while I'm still alive. "I don't want to go to hell," I finally say.

Her eyebrows tilt upward just a tiny bit in another micro expression of what I assume is pity. "I want to give you full disclosure that I'm not a religious person, but for the sake of this exercise I'll speak as if your experience of Catholicism is the objective truth, all right? With that said, would you mind if we explore this a bit?"

"Okay . . ." I go back to tossing the ball. I'm not trying to have a religious argument during therapy, so maybe her pretending she believes what I believe for "the sake of this exercise" is best for now.

"Can you tell me what it is that makes someone worthy of a fate like hell?"

I squint at her skeptically, not really sure where this is going. Still, she seems to have an end goal and not just random questions, so I humor her. "Sinning. If you don't confess and repent for your sins before you die, you go to hell."

"I see." She nods her understanding. "And do good deeds have an effect as well, or only sins?"

"Well, it depends. Like, if you're so well-known for being good that you get canonized as a saint, then you're guaranteed to get into heaven. And if you do something so bad that it's a mortal sin, then you're pretty much guaranteed to go to hell unless you confess to a priest and repent."

"And is your sexuality a mortal sin?"

"Depends who you ask," I say automatically, still tossing and catching. I've been trying to figure that out for so long, but none of the nuns or priests I've asked can seem to agree. "To be a mortal sin, it has to be grave, done intentionally with full knowledge of the impact and consequences, and done with full consent of the sinner," I say, basically from memory. The grave part, I think is what gets everyone hung up. Like, what qualifies a sin as being grave? Everyone agrees on murder, but that's pretty much the only consensus we've all been able to come to.

"I see," she says again. "Did you fall in love intentionally with full knowledge of the consequences? Did you consent to falling in love?"

Her question surprises me so much that I miss the ball and it bounces right off my forehead before rolling away on the ground. I laugh a little. "I guess not."

No one's ever focused on *that* part of the equation when it came to this whole mortal sin debate. Another point for Dr. Lee. If me loving Jamal isn't an unforgiveable type of sin, then maybe there's hope for me. But is it the type of sin that can be canceled out with a good deed?

"I think, in general, good deeds should also count," I add.

Another micro smile. "So maybe you can focus on the good deeds you know you can do, like treating people with love and being generous and kind as much as possible, instead of focusing on something you can't control."

"You know what, yeah," I say, feeling a little pumped up. I think back to that conversation with Yami from the hospital. She told me she loves herself *because* she loves me. Because we're the same. Maybe loving Jamal will be like that for me. If I love someone I can see myself in, maybe I'll hate myself a little less. And with hell out of the picture, the only consequences of being out are other humans, who I can handle for sure. "Fuck what anyone else thinks. Who cares if people don't like it? It's my life, not theirs."

Micro smile. "I think you found your answer, Cesar."

She's right. The answer was so obvious all along, I don't know why it took this conversation for me to figure it out. The answer is him.

I'm ready.

5

WHEN YOU FIGURED OUT HOW TO AVOID GOING TO HELL

bargaining

I spend the car ride home from therapy writing out a poem for Jamal in my notes app, vaguely aware of my mom talking to me. Something about a pop-up market in Sedona.

"Are you sure you'll be all right this weekend?"

"Yeah, mhmm," I respond on autopilot.

"I'll only be a couple hours away, so if you need anything, just call me, okay?"

"Okay, yeah," I say, still typing away. I want to show Jamal this little piece of me I've been keeping from the rest of the world. He deserves a straight answer from me, for once, but I don't want to send it over text.

So, as soon as I get home, I write the poem out in the Jamal section of my notebook, so I can give it to him in person. Once it's done, I tear out the page and read it over one last time. Not to make sure it's good enough, because that never mattered with him. He's the only one who doesn't expect me to be perfect. It's almost better that this particular poem is straight from brain to paper—or brain to notes app to paper. He'd like it best that way, I'm sure.

The first time I fell, I accidentally found that the
Answer to all the questions burning in my head were the same.
Is it possible to be seen completely and still loved? Does he
  really want me, out
Of all the people in the world? When we're old and gray, and our
  lives have run their
Course, will he still want me? Will I want him?
Yes, obviously.

I've barely had time to read the full poem before Jamal calls me at our usual time. I have to resist the urge to ask him to be my boyfriend right then and there. No, I want to do things right this time. I should ask him in person.

"What are you doing this weekend?" I say as soon as I pick up the phone. I'm already googling movie times for something he might be into.

"Probably whatever you're about to invite me to." His words have a certain lightness to them that makes me think he's smiling.

"Wanna go to the movies?" I say, trying not to sound as eager as I am. "They're playing *Battlestar Galactica* at the dollar theater on Saturday." I don't know much about the franchise other than that Jamal used to watch it on repeat as a kid.

"Really?" he asks, his voice a little higher pitched than usual.

"Yeah," I say with a little laugh. With my microscopic attention span, I've never been big on watching movies, but Jamal loves them. I don't know, it seems like a nice gesture. "Is there anything I need to know going in?" I ask, knowing Jamal is probably itching to tell me all about it.

That question is all he needs to unleash a massive info dump of all his hidden Battlestar knowledge. It's times like these I can put my audiographic memory to use. I quietly file away the unfamiliar terms and names in my brain while Jamal gets progressively more and more excited. *Battlestar Galactica* isn't particularly up my alley, but I could listen to Jamal get this hyped up over something for literally any amount of time, any day.

Or all night, apparently. I'm not sure who fell asleep first, but the call is still going when I wake up a few hours later, Jamal's rhythmic breath just heavy enough to tell me he's been passed out for a while.

"Good night," I whisper before hanging up and falling back asleep.

I spend the rest of the week brushing up on Battlestar knowledge and playing out different scenarios of how I might ask Jamal out in my head. In Mr. Franco's class on Friday, I'd rather daydream than fall asleep for once. I'm not even catastrophizing this time.

In fact, I'm imagining all the ways this could possibly go *right*. If he says yes. If we could be even better together now than we were before. Maybe it can last this time. I'm in the middle of running through all the ways I can phrase the big question when David and three other guys walk in.

Mr. Franco claps his hands together and stops droning on long enough to introduce them. "All right, everyone can wake up now, the main office told me we had some free entertainment coming our way, courtesy of the drama class. What's your skit about today?"

"It's an anti-drug PSA from Father John," David says.

"A heavy topic, huh?" Mr. Franco presses his lips together like he wants to say more, but just gestures to the guys up front. "The stage is yours."

David takes the cue and goes to one side of the room while the other three go to the other. Then David starts walking past them.

"Hey kid, do you wanna get high? 'Cause I have free drugs," one of the guys says as he pretends to open up an imaginary trench coat full of said drugs. "It's the good kind."

"I love getting high, but I don't need your drugs," David says, and I can already tell he's trying to keep from laughing. "The only thing I need to get high on is Jesus's love for me."

There are a few stifled laughs at that, but David stays impressively in character. Him being an atheist makes this a hundred times more hilarious. If only it was the norm to be offered free drugs by random students, like every adult at this school somehow thinks it is. I bet Father John wrote the script himself and thinks it's great.

"Only losers don't do drugs," one of the other actors says, and they pretend to laugh at David while they all give him a thumbs-down.

"Doing drugs is a sin, and sinning isn't cool," David says with his arms crossed in a challenge.

"Whatever, it makes me feel good," one of the guys shoots back. So far, that's the only realistic part of this skit.

"If you really want to feel good, you go to confession and repent. Forgiveness feels better than drugs," David says with prayer hands. Mr. Franco cuts in at that, making the time-out signal with his hands and stepping forward.

"We also have an excellent guidance counselor for anyone who's struggling to feel good. There are plenty of adults at this school you can trust if you need help," Mr. Franco says, bringing the vibe of the room down for a moment. I almost scoff at the comment.

I've gotten detention for chewing gum, so I doubt anyone could admit to doing drugs here and not get in trouble. "Consider dropping by for a counseling session after confession." He goes back to the sidelines, then gestures at David. "Go ahead."

"Do you even know the sacraments, bro?" David jumps back in without skipping a beat, as the other actors just stare at him like they've never heard the word "confession."

"I know the sacraments!" one of the guys insists, while holding back a laugh at David's ironic earnestness.

I know it's all kind of a joke to them, but it does give me a twinge of guilt. Like, maybe I should talk to Father John about Jamal again, just in case. Maybe it doesn't have to be like last time. I can present my case like I did with Dr. Lee.

"Oh, good! Because Father John opens up the confessional before school and at lunch every Friday. Peer pressure is bad, so peers, press your palms together and pray for forgiveness. Amen."

"Amen," the rest of them chime in.

They all bow, and David finally breaks character as he grins at me and waves. I give him a thumbs-up and he makes sarcastic prayer hands at me before they shuffle out, bursting into laugher once they're out of the room.

Mr. Franco clears his throat. "All right, speaking of forgiveness . . ." He doesn't waste any time before he starts passing our tests back from Monday. "Some of you might want to repent when your parents see these scores."

"Tests aren't cool, the sacraments are," someone says, followed by a few laughs, and then everyone starts dramatically quoting the skit to Mr. Franco when they get their marked-up tests.

"Do you even know the sacraments, bro?"

"Only losers give pop quizzes."

"I don't need to get high, my test score does it for me."

"All right, all right, very funny." Mr. Franco rolls his eyes as he hands me mine. As expected, my score of 65 percent is crossed out in red ink and replaced with a 100 percent, meaning my test set the curve.

"We basically tied on this one," Jeremy says when he sees my score, proudly showing me his test with an original score of 63 percent.

"I won't go so easy on you next time," I taunt playfully, and he laughs.

"No, please do, Mr. Franco sure as hell won't."

At that, Mr. Franco shushes us to start reviewing the correct answers, and I find myself dozing off a bit. I didn't sleep well last night, and Mr. Franco doesn't make staying awake easy. Lucky for me, he doesn't bother me, and I wake up to the sound of the bell.

It's not like I was intentionally taking David's skit seriously, but for the rest of my morning classes, I can't help but feel like maybe the timing wasn't a coincidence. Maybe there's a reason I was supposed to get that reminder to talk to Father John. So when lunch comes around, I find myself walking toward the chapel.

Getting advice from Father John might be a good idea before I ask Jamal out. The more I think about it, the more it makes sense. If Dr. Lee is right, then good deeds count toward whether I go to heaven or hell just as much as sins do. That means Father John can do some quick priest math and tell me exactly what I need to do in order to be with Jamal and still make things right with God. It's the perfect opportunity for me to get answers before my date tomorrow.

When I get to the chapel to meet Father John, it doesn't really surprise me that I'm the first and probably only one to take him up on his offer. I'm sure almost everyone else at Slayton has the chance to go to confession every weekend, so they'd have no need to go at school. But since my mom and Yami work so much, we don't really go to church at all.

There's no line, so I walk right into the booth and sit across from the priest, who I can't really see behind the screen.

"What's up, Father John?" I say as I do a quick sign of the cross.

He sighs a little. "Hello, my son. What sins weigh on your heart today?"

I sit on my hands to keep from fidgeting too much. "I actually just came here to ask you a question."

"Ask it."

"Or, maybe, like, two questions. Three, tops."

The pause is too long for comfort, so I take his lack of response as my cue to go on.

"Okay, so, hypothetically speaking . . ." I don't know why I'm starting out with hypotheticals when this is obviously about me. "If a guy falls for another guy, what exactly would he have to do to cancel out the sin?"

"Cancel out the sin . . . ?" He repeats my last few words, as if they were in a different language.

"Right. Like, what if I go volunteer at a food bank every time I have sex—"

He clears his throat like that caught him off guard, but I keep going.

"I mean, since you can't just stop doing certain sins . . . like if I like another guy, but I'm also, like, a *really* good person, I don't have to go to hell, right?"

He pauses again, though not for as long this time. "Your focus is in the wrong place, my son. If good deeds cancel out sins, then what is there to save us from sin? Actually, it's the opposite. A good deed means nothing if done with sin in one's heart."

I swallow the lump in my throat. This is not going according to plan. "But what if it's not a mortal sin? It's not a conscious choice, I can't really help it. What then?"

By now I've dropped the hypothetical act. He's the one who told me to break up with Jamal for my penance last year, so he knows exactly what I'm talking about.

"You always have control over yourself, my son. You only have to resist the temptation."

"No, you're not getting it," I start, my voice raising more than I mean it to. "I can be a better person! I'll be really, *really* good, I promise—" I stop myself when my voice cracks. I wasn't expecting to get so mad, but I also really wasn't expecting our talk to end up this way.

"A good person who refuses to rid himself of the devil's influence will find himself again with the devil in the afterlife."

"But I . . ." I stop myself before getting choked up again. I have to go back to class soon, I can't go getting emotional. "I have to go," I blurt out, and bolt from the confessional before he has a chance to respond.

I thought Father John having that priestly connection with God would mean he could give me some kind of answers, but I was wrong.

No, he's the one who's wrong. He must have mistranslated or something. He's *wrong*. There has to be a way to prove him wrong.

6

WHEN RESISTING THE ROUTINE FEELS LIKE FREEDOM

grasping for control

I do a double take when Doña Violeta shows up to take me and Yami home from school instead of my mom. The woman is basically our surrogate grandma, for all intents and purposes, since Yami and I haven't seen or heard from our abuela in years. On the rare occasion Abuela comes up in conversation, Mami either changes the subject or says something about how crazy she is. Growing up, Doña Violeta was there instead. She helped raise Yami and me, and practically every other kid on our block.

"What's she doing here?" I ask Yami as we walk toward her car.

"Mami's in Sedona this weekend, remember?" Yami raises an eyebrow. "She's been talking about it all week."

"Oh, right," I say, pretending I remember her bringing it up. Somehow my brain only manages to remember useless things, like textbook glossaries and differential equations. When it comes to real life, I always come up blank.

Maybe that has something to do with The Thoughts I keep having to push down whenever my brain tries to leave robot-student mode. Those thoughts being particularly persistent after that conversation with Father John.

I pretend to pay attention to Doña Violeta's story in the car, but all I can think about is how I have to prove Father John wrong. There has to be some kind of loophole. If Father John can't tell me what to do in order to be with Jamal without going to hell, I'll bring my case straight to the source. I may not be able to hear God's voice in my ear like a priest, but I can still get my message across.

As soon as we get home, I go straight to my room and pray harder than I have since my hospital stay. I know most people pray before bed, but my usual time is after school. Since I go to bed at inconsistent times, if at all, it's easier to make a habit of it if I can do it at the same time every day.

I pull my cross necklace out of my shirt and close my fist around it tight. When I'm not in school, I'm usually wearing that one and my jaguar necklace, which both feel spiritual to me in different ways. But with the dress code, I can only wear the cross to school.

I'm not proud of it, but this particular prayer is not pretty. I find myself straight up groveling, begging for some kind of sign that I missed something—that Father John missed something—and I don't have to spend the rest of my life pretending not to love Jamal.

I beg for some kind of sign, for God to just tell me what to do to make it right. To tell me it's okay to be with him. There has to be a way to make things work. With trembling prayer hands and faltering confidence, I end up lying in bed staring at the ceiling all night instead of sleeping.

✦ ✦ ✦

When Jamal picks me up for the movie the next day, I shoot up one more quick prayer before opening the door. All I need is a sign of some kind that this is okay, and I'll know I can completely ignore what Father John said.

I cross myself and open the door to find Jamal standing on the other side, hands folded behind his back and a smile on his face. He's never been the type to just text me saying he's here so I can come out to his truck. Instead, he comes to the door every time, walking me to his truck and opening the passenger door for me.

"Thanks," I say, unable to keep from smiling as I climb inside. It's hard not to feel lighter around him, even with Father John's words weighing me down.

"Question," Jamal says as he pulls the truck off into the road.

"Yeah?" I say, wondering if he'll ask again about getting back together so early in the date.

"If you had to choose how the world would end, what kind of apocalypse would you pick?"

I let out a little laugh. There really is no telling what kind of question he's got in his head at any given moment. "Um, what are my options?"

"Like, alien invasion, zombies, animal uprising, the rapture, nuclear war . . . it can be anything, really."

"Definitely not the rapture," I find myself saying with an involuntary shudder. "Maybe animal uprising? I've been pretty nice to animals, I think. Maybe they'll spare me."

"Yeah, that's probably the best one for the sake of the planet, too," Jamal says thoughtfully. "I'd pick the alien invasion."

He doesn't elaborate on his answer, but he doesn't really need to. Being both a sci-fi and astronomy enthusiast, I'm sure getting abducted by aliens and taken to see space is up there on his wish list.

We pull up to the theater then. It's a small dollar theater in the middle of the day, so we basically get the entire place to ourselves. I planned to pay for everything, but Jamal sneaks over to the concession stand while I'm getting the tickets, and by the time I have them, he's balancing a large popcorn and two sodas in his arms.

I try to keep my eyes open for one of those signs from God that I either will or won't go to hell for even being here with him, but nothing feels out of the ordinary. I take the drinks from him, so he only has to carry the popcorn, and we take our seats in the very back of the theater.

Most of the movie goes right over my head since I'm overthinking so hard. I have to be hypervigilant, so I don't miss whatever signal I'm supposed to get.

Jamal rests a hand on the armrest in between our seats, and without thinking, I find my hand instinctively going to meet his. He turns his head, looking surprised but happy as he turns his palm upward to take my hand.

My stomach does a somersault, and I'm not sure if it's because I missed the warmth of his hands, or because I acted without getting my sign first.

It's just hand-holding, though. I haven't asked him to be my boyfriend or anything, so technically I'm still in the clear, I think.

Part of me wonders if the *feeling* of his hand in mine is a signal in its own right. I can't deny the safety of it. How this simple touch relaxes my shoulders and tugs at the corners of my lips. That can be a sign, right?

As soon as I think it, the screen lights up with a fiery explosion, the sudden booming in my ears making me pull my hand away in a flinch.

Is *that* a sign?

My head pounds the rest of the movie trying to make sense of it. I do my best to weigh the two conflicting signals against each other, but by the time the credits roll, I'm no closer to an answer. At least, not one I can be confident I'm not misunderstanding.

I try my best to listen to Jamal raving about the movie on the way home, but I have a hard time concentrating on his words, especially since I barely absorbed any of that movie. I was supposed to ask him to be my boyfriend today in person, but the longer I go without some kind of hint that it's all gonna be okay, the harder it is to get any words out of my mouth.

I haven't said anything by the time we pull up to my house, and I don't know if I can.

"Thanks for today," Jamal says, turning toward me with a genuine smile. At least he doesn't seem to be freaking out as much as I am. "I had a good time."

"Me too," I admit. I always have a good time with him, no matter how much my own brain tries to sabotage it. I find myself subconsciously leaning the tiniest bit forward. I have to admit, I don't want today to end.

He leans in too, and I glance down at his lips, wondering if the skip in my heart is enough of a hint.

Before either of us gets too close, Jamal's phone goes off. He pulls it out of his pocket and frowns at the screen. "Sorry, I should really answer."

"It's okay, I have to go anyway," I say a bit too quickly, opening the door and hopping out of the truck in one movement. "Bye!"

I shut the door, and he waves behind the window as he answers his phone. Like always, he doesn't drive away until after I get the door open. The sun is still up, but he's always making sure I get in safely before driving off.

When I get inside, I lean my back against the door and sink, running a hand down my face. The phone call wasn't necessarily a sign, right? It doesn't have to mean anything just because it happened when I *maybe* thought about kissing Jamal . . . right?

It doesn't occur to me that I forgot to take my meds until Sunday morning, when I pass by the pill counter and realize both the Saturday and Sunday pills are still in their slots. My stomach drops as I rush to get the missed pills out of the counter. Not because I missed them, but because I could have gotten *caught* missing them.

If Mami or Yami had noticed before I did, they'd never let me go a day without hovering over my every move again. This weekend is the first time Mami's dared to leave me relatively unsupervised since my inpatient stay, so she definitely can't know.

I drop the Saturday and Sunday pills in my palm and go straight to the bathroom, immediately flushing the one I missed. I pop the Sunday pill in my mouth, but I hesitate before swallowing.

Aren't I supposed to be spiraling after missing a dose? I don't really feel all that different today than I normally do. I feel . . . fine?

I don't really know what pushes me to do it. Maybe it's because I'm genuinely doing better. Maybe because I'm sick of being watched while I take my meds like some kind of prisoner. Or that I want to feel in control of one fucking thing in my life.

And if I already missed a dose and I feel fine, then what's the harm in just . . . pausing?

Whatever the reason, I spit the pill out in the toilet, satisfied in the knowledge that maybe everyone is wrong about me. Maybe I don't actually need to be babied for the rest of eternity. Maybe this is the beginning of me taking control of my own life.

I'm about to head back to my room when the door on Yami's side of the bathroom opens and she walks in, rubbing her eyes.

"How was the movie?" she asks through a yawn.

"It was—" I start, but my phone dings mid-sentence with the email notification sound. "Good . . ." I trail off as I pull my phone out and check it, but the email's preview makes the blood in my ears pump loud enough to hear my own pulse.

Subject: Re: miss you papi
I know it's taken me a long time to explain . . .

"Uh, I'm gonna go back to sleep." I give Yami a half-hearted excuse before going straight to my room so she can't ask any questions.

I close and lock my door and sit at the edge of my bed, trying my best to hype myself up to open the damn email. The blood pumping in my ears turns to slush, and I'm suddenly dizzy. I have no idea what to expect from his response. Is he going to apologize? Will he say he misses us too? Or will he just confirm he's disowned us?

Part of me wants to just delete the email without reading it, but I know if I do that I'll always wonder what could have happened. And if I wait until I'm not scared, I'll never be able to read it at all. So, I force myself to take three deep breaths, and open the email.

Subject: Re: miss you papi

I know it's taken me a long time to explain my thoughts here, and I apologize for that. I thought maybe if I gave it some time, things would work themselves out on their own, but I guess I can't make you change. I got your email and thought, it better be good. But you're both still doing what you're doing.

I can't lie to you. I'm very disappointed.

You and your sister have been brainwashed, and I can acknowledge that my absence in the last few years has made this harder on all of us. But I can't pretend to support what I know in my heart is not right.

If you only take one thing I say to heart, let it be this: It doesn't matter what anyone has tried to convince you until now. What you're doing is a choice. And you're making the wrong one. I can't just sit around and enable my kids to choose this lifestyle over family, and over God. You're both throwing away my legacy and your own futures.

I won't force you, but whatever you choose, you have to live with the consequences.

I stare at my phone until the words blur. I know what I have to do now. Or, what I have to *not* do.

Father John was right. Maybe I can't control my feelings, but I can control my actions. I can choose what to do about my feelings.

This was the sign. I can't be with Jamal. Not without facing the consequences.

7

WHEN THE PERFUME LABELED "FOR COUPLES" SMELLS BETTER BUT IT'S NOT A DATE

cognitive dissonance

Since Mami wasn't sure exactly what time she'd be home, she told me and Yami not to worry about our New Year's resolution of making Sunday dinner. I'm not proud of how relieved I was to get that text. After the email from my dad, I don't know if I could have spent time making food with Yami without telling her about it.

What would be the point in telling her? Knowing what my dad thinks would just piss her off and make her feel bad. Besides, if Yami knew he'd emailed me—or worse, that *I* had emailed *him*—she'd never let me live it down.

I planned to spend the rest of the evening in my room, but Mami gets home too early for me to pretend to already be asleep. Since the sun isn't even down yet, I have no choice but to socialize.

I go out to the living room to find Yami and my mom hugging, which seems to happen a lot more now than when we were growing up. If I had to pinpoint when Yami and our mom started getting closer, I'd guess it had something to do with Yami coming out to her last year.

Mami gives my sister a final squeeze before letting go and pulling me in for a hug of my own. "How was your weekend of freedom?"

I know she's making a joke, but something about it feels off. Does she know I abused that freedom by not taking my meds?

"It was good," I say, trying my best to sound chill about it. Like I didn't do anything wrong, I didn't get an email from my dad, and I didn't just decide to burrow myself further in the closet for potentially the rest of my life.

She kisses my head before letting me go and clapping her hands together.

"So, Yamilet, how behind are we from this trip?"

I take that as my perfect chance to check out of the conversation, since they'll probably be spending the rest of the evening catching up on their jewelry orders. I slip away to my room and lie in bed with my eyes closed, as if that could possibly help me sleep.

I don't get much rest before seven rolls around, and I stare at Jamal's contact in my phone until practically the last second before answering. By now, I've made up my mind. We can't get back together.

Still, that doesn't mean we can't be friends, right? I really don't want to lead him on—but I can't lose him either—but I can't date him again—but I *want* to—but I *can't.*

I have to tell him.

"Hey, b—you," I say, resisting the urge to call him babe. Even with all these months being single, it still feels natural to call him that. But it was naive of me to think we could go back to it.

"Hey, you." I can hear the smile in Jamal's voice, and despite how much I should be dreading talking to him, it immediately relaxes me. "How are you, Cesar?"

He usually starts out our calls this way, but from him, I know it's not just small talk. He genuinely wants to hear whatever might be bothering me, how my day really was—unfiltered.

My phone buzzes with a text before I can answer, and I open it to find a stream of texts spread out from New Year's Eve to today.

Hunter: Hey man how've you been?

Hunter: How's it going bro?

Hunter: Dude you okay?

Shit. I don't mean to ignore Hunter, but what am I supposed to say to "How's it going?" when it's going bad? I feel like shit, but I can't exactly tell him that without having to explain why. And I'm not trying to think about it any more than absolutely necessary.

"Cesar?" Jamal asks when I take too long to respond to *him*.

Right. I think about telling Jamal I don't feel the same way about him anymore, or that I don't want to get back together, but "Eh" is all I end up saying, since I'm not the best at lying to Jamal. I know I'll have to tell him soon, but I just change the subject like a coward. "You still doing that open mic next Friday?"

"Of course," Jamal says. "Why? Did something come up?"

Even though I can't get back together with him, and being around him knowing that will be absolute hell, I can't bring myself to let him down. I'm not about to let him come out to a strange crowd without some kind of backup.

"If you're there, I'm there. You know I'm your biggest fan," I say, despite my better judgment.

"My one and only." He laughs with a tiny little snort that shouldn't be cute but is. "So, question."

"Yeah?"

"How are you? Like, actually."

Dammit. I almost thought he'd let me drop the subject.

"Hungry," I say. Sure, I've already eaten, but my stomach has a mind of its own. I decide Jamal doesn't need to know I've been desperately praying about him—and failing.

He chuckles. "I can bring you some Takis?"

The thought makes me grin. "That would solve literally every single problem in my life," I say dramatically, and somehow, it really feels like it would.

"Give me ten minutes. Then you can tell me what's *really* going on."

He hangs up before I can protest. He's always so good at catching my deflections.

Sure enough, there's a knock on the door exactly ten minutes later, and I rush to grab it, trying to beat my mom. I quickly pass her and Yami on the couch making jewelry.

"Expecting someone?" Mami asks as I hop over some necklaces on the floor.

"Just Jamal," I say as nonchalantly as possible. Mami always freaks out when Jamal comes over. She might love him even more than I do—I mean, she definitely does. Because I can't love Jamal. Not anymore.

I open the door to find him standing up straight with his arms folded behind his back. He's got on a smooth long-sleeved striped button-up tucked into his pants. If I didn't know better, I'd think he got dressed up just to come here, but no, that's just how he always looks.

"Jamal! Come in, come in!" Mami's voice from right behind me makes me jump.

"Wah! ¡Me asustaste!" I say with both hands on my chest, trying to calm my heartbeat. I'm not usually so jumpy, but I must still be on edge from the email. Mami just ignores me and tries to pull Jamal inside.

"Actually, Mami, we were gonna go for a ride, right, Jamal?" I give Jamal a please-play-along look. I'd rather eat Takis in Jamal's truck than be forced to hang out as a family.

Weirdly enough, when it's just me and Jamal, I have a chance at pretending it's not real. That we're just in our own little world, and nothing else matters. But when he's hanging out with me and my mom and Yami, there's always been this awkward tension regarding the breakup. Like they've both been waiting for us to get back together since the day we split.

"You have to come in for at least a minute! Just to say hi!" Mami coaxes, and Yami comes to the rescue from her spot on the couch.

"Let them go, Mami. We don't have slacker money." She looks back at me and does a dramatic wink, which I pretend I don't see. Mami frowns, but agrees and finally lets me out the door with Jamal.

He moves his hand from behind his back to reveal a bag of Takis, handing them to me with a smile.

"You just saved my life, do you know that? Taki withdrawals are no joke." I pop open the bag and stick my hand in before we make it out of the entryway.

He just grins and leads the way to his truck. From outside the house, we can hear Doña Violeta's music playing from her spot on her porch. The upbeat ranchera blasts throughout the neighborhood while she sits in her chair nodding on beat and people watching.

She waves when she sees me and Jamal walking outside, and Jamal waves back while I blow her a couple of kisses. Jamal opens the passenger-side door for me when we get to his truck, which makes me hesitate. When we were together, he always opened the door for me, and he started doing it again after we kissed on New Year's Eve.

My dad's words echo in my head.

What you're doing is *a choice, and you're making the wrong one.*

I quickly get in the truck so Jamal's not standing there waiting for me, and he walks around to his side.

I try to hype myself up to have the conversation. To tell him we can't be together again, that we can't kiss anymore or hold hands or open doors for each other. But when he sits down in his seat, the words get caught in my throat.

"Want to go to the mall?" I say, instead of anything useful.

"Sure," Jamal says as he starts the car.

The mall was . . . a bad idea, to say the least. First of all, I have no money to be buying anything, but more importantly, it's a lot of walking around side by side. Jamal knows not to straight-up hold my hand in public since I'm not out, but we used to "accidentally" brush our hands together whenever we'd walk side by side out in the open. It used to be a reminder that, even though we couldn't be "out" in the open, we still had each other.

Now it's just a reminder of how shitty I've been to him. I pull out my phone, making sure to hold it in the hand closest to Jamal so neither of us are tempted to "accidentally" brush hands.

"Are you single, or are you taken?" Some mall kiosk lady is looking at Jamal, holding out two different perfume bottles.

An unwelcome wave of jealousy flows through me for a split moment before she keeps going.

"This cologne will make your girlfriend feel cozy snuggling up to you," she says, holding out the bottle to the right. "And this one is guaranteed to attract all the single ladies. What will it be?"

My instinct is to ignore her and keep walking, but Jamal is stuck in place. He eyes both colognes like this decision is going to make or break world peace. His eyes catch mine for a split second before he turns back to the cologne.

"Taken?" the lady asks, looking back and forth from Jamal to me. "It also works for boyfriends." She winks.

That's when I panic and snatch the "single" cologne from her hand, taking in a deep whiff.

"This one smells better," I lie. It makes me cough. The "taken" cologne isn't as overbearing, but I guess if I'm gonna stay single I should get used to the smell.

Jamal's shoulders slump ever so slightly. At least compared to his natural perfect posture. He only lets it show for a moment before straightening up and politely asking the lady for two of the "single" colognes.

She happily bends over to grab a couple bottles of the stuff, then bags it up and hands it to Jamal. We turn away from her and start walking out to the car.

Back at the truck, Jamal holds the door open for me again, which kills me. He looks at me just a second too long when we get in, then he reaches in the bag with the two bottles of cologne.

"For you." He hands me one of the bottles.

"Are you saying I smell bad?" I try to sound playful, taking the cologne and shoving it in my pocket. I laugh to hide the sting because hygiene is actually a sore subject for me. When I go through my depressive episodes, as Dr. Lee calls them, taking care of myself kind of goes out the window, and showering is one of the harder tasks to accomplish. I try not to go around smelling. The most I can usually manage is to scrub my crevices with a washcloth every couple of days and wear deodorant and dry shampoo, but . . . yeah, I'm not proud of it.

"Of course not." Jamal doesn't laugh back, or even smile. He knows this is a problem for me, so I know this is his way of helping. It just makes me feel that much shittier for stringing him along.

"We can't get back together," I blurt out.

He's quiet for a moment, his ever-intense eyes searching mine for an answer I can't give. I never told him why I broke up with him in the first place. I couldn't. Can't.

"I understand," he finally says. He sounds sad but not angry. He's never angry with me, even when he should be. Anyone in their right mind would have dropped me a long time ago.

"You do?" I ask, tentatively reaching for another Taki from the bag he gave me earlier. "Is that all you have to say?"

He doesn't say anything for a bit, but I'm used to Jamal's long pauses by now. I used to think he wasn't listening, but now I know he's just super intentional about what he does say. He takes his time to choose his words. I love—uh, have noticed that about him.

"I'm sorry," he says, shaking his head, which throws me off. "I shouldn't have kissed you. I crossed a boundary." I can hear the pain in his voice. He really thinks this is his fault.

"Shit, Jamal," I say, not knowing what else *to* say. It wasn't like Jamal kissed me all on his own. I was every bit as into it as he was. I can't have Jamal feeling guilty on top of everything else. "I crossed my own boundary," I finally add, hoping he really gets it.

Another long pause. "Why?"

I don't know how to answer that. Because I wanted to? Because I missed him? Because I love—

"Because I wasn't thinking," I say, and Jamal adjusts his glasses, which he usually does when he's trying to figure something out.

"I understand," he says again.

My head hurts. How can he understand?

You should apologize.

"Shit, Jamal . . . ," I say again, letting the "sorry" be implied. "Why do you put up with me?" I ask, feeling heat rise in my chest.

Jamal just looks at me with those intense eyes like the answer is obvious. "You know why, Cesar." His voice is soft. Too soft.

An unexpected wave of anger bubbles inside as I realize what's really going on here.

"Do you feel sorry for me or something? Because of what happened last year?" I ask defensively.

"What? No, that's not—" Jamal starts, but I don't let him finish.

"I can take care of myself." I start laughing. "Just because I got sent to the land of the sticky socks *one time* doesn't mean I'm some fragile little child."

"That's not what I meant." Jamal doesn't take his eyes off mine.

"What did you mean, then?"

"I mean I love—ugh!" He runs a hand down his face. "I'm sorry . . . I . . . I care about you, okay? Is it so hard to accept that some people just . . . genuinely care about you?"

I shrug and eat another Taki.

It really is.

8

WHEN YOU STAY UP ALL NIGHT CONTEMPLATING RUNNING AWAY WITH OLIVIA RODRIGO

lack of sleep

This whole week and into the weekend, it's been the same every night. The Thoughts creep their way into my brain while I lie in my bed desperately covering my ears with my pillow. But like every other night, The Thoughts bleed through the fabric.

If I don't hurry up and think about something else, I might do something I can't take back, so I take a deep breath and think about solutions instead of focusing on the problem, just like therapist number three suggested. Jamal said he understood, so I should take him at his word. And I can't date him again, so I might as well move on, right?

I just need to find a girlfriend to get all this guilt off my back.

But I don't want a girlfriend.

I want a Jamal.

But I also can't want a Jamal.

I need a girlfriend.

Ugh.

I try a different approach, plugging my ears with my AirPods and playing Olivia Rodrigo.

It's easier to listen to breakup music and imagine that Jamal did something wrong so I can get over him. Maybe one day I'll find myself an Olivia Rodrigo to run away with. Maybe I won't have this empty hole in my chest forever.

I'm still awake when the sun comes up on Monday, but I eagerly jump out of bed and put on my Slayton uniform. It's a lot easier to shake off The Thoughts when the sun is up.

I go to the bathroom and find myself staring at the Mayan Code of the Heart, In Lak'ech Ala K'in, on the mirror. I typed the famous poem out underneath it and put it up there after my dad got taken away, and I haven't been able to touch it since.

In Lak'ech
Tú eres mi otro yo / You are my other me.
Si te hago daño a ti / If I do harm to you,
Me hago daño a mí mismo / I do harm to myself.
Si te amo y respeto / If I love and respect you,
Me amo y respeto yo / I love and respect myself.

When I first put it up, it was my way of trying to reconnect with my dad since he was obsessed with that poem. Him being the reason I put this up makes me want to tear it down, but I can't bring myself to do it. Over the years, it's kind of taken on a life of its own, and it's more of mine and Yami's thing now than my dad's.

I shake off all thoughts of him and check myself out in the mirror to make sure I don't look as sleep-deprived as I am. My bloodshot eyes are the only things that really give me away, so I splash some water on my face and put in some eye drops. Voilà.

Looking at my bad self, you'd think I would've had at least eight sweet and dreamy hours of beauty sleep.

The door that leads into Yami's room opens, and she groggily walks into the bathroom. Yami, on the other hand, looks like she slept a good twenty, but "beauty" is not the word I'd use here. Her hair's all disheveled and one eye is still half closed.

"You look like if a mop and the chupacabra had a baby on your head." I offer her a brush, then wipe the eyedrop tears from my cheeks. Her mouth twitches into a smile, and she shoves my shoulder.

"I know it can be overwhelming looking at such unfiltered beauty, but you don't have to cry about it." She takes the brush from my hand and starts working on her hair.

I just laugh, rolling my eyes as I reach for the toothpaste.

"Anyways, you sleep okay?" she asks through a yawn. I stick my toothbrush in my mouth instead of answering her straight, and shrug. She must have noticed something's been off with me lately. I think this is her way of asking if I'm okay since she knows it makes me less prickly than outright asking.

I spit into the sink just as my second alarm goes off.

7:00 a.m. take meds

Yami keeps working on her hair, and I head over to the kitchen, where my mom is waiting for me with a plate of chorizo and papas. I reach for the pill counter and take out the pill for Monday, staring at it for a bit before doing anything.

Something in me is resisting going back to the routine hard, even with my mom back. It's like, everything in my life feels so far out of my control right now. I don't have a choice but to go to school every day. I have to do my homework and ace every test to live up to everyone's high expectations. I'm forced to go to therapy every single week. I don't even get to date who I want. But this, I have control over. This, I can choose.

I put the pill in my mouth and pretend to swallow, then go to the bathroom just as Yami's walking out. I close the door behind me and spit the pill out in the toilet.

At school, it's more of the same boring shit I'm used to. Every class is almost impossible to stay awake in. I'm acing them anyway, so it really doesn't matter if I'm awake or not. I've got a practically photographic memory, so as long as I skim whatever chapter we cover in the textbook later, there's not really any need to take notes.

The teachers and I both know I'll get all my homework right and do great on the tests. Some of them don't even care if I sleep in class anymore as long as I keep my grades up. There's really only two teachers who have actually tried to do anything about it. Mrs. Perry, the English teacher, never fails to give me a detention if she catches me, but I've gotten sneaky. Then there's Mr. Franco. He catches me almost every time, but I never get in trouble. He usually just wants to talk. Still, it's best to be stealth if I can help it.

It's not that I don't *try* to pay attention, but even when I do, it's all so boring. Mr. Franco has this slow, soothing, almost melodic voice. It's like he *wants* me to fall asleep. Luckily Jeremy's the tallest guy in this class, so sitting behind him is about as safe as I can get. My eyes grow heavier and heavier, and finally I give in and close them. . . .

"¡Oye maricón!" someone calls out. I flinch, not because of the word but because of who's saying it.

I turn around to get a look at Nick and see he's with all of them. Avery, Marcos, Antonio, Joseph, and Daniel all stand behind Nick like his little henchmen.

I don't wait to be called that word again. I swing and hit Nick right in the nose. He hits back, but I dodge him all right. There's a reason they always come at me all six of them. Before I know it, Avery has my arms pulled behind my back while the rest of them rush me. I flex my stomach, preparing for impact.

Nick wipes his bloody nose, then swings for my face.

BLAM!

My eyes shoot open to the sound of a textbook being slammed on my desk, making me fall out of my chair. Everyone cracks up, and I force myself to laugh with them, letting them believe my flushed face is from laughter and not that dream flashback.

"Asshole!" I playfully yell at Jeremy, who's wheezing and wiping a joyful tear from his eye. I make myself get up and sit back down, even though my fists are still balled from the dream fight, and all I want to do is punch *someone*. It takes everything in me not to lash out. Instead, I laugh along, heat heavy in my ears.

The only person not laughing is Mr. Franco. "Language, Cesar," is all he says before getting back to his lesson.

Everyone stops laughing when he goes back to teaching, but my ears ring so loud they all might as well still be mocking me, and those laughs might as well be coming from Nick and them. I can barely hear the bell signaling the end of class over the sound of my ears ringing.

"Cesar, will you stay a moment?" Mr. Franco asks, just when I stand to leave.

I pack up my bag and walk over to his desk, but he waits until everyone else is gone before saying anything.

"Didn't sleep well last night?" he asks.

I shrug. "You know how it is," I say casually.

"No, I don't, actually." His eyebrows knit together in a concerned expression, which I hate. "Is everything okay at home?"

"Everything is great," I say truthfully. My mom and Yami are more supportive than I could ever ask for. Jamal is still my best friend, and he's amazing. I have friends and straight As and I'm lucky enough to be here on scholarship and . . . and, and . . .

And I'm miserable.

The fuck is wrong with me?

"Are you sure? Everything all right with your mom and dad—"

"I don't have a dad," I interrupt, surprised by my own firmness.

Mr. Franco doesn't stop with that pitying look. "I hope you know my door is always open if you need to talk. And if you don't want to talk to me, we have a school counselor here who would be happy to—"

"Can I go now?" I cut him off, but when his eyebrows knit together again, I force a smile. "My next class is across campus. Don't wanna be late."

He finally smiles back. "All right, Cesar. Go ahead."

I turn around, immediately putting back on my usual persona. I'm obviously doing completely and totally great and anyone who says otherwise is getting sued for slander.

Between second and third period, the first thing I do is find

Yami and her friends in line. We have a fifteen-minute break right now where we can get cookies and coffee, but I never have any money. Yami, on the other hand . . .

"Buy me a cookie, my sweet, beautiful sister?" I say as I walk up to Yami, who's already standing hand in hand with Bo. Next to them, David stands behind Amber, hands resting on her hips. Their other friend, Emily, looks relieved to see me, probably because we're the only two single people in the group. Yami stares at me deadpan despite my puppy face and pouty lash fluttering, so I add, "I'll pay you back."

"No, you won't," Yami says but still picks up two cookies when we get to the front of the line.

I thank her with a big smile, not walking away after she hands me the cookie. She doesn't ask questions, either. Most of my friends were seniors last year since I was in a lot of the senior classes, but this year they're all gone and I'm in tiny classes with just the other "gifted" seniors.

Sure, I have lots of acquaintances. Lots of people who would call me a friend. But I don't know, I prefer hanging out with Yami's group. I've kind of been hovering around them all year. None of them seem to mind, and Yami's never said anything, but I still feel a little out of place. Like I'm intruding on her life and being a big fat burden.

I don't know why I feel so attached to them. Maybe they just feel safe because they've already been vetted by Yami. Plus, besides Hunter, Jamal, and my mom, they're the only ones who know I'm bi. For a long time, that felt like a comfort, but now I'm not sure how I feel about it.

"How's your ass, bro?" David asks me out of the blue. He doesn't call me bro in the way some guys call each other bro, but because everyone literally thinks we're twins since we're two short-ish Brown guys at a mostly white Catholic school.

"What?" I ask.

"Jeremy told us you fell out of your chair," Bo fills me in, chuckling.

Well shit, news travels fast around here. I put on that laugh again. The one no one can ever tell is fake. "Oh. My ass is fine."

"You're damn right it's fine," David says, miming himself slapping it, which brings a real laugh out of me. I don't know how to explain it, but it's like, there's that weird way straight guys like to pretend they're gay, right? Like, pretending to hit on other guys and making jokes about being into each other. But they usually only do it with other straight guys, in situations where everyone knows they're straight, but I don't know. There's something euphoric about a straight guy pretending to hit on me when he knows I'm bi. Like he's not going to treat me any different or be weird around me just because we're both guys and one of us isn't straight.

And maybe I'm doing some Olympic-level mental gymnastics here, but David pretending to hit on me means I definitely give off straight energy, right?

We all laugh, and for just a moment, I forget that this isn't really my life.

That these aren't really *my* friends.

Then I catch a glimpse of Father John walking to the chapel, and the laugh gets sucked out of me. I catch Yami glaring at him from the corner of my eye, and I know she hates him because of me. Even if she won't say it, I know she blames him in some way for my spiral last year, since it happened after my penance of breaking up with Jamal. She doesn't know about our most recent conversation, and I'm definitely not going to tell her.

When Father John looks at me and nods his acknowledgment, I'm suddenly aware of how gay my laugh might sound. I could give off all the straight energy in the world, but it wouldn't matter. He would still know. The smile is wiped from my face, and my heart falls to my gut.

9

WHEN NO ONE WILL LEAVE YOU THE FUCK ALONE

irritability

I spend the rest of the day catching up on sleep, except for English with Mrs. Perry. I'm not trying to get detention again and have my mom get on my ass. Yami used to cover for me whenever I got detention last year, but Mami eventually found out. Now I have to be smart about it and only sleep in the classes where the teachers don't care.

To my horror, Mrs. Perry puts a video up on the projector after roll call. How am I supposed to stay awake for *that*?

I try my best to keep my eyes open, but I haven't slept well in a while, and it's really trying to come for me right now. I don't remember consciously deciding that I don't care about detention, but I must have at some point, because the next thing I know, the sound of the bell ringing jolts me awake and a detention slip is resting on my desk. At least she didn't wake me up.

I know better than to keep from telling Mami, or at least Yami, when I get detention now. Trying to hide it last year didn't exactly end well. When The Event happened, my mom went through my phone and found out everything. No point hiding it anymore, so

I shoot Yami a quick text before the end of the day. I'm cutting it a little close, since school's almost over, but whatever. Better late than never, I guess.

Cesar: got detention

Yami: want me to tell mami?

Cesar: 👍

While I'm on my phone, I notice I have another text from Hunter.

Hunter: want to hang out this weekend?

Since I keep forgetting to respond to him and he didn't ask how I'm doing this time, I decide to text back before I have a chance to get distracted and forget.

Cesar: Jamal has an open mic on Friday, want to come?

Hunter: He told me! I'll be there for sure.

Sometimes I forget that people I know are friends even when I'm not around. I've always wanted my friends to like Jamal, but since he can be a little socially awkward, they don't always warm up to him. It's nice to know Hunter's an exception.

Even if me and Jamal can't be together, I still want to be there for him. With Hunter there, it'll be nice to have him as a bit of a buffer so things aren't weird.

I grin as I shove my phone back in my pocket before dipping into the cafeteria for detention. I take advantage of my time in there by doing my homework, half listening to whatever animated story Coach V tells everyone else this time. Ever since he started overseeing detention, it's been a lot more interesting since he doesn't believe in silence.

Today, he's telling us about how his girlfriend's abusive ex-boyfriend got him arrested ten years ago.

"Now, don't get me wrong, violence is wrong. Always. That's why I shot that mother trucker in the foot."

I choke on a surprised laugh as I solve the last problem in my Calculus II worksheet, finishing just in time for the clock to strike 3:30 p.m., signaling the end of detention.

"Remember, kids, don't hit your partner. That way, you won't get shot in the foot!" he says loudly over the sound of all of us packing up our bags and rushing out the cafeteria doors.

Yami's waiting for me at one of the tables in the quad, and thank God, she's with Bo. Which means Bo is giving us a ride home again today. Which also means I can put off the lecture just a little longer.

Yami and Bo get up from the table hand in hand but let go when I approach. They swarm me on either side, grabbing onto my hands as we start walking toward the car. It's like I'm a toddler and they're protectively keeping me from running into the street, but I know they're just doing this to make sure I don't feel like a third wheel. True to my everything-is-great persona, I milk it, swinging my hands back and forth and practically skipping.

"So are you guys my moms now?" I laugh.

"We hereby adopt you," Bo says.

"Hell no," Yami says at the same time, then she laughs. "Sorry, Bo, but I'm not ready for kids just yet. At least, not ugly ones." She pats me on the head.

Bo pouts. "But he's so cute!"

"But I'm so cute!" I echo, making the cutest puppy face I can manage. "You said it yourself, remember?"

"Well, sure, but I meant in that so-ugly-you're-cute kind of way. Like Bo's dogs." Yami laughs, and I can't help but laugh too. Bo's dogs are a little ugly.

"I mean, you have my face, so who are you really calling ugly?"

Yami gasps and clutches her imaginary pearls like she's about to have a heart attack. "How very dare you!"

"Shhh, you're both beautiful," Bo says, giving my hand a squeeze and blowing Yami a kiss.

I pretend to savor every moment of Yami and Bo's attention. Really, though, it just reminds me they're giving up their alone time to make me feel comfortable. However big or small, everyone's always making sacrifices for me, and they all think I don't notice. I ignore the twinge of guilt in my gut and take the back seat for once, sticking my AirPods in my ears so I can at least give them the illusion of some time alone.

When we get home, Yami cushions the blow from my mom by distracting her. Mami's sitting at the kitchen table waiting for us, obviously disappointed in me, but Yami walks in first and immediately brings up how much work she and my mom have to do.

"Did you see we got a bulk order today? What if you get started on that while I work on our existing orders, so we don't fall further behind?" Yami's already walking to the living room, aka their workspace, like she expects Mami to follow her, but Mami just sits there staring at me with sad eyes.

"I thought we were past this, mijo."

"It's not like I cheated on a test or anything," I say dismissively. "It's not my fault I fell asleep."

"I never said it was your fault—"

"Then why are you on my ass?" I snap unexpectedly, and she looks taken aback.

She doesn't say anything at first, and I just stand there, squirming under the ever-familiar pitying look she's giving me. I don't know why she lets me talk back to her now. It's like she's walking on eggshells around me ever since The Event. Everyone does, really. Like she's afraid she'll lose me if she disciplines me like she used to. I won't lie, I've been talking back more and more, trying to get *some* kind of reaction out of her, but no. All I ever get is that look. It's so much worse.

"So you're still having trouble sleeping at night, then?" she asks, eyes starting to shine.

"I guess so," I say, shifting my weight uncomfortably. Why does she have to *look* at me like that?

She finally forces a smile. "It's okay, mijo. I still have money on you being the next Jeff Bezos."

"Ew, that's not a compliment." Yami gags.

Mami clucks her tongue. "You know what I mean," she says, and I do.

She means I'm supposed to have a bright future. That I'm the always-exceptional straight-A student who can do no wrong, no matter how much detention I get. Being a prodigy is a lot of pressure. Sometimes I wish I could just be mediocre. That I could just be *okay* at something, let alone bad at it.

"Are your meds working all right?" She changes the subject when I don't respond to her whole Jeff Bezos failure of a compliment.

"They're fine," I lie, almost interrupting. My meds weren't doing shit when I was on them, so it's not like there's anything different to report. Besides, I don't want my mom worrying about me any more than she already does. "Can I go now? I have homework." I lie again; I finished my homework in detention.

"Okay, mijo," she says, all sad, then pulls me in for a tight hug before going to join Yami in the living room. I let her hug me even though I don't know why she's doing it. I just got detention for the however-manyth time this year. I should be getting grounded, not hugged. It's all just so much worse.

She gives me one final squeeze before letting me go, and I get the hell out of there as quick as I can. I stay in my room through dinner, counting down the minutes until Jamal calls me.

I know I shouldn't be looking forward to talking to him. Usually, hearing Jamal's voice makes me feel better, but it got complicated after talking to Father John and getting that email from my dad. That light, fluffy feeling Jamal usually gives me is still there, but now it's mixed with a heavy dose of guilt and shame.

So when seven finally hits, I let the phone ring a few times before bringing myself to answer it.

"Hey, you," I finally say.

"Hey, you," he responds. "How are you today?"

"I'm good!" I say automatically. "You?"

"You sure?" Jamal asks. "Yami told me you got detention."

"Yeah, and?" I say, rolling my eyes. Goodbye three-second-long light fluffy feeling. This time it's not even replaced with shame or guilt, but annoyance. I don't need Jamal *and* Yami *and* my mom to be on my ass. And I don't appreciate Yami talking about me to Jamal behind my back.

"And you're deflecting. Are you okay?"

That's when a wall builds up around me, and I suddenly don't want to talk to Jamal anymore. "Okay, well, deflect *this*," I say as I hang up the phone.

And *now* the guilt and shame kicks in.

10

WHEN YOU HAVE ABSOLUTELY NO REASON TO BE JEALOUS SO OF COURSE YOU'RE NOT AT ALL JEALOUS

inflated self-image

Every day, I pretend to take my meds before spitting them out in the toilet. Every day, I'm more and more suspicious of the circumstances that made me have to go on them in the first place. Like, if the meds weren't making me feel better, what *were* they doing?

Jamal's interest in sci-fi pops into my brain, and I feel like this all being some kind of dystopian brainwashing plot isn't as far-fetched as I used to think. Part of me knows I'm probably being paranoid. That this fear is ~~definitely~~, ~~most likely~~, ~~probably~~, maybe irrational.

But it's better safe than sorry, right? Besides, sometimes not taking my meds in the morning is the only solid win I have in a day, and I'm not about to give that up.

So I have a new routine now. One I'm fully in control of. Every morning, I stick the pill in my mouth and pretend to gulp, then go to the bathroom as soon as my mom looks satisfied and spit it out in the toilet.

Of course it doesn't change much. I still fall asleep at school instead of at night. I still get detention more than I should. My mom still looks at me like I'm a kicked puppy. But at least *I* did something.

It's not until several days into the new routine on Thursday when something *does* change. I reach for my bag to get my homework out while Coach V tries to entertain us in detention, but a thought stops me: What's the point?

I already know all this shit. Even if I don't do the homework, I know I'll ace the tests. It's not like homework itself counts for enough of my grade to make me lose my scholarship on its own, so does it even matter? I'm sure it'll be fine. Instead of working on something productive, I just stare at a stain on the wall listening to The Thoughts.

The Thoughts haven't come during the day in a while, but I welcome them now because maybe it'll mean tonight will be peaceful.

I decide to start doing a technique Dr. Lee taught me in our first session and respond to the voice in my head like it's a real person. Someone mean enough to say whatever it's saying. Since I wouldn't take that shit from a real person, I guess it does kind of help to respond to it in the same way.

You're a burden to everyone around you.

Yeah, no shit, me. You've really got to come up with some tougher insults if you want to actually hurt my feelings.

Everyone you love secretly resents you.

A swing and a miss. It's not like any of them can resent me more than I do. Besides, I already knew that.

Of course they resent me. I'm the whole reason Yami has to go to Catholic school in the first place and why she and my mom have to work their asses off every waking minute to try to pay for her tuition. I broke up with Jamal, then strung him along. He has to be pissed at me for that. Then there's my dad . . .

They're better off without you.

Aren't you supposed to be antagonizing me, me? I don't think this is going to work if we *agree* on everything.

And finally, silence.

I can't believe that actually worked.

Guess therapy has its perks, *some*times.

When seven on Friday comes around, the doorbell rings instead of my phone, and I hop out of bed to meet Jamal at the door. I almost didn't expect him to come. We haven't talked much since I hung up on him a few days ago, which is really not normal for us. I texted him sorry and lied saying I was swamped with homework this week to avoid getting into anything deeper, so he hasn't been calling me at the normal time. He's not the type of person to try to talk things through over text, so I was hoping to wait out the confrontation until it went away.

I just need to act like everything is fine. If Jamal's mad at me for hanging up on him, he wouldn't be here to get me for his open mic, right? Hopefully it's been long enough not to matter anymore. And if it hasn't, then maybe if I pretend there's nothing wrong, he'll follow along.

"Bye, Mami! Bye, Yami!" I shout before darting out and shutting the door behind me, so they don't ask questions and make us late. I already told Mami about the open mic, but I wouldn't put it past her to hold us up trying to make conversation with Jamal. Not that we'd be late; we still have awhile before the open mic starts, but Jamal wants to get there early to make sure he can sign up and guarantee himself a spot. If it wasn't for him coming to get me first, he'd probably get there even earlier, considering the coffee shop is right outside his neighborhood.

"You hung up on me," Jamal says instead of a hello. So much for brushing it under the rug. "I thought you were mad at me."

"Oh, uh, no . . . ," I say, starting the walk to his truck to make the conversation feel more casual. I don't want it to feel like a big deal, but I also don't want him to feel bad for any part of this. "I was just off that day, I guess."

"Do you want to talk about it?" he asks when we get to his truck. He starts to reach out to open the door for me before pulling his hand away.

"Nope, I'm good," I say, opening my own door and climbing inside so he doesn't push the subject.

It's not a long drive, so we don't have a lot of time to talk before we get there, which is probably for the best. The venue isn't exactly what I was expecting. It's got that hipster-Christian vibe a lot of youth ministry volunteers tend to have. It's a ritzy-looking coffee shop filled with white people who look like they claim to have listened to all the popular artists "before they were cool." I find myself walking a little bit closer to Jamal as we enter, and I realize he's doing the same.

We're definitely out of our element. Still, hearing Jamal perform will make tonight worth it. When I glance over the menu, I realize it's full of Bible puns.

Between the extra-caffeinated white coffee called the Resurrection, the Ten Command-mint iced mocha, the red velvet cold brew called the Red Sea, and the Virgin Bloody Mary, this place feels like the acid trip of every pothead youth pastor's wet dreams.

I glance over at Jamal, trying to gauge if he already knew this was a Christian coffee shop. He looks a little nervous, but that could just be a regular amount of pre-performance nerves.

"You still down to do this?" I ask.

"Yeah." He lets out a little huff like he's pumping himself up. "I'm about to make a bunch of people really uncomfortable, but I might as well get some exposure therapy, right?"

"We can leave whenever if anything happens," I offer, and he nods.

A hand slaps against my back, and I whirl around ready to start swinging until I see the body attached to the hand.

"Missed you, bro! Where the hell have you been, loca?" Hunter says as he pulls me in for a hug, then gives one to Jamal.

I resist the urge to tell him it's loco or react in any way to being called crazy. Even if it is just a quote from one of the Twilight movies he's probably never seen.

"Sorry," Hunter says before anyone gets a chance to respond, retracting his neck like a scared turtle.

I just laugh. He may have been one of the most popular guys at Slayton, but college must have humbled Hunter enough for him to actually feel an ounce of embarrassment at what comes out of his mouth.

"This is my friend Sasha." Hunter clears his throat and gestures at the tall brunet guy next to him, who waves. "I thought you might want some backup, since you're doing a, uh, coming-out poem, and Sasha's, well . . . like you."

Hunter glances at me before continuing a little faster, like he thinks I'll be annoyed or something, "I mean, like, he's done this part already. If you know what I mean." He stumbles over his words a bit, and a little tingle of panic rushes blood to my ears. Hunter's not exactly being subtle, and I don't know Sasha like that.

Did he see Hunter look at me before adding the caveat about Sasha already being out?

I push the panic down, and a small pit of jealousy swells up in its place. I wonder if Sasha feels comfortable with being the official queer moral support of the night.

Jamal looks at Sasha apologetically and asks what I'm thinking. "Did you know what you were getting yourself into when Hunter invited you?" He gestures at the Bible-themed drinks menu.

"Honestly, I wasn't loving the idea at first, but he showed me your picture, so obviously I had to make an exception," he says with a flirty smile that makes my insides churn.

"I don't understand," Jamal says, the line clearly going right over his head. "Do we know each other from somewhere?"

I try not to visibly gloat at Jamal not picking up on what Sasha's doing. Jamal rarely says he doesn't understand *me*. Sasha has game, but it's a shame there's no spark. How sad for him.

"You're cute." Sasha laughs. "No, we don't know each other. I just thought you were hot enough to try and fix that."

I don't want to hear Jamal's response to that, so I quickly shake away the jealousy and go to the counter to order an iced caramel mocha, Jamal's favorite. Sasha may be hot, but does he know Jamal's favorite coffee order? I think not.

God, I'm annoying myself. Why am I even jealous? I already told Jamal we can't get back together. Who cares if Sasha likes him? It has nothing to do with me either way.

I hurry and pay for the caramel mocha while some white dude with a guitar gets set up at the mic. As soon as Jamal's drink is ready, I grab it and head to the table where the three of them are sitting now.

"Thanks, Cesar," Jamal says when I hand him his coffee. "You didn't want anything?"

"Stomach hurts," I answer honestly. It's the anxiety, I think. Why I'm anxious when Jamal's the one performing is beyond me. Still, I'm not really in the mood to drink caffeine and have yet another reason to stay awake tonight.

Jamal nods his understanding before leaving me alone with Hunter and Sasha to go find the sign-up sheet.

"So how do you all know each other?" Sasha asks.

"School," I say flatly.

"Cesar and I went to Slayton together last year, but before that, he went to the same school as Jamal, so he introduced us," Hunter clarifies.

Sasha leans forward, propping his elbows on the table like he's about to share a secret. "So, Cesar, I have to know, is Jamal single? Hunter couldn't tell me."

"Yeah." I swallow the lump in my throat. "But I don't know if he's looking right now," I find myself saying. Which isn't really fair of me. I have no right to keep Jamal from dating whoever he wants now. Still, being his wingman isn't exactly a skill I was prepared to hone.

"I'm fifth in the lineup." Thankfully, Jamal cuts the conversation short when he comes back to our table. He's holding a couple pieces of paper in his hands with his poems written on them. I can't help but notice the slight tremble of the paper in the air, which makes whatever annoyance I had completely dissipate.

"You're gonna do great," I say, offering Jamal a reassuring smile. He lets out a breath and sits down next to me.

Before we know it, the MC is announcing the rules of the open mic: Each performer has five minutes on stage, no disrespecting each other, no heckling, etc. etc. etc. Just as they're about to introduce the first performer, someone pushes their way forward, stealing the mic from whoever was about to go first. I don't get a good look at his face until he turns his cap backward.

My stomach drops. My fists tighten. My ears ring.

Someone's trying to usher him off the stage, telling him there's a set order, but he just ignores them and shouts into the mic, holding it so close to his mouth he's practically making out with it. "Hello, my name is Nick, and my pronouns are fuck and you!"

I quickly scan the room for any sign of the rest of his entourage, but only see Avery. Thinking about it now, I shouldn't be surprised Nick's here, considering how close we are to his and Jamal's neighborhood. This might actually be the right kind of crowd for his whole anti-pronouns spiel, too, if it weren't for him breaking the rules first.

"Oh, great. It's gonna be *that* kind of night," Sasha says under his breath.

Even Nick's little minion Avery looks embarrassed, trying to signal for him to leave from off the stage. Nick spouts some bullshit for another few seconds before Avery joins him on stage and tries pulling him off.

"One Holy Grail for Nick!" the barista calls out, and Nick finally lets Avery lead him to the counter.

The useless MC then apologizes to everyone and introduces the actual first performer. The musician starts singing a love song that makes me feel way too mushy. I want to grab Jamal by the hand and take him away from this place. Away from Nick and Avery and Sasha, and just bring him somewhere safe. I'm about to ask if he wants to bail since Nick and Avery showed up, but before I get a chance, a hot drink spills right in my lap.

I jump to my feet and find myself face-to-face with Nick.

"Whoa, not cool, dude," Hunter says as he grabs for some napkins across the table.

"It was an accident." Nick sizes me up, chin raised. Like he's challenging me. He wants me to be the one to pick the fight, and I'm not giving him the satisfaction.

"Not now, bro, you're drunk," Avery mutters, looking fully exhausted. I'd be exhausted too if I had to keep Nick's ass from causing a scene every time I turned a corner. Avery's always been Nick's right hand, and the only brain cell among basically their entire group. At least he's smart enough to know when they're the ones outnumbered.

Nick holds my stare for a few more seconds before finally smirking, as if he's somehow won this encounter. He walks off, making sure to shoulder check me on his way out.

"Assholes," Sasha mumbles. "Thank God they left."

"You know those guys?" Hunter asks, still wiping the table with napkins. He's about to start dabbing at my lap, but I stop him.

"I got it," I say as I grab the napkins from him and wipe myself off.

"They go to Rover." Jamal answers the question for me. I'm glad he doesn't give them any more information than that. They don't need to know that they bullied me so bad my mom switched me and Yami to Catholic school.

After that, I pretend to focus on the poet on stage, so no one thinks too much about what just happened. But this girl's poems are nowhere near on Jamal's level. And yeah, yeah, I know this is an open mic and not a competition, but Jamal is about to crush these fools.

After a few more performances, Jamal gets introduced. He hesitates before standing up. I wish I could rub his shoulders or back or squeeze his hand. Anything to tell him I'm here for him and not to be nervous. But the truth is, I don't know this crowd, and I don't want them making any assumptions about me and Jamal. Nick might be gone, but I don't know who else might be just like him here.

Once he's on stage, Jamal closes his eyes for a moment, clears his throat, and steps to the mic.

"This one isn't really a poem, actually. I don't really know what it is," he starts, then takes a deep breath and reads from his paper. *"A letter from the closet to the queer."* He pauses, and I find myself mesmerized already. He looks at me nervously, and I give him a reassuring smile and a thumbs-up before he continues. *"You said you didn't need me anymore. You said you felt trapped, but I know you better than that. Between bitter breaths, you released a sigh of relief because you've always been safe with me. And no matter how scary it is being* out, *you know I'll always be your safe place.*

"But . . . you wanted to see the world. To go to Pride. To love someone out loud. To love a boy." He glances at me at that part, but quickly looks away. Jamal's never been able to do that part with me. Not out loud, at least. *"When you pick out your clothes every morning and look into my eyes, you make the same choice. Every day you wear the armor I provide you, and you leave me so you can see the world. You look into my eyes, my gentle reminder of safety, and you turn it down.*

"*But I'll always be here. I was here when you came back after your first time venturing outside.*" I happen to know the "first time" he's talking about is when he told me he loved me. When we shared our first kiss. My chest gets tight.

"*I remember the next time you came back. You stood in front of me, beaten and bloody with tears tracking down swollen cheeks. No matter what garments I offered to soak the salt water from your face, you cried still. You cried because, while you love the outside, it didn't love you back.*" This time I know he's talking about when he got kicked out of his mom and stepdad's house after coming out to them.

I'll never be as brave as Jamal. Every time I came out of the closet was a mistake, besides that fluke during anti-prom when I came out to Yami's friends and Hunter. Even if I can be out to Jamal, and Yami, and my mom, I could never just talk about my queerness plainly in front of a crowd. Especially one like this.

This crowd isn't outright heckling or anything, but most of them aren't snapping in support like they did every other line of the first girl's poem. And when his piece is done, they give polite, unenthusiastic claps.

But I'm still breathless by the time Jamal walks off stage and back to our table. Not because his piece was good—I know nothing about poetry, or what makes it good—but because of how real it was. How real it could be for me, if I ever wanted it to be.

But I don't. Not now. Maybe not ever.

On the car ride home, Jamal can't stop smiling.

"I'm proud of you," I say, his smile contagiously rubbing off on me.

"Me too," he admits. "It probably could have gone better, though."

"What do you mean? You were perfect."

"I mean, it was kind of weird, you know? The crowd didn't really seem like they were feeling it. Who knows, maybe they were homophobic or something. Maybe my letter sucked. Maybe Nick just threw off the vibes."

"Okay, no, your letter did not suck. It was probably just the crowd. I think the only queer people there were at our table."

"Yeah, maybe . . . I wish there were more open mics around here." Jamal slumps his shoulders. "I don't even know if I want to go back to that one."

"Why don't you start your own?" I ask. "You can make it explicitly queer friendly if you want."

Jamal lets out a small breath through his nose. "We're in Arizona. Is there even a market for that kind of thing?"

"There has to be," I say with more confidence than I expected. "Especially here, people are probably starving for that shit."

Jamal pushes his glasses up his nose like he's considering my words. "You know, that could actually be an option."

"Why not?" I shrug. "You can do whatever you put your mind to."

And no, I'm not saying that because I believe in mind over matter or thinking things into existence. I'm saying it because *Jamal* can literally do anything he sets out to do. He's determined like that.

"I'll look into it," Jamal says tentatively, but he's still smiling.

I look down at his hand, which is resting on the center console.

I want to take it in mine. Want to pull his palm to my lips and kiss it and tell him he's amazing and that he deserves everything he wants, but I don't.

My closet isn't as loving toward me as Jamal's. Mine is dark and stuffy, and I feel like I'm locked in. My dad and Father John and God Himself have their backs against the door so I'd have to push through all of them to make it out. They all chant those ever-familiar words on repeat from the other side.

What you're doing is *a choice. And you're making the wrong one.*

Unfortunately, I've never died before, so I'm no expert in how to get into heaven, but I still can't make sense of it. How can loving Jamal be wrong when being with him has felt nothing but so, so right?

My fingers find the necklaces dangling from my neck. The two have always felt contradictory somehow, cross and jaguar. Catholic and indigenous symbolism. All I want is for those two pieces of myself, those two necklaces, to go together. To coexist.

But how can they?

The jaguar says to face my fears, while the cross says not to sin. For the tiniest moment, the chanting fades, and I peek through the crack in my closet door where the light seeps in. It creaks open ever so slightly, inviting me to take an exploratory step outside. If I could just give it a push . . .

Instead, I grab the handle and shut it tight.

11

WHEN YOU'D RATHER GET A PAPER CUT IN SHARK-INFESTED WATERS THAN DO YOUR HOMEWORK

low motivation

Jamal calls me at the usual time on Saturday, but I can't bring myself to answer. I don't know if it's because his closet letter touched a nerve I don't know how to address, or just that the open mic was too socially exhausting for the miniscule amount of sleep I got.

All I know is I need to feel like I don't exist for a little bit longer. So I stay in bed and close my eyes. Unsurprisingly, sleep doesn't come, but being conscious doesn't make me any more capable of being a human person. It kind of feels like all the hours of sleep I've been missing teamed up and personified—not to help me sleep, but to beat the living shit out of me.

It isn't until the next day that I even consider getting out of bed. Well, consider is maybe a strong word. The thought crossed my mind, but I can't do it. I know I promised to make dinner for my mom on Sundays, but I'm sure the food tastes better without my influence anyway. Besides, Yami's probably grateful not to have to fix all my fuckups. It's better this way for everyone involved.

I may have successfully gotten The Thoughts to shut up the

other day, but I'm having a harder time right now. The Thoughts are mean, sure, but not wrong.

Jamal calls again at the usual time tonight, too. I want to ignore him. I want to answer. I want to go into a coma, so I don't have to make any decisions for a while. At least then I'd have a good excuse to lie down and do nothing.

But if I ignore Jamal too much, he might realize I'm not actually worth talking to and stop calling. And I know that would probably be for the best, but it would probably also be the actual end of the world. Worse than the animal uprising, alien invasion, or any of the other options he gave me to choose from. So I gather all the energy that's been accumulating from my hibernation and answer the phone.

"Hey, you," I say, as if I hadn't just ignored him yesterday.

"Hey, you," he says, and as usual, I can hear the smile on his face. "How are you, Cesar?"

"Good, what about you?" I quickly throw the question back before he has a chance to catch my deflection.

"I'm great!" he says enthusiastically. "I wanted to tell you yesterday, but I found a coffee shop that will let me host an open mic! It's happening in two weeks!"

"Already? That's awesome!" I say, a genuine smile tugging at my lips.

"Thanks. Apparently, this place is queer owned, and they loved the idea of a queer-friendly open mic, so it was really easy to plan." He's talking faster than usual, like he's too excited to hold it in.

"I knew you'd make it happen."

"So, question," he says, sounding nervous.

"Yeah?"

"Do you . . . want to come?"

At first I'm not sure why he's asking as if I *wouldn't* want to come, or why he sounds so nervous. But then I realize this open mic is different. It's a specifically queer space, and he wants to make sure I'm ready for that.

I want to question why he even wants me there. Why he's still putting up with me. But if he's under some false illusion that I'm worth keeping around, I don't want to go shattering it. Besides, it's not like I have to come out in order to support a friend. "I'll definitely be there."

"Thanks, I appreciate you."

For some reason, the familiar line makes my heart ache. For all the times Jamal insists he *understands* everything about me, I can't get a grasp on him at all. To him, it's like I can do no wrong, and I don't have a single flaw. I have no idea what he sees when he looks at me, but whatever it is, he must be kidding himself.

I'm not perfect like everyone thinks, and I'm tired of pretending to be.

Maybe that's why I haven't been doing my homework. Maybe that's why I stopped bothering to hide it when I fall asleep in class.

I'm done living up to everyone's expectations.

The days start blending together like one dull, meaningless blob. I'm almost grateful to get called out of class and into the guidance counselor's office on a Monday, if only because it breaks up the monotony for a bit.

The counselor's office is full of feel-good posters that say things like Jesus Loves You and Blessed Not Stressed, which both feel hilariously off-base at the moment.

"Good morning!" I say cheerfully, doing my best to channel the Not Stessed part.

"Good morning, Cesar." She grins and gestures for the seat in front of her desk, waiting for me to sit before speaking. "It's your senior year. Have you given any thought to what college you want to go to? Applied for any scholarships?"

"Can't say that I have," I say truthfully.

She quirks an eyebrow. "Really? If you'd asked me last year who between you and your sister would be going to college, I'd have had my money on you." I have to suck on my lips to keep my face from twisting at that comment. It's not like she's in the minority with that assumption, but it still bothers me. Hopefully she didn't say the same thing to Yami. Part of me wants to ask Yami myself, since that comment kind of implies she *is* going to college, and she hasn't said anything about it to me. "I'm sure you could get several scholarships if you start applying!"

"What if I just don't go to college?" I ask the forbidden question. I haven't had the energy or motivation to apply for any scholarships, and I don't see that changing anytime soon. My mom probably wouldn't care if *Yami* didn't go to college, but me? I've been being prepped for it my whole life, basically, just because of my unusually high IQ. Which, let's be real, is bullshit and unfair for all parties involved.

"Well, do you know what you might do instead of college?"

I just shrug. Why do I always have to be doing something? It's exhausting.

"Well, either way, it's a good idea to keep your options open. Which brings me to our next conversation. Do you know the real reason I called you here?"

"Because you missed me?" I say, trying to get a grin out of her so she stops looking at me all concerned like that. Usually, the older office-lady types are all over the banter, but she just sighs and goes on.

"I just wanted to remind you that your scholarship requires you to maintain your GPA at a certain threshold. I'm worried you might be putting your scholarship in jeopardy if your grades keep dropping like this."

I resist the urge to roll my eyes. "I already did the math. It shouldn't be a problem as long as I keep acing my tests." Logically speaking, I know it's bad if I lose my scholarship. I'd have to go back to Rover, and I'd be in a shit ton of trouble, but honestly, I feel like it's what I deserve.

"You can't count on that, Cesar." She folds her hands together on the table and looks at me with another one of those pitying looks I fucking despise. "Lucky for you, I talked to your teachers, and we came up with a plan. If you can make up all the homework you've missed, you can get 60 percent credit on it. That'll be enough to bring your grades back up to a safe level."

"Thanks," I say, knowing I won't be bothered to do that much work with the low amount of energy I've had lately. Not that I'll need to, if I keep acing my tests. "Can I go now?" I ask, feeling irritation starting to simmer, which isn't a good sign.

I don't know why, but lately any small inconvenience lights an angry fire in my chest. I try not to come across as an angry person, but the truth is, sometimes I just want to blow up on literally everyone all the time. I know better than to do that to the school counselor, so it's best if I leave before the annoyance turns into full-blown rage.

"Not so fast, Cesar. Let's talk for a bit, okay?" She seems to soften up at the first hint of me not being all smiles and rainbows, for some reason.

"Okay?" I say, knowing I don't have much of a choice.

"How are things at home?" She asks that same question Mr. Franco is always bugging me with.

"Things are great!" I say in my best cheery voice, trying to push down the bubbling irritation.

"I hope you know that if you want to talk, or need anything, that's what I'm here for, all right?" She finally smiles, but it's a sad smile, like she feels bad for me.

"Everything's fine, seriously," I say, voice as even as I can manage.

"All right. Well, I can't force you to open up. But know if your grades dip any lower, we'll be talking again very soon."

"Got it," I say curtly, then get up and walk away before she can ask any more questions.

Between second and third hour, David approaches me.

"Hey, did you study for the English test today, by any chance?" he asks.

I shake my head. I barely have the energy to shower these days, let alone use my brain.

"Shit," David says. "Me either. Totally forgot it was today. Want to cram at lunch?"

"No, thanks." I shrug. "I have to . . ." I trail off. God, usually I'm good at coming up with excuses, but my brain is just not working lately. Way too foggy. "I have to do my homework," I finally say, then turn around and walk away before he can get too suspicious.

When English comes around, our tests are already on our desks. I walk in and confidently start filling out the top of the Scantron, then get to reading the test questions. They're way too easy. It's so simple, it's boring. So boring I could do it in my sleep . . .

I fill it out like muscle memory, almost like I'm in a trance.

I don't realize anything's wrong until the bell signaling the end of class wakes me up, and I'm horrified to see an almost completely empty Scantron in front of me.

I slept through the test.

12

WHEN YOUR FISTS HURT FROM CLENCHING THEM SO HARD

anger

Yami goes home with Bo today, so she can't shield me from Mami the way she usually tries to. Good, honestly. I don't need her protection. Everyone worries about me too much. They'd all be better off if they'd just give it a rest.

The second I'm let out of detention, I go straight to my mom's car. I'm not scared to face her. In fact, I'm looking forward to it. Maybe if she has to see me after detention without Yami to cushion it, she'll actually get mad.

I make no apologies when I get in the car. I want to see what she'll say.

"Mijo, I talked to your counselor today." She sounds more worried than angry, so I'm really not loving this start. At least she decided to have this conversation while she's driving, so I don't have to deal with that *look* she always gives me.

"Whatever Dr. Lee said, it's—"

"Your *school* counselor," she interrupts.

Great. It's not like Mami needed another reason to get on my ass about my grades or anything.

"It's fine, I have it handled," I lie.

"Do you need a tutor? Is there anything I can do to help?"

I frown. We both know she has no way of helping me with Calc II. "I did the math. As long as I keep acing the tests, my grades won't dip below the scholarship level. I'm doing just fine, I promise." I intentionally leave out the part about me failing the test today, which kind of throws my whole plan on its head.

"Well then, what's going on with your grades?" she asks, and even though she's looking at the road and not at me, there's concern etched into her features. I shift in my seat so I'm facing the window instead of her. "Mijo?"

"I have it handled!" I snap, expecting—*hoping*—she'll blow up right back.

Instead, she just lets out a shaky breath. "I'm going to get you a tutor."

"But I don't need—"

"I'm your mother, and I'm telling you you're getting a tutor."

At that, the little bubble I usually push down bursts.

"You don't know what's best for me!" I whirl around so I'm looking right at her, and she finally snaps her head in my direction.

"No, *you* don't know what's best for you!" she yells back, which feeds the anger. I've been waiting for a fight for *months*, and I'm finally close to getting one.

"That makes no fucking sense!" I shout. "So everyone knows what's best for me but me?"

And then, just as quickly as she blew up, she deflates. "That's not what I meant."

"Ugh!" I ball my fists, trying my best not to punch the dashboard and get us in an accident. "Why are you always walking on eggshells around me? Just tell me I'm a piece of shit! Tell me you're disappointed! That you're pissed! *Something!*"

"I'm not any of those things, mijo." She reaches a hand across the center console and takes mine. The touch grounds me just enough to relax my clenched fists and let her hold on.

"Why not?" I ask, my voice catching this time.

"Because I . . ." She squeezes my hand as her voice cracks, too. "I couldn't bear it if something I said or did made you—"

"Made me kill myself?" I interrupt. We've been dancing around the subject since I almost did it last year, might as well get to the point.

She lets go of my hand to wipe a tear from her eye. "Yes, Cesar. I don't want to lose you, do you understand?"

I let out a deep breath. "My life is not your responsibility."

"Of course it is, mijo. I'm your mother."

And that, that just fucking kills me. It's not like I'm going to off myself tomorrow, but I don't know . . . I'm pretty sure that's how I'll go. The thought of my mom blaming herself, of Yami or Jamal blaming themselves, makes me feel so fucking hopeless. Like I can't even have the distant idea of a release from this world as a comfort because I know it'll completely wreck them. And despite how I treat them, I do actually care.

When we pull up to our driveway, there are two people standing on the side of the house, peeking in through the side window.

"Who the f—" my mom interrupts herself by honking her horn to get the peepers' attention and rolls down the car window. They both jolt at the noise and whirl around, and Mami lets out a relieved laugh. "Ay dios mío, I thought we had some stalkers! Why didn't you tell me you were in town?"

Now that I get a better look, I still can't put names to faces. One is a vaguely familiar-looking girl with short, straight black hair around my age, and the other is a bald guy probably in his late thirties, also vaguely familiar. The girl perks up and waves enthusiastically when she sees me, but it isn't until the guy starts talking that I realize who they are.

"We happened to be in town, so I thought we'd stop by to surprise my little sister!"

Mami parks the car, not wasting any time before getting out and giving my tío Paco a huge hug. Her face is smothered by his shoulder so I can't really tell, but I think she might be crying. I undo my seat belt and get out of the car to say hi to my cousin Moni, who I haven't seen since I was like ten.

I'm about to go in for the socially mandated familial hello hug, but Moni holds up the palm of her hand to stop me.

"Sorry, I don't usually do hugs. High five?"

I happily trade the hug for slapping the palm of her hand.

"I'm so rude! Come in, come in!" Mami says through sniffles as she unlocks the door and leads us all inside. "Cesar, why don't you show Monica your room? Your tío and I have a lot to catch up on."

"Sure," I say as I start down the hall.

"Leave the door cracked!" my tío calls out, and I throw a thumbs-up over my shoulder in response.

Moni makes herself comfortable on my bed right away, and I take the desk chair.

"So what are you guys doing in town?" I ask, not really knowing what else to talk about. We haven't talked in years, but Moni and I used to be pretty much inseparable when we were little.

Moni scoffs. "I got in trouble, so my dad's sending me to Abuela's to set me straight."

"Oh, shit, they were serious about that?" I ask. My mom and tío used to threaten us all with being sent to Abuela's if we got in trouble, but Mami never made good on it. Considering my mom and abuela rarely talk and my mom can't stand her, I never took the threat seriously.

"Are you forgetting I'm the problem child?" Moni says, though she doesn't look convinced by her own words, and honestly, I'm not convinced either.

Even when we were little, Moni's always been somewhat of a musical genius. Sometimes her dad would go hunting for an instrument she'd never played so he could give it to her as a party trick. He'd play a recording of some song from that instrument, then we'd all watch while she tinkered for a few minutes before playing the same song by ear. They moved to L.A. when she got into a fine arts middle school, which I didn't even know was a thing.

"You too?" I laugh humorlessly. Maybe we have that whole prodigy-turned-disappointment thing in common. I think about how Tío Paco only called the visit a "surprise" and said that they just happened to be in town. "Why do you think your dad didn't tell my mom what happened?"

She shrugs. "He probably will, but I guess he's nervous. I bet he just doesn't want to admit why he's sending me with Abuela."

"Why's that?" I ask, leaning forward in my chair. I forgot how nice it was not being the only family disappointment ever since they moved to L.A. and my mom stopped talking to my abuela. Despite Moni's genius, she's always been pretty rebellious.

"To get me away from my *negative influences*," she says the last part with finger quotes. "Which is silly. My business is where I am, I'm just excited to tap into a new market. I'm the influence! If he's so worried about negativity, maybe he should be more supportive."

I nod as if I have any idea what she's talking about, but luckily, she keeps going, so I don't have to ask.

"Seriously, he should be proud of me! I'm an entrepreneur! Just because my business isn't *technically* legal doesn't mean it's not ethical, and just because the work he does *is* legal doesn't make it right."

I vaguely remember my tío having some kind of job in the pharmaceutical industry, but other than that I have no idea what she's referring to. "Uh, what's your business, exactly?" I ask once I remember how Moni's always been. She kind of forgets that not everyone has all the same context going into a conversation. She probably doesn't even realize I don't know what she's talking about.

"Oh, I sell weed." I laugh involuntarily, but she doesn't crack so much as a smile. "But my dad's just as much of a drug dealer as I am. I want to save up and open my own dispensary when I'm old enough. If he wants me to stop selling the 'wrong' way, he should help me fund my dispensary with *his* drug money. But *no*, he'll only give me money if it's for a music program.

"He says he invested too much in my career to let me throw it away by focusing on something else. So I said he doesn't have to throw my career away, I'll do it for him." She smiles and sits up straighter. "He should learn from me. It's never too late to leave a soul-sucking career. Anyways, where's Yami?" she asks, but keeps going before I can answer. "I'm kind of relieved she's not here, honestly. Probably wouldn't be able to talk about this stuff around her, you know?"

"You don't like Yami?" I'm a little surprised since I always thought Yami and Moni got along. They were never as close as me and Moni, or me and Yami, but the three of us still had fun.

"More like she probably doesn't like me. At least, she won't when she finds out why we came back. She'll probably think I'm a bad influence on you."

I'm about to respond that Yami never said anything bad about her, but Moni shushes me before I can get a word in.

"Did you hear that?" She's whispering now.

"Hear what?" I say quietly, trying to listen for whatever.

"That was your name. I think they're talking about you; let's go listen."

She doesn't wait for me to agree before slowly pushing the door open and creeping into the hallway. I follow because, I mean, I do want to know what they're saying about me.

My mom and tío's voices are coming from the kitchen on the other side of the hall. They're talking kind of quiet, but it's still easy enough to make out.

"I just don't know what to do with that boy," I hear my mom say. I clench my jaw, trying not to let Moni see any emotions on my face. "What am I supposed to do?"

"Have you talked to Mami? She's been a huge help getting through to Monica—"

"We don't speak," my mom responds harshly.

"Don't be so hard on her. She's doing a lot better now. She might be able to help."

They argue in hushed tones for a bit over whether my abuela is worth reaching out to. I don't even know what happened between my mom and abuela. All I know is they haven't spoken in years, and every time I overhear my mom talking about her, it's about how crazy she is and how she can't be trusted.

Before they say anything too juicy, their voices start moving in our direction, so Moni and I rush back to the room as stealthy as possible, barely managing to push the door to its almost-closed position before our parents turn the corner. Not long after that, Moni's dad knocks on the door saying it's time for them to go. I give my tío a goodbye hug and Moni another high five, and they're gone. Hopefully it won't be another seven years before I see them again.

I flop face-first down on my bed as soon as I'm alone and stay like that for who knows how long. I try not to let it bother me too much that my mom was venting about me. That she "doesn't know what to do" with me. I just cover my ears with my pillow, like that'll block out the memory of what she said and what that might mean.

Eventually, seven o'clock hits and Jamal calls.

"Hey, you," I answer on reflex, even though it's probably not a good idea to talk to him when I feel like shit.

"Hey, you. How are you doing?" I knew the question was coming, but somehow, I'm never prepared for it. I don't know how to lie to him, but I don't want to be an asshole and hang up on him again or anything either.

I sigh. "Can we not talk about it today?"

"Okay." He takes a few seconds to say anything else. "Question."

"Yeah?" I find myself smiling.

"Do you want to go to a party together on Saturday?"

"Why?" I find myself saying. Jamal has never been the party type. He only ever goes when *I* want to go, so I don't have to show up by myself.

"I just thought, since the open mic I'm throwing is the next day, maybe you can stay the night at my place, or I can at yours, and we can go together?"

"What kind of party—"

"I mean, not *together* together. Just, like, at the same time, together. Like, ride in the car, together."

"It's okay, I know what you meant." I laugh a little. "Is it a Rover party?"

"It is, but if you ever missed Rover parties, this is the one to go to. According to Avery, Nick and Bianca are apparently a match made in hell, and they'll be on a date that night. So we can invite Yami too. And you two could come without running into them. I can pick you both up. If you want to go, I mean."

"Wait, you talk to Avery?" I feel like my brain just short-circuited hearing that name out of Jamal's mouth.

"Not *really*. We have a class together, so I just asked him if they'd be at the party. He's kind of a different person without his friends around. It's weird."

I know Jamal's intentions were good here. I'm almost certain I know exactly what went down. Jamal's probably worried about me since I've been weird lately, and inviting me to a party outside his comfort zone is his idea of cheering me up. But he couldn't invite me to a party Nick and his friends would be at, so he outright asked Avery if they'd be there. Which, in theory, is nice. But . . . "You didn't tell him you were inviting me, did you?"

"I didn't."

I finally relax my shoulders. I wouldn't put it past Avery to lie and say they wouldn't be there just to get me to show up while they have enough bodies to actually do something.

"Okay, good. As long as Nick won't be there, we can go. I'll invite Yami."

I can hear his relieved sigh blowing into the phone. "Great. I'll pick you guys up then."

"Thanks," I say, hoping he hears the unspoken part. That I appreciate how he looks out for me and wants to cheer me up. Unfortunately, Jamal isn't an expert in reading between the lines, so I find myself adding one of his go-tos. "I appreciate you."

Dr. Lee thinks we're having a staring contest, but no matter how long her eyes bore into mine, she can't make me regret a single thing.

Clearly my mom told her about our kind-of sort-of fight. Dr. Lee knows my grades have been dropping, and she knows I've been irritable with everyone lately. What she doesn't know about is the email from my dad. She doesn't know I've been off my meds. And she doesn't need to.

I feel like she's goading me into apologizing to everyone, but what she doesn't get is that I can't. I don't really know how to explain it. It's like . . . someone might not even be that mad at me, and we could just as easily let the incident pass and forget about it. But if I apologize, that brings all the bad things I've done right to the surface for everyone, dangling my bad decisions in our faces like a carrot in front of a Minecraft pig.

I already know I'm a horrible person, but Jamal? Yami? My mom? They've never seen me in that way. How am I supposed to live with myself if a simple apology makes them see me the way I see myself?

Yeah, there's no way I'm apologizing.

"Do you think you might be sending your loved ones mixed messages?" Dr. Lee asks, folding one condescending leg over the other. "It seems like your mom is trying to respond to your cries for help—"

"Aren't you supposed to make me feel *better*?" I snap. And okay, okay, she's not *wrong*, but she has absolutely no right. I don't tell her my business so she can make me feel like shit about it.

She scribbles something down on her notepad patronizingly. "My job is to help you improve over time. Sometimes that involves exploring things that might feel uncomfortable."

"What, so I can't be annoyed at my family now?" I say, attitudinally crossing my legs to mirror hers before continuing. "Am I supposed to be *happy* my mom's always on my ass about everything I do and say?"

"Of course not," she says, eyes flickering up from her notepad. "Maybe this is a sign that it might be worth reexamining those boundaries we talked about before. Do you remember?"

The only boundary I can remember setting for myself is the most recent one about Jamal. I decide to just fuck it and tell her. "Yeah, so I do have a new boundary now. I decided to only date girls from now on. So, me and Jamal aren't getting back together."

She does a bad job hiding her concerned micro expression. "What changed?" is all she asks.

I clench my jaw. Nothing's changed, really. But at the same time, everything has. Every time I think about Jamal *like that*, I can't get my sperm donor's email out of my head. It's obviously too late to fix my relationship with my dad, but God? God, I do want to get right with.

I find my hand traveling to the cross hanging around my neck and the jaguar necklace behind it. My mom says God accepts me the way I am, but Father John says otherwise, and that guy's, like, a professional God salesman. Theoretically, I could date a girl and even be happy with one. That is, if I could just bring myself to get over Jamal . . .

"Nothing's changed," I finally say.

"I see." She pauses and writes something down in her notepad again, then looks back up at me. "I won't press you to change any boundaries if you're not comfortable with that, but I want to urge you to examine the reasons why you set this boundary in the first place. Maybe that's worth taking a look at."

"I have a good reason, but it's none of your business," I say reflexively.

"I believe you," she says, without pressing the issue further. "Now, back to our earlier conversation. Would you consider your sister, your mom, and Jamal to be your main support system?" Dr. Lee asks, which kind of throws me off.

"Um, yeah, I guess so," I mumble.

"It seems like the three people who are there for you the most are the people you get the most frustrated with. Why do you think it is that you feel negatively about your support system, well . . ." She stops writing in her notepad for a moment to look up at me. "Trying to show you support?"

There's that feeling again. That twinge in my chest.

"Guilt," I find myself saying truthfully.

She writes something down again. "You don't feel like you deserve their support?"

I just shake my head, since I can't bring myself to say the words. I *don't* deserve their support. They spend all their time trying to make sure I'm okay while I'm just . . . *me*. There's no reason they should be spending so much of their energy on my mental health. It doesn't make any sense.

"Now we're making progress," she says, giving me a reassuring smile.

And maybe that's true. Maybe I'm not the type of person who can just apologize whenever I fuck up, but I *can* do something.

Maybe I don't deserve their support right now, but somehow, I need to find a way to fix that.

13

WHEN YOU MAKE UP AN ENTIRE SEMESTER'S WORTH OF HOMEWORK IN ONE NIGHT

hyperactivity

I don't sleep tonight either, but this time instead of lying down and trying to ignore The Thoughts, I don't even bother closing my eyes. It's almost like I was a dying car battery that just got jumped. All the energy I've been missing for the last couple weeks is suddenly in my grasp.

I remember the counselor's offer from before. If I finish my overdue homework, it'll probably be enough to get my mom to ease off, even with me having failed a test. Which will hopefully get Yami and Jamal to stop worrying, too.

I sit at my desk and get started.

While I know this stuff, it's still not exactly quick work. I feel like they make this shit purposely time-consuming just to steal our lives away. Still, I'm faster than most, so by the time I finish, the sun still isn't up. I check my dying phone. Three in the morning.

What else can I do to make things up to my mom and Yami?

I jump up and quickly start cleaning my room, which I've been putting off so long I'm surprised my clothes haven't fossilized on the floor. With how much energy I have, though, it only takes me a half hour or so to organize everything and put away my laundry. But now I'm in a cleaning mood, so I expand my chores to the rest of the house.

First up, dishes. I do them as quietly as I can manage. I sweep next, then scrub the floors. I do it on my hands and knees with a washcloth instead of with the mop, since that's how Mami does it when she wants to be extra thorough. Once the floors are spotless, the couches fluffed, the surfaces dusted, the windows cleaned, and the mess in the living room reorganized, there's still about an hour before my alarm goes off, so I go ahead and clean the bathroom too, making sure to even scrub the shower.

Suddenly I feel gross, being the dirtiest thing in the bathroom. I don't even know when the last time I showered was. Today is different, though. After cleaning the rest of the house, the last thing to wash off is myself, so I hop in the shower for the first time in too long.

For once, I feel the way everyone else says they feel when they shower. Refreshed, energized, creative. I even find myself singing a made-up song while I shampoo. I don't know what's wrong with not-today me, but usually showers *take* energy instead of giving it. Everything takes energy most days. Getting out of bed, getting dressed, social interaction, and, yes, showering.

Today, though. Today, ha ha! Today is the shit. *I'm* the shit. Today I'm showered and dressed before Yami even manages to make it to the bathroom at all.

Mami's not up yet either, so I decide to make pancakes before she wakes up as a surprise. I'm not making them from scratch or anything, but this pancake mix and milk are working their asses off. They smell better than any breakfast I've ever made. Hell, better than most Mami's made. I can't help myself. I eat the first one I finish, just to make sure it tastes as good as it smells.

And, oh my God, how the fuck does it taste even *better*?

Who says I can't cook? I'm Gordon fucking Ramsay, bitch!

"Cesar?" Mami comes into the kitchen, looking around the house in awe. I grin at her.

"I'm making pancakes!" I say proudly.

She tilts her head to the side. "You didn't have to do all this, mijo."

"I wanted to!" I say eagerly, almost interrupting, but this time it's because I'm excited and not angry.

She finally smiles and holds her arms out for a hug. I put the spatula down and fall into it.

"Love you, Mami," I say softly.

"I love you too, mijo. So, so much. Thank you for this."

"Um, what happened in here?"

Mami and I pull away to find Yami wandering the living room and looking around. Her eyes catch the coffee table, where I've organized all their jewelry by color.

"I cleaned!" I beam.

"You rearranged the jewelry?" She sounds like she's biting back some kind of emotion. Happiness? Relief? "How are we supposed to know which order is which?" Her voice is a little louder now. Okay. Um, maybe that's anger.

"Oh, I . . . I didn't realize—" I start, but Mami interrupts.

"It's okay, mijo. We'll figure it out! Thank you for cleaning!"

Then I realize her smile is forced. Like she's *still* walking on eggshells.

"Yamilet, thank your brother for his hard work," Mami says, enunciating through her fake-smiling teeth, eyes darting from me to Yami like she's afraid a bomb might go off.

"You don't have to thank me," I say before Yami has to swallow her pride to thank me for giving her more work. "I'll fix it, okay?"

"I know you were trying to help, but . . . this is gonna take *hours* to figure out," Yami says, rubbing a frustrated hand down her face.

"I said I'll fix it. There's nothing to worry about, okay?"

"Thank you, Cesar," Mami says, putting a hand on my shoulder and squeezing.

I don't know what it is about the touch, but it's like she detonated that bomb she was so afraid of setting off. I shake her hand off, unable to control my outburst. It's like all the high energy that kept me feeling so good all night turns on me out of nowhere. The energy is there, but now that there's nowhere productive to channel it, it turns sour and uncontrollable.

"Don't touch me!" I shout, then run to my room and slam the door.

Okay, logically I *know* I'm overreacting. I know something isn't right here, but I can't help it.

Even when I try to make things right, all I'm capable of is fucking everything up.

14

WHEN EVERYTHING IS PERFECT UNTIL IT'S NOT. UNTIL IT IS AGAIN! UNTIL IT'S NOT

mood swings

By the time I get to school, the events of the morning have slipped through my hands like a wet bar of soap. I don't even remember why I was mad, and I don't care. It doesn't matter anymore. All that matters is that my grades will go up now, which means Yami and my mom have to be at least a *little* relieved, even if I am a fuckup.

I don't even fall asleep in class all day. It's like the colors are brighter, the food tastes better, the air is crisper. Hell, Mr. Franco's voice even sounds nice for once.

In the car on the way home, Mami looks at me like she's worried, but my smile makes her relax a little bit. I feel like she's about to bring my mood crashing down by mentioning this morning, so I start talking first.

"I finished all my late work! My scholarship is officially safe."

"¡Eso!" Yami says from the back seat, and Mami beams.

"I knew you would," she says, even though I know it's a lie. Still, it doesn't matter right now.

When we get home, the first thing I do is help Yami and my mom fix the jewelry shit I fucked up. It only takes about an hour and a half with all three of us working, then I get straight to my homework, which I'm already ahead on after last night.

Yami knocks on my door a bit after I finish. She doesn't wait for me to answer before opening it and coming right in.

"So when were you planning on inviting me to that party? If you wait too long, I might have plans . . . ," she says as she plops down on my bed.

"You don't have plans." I laugh, rolling my eyes. I was *planning* on inviting her right after Jamal invited me, but it must have slipped my mind. Jamal probably figured I'd forget and texted her himself. "So, want to come? Your nemesis won't be there."

"Do you really want me to go?"

"I'll only go if you go," I say, not realizing until then that I really *do*. If Jamal is the only one at the party I'm comfortable around, I don't know if I trust myself not to let my feelings get the better of me. Yami would be a good buffer, but I don't want to *tell* her that.

"Well, you *definitely* have to go, so it'll be a worthy sacrifice."

"What do you mean?" Why would Yami care if I went to a party or not?

She raises an eyebrow like I should know. "You've been . . ." She pauses, probably choosing her words carefully. "Broody lately."

Despite my conversation with Dr. Lee about how my support system being supportive is a good thing, an immediate pang of annoyance clangs against my temples.

"I'm fine, seriously. You don't have to worry about me."

Yami gives me a skeptical look. "I don't believe you. You're getting detention almost more than last year at this point. Even then, your grades never slipped like this. You haven't gone anywhere but school since that open mic. You need to get out there. I miss having fun with you!"

"Is going to a party supposed to help my grades come up?" I ask, laughing. She's really grasping at straws here if this is her idea of a solution.

"It's not about your grades." Yami shrugs. "Have you ever considered that getting out of the house will make you feel better, and if you feel better, maybe you'll be more motivated."

I roll my eyes, not buying Yami's little speech. "Of course it always comes back to my grades."

"Fine." Yami rolls hers right back. "Well, you *do* have a scholarship to maintain."

"What if I don't want to maintain my scholarship?"

That seems to push one of Yami's buttons, because she stops with the peppy-big-sister act. "Do you realize how lucky you have it? I'm working my ass off every day just to make a dent in my tuition, and you have a *full ride*. That's huge! And you're practically throwing it away!"

"You're the one who has it lucky!" I shoot back. "You *like* Slayton, but you wouldn't even be going if it wasn't for me. I don't even want to *be* here!"

Yami looks like I just slapped her in the face, which I might as well have, but I can't stop.

"No one asked me if I wanted a scholarship. No one asked if I wanted to go to Slayton in the first place. No one ever asks what *I* want! You all just drop your whole lives for some *idea* of what you *think* is best for me!"

Yami's quiet for a while, her eyes shiny with tears. Then finally she softly asks, "What do *you* want, Cesar?"

And since it's the first time anyone's ever asked me that, I don't have an answer. Do I want to go back to Rover? Do I really want to lose my scholarship to Slayton?

I do know I want to rewind this conversation. I want to stop making everyone around me miserable. Sometimes I want to just stop existing.

"I want you to come to the party," I say, grasping at the remnants of the lighthearted conversation this started as. It's the closest I can get to a peace offering without acknowledging everything that went wrong.

She pauses for a while, and I can only hope our sibling telepathy is enough to get my message across. Casual conversation. No tension. We're chill.

"Fine." She gets up and starts walking out but pauses at the door, a tiny smile on her lips. "But I'm bringing Bo."

My shoulders relax. I think she got it.

On Saturday, our doorbell rings at exactly seven forty-five, even though the party is only five minutes away and starts at eight. Jamal is never one to be late—doesn't matter if it's a party where you're *supposed* to be late. Yami and I share a quick look before I get the door.

"Don't worry, we still have to wait for Bo to get here," Yami says, reading my mind like she always does.

When I open the door, Jamal is standing in the doorway looking even nicer than usual. His button-up shirt is long-sleeved and solid white instead of his usual plaid or stripes.

"Hey, you," he says with a small grin as I open the door.

"Hey, you," I say back, the sight of him pulling my lips into a grin of my own. It's not like I was in a particularly good mood before he got here, but something about him just makes me feel lighter.

"Hey, *Yami*," Yami says, inserting herself into whatever moment Jamal and I definitely were not just having. She walks out the door and hugs Jamal, which kind of gives me permission to hug him too. It's a quick hug. Something that says 'We're friends,' I think. Still, I can't help but notice he's wearing the "I'm single" cologne we bought together. And, really, is it still singles cologne if we're wearing it together? Fuck, my head hurts.

Yami practically pushes past Jamal and me on her way out the door when she hears Bo's car pull up next.

Jamal and I turn around to see Yami run into a hug, and Bo picks her up, squeezing her tight. Jamal clears his throat awkwardly.

"Should we give them a minute?" he asks.

"Nah, let's go bug 'em," I say mischievously, and run past Jamal to hug Bo.

I'm sure it's not lost on Jamal that I hug Bo tighter than I hugged him, but he doesn't show it. What he does show is a whole life-time's worth of awkwardness on the ride to the party. He's keeping both hands on the wheel instead of resting one on the center console like he did when we were together. That was always his way of inviting me to hold his hand, but obviously that's off the table right now. Which shouldn't bother me because this is what *I* wanted.

Ugh. I need a drink.

Luckily, there are plenty of those where we're headed. There's a sign on the door that says to go through the backyard gate, so we go that way. The music shakes the blood in my veins like I've had too much caffeine.

Once we're in the gate but before we get to the crowd, Yami takes out her phone and pulls us all in for a selfie. I throw one arm around her and one around Jamal, and Bo kisses Yami's cheek as the flash goes off. Then Yami and Bo slip away, and a few seconds later, I get a notification that I'm tagged in her story.

I share it absent-mindedly, and I swear it's not even a full five seconds before I get a like from Bianca, of all people. I'm glad Yami's already ahead of us, because I don't hide my reactions that well. Pretty sure Bianca has her notifications turned on for me since she likes basically anything I post involving Yami. Not sure if that's her way of trying to be nice or passive-aggressive or what, but I'm staying out of it.

I pocket my phone and follow Jamal toward everyone else, but we don't get far before he suddenly stops. "Shit, I didn't realize . . ." He turns to me. "Do you want to leave?"

I look behind his shoulder to see that while Nick isn't here, Avery and two of their other friends are. I don't blame Jamal for assuming they wouldn't be here without Nick, since I've barely ever seen them without their ringleader. I accidentally catch Avery's eyes, but he just goes back to his conversation like he didn't notice me at all.

"Nah, we're already here," I finally answer. Without Nick or even the whole group, I doubt Avery's stupid enough to go starting shit. "Let's do some shots." I nod toward the sliding door, and Jamal follows me inside to the kitchen.

I pour one out for me, then one for Jamal.

"I'll stick with water since I'm driving," he says, and I shrug and take both shots in my hands.

"Cheers to me, then," I say, clinking the two shot glasses together and downing them one after the other. It's crowded enough that the kitchen is pretty much the only place to hang out without having strangers breathing on your neck, so I lean against the fridge while Jamal hops back to sit on the counter behind him.

I catch a glimpse of Yami and Bo from the living room. They're dancing together, but Yami is looking around the room instead of at Bo. Her eyes find mine, and she holds a thumb up at me. Then Bo puts a gentle hand on Yami's cheek to coax her to look back at her girlfriend. I roll my eyes. We're at a damn party, and Yami still can't stop worrying about me.

I pour another shot for myself and down it.

"Question," Jamal says, leaning toward me with a curious look in his eye.

"What's up?" I can't help but smile. I love his random questions.

"If you had to battle any cryptid, assuming the terrain isn't deadly for either of you, which cryptid would you pick?"

"Can it be a battle of wits?" I ask. "Because in the ring is one thing, but put me in a battle of wits against Bigfoot, I got that in the bag."

Jamal's eyes widen. "Trust me, you do *not* want to challenge a sasquatch to a battle of wits. I don't care if you're Albert Einstein, those things are scary smart."

Part of me wants to ask about it, because I'm sure Jamal has a wealth of Bigfoot knowledge *about* Bigfoot knowledge ready to go.

I keep my question to myself, though, since his hypothetical came first. I take another shot before giving my answer another go.

"Okay, then I'll go with a regular battle against a jackalope. They're a little too cute to hurt, but I feel like I could scare it away before it came to that."

Jamal nods his approval. "I'd pick the Loveland frogman. It'd probably take one good punch to his soft belly for him to throw up."

I'm about to ask what the hell the Loveland frogman is when the door to the yard opens, and I feel like *I'm* gonna throw up.

I figured Bianca knew whose party we were at since she liked my story, but I didn't think she was obsessed enough to leave her date and bring Nick here.

He stumbles in with one hand around Bianca's waist until he gets to Avery and them, who've made their way inside by now. He practically pushes Bianca away to say hi way too loudly and give them all handshake hugs. I don't know what the nature of their date was, but they're both clearly already drunk.

My eyes dart to Yami, who hasn't seemed to notice them just yet, but Bianca is already scanning the room. Unfortunately, she spots me before she finds my sister and eagerly makes her way to me and Jamal, officially making it impossible to avoid Nick. He grins when he sees where she's headed and follows her with the rest of them.

Jamal hops down from the counter and stands next to me defensively, but Bianca seems completely oblivious to the tension.

"Hey, Cesar!" she says cheerfully as Nick crosses his arms with a smirk. "Where's Ya—"

"What's up, joto?" Nick taunts without letting her finish. She frowns but doesn't say anything. I'm about to punch Nick when Jamal puts a protective arm in front of my chest.

"Leave him alone, Nick." His voice is low and firm. It'd be hot, honestly, if I wasn't so heated myself.

Nick stumbles forward and grabs the shot glass out of my hand, spilling most of it before downing what's left. He's clearly way drunker than I am, but hopefully not for long.

"He's not worth it, Cesar," Jamal says under his breath, a steadying hand on my tense shoulder. If it wasn't for Jamal right now, I'd have already clocked Nick in his annoying chin three times over.

Before Nick has a chance to do anything, Yami and Bo have already pushed their way in between Nick and me, both of them pointedly ignoring Bianca. I want to shove past Yami and deck the dude, but one look at Jamal's concerned face, and I know I have to resist the urge. He's worried about me again. It takes everything in me to get the angry fireball inside to simmer down.

Nick laughs. "Aw, you got your sister to protect you?"

"Will you shut the fuck up?" Bianca finally bursts out, surprising everyone.

I don't know if a face can physically get redder than Nick's right now.

"You don't talk to me like that." He says it more like a threat than anything, but she doesn't seem fazed.

"What, like how you talk to literally everyone all the time?"

Jamal and Yami take the opportunity to pull me away from the kitchen while Nick and Bianca start full-on screaming at each other in front of everyone. Even Nick's friends eventually leave them to their fight.

"You okay?" Yami asks, and I nod. I know she's actually asking if I want to leave.

"Are you?" I glance at Bianca, who's screaming so hard her neck veins are popping out. Yami just laughs.

"Actually, it's kind of amazing seeing her this mad."

By now, Nick is storming outside, followed by his friends, while Bianca raises both middle fingers in the air shouting how they're over.

Jamal looks down at my fists, which are clenched so hard I might break them. I know what he wants to do. When we were together and I was this stressed, he'd take one of my clenched fists and coax it open until he could slip his hand inside.

"Squeeze all you want," he'd say.

When I notice his fingers twitch as he looks at my fists, I can't handle it. I turn around and rush past him, past Yami and Bo, and past the crowd. I run until I find the bathroom and shut myself inside.

I'm not even that drunk yet, but I feel like I'm flying, and not in a good way. It's like when you get on a plane and it's all shaky before landing and you're afraid everyone's going to crash and die. I feel my heart pounding against my ears, which makes the room spin even more than it already was. I press my back up against the bathroom wall and slide down to the floor, hugging my knees and taking deep breaths. Am I having a panic attack or something?

After a while, there's a knock on the door, and it just makes it harder to breathe.

"Is anyone in here?" It's Jamal.

I let out another breath, trying to tame whatever outburst might be trying to force its way up. I can't tell what's going on inside me right now. Is this anger? Anxiety? Fear? Excitement? Whatever it is, it's hard to get it to shut up.

There's another knock.

"Is that you, Cesar?" Jamal's voice again. Shit. He must have seen me come in here.

"It's unlocked," I say back, putting my head between my knees. The door opens, and Jamal comes inside, closing it behind him.

Without a word, he sits right across from me, waiting. I don't realize I'm hyperventilating until I hear his voice again.

"Breathe, Cesar. Can I touch you?" he asks, and I nod without lifting my head from between my knees. He puts a hand on my calf, rubbing his thumb gently against my jeans. "You're safe, okay? Me, Yami, and Bo are here. Nick already left. No one's gonna hurt you, okay?"

That's when I lift my head to look at him. "You think I'm scared?"

Jamal shrugs. "You're not?"

"Pfft. I'm not scared of Nick."

He raises an eyebrow, and he doesn't have to say what I already know he's thinking: *Then why did you come hide in the bathroom?*

And part of me wants to tell him exactly why, but the problem is *I* don't know. I don't know why I ran in here. I don't know why I've been getting so damn angry lately or why I haven't been able to control myself or why I've had so much fucking energy after not sleeping at *all*. All I know is . . . I don't want it to stop. And that kind of scares the shit out of me.

"What?" I finally answer his nonverbal question, pretending I don't know what he wants to ask.

"Question," he says without taking his eyes off mine. I just nod for him to go on. "Do you want me to leave?" he asks, and I'm about to answer no when the door swings open, and Bianca stands on the other side of it, holding a bottle of tequila.

Fuck.

I hop to my feet so fast I probably hyperextended something.

"Oh . . . am I . . . interrupting something?" she asks, looking at us all judgy.

No. Fuck, this is not happening right now. If Bianca outed Yami, she'd definitely do the same to me. Sure, Nick and his friends knew about me, but they didn't really go around gossiping about it. It's not that Jamal and I were doing anything in here anyway, but I definitely can't let *her* think that.

"Nope!" I say as casually as I can muster.

"I was having a panic attack, and Cesar came to calm me down," Jamal lies, thank God. A panic attack is a good reason to be locked in a bathroom with your strictly platonic best friend, right? "I'm just gonna . . . ," Jamal starts as he slides past Bianca and out the door.

"Do you need the bathroom?" I ask.

"I mean . . . not really. I was just . . ." Bianca's playing with her hair as she talks, and she's not making eye contact. She looks like she might have just been drunk crying.

"You okay?" I ask, even though the last thing I should care about is whether or not Bianca is okay. She sits down next to me and hands me the bottle, which I gladly take a few generous swigs from before handing it back.

"I'm fine. I'm just so *mad*!"

"Yeah, breakups are rough," I say with a nod, relating to her more than I'd like. "Fuck Nick."

"Yeah, I'll pass." She laughs for a second before going back to looking sad. "But no, it's not about him actually."

"What is it, then?" I ask, stupidly.

She pauses for a second. "Why is Yami still mad at me? Like, I just chewed Nick out in front of his friends for her!"

"Wow," I say under my breath, trying to ignore the implication that I had nothing to do with that whole scene. "So, you brought your boyfriend who you *know* used to jump me to a party you *knew* I was at just so you could talk to my sister? And when shit almost popped off you only stepped in so you'd look good . . . to my sister?"

I expect her to roll her eyes and defend herself, but she just sighs and gulps down some more tequila. "I guess I didn't really think it through."

She hands me back the bottle, and I take it. For some reason, that response makes me soften up. I'm no better than Bianca when it comes to being impulsive and hurting other people. I've been hurting everyone around me basically every move I make. They'd all be so much better without me. Maybe me and Bianca are more alike than I thought.

The only person who seems to get any kind of enrichment from my existence is Nick. Specifically, when he's beating the shit out of me. I take another swallow from the bottle before looking back at Bianca.

"Do you think Yami really loved me? You know, like that?" Bianca looks sad as she says it.

"I mean, why wouldn't she?" I ask, my words blurring together.

I meant it more like, why would Yami lie about that, but Bianca gets all smiley like I just gave her a compliment. She grins and takes my hand. "Come on, let's go."

She pulls me to my feet and out the door, and I let her. We go out to the living room, where Bianca picks up a red cup from the coffee table, which she apparently abandoned for the tequila bottle we forgot in the bathroom. She's about to put the cup to her mouth when I stop her.

"Don't drink that," I say, coaxing it away from her lips.

Her eyes widen. "Do you think someone put something in it?"

"No way to know, but better safe than sorry." Bo's parents drilled into me and Yami the rules of party going. Don't leave your drink unattended, and don't drink something that you haven't had your eyes on, etc. etc. "Let's just make a new drink."

She nods and pulls me along to the kitchen, where she grabs another bottle of tequila and takes a few swigs straight from the bottle, then hands it to me. I shrug and gulp down a swallow or two. Bianca gets out her phone to take a selfie with me and the bottle. I look around anxiously. If Yami sees a picture of me with Bianca, she'll be pissed. But . . . maybe that's not a bad thing. Maybe she needs a reality check about me. That I'm not just some innocent little kicked puppy that needs taking care of all the time. Maybe she needs to see me for who I am.

I kiss the bottle for the camera, and Bianca kisses the other side of it, so the bottle is the only thing between our lips. A guilty chill runs down my spine, but I ignore it.

Next, she pulls me back to the living room where people are

dancing and Jamal is standing alone in a corner. He sees me and lights up, then sees Bianca and pushes his glasses up his nose like he does when he's trying to figure something out.

Bianca wraps her arms around my neck and closes the space between us. Before I know it, our hips are pressed together, and she's grinding them to the music.

"What are you—"

She interrupts me with a kiss. It catches me so off guard that I don't stop her right away. When I finally pull away, I see Jamal standing across the room with an unreadable expression.

No matter what I do, Jamal and Yami and even my mom keep getting hurt, but they still can't stop with all the babying. Jamal and Yami haven't even been having fun at this party. And Dr. Lee was right. I don't like it because I *don't* deserve it. Even when I tried to deserve it, all I did was mess shit up, so what's the point? If there's no hiding that I'm a shit person, I might as well make it more obvious so everyone can stop fooling themselves.

Then there's Nick. He'd probably beat the shit out of me if he knew about this, but he'd do that anyway. At least this way I can hurt him back.

Bianca grabs my chin and pulls my face back toward hers so we're eye to eye. And that's when I know what I have to do.

I lean forward and kiss her again.

15

WHEN YOU DANCE WITH THE LITERAL DEVIL

reckless behavior

I open my eyes halfway through the kiss, scanning the room for Yami, but I don't see her or Bo anywhere. Jamal, on the other hand, makes eye contact with me for just a moment before he turns around and leaves the room.

"Want to go somewhere more private?" Bianca asks, and I nod, following her into one of the bedrooms.

Don't get me wrong. I know I'm "mentally ill." I know that. But it's not like I'm not in control of my actions. Sure, we're both a little tipsy—maybe more than a little tipsy—but I know exactly what I'm doing, and I'm doing it of my own free will.

I know how messed up this looks. How messed up it *is*. I know there's only so much I can be forgiven for. There's no turning back from this, but I'm doing it anyway. And if I wanted to, I could stop at any moment.

But I don't stop.

Bianca's lips move to my jaw, and her hands travel from my chest down my stomach, and finally to my zipper.

"Your sister would be pissed if she knew what we were doing, wouldn't she?" Bianca asks as she unbuttons my jeans and slides the zipper down.

I keep my thoughts to myself about how weird it is that Bianca is thinking about Yami right now.

Bianca pulls my boxers down and gets on her knees.

"Probably, she'd—oh . . ." The words get sucked out of me. Like, literally.

And then the door swings open, and another hungry-for-each-other couple stumbles in sucking face.

Bianca jumps to her feet, letting out a startled noise. That's when the couple notices us. And when I really notice them.

Yami and Bo.

I quickly pull my boxers back up and zip my pants. Yami just stares at me and Bianca. I know I should be trying to explain myself, but what is there to say? I did what I did, and I did it for a reason. Finally, it seems to click for Yami, and whatever rage I felt over the last few months is multiplied tenfold in her.

There's silence and then, "You fucking bitch!"

Yami rushes Bianca, lunging at her and tackling her to the ground. Bo rushes in and tries to pull Yami away, but Yami has Bianca's hair in a death grip, and she doesn't look like she has any intention of letting go.

I'm honestly too stunned to move. Yami's never gotten in a fight before, especially not with Bianca, her ex-best friend. Especially not over me.

Bo eventually manages to pull Yami away from a seething Bianca, but then her rage is turned toward me.

"What the fuck are you doing with *her*?" she shouts, but I have nothing to say for myself.

Bianca hurriedly pats down her fist-tangled hair. "Isn't it obvious?" she says, but not before running to the other side of the bed so Yami can't reach her.

"Yami, she's not worth it," Bo says, and I'm not sure if she's hugging Yami or trying to hold her back. Maybe both.

Then Yami lets out a deep breath to calm herself. "You can let go now, Bo."

Bo lets her go.

"Bianca, you should go," Yami says, too calmly. Then panic sinks in for me. She wants to talk? *To me?*

It all comes to the surface now. I just hooked up with Yami's worst enemy. I *hooked up* with the girl who outed Yami last year. The girl who made my sister's life a living hell. However much I hate Nick, Yami hates Bianca even more. They were best friends. They grew up together. We all did. I *saw* how much they meant to each other before the betrayal. Even if Yami didn't talk about it, I saw firsthand how messed up she was over losing Bianca. I knew hooking up with Bianca would hurt my sister. I *wanted* it to.

Now Yami knows without a doubt who I really am. Now she knows she can walk away, and anything that happens to me won't hurt her anymore. Same with Jamal. All this time, I've been looking for a way to save everyone from the grief of losing me, and I found it. They're free of me now. I finally did it.

So why does she want to talk?

A vortex of guilt and terror rushes over me. This is what I needed to happen, but I can't just talk about it.

"No, I'll go," I say as I run out the door as fast as I can. I don't stop when Bianca tries calling out to me. I don't stop when I pass Jamal sitting alone in a corner.

I just run, as if I can outrun the consequences of what I've just done, just for a fleeting moment. I run as if I can escape my own body. I run until my calves hurt. Until I don't know where I am. Until I'm completely alone. I run. I run. I run.

Eventually my legs give out and I collapse onto the asphalt on my hands and knees. That's when I finally break down crying.

16

WHEN EVERYONE YOU KNOW IS DEFINITELY CONSPIRING AGAINST YOU

paranoia

The next day, just before Jamal is supposed to pick me up for his open mic, dread fills my stomach at the realization that I can't go. I can't hang out with him anymore. I can't do any of it.

I haven't spoken to Jamal or Yami since last night, not that either of them have tried. I wouldn't be surprised if Jamal didn't show up to pick me up at all. Then again, it's Yami I'm more worried about, because Jamal hasn't been expecting us to get back together since we talked about it.

Instead of waiting for him to pick me up, I leave the house just in time so that when he gets there—if he even comes—I'll be gone.

I make a run for it from my room—where I've been hiding all day—so I don't have to bump into Yami either.

"I'm going out," I call to my mom, then slip out the door before she can respond.

But just as I make it off the driveway, the rumble of Jamal's engine gets louder as his truck appears turning right onto our street.

Without thinking, I dive behind the nearest bush and wait as Jamal gets out of his truck and walks toward our front door. I hold my breath as he rings the doorbell. It opens just moments later, and I can hear my mom's surprised voice answer him.

"I thought you and Cesar just left?"

"No, I just got here. He left?" Jamal asks, sounding hurt.

"He just left, I'm sorry. He couldn't have gone far, though. Maybe you can catch up to him?"

I peek from behind the bush to see Jamal turning around to look down the street, as if trying to solve the mystery of where I went. Then he gets out his phone, types something, and presses it to his ear.

Shit.

My phone starts vibrating way too loudly, right here behind the bush. I rush to silence it, but it's too late. Jamal walks up to the bush, a confused look on his face.

I guess there's no avoiding him now. I stand up and brush myself off, not knowing what to say. I expect him to be like "Question. Why are you avoiding me?" but instead he just states the obvious.

"That was weird." For some reason, I'm annoyed that all he has to say about this is that it's weird. What I did with Bianca could be described a lot of ways, but "weird" wouldn't be my first choice.

"Why?" I start defensively. "We're not together, I can hook up with whoever I want. It's not *weird*."

There's a hurt look in his eyes for a tiny fraction of a second before he nods. "That's true. I was talking about you being in a bush. That was weird."

"Right . . ." I sigh. I guess the truth will get the job done. "I was avoiding you."

Jamal's eyebrows furrow in confusion. "Why?"

I clench my jaw, trying to figure out how to say what I need to say to get him to leave me alone.

"Did I do something to upset you?" he asks. "I won't know unless you tell me."

"Look, I don't want to go to your stupid thing, okay?" I blurt out, and he takes a step back.

"My stupid thing . . ." He repeats the words like they're in a different language, pushing his glasses up his nose.

I just stand my ground, holding my breath. I can't bear to say anything else to him, but I can't take back what I've already said. If what happened at the party with Bianca didn't do it, I need another way to get Jamal to see me for the horrible person I am. Need to get him to leave me alone, so he won't feel guilty when something happens to me.

"Understood," he finally says and walks back to his truck without another word. It's a subtle, but noticeable, change from his usual "I understand." More distant. Which can only be a good thing—for him, at least.

I run back in the house and into my room, ignoring my mom's questions and slamming the door behind me.

I stay in my room until the next morning, when my alarm goes off to take my meds. I don't even know how long it's been since I stopped taking them. A week? A month? Time doesn't really mean anything to me anymore.

I'm not trying to cross paths with Yami, so I rush out to pretend to take my meds, then head back into hiding until it's time to go.

When I finally have to leave my room again and go to the car, I almost shit myself at Yami standing right in front of my door when I open it.

I'm expecting her to tear into me, but she looks more hurt than angry. My eyes shoot to the floor.

"Isn't that jaguar necklace you're always wearing supposed to be for facing fears? You can't even look me in the eye. Fine then . . ."

She doesn't give me the chance to say anything back, because she turns around and walks down the hall toward the car before I can process what she said.

I look over to my desk, where the jaguar necklace, the cross necklace, and the promise ring Jamal gave me last year are all sitting. Yami's right. I definitely don't have the right to wear any of those things anymore. Instead of staring at them, I rush over and yank the desk drawer open, then take all three pieces of jewelry and throw them inside, on top of my abandoned poetry notebook, so I never have to look at them again.

When I get in the car, I sit in the front seat and blast music loud enough that I won't be able to hear anything else Yami says to me. Who cares if she's right? I can avoid her all I want.

I don't even bother going to my usual table at lunch. Well, not *my* table—Yami's table. Instead, I sit with Jeremy and his friends, and I joke around with them and laugh when it's expected. I don't allow myself so much as a glance in Yami's direction, and I hope she's not glancing in mine either.

It's hard enough to be in the same building as her at lunch, but in English, I have to sit next to one of her best friends, who probably hates me now.

"Hey, you okay, bro?" David asks.

I squint at him. Did Yami not tell him what I did? Or maybe she did, and she's using David to try to get information out of me? Well, she's not getting any. "Yeah, I'm good," I say nonchalantly.

Then, just as class is about to start, Mrs. Perry gets a call from her desk. When she hangs up, she looks right at me.

"Cesar, you're wanted in Principal Cappa's office."

A chorus of hushed *ooooo*s rings out, but Mrs. Perry just looks at me expectantly. I've never been sent to the principal's office, no matter how many times I've gotten detention. I couldn't have dipped below the scholarship threshold, right? No, I turned in my late homework, so that can't be it.

"Mr. Flores," Mrs. Perry says, reminding me that she's waiting for me to leave to start her lesson.

I pretend I'm not bothered as I get up and head out the door. The walk to Principal Cappa's office is excruciating as I try to figure out what could be going on.

Maybe Mami found out about what I did and she's taking me out of school for the rest of the day so she can kill me?

When I finally get there, the office lady tells me to have a seat until Principal Cappa's ready for me. I sit and bounce my legs, resisting the urge to get out my phone and text Jamal, since he probably wants nothing to do with me now. Which is good. That's what I wanted. Right?

"He's ready for you," the secretary says, and I get up on wobbly legs, not bothering to appear confident anymore since there's no one to perform for. But as soon as I reach for the handle, I regain my composure. It's like an instinct for me around adults to be as charming as possible. It's worked out for me most of my life, so I'm not about to stop anytime soon.

"Hey, Principal Cappa," I say cheerily as I open the door and walk in, but the charming facade vanishes the second I see who's in the room. "Mom?"

"Have a seat, Cesar," Principal Cappa says, and my mom nods to acknowledge me. She looks pale, like she just got food poisoning or something.

I sit in the empty seat next to my mom. "What's going on?"

"I'm sure you're aware we have a no-tolerance policy when it comes to illegal activities." Mr. Cappa turns to his computer and types for a second, then tilts the screen toward me.

Oh. Fuck.

The picture of me and Bianca kissing the tequila bottle is pulled up on my Instagram. Bianca must have posted it and added me as a collaborator, and I must have accepted like a dumbass. I don't remember doing that. Why would I do that? Bianca probably didn't think twice about posting it, but this is Slayton. Here, people have no shame about snitching, so it was only a matter of time before the administration got ahold of that picture.

"He's a good kid, Principal Cappa. It won't happen again," my mom pleads, and he looks at me with a raised eyebrow.

"Is that true, Cesar?"

I just shrug. I don't care to lie right now, so I don't. "It's not like I was drinking on campus. What's the big deal?"

"The *big deal* is that by attending this establishment, you are representing this school and our values whether you're on our campus or not. Not only that, but we're *paying* you to do it. Cesar,

I'm afraid I can't let this go unpunished."

"Please, he's worked so hard for his spot here. He's been at the top of his class every year since he started high school until . . . well, he's been through a lot recently. Trust me, you've never met a harder-working kid."

I let out an involuntary laugh at my mom's inability to see what's right in front of her. Since when was I a hard worker? I got good grades because it was *easy*, not because I tried. Both she and the principal look at me like they expect me to say something, but I just clear my throat like I didn't just laugh out loud at my mom.

"I promise you he won't do anything like this again," Mami continues, her voice more desperate now.

Mine comes out like ice. "You can't make promises for me."

She shoots a fierce glare in my direction. She probably *is* gonna kill me, but I don't care. I don't care about any of it. Mami turns back to Principal Cappa. "Obviously he's not himself right now. You can see that, can't you? If you just give him another chance—"

"You can't fix everything for me!" I snap, surprising all three of us. "I don't need you to fight my battles! That perfect version of me you have in your head is made up, okay? He doesn't exist!" I turn to Principal Cappa, so I don't have to see my mom's reaction to what I say next. I already convinced Yami and Jamal they're better off without me, but my mom might need an extra push. "Just because she says I'll be good doesn't mean I will. I'm not her puppet. I did that shit, okay? Don't coddle me for her sake."

"All right, then. I think it's settled." Principal Cappa shakes his head, like he's not looking forward to whatever he's about to say. "I'm sorry, Cesar, but I'm going to have to expel you from this school."

My mom bursts into tears, but I don't react. I knew I was gonna be in trouble, and even if an expulsion isn't what I was expecting, I somehow can't bring myself to care. None of it matters.

"And to be quite frank with you, you're lucky I'm not getting the authorities involved. You're both free to go."

He gestures toward the door. I don't wait for my mom to say anything or to move. I just get up and walk out the door. It takes my mom a few seconds to follow me out. When we get to the waiting area, my mom stops by the front desk.

"Will Yamilet be coming down?" she asks the lady behind the desk.

"We got ahold of her, but she asked if you wouldn't mind her staying the rest of the school day." The office lady types away while she talks. Getting my sister out of class is probably not the highest on her list of priorities. It's no wonder Yami doesn't want to come home early. She probably wants to spend the least amount of time with me as possible.

The bell rings, which means I'll have to walk past everyone with my mom. They'll probably all know I'm expelled before I even make it off campus.

"Did you tell her the situation?" Mami asks anxiously.

"She's aware." The lady nods. "Should I call her down here to talk with you?"

"I'll be by the car," I say, not bothering to hear the rest of the conversation. I don't want to be in the room if Yami comes in here. I walk out the door without giving my mom a chance to answer. Maybe at least this way I can save face by going to the car alone.

I pretend to just be walking to class like everyone else, and no one seems to notice anything's off. At least, not until I see Mr. Franco standing outside his classroom. He sees me right away, and the sad look on his face says he knows exactly what's going on.

I don't know if my teachers were notified or if he just heard from whoever snitched, but it pisses me off either way. So much for there being trustworthy adults at this school. It was all "We're here for you" and "We care about you" until they had the smallest excuse to get rid of me.

I walk past Mr. Franco without looking at him twice, perfectly content with the fact that I'm never coming back.

The ride home is silent. I don't dare turn on music, since I'm hanging on waiting for Mami to just *say something*, but she doesn't. I have no idea what to expect. Is she gonna whoop me? Yell at me? Kick me out? I probably deserve all three.

She was crying so hard when I left her in the office, but she's fully stone-faced on the ride home. I search her body language for some sign of what's to come, but there's nothing. She's not even gripping the wheel harder than usual. In fact, she looks like she's driving on autopilot.

The silence stretches to practically half of our forty-minute drive home before I finally break it.

"Are you gonna kick me out?" I had to ask. I don't know where I'd go if she did. If I hadn't blown Jamal off yesterday, I'm sure I'd be welcome to stay with him at his cousin's house. But there's no way I could ask that of him after what I did.

Mami doesn't answer. It's not that I can't read her expression, there's nothing *to* read. I've never seen her look so . . . empty.

She doesn't react when I finally turn on the radio to let the music drown out the silent tension.

I don't have to be told to go straight to my room when we get home. I throw myself onto my bed and hide my face in a pillow, wishing it was humanly possible to suffocate yourself. I lie there trying not to think about what happens next. I don't know how long I'm pretending not to exist before I get a phone call. It takes every ounce of effort from each individual cell in my entire body to exist as a person again and answer the phone.

"Hola, Doña," I say, falling back into my cheery talking-to-adults voice, but it feels like I'm hiding the wound from today with duct tape. She doesn't seem to notice I'm off, though.

"I heard you're home today, mijo. Since you're free, would you mind coming with me to a doctor's appointment?" Doña Violeta asks me to come with her to appointments every so often, since I'm good at talking to doctors and getting answers. Even though socializing is less than ideal right now, I'll do anything to get out of this tension-filled house.

"I have to ask my mom," I say, realizing I might actually be grounded.

"I'll wait," she says, so I open my bedroom door and walk out to the living room, where my mom is making jewelry.

"Can I go with Doña Violeta to a doctor's appointment?" I ask.

But she just keeps working silently, completely ignoring my question.

"Okay, I'll take that as a yes." I roll my eyes and put the phone back to my cheek.

"I'm coming," I say, then head out the door ready to walk over to Doña Violeta's house down the street, but she's already parked in our driveway. I hop in the passenger seat, eager to drive far, far away from this house.

Well, not that the doctor's appointment is that far, but still.

Except she doesn't drive the usual route to the doctor's that I'm familiar with. We eventually turn down a street into what looks like a residential neighborhood with dirt roads.

"Um, did you get a new doctor or something?" I ask, not sure if this is some kind of work-from-home-doctor situation going on.

The car stops in front of a house I don't recognize.

"I'm sorry for this, mijo," Doña Violeta says sadly. "But you're going to be staying here with your abuela for a little while. Someone will come tomorrow to drop off your things."

"*What?*" I don't unbuckle my seat belt or make any moves to get out of the car. I've never been to my grandma's house. Haven't even seen her since right after my dad got deported, when she came to try and take care of us while Mami was grieving. But even then, all I remember is her and my mom fighting.

And Doña Violeta's in on it? Did Yami know I was getting sent away, too? Is that what Mami meant when she asked if Yami "knew the situation"?

How long were they all conspiring to get me out of the picture? If Mami is sending me here of all places, and she couldn't even bring herself to drive me personally, she must really hate me.

Maybe I just got disowned by both my parents.

And maybe that's exactly what I wanted.

17

WHEN YOU PICTURE THE LIGHT AT THE END OF THE TUNNEL

suicidal ideation

Doña Violeta takes my hand as she leads me to my abuela's front door like I'm a scared toddler, but I don't react. Instead, I just let my hand lie limp in hers.

Doña Violeta is basically my grandmother. She's more of a grandma to me than my abuela ever was. But I don't know if that's because Abuela didn't want to be there, or because my mom didn't want her to be.

I find myself standing in front of the door with Doña Violeta like a zombie. None of this feels real. Doña Violeta knocks, and a few seconds later, an older woman with brown skin and a chihuahua in her arms opens it. She looks taken aback, but not at seeing me. There's a brief pained look on her face as she looks at Doña Violeta before she switches into a nasty-looking stink eye. Do they know each other?

"Violeta," Abuela says curtly as she pets the shaking chihuahua, then looks to me and gives me a different kind of stink eye. One that says "You're in big trouble." I shrivel under the look.

"Be gentle with him, Graciela. He's going through a hard time," Doña Violeta says, not seeming to care that I'm right here and can hear every word.

"How I care for my grandson is none of your concern." Abuela shoots her another glare. "Why are *you* even here?"

"I'm sorry," Doña Violeta says softly, her tone hinting at some deeper meaning I'm not privy to.

"You can go now, Violeta. Cesar?" She opens the door wider and steps to the side, allowing me to enter. I look to Doña Violeta, who nods in reassurance, then backs away while I take a step inside.

Abuela doesn't put the dog down to hug me or anything in greeting like Doña Violeta would; she just silently steps aside for me to enter.

The house looks bigger from the inside. The living room is slightly larger than ours, and it looks like there's a main bedroom on one side of the house with a hallway and one other bedroom at the end of it. Abuela finally puts the chihuahua down once the door is closed, and the little thing runs right past me and onto the couch, where someone is sitting and working on some kind of worksheet on the coffee table. At that sight, my whole mood is saved.

"Moni?" I rush over to get a better look. I completely forgot she got sent here too!

She looks up from her worksheet, then her face lights up with recognition. "Cesar! Holy shit, you too?" she asks as the dog hops into her lap. "What'd you do to end up at the problem-child house?"

I shrug. It's not like she needs to know everything.

Abuela claps her hands, snapping Moni and I out of our conversation. "Ándale, let's get to work. The floors won't sweep themselves." She materializes a broom seemingly out of nowhere and hands it to me. "Monica, don't get distracted. No dinner until your homework is done. Cesar, no dinner until the floors are swept and mopped."

I let the broom fall to the floor when she holds it to my chest. "I don't even know you; you can't tell me what to do."

Moni's eyes widen, and she swipes her hand across her throat in a cut-it-out kind of gesture. I ignore her, crossing my arms and giving my grandma a glare.

"Let's try that one more time before I sic Lareina on you." She gestures to the tiny chihuahua in Moni's lap. Is she really trying to joke around after I just got kicked out?

"My room's over there, right?" I roll my eyes and point down the hall. "I'm going to bed."

Before I can turn to head in that direction, my grandma points at me with her whole arm and shouts, "Lareina, he's not listening to me!"

I expect Moni to laugh or my abuela to crack a smile, but instead the chihuahua flings itself off Moni's lap and darts toward me, barking viciously like I'm her next meal.

"What the fuck!" I yelp as I book it away from the tiny monster. I almost trip over my own feet as I scramble toward the bathroom and slam the door behind me, locking it for good measure.

The dog keeps barking outside the door, and I can practically hear her mouth foaming. I think my abuela's plan backfired on her because I'm definitely not leaving this bathroom. How is getting me killed by a rabid dog supposed to make me do chores?

"Lareina, leave it." The dog actually quiets at the command, and footsteps approach the door. "You can either come out and get to work or stay in there as long as you want, but no one is having dinner until the floor is clean. Your prima wants to eat too, you know."

I ball my fists and try to breathe through the budding anger. Using Moni against me is fucked up. She's the only person I know who might actually get me, being a fellow "problem child," like she says.

Fuck it. I unlock the door and shove it open to find my abuela standing just outside, waiting for me with the broom in hand.

I grab it from her and stomp back to the living room without making eye contact. Moni mouths a "Thank you!" before getting back to her worksheet.

"And, Cesar." Abuela raises a hand toward my shoulder, then retracts it. "I'm not your mami, okay? We all have shit we're going through and all of our heads are a little messed up, but that doesn't mean we don't have to take accountability for our actions. That's what you're here for."

"Fine," I mumble.

"Oh, and your phone," she says, holding her hand out expectantly. I think about resisting, but one glance at the chihuahua from hell sets me straight. I reluctantly pull my phone out of my pocket and hand it to her. Then she walks off to the kitchen to make dinner.

Despite how annoying it is, this is probably a good thing. I got exactly what I wanted, right? Mom, Yami, and Jamal are so mad at me they'll never want to speak to me again, and they're all much better off that way. Now they can live their lives without having to babysit my mental health. I'm not going to Slayton anymore, so no one has to worry about me maintaining my scholarship. I don't have to face Yami at school, either.

And Rover isn't all bad. Sure, Nick and his minions are there, but it's a big enough school that I can probably avoid them. Jamal, on the other hand, might be a little trickier to avoid since we'll probably be in all the same honors classes.

Still, it'll be fine. Jamal will probably just ignore me like my mom did. I gave him more than enough reason to.

It's actually a perfect situation. This way no one will have to feel guilty if anything happens to me. Whatever happens to me will be my responsibility and mine alone.

For the first time in a long time, I feel good about the future. A future I hopefully will have no part of, and everyone will be better for it.

18

WHEN YOU CONSTANTLY FEEL LIKE YOUR CHAIR IS ABOUT TO TIP

anxiety

Mopping while I can smell the quesabirria Abuela is making is torture. I think she's making the food smell extra good just to tease us.

"Finished!" Moni says, jumping up from her spot on the couch and rushing over to the kitchen.

"Not so fast." Abuela holds her palm face out to Moni. "No one eats until we all eat. Besides, I need to check your work, and you still have violin practice to do."

Moni slumps her shoulders and goes back to the coffee table, where she picks up her worksheet and hands it to Abuela, then goes off to the corner to get her violin.

"Bueno. Monica, this looks good," Abuela says, clapping her hands together just as I'm finishing up the floors. "Let me check your work, Cesar."

"You have to check mine too?" I ask, suddenly regretting the lackluster job I did.

Not only does Abuela point out every individual spot I missed and make me do the whole thing over again; she then grabs a paper towel and wipes the floor to test if it's completely pristine. Since the paper towel obviously comes back less than pure white, it's a fail. After having to re-mop three times over, once with Moni's help after she's done practicing, we finally get it clean enough to where she's satisfied.

"All right, time to eat."

"*Finally*," Moni says, and we both hurry to the kitchen, where we each put together our plates and bring them over to the dinner table.

Something feels slightly off, so I glance down to see the bug-eyed demon spawn staring at me and licking her lips between my legs. I tense up and slowly pick out a tiny piece of meat from my plate. I'm about to toss it under the table far enough away from my crotch so Lareina stops threatening me when Abuela notices.

"Lareina! No begging!" She snaps her fingers, and the dog slowly walks away from the table and sulks on the couch. I let out a relieved breath.

Abuela doesn't waste any time eating. Instead, she gets straight to business.

"Cesar, you're new here, so here's how this is going to go. I'll answer the question I know you're thinking first: I don't know any better than you do how long you'll be staying here. That will be entirely up to you. We'll need to enroll you back at Rover, which might take a few days, so until then, you'll be working in the house with me during the day while Monica goes to school. We eat breakfast and dinner as a family. Our mornings start early with a daily horoverse reading—"

"I still think they missed an opportunity with that app name," Moni interrupts.

"What is it, like a scary book?" I ask. Why the hell would Abuela have us reading horror novels before school?

"More like Bible astrology," Moni says. "I personally think they'd have a better chance at reaching their target audience if they called it horoscripture. Or better yet, holyscope. Godstrology, even." Moni clicks her tongue and shakes her head. "Seriously, it's like they didn't even try. And what's with that logo? I could design a better one using clip art, it's not even—"

"As I was saying." Abuela clears her throat, and Moni becomes the embodiment of the grimace emoji. "Every day you'll get a list of chores to do, and once you finish those and I check to make sure you did them well, you can have the rest of your time to yourselves."

"It's not a lot of time. Don't get your hopes up," Moni says under her breath.

I nod, taking another bite of my quesabirria taco.

"You're both essentially grounded while you're here, so no leaving the house, no phones, no computers—"

"No TV, no video games, no fun," Moni adds, copying Abuela's voice with a finger raised like she's lecturing both of us.

Abuela shoots her the stink eye, but there's a tiny hint of a smile that cracks for just a split second. "You can have all the fun you want, as long as you get your chores done and follow the rules."

"Really?" Moni claps her hands the way Abuela does, and I can't tell if she's making fun of her or if she's genuinely picked up some of her mannerisms from staying here. "Can we have a game night?"

"Why don't we let your primo settle in for tonight, and we can talk about something like that another day."

I raise an eyebrow. Board games with Moni and my grandma doesn't exactly sound fun, but whatever. Anything to keep me from dying of boredom, I guess.

After dinner, Moni shows me to our shared room, which is completely empty except for a bunk bed in the corner.

"I'm on bottom," she says as she crawls into the lower bunk.

"Fine by me." I didn't bring any pajamas with me, so I climb into the top bunk fully clothed.

We're quiet for a few minutes, and I'm starting to think Moni has fallen asleep when she finally breaks the silence.

"No one appreciates ingenuity in my line of work," she says, all fast like she's been holding it in since we got in bed.

"Oh," is all I say, since I'm way too tired to make more words than I absolutely have to. Moni doesn't seem to have that problem.

"I came up with an innovative product packaging idea you can't find anywhere else on the market, but all my dad cares about is a failed drug test! What a hypocrite, right? Unlike him, I actually try my own product to make sure it's good. That's why my customers are happier than his."

"That sucks," I say, still not really knowing how else to respond.

"That's why I'm here," she continues. "Because of the drug test. He didn't even want to know the rest of the story!"

I know she probably wants me to tell her why *I'm* here now, but instead I ask, "How long are you staying here?"

"No idea. Long enough I'm going to school here for now. I think my dad's trying to teach me a lesson about public schools being bad or whatever, but I actually really like it here!"

Great. I'll be here until I die, probably.

"So what got you sent here?" She asks outright this time.

I roll over, as if to roll away from the question. "You're really persistent, you know that?"

She laughs. "I mean, I'm curious. I've been here by myself for a week. It's nice to have someone else to talk to. I mean, it's obviously not good for you that you're here, but it's good for me, and that's good enough for me."

I can't help but let out a small laugh. "Fine," I say. I guess there isn't any point to hiding it, really. "I got expelled from Catholic school."

"What'd you do?" she asks, not even pretending to feign sympathy. I kind of like that.

"You ask a lot of questions."

"What can I say, I'm a nosy bitch."

I let out another little laugh. Normally, I'd be really annoyed at all the questions, but something about Moni makes me feel less on edge. Maybe it's because we're kind of the same. As a musical prodigy turned drug dealer, she's just as much of a disappointment to her dad as I am to my mom. She knows what the pressure is like, and what it's like not to live up to it.

"I got tagged in a picture on Instagram of me with a bottle of tequila, and I added it to my page like a dumbass," I finally say.

I can hear Moni draw in a breath through her teeth. "That sucks. Can they really expel you for that if it wasn't on school grounds, though?"

"Yup," I say. I know in public school they wouldn't have been able to do shit about that, which is probably why Bianca posted the picture in the first place, but Catholic schools have a different set of rules. They have no problem using social media and your personal life against you.

Moni doesn't answer. I'm about to start being nosy myself and ask *her* a question when she starts snoring.

Guess I'll have to wait until tomorrow.

19

WHEN YOUR THERAPIST DOESN'T KNOW WHAT THE FUCK SHE'S TALKING ABOUT

denial

If there's any upside to being here, it's that I don't have to fake taking my meds every morning. Abuela has no reason to think I wouldn't take them, so my meds get to stay in the bathroom where I can do with them what I want. That little bit of freedom makes me just a little less grumpy when Abuela wakes me and Moni up before the sun even comes out. Apparently, it's time for our horo-verse reading. Once we're all sitting in the living room, she hands both me and Moni a piece of paper and a marker each.

"I like to print off our verses so we can write notes in the margins. I underline stuff that sticks out to me, but you can mark yours up however you like."

I look down at my paper to see the famous "love is kind" verse.

> Though I speak with the tongues of men and of angels, but have not love, I have become sounding brass or a clanging cymbal. And though I have the gift of prophecy, and understand all mysteries and all knowledge, and though I have all faith, so that I could

remove mountains, but have not love, I am nothing. And though I bestow all my goods to feed the poor, and though I give my body to be burned, but have not love, it profits me nothing.

Love suffers long and is kind; love does not envy; love does not parade itself, is not puffed up; does not behave rudely, does not seek its own, is not provoked, thinks no evil; does not rejoice in iniquity, but rejoices in the truth; bears all things, believes all things, hopes all things, endures all things.

Love never fails. But whether there are prophecies, they will fail; whether there are tongues, they will cease; whether there is knowledge, it will vanish away. For we know in part and we prophesy in part. But when that which is perfect has come, then that which is in part will be done away.

When I was a child, I spoke as a child, I understood as a child, I thought as a child; but when I became a man, I put away childish things.

For now we see in a mirror, dimly, but then face to face. Now I know in part, but then I shall know just as I also am known. And now abide faith, hope, love, these three; but the greatest of these is love.

Abuela reads it out loud to us while I start immediately marking it up. Instead of underlining stuff I like, I find myself crossing things out.

I don't hear what Abuela and Moni say next. It's a few minutes before I'm done blocking out the parts I feel like and making this whole verse actually relevant to me. I look down at the page one more time.

1 Corinthians 13

Though I ██████████████████████
███████ love ██ h ████████████ i ██
█████████ m ███
████████ I █████████████████ understand ███████████████████████████

████████ I am not ████████████████
██ good ████████████, and ██████ I █████
██ burn ██████████████████████
Love ████████████████ does not ████
███████████████████████████████
behave █████, does not ████████████
███████████ rejoice in ████████████
█ the truth ███████████████████████
██████████████████

Love ████ fails ████████████████
███████████████████████████████
███████████████████████████████
For we know ████████ we ██████████
███████████████████████████████
████████ will be done away.
█████████ I thought ████ h ████ I ████
m ███████████████████
████████████ a mirror, ██████████ face to

face. Now I know  just as I ▮ am known. ▮▮▮▮▮▮▮

After we drop Moni off at school, Abuela and I spend the rest of the day cleaning the house and doing odd jobs, like taking down the Christmas lights, which have been up for *way* too long since it's almost February.

Still, I'd rather clean than go to therapy, and with this all being so new, I get to skip therapy exactly one time. Unfortunately, the week somehow goes both excruciatingly slowly and too fast to process a thing. All that exists is cleaning and being kept awake at night by Moni talking about literally anything. I guess I wouldn't be sleeping much, anyway. Before I know it, I have to go to therapy again, and I'm more than exhausted. I can't believe I even still have to go to therapy after everythig I've done. If my mom is really disowning me, why would she still make me go? Just to be cruel? I wanted her to stop caring and forget I existed, not keep tabs on my suffering.

In the beginning of today's session, therapy is mostly small talk. I'm not usually bursting to talk or anything, but I guess there's usually *something* to say. Eventually, Dr. Lee asks a more specific question than her usual open-ended "How was your week?"-type bullshit.

"Can you tell me a little bit about why you're staying with your grandmother now?" I guess either my mom or grandma must have filled her in, at least partially, for her to know that.

"I got expelled" is all I say at first, but she just keeps looking at me like there's more to it. And yeah, there is, but that doesn't mean I have to tell her. Still, her hot stare feels like it's trying to sweat the answers out of me, and it's succeeding. "There was a picture online of me drinking at a party, okay?"

"And that's why you got expelled?" she asks.

"That's what I said, isn't it?" I shoot back.

She writes something down. "Your mom mentioned a new conflict between you and your sister. Do you want to talk about that?"

"No," I say automatically, but I have a feeling she won't drop the subject, so I deflect. "I stayed up all night a while ago and cleaned the whole house and made breakfast and caught up on all my homework and all that." I almost mention that I even showered, but the shame in admitting I don't do that as regularly as I should eats at me and keeps my mouth shut about that part. "And I rearranged Yami and my mom's jewelry stuff by color, which I guess was a bad idea, because it means they wouldn't know whose order is whose. . . ." I trail off, hoping this explanation is enough.

She writes something down in her notepad as she speaks. "Do you find you have those bursts of energy often?"

I shrug. "Recently, I guess, yeah. But it doesn't happen all that much usually."

"I see." She writes something else down. "And this caused a big enough rift in your relationship with your sister for your mom to bring it up?"

My instinct is to deflect again, but now I'm having second thoughts. It's not like I have anything left to lose, right? I guess the only reason I usually don't like telling Dr. Lee all my business is because I thought she'd go blabbing to my mom. But now that my mom doesn't give a shit about me, I can say whatever I want. "Anything I tell you is confidential, right?" I ask, just to be sure.

She looks up from her notepad with a micro-pleased expression. "As long as you don't express any instance of hurting yourself or others, or any plan to. That kind of thing I would have to report. Your guardian will know about your medications and diagnosis, but everything personal you tell me is confidential."

"I hooked up with the girl who outed my sister. Jamal and Yami both know about it, so they want nothing to do with me anymore, and my mom hates me now because I got expelled."

She's quiet for a while as she writes something else down.

"What are you always writing about me?" I snap. The writing didn't bother me at first, but now I can't help but imagine she's documenting all her judgy thoughts so she can make fun of me to her therapist friends, I don't know.

"It's just a memory aid, so I can refer back to it later if I need to identify any recurring patterns. Which brings me to my current theory . . ." She flips through her notebook at that, like she's double-checking something before saying it out loud. "I think you might be experiencing a manic episode."

"The hell does that mean?" I shift uncomfortably on the couch.

"It means you're experiencing a period with a high intensity of emotions and energy."

"Are you saying I'm crazy or something?" I ask, gripping tightly to the arm of the couch.

"'Crazy' isn't the word I'd use for it," she says. "But based on your previous records, and what I've learned from our sessions, I'm diagnosing you with bipolar disorder. Bipolar can cause these types of long shifts in mood and energy, which we categorize as mania and depre—"

"I know what bipolar is," I interrupt, rolling my eyes. I'm definitely not that.

"Okay, that's good. You're already ahead of the curve then. You should also know there's a support group for teens with serious mental illness that meets here every week after your session. I recommend you check it out."

Serious mental illness. Bipolar. The words feel foreign, like they can't possibly be used to describe *me*. I'm supposed to be that happy-go-lucky guy with straight As who falls asleep in class sometimes. I'm supposed to be good at everything I try. I'm supposed to be the golden boy. Not the fuckup. Not the problem child. Definitely not *this*.

"I'm not fucking crazy," I say.

"Again, that's a loaded word. I wouldn't call anyone crazy who didn't self-identify that way." God, she's so condescending it makes me sick. "I'm here to answer any questions you might have. How much do you know about bipolar disorder?"

"I know enough," I say. Enough to know I definitely don't have it.

"Well, I think this diagnosis could actually open a lot of doors for you and answer a lot of questions. Now we know where some of your impulsive decisions might be coming from. We know that when you go through a period of this much energy, or a period of depression, that it's only temporary. I hope that can bring you some peace the next time you experience that."

"I'm not that impulsive," I mumble. She doesn't know what the fuck she's talking about.

I just tune her out while she goes on explaining irrelevant shit to me about a disorder I don't have. Eventually she looks at the clock in the corner of the room. "That's about our time for today. The group session starts in a few minutes, would you like to stay for that?"

"Nope!" I say as I get up and walk out.

Dr. Lee is wrong. She doesn't know anything about me. I'm not going to that group today, or ever.

Since I won't be officially reenrolled at Rover until Monday, the rest of the week drags on while Moni's at school. The chores feel endless, and I swear time flows backward at one point. Even on Friday, the boredom doesn't end when Moni's done for the week, since she has her own chores, homework, and violin practice to do.

Lucky enough for her, though, she gets out of practice early since her dad called to talk to her. I know Abuela's been talking to both Tío Paco and my mom with updates about both of us, but my mom hasn't asked to talk to me the way Tío Paco does with Moni. I have to keep reminding myself it's a good thing.

Moni puts her dad on FaceTime, so I do my best to mind my business while I scrub the grout between tiles with a toothbrush. Still, neither of them is exactly discreet, and like I said . . . I'm bored.

"So have you made up your mind about which college you want to—" Tío Paco starts, but she doesn't let him finish.

"I already told you I'm not going to school for music anymore."

An audible sigh. "Mija, do you know how many young girls would kill for a scholarship to Curtis? How many would kill for your spot at *Juilliard*? You can't throw away your chance at a future just to make a point."

I cringe at how familiar this conversation is. It honestly makes me relieved my mom is so done with me. Abuela starts making dinner quieter, like she's also pretending not to listen.

"And what point would that be, exactly?" Moni tilts her head in an innocent question mark.

"You know very well what I mean, Monica."

"Aww, it's so sweet how much you care." She puts her hand over her chest. "I know you're just worried about my future, Papi. I would be too, if I was you! I know some people these days have to go by a pasty Anglo name in the office and kiss their boss's greedy white ass to find success, but you don't have to worry about that with me, *Patrick*. Not everyone can be success-ful without selling out to a giant pharmaceutical corporation that punches down on the vulnerable, but *I* run my business *ethically*. So thank you so much for the concern, but I don't need your career advice."

I let out a cough to keep myself from laughing, but no one seems to notice I've been cleaning between the same two tiles this entire conversation. Abuela is still pretending not to listen, though she's somehow not making a sound in the kitchen. My guess is that she actually *agrees* with Moni about Tío Paco's job.

"Very funny, Monica." My tío doesn't even sound taken aback, like this is just another regular conversation with his kid.

I almost want to ask what Moni means by the whole punching-down thing, but I figure it's a conversation for later. For now, I just clean quietly while Moni and her dad bicker over her future.

It isn't until we're in bed for the night that it comes back up, and I'm not even the one to say anything.

"Ugh . . . ," she groans. Moni seems to love waiting until I could plausibly be asleep to make conversation.

I wait, expecting her to follow up her groaning with an actual complaint, but she just groans louder. "Uggghhhhh . . ."

"You okay?" I ask before she decides to start kicking my mattress again.

"Can you believe my dad? What is his problem?"

"Yeah, I feel you," I say. "My mom's kind of the same way. At least, she was . . ." I trail off before mentioning my mom wants nothing to do with me anymore.

"Can they both just chill the fuck out? If my dad has enough money to pay my way through Juilliard, why not ASU? But *no*, he'll only pay if I do a music program. If he doesn't want me to make my own tuition money, he should fucking help me! Like I know my dad invested a lot in my music, but it was never what *I* wanted."

"They don't care what we want," I say, but the realization doesn't hurt as much as it should. I feel for Moni, but I did this to myself.

"You'd think he'd understand that. I doubt his dream job was to pay off doctors to prescribe a specific medication regardless of a patient's needs."

"Wait, what?" I knew Moni's dad didn't have the most virtuous of jobs, but I didn't even think something like that was a thing. "People do that?"

"Yup, and they all get to profit without actually helping the people they're burying alive in medical debt. And *I'm* the one who needs to rethink my priorities?"

I haven't been taking my meds for a while, but if I ever had an inkling to go back on them, it's gone now. If doctors can be paid off like that, then there's no way I can trust Dr. Lee. And if I can't trust my therapist, who *can* I trust?

I can't rely on therapy or medication or any kind of support system. I pushed everyone else away, so all I have is me.

And I know better than anyone how shit my own company is.

Even I don't want it.

20

WHEN YOU FINALLY FIND THE ANSWER TO YOUR PRAYERS

losing touch with reality

Even on the weekend, it seems like Abuela has an endless list of things for me to do while Moni does homework and music practice. I go through the motions monotonously to the sound of Moni's pro-level violin skills. I try to let the music distract me from thinking about what day it is.

Yami's birthday.

I don't ask Abuela for a phone to call her, though. Yami wouldn't want me calling her anyway. She'd probably just ignore it. She needs space from me right now, and I'll give it to her. I try to make myself feel satisfied that my plan worked so well. It literally went perfectly, but for some reason everything just aches.

I push through it and do my chores without saying a word to Abuela. After I power wash the plastic chairs outside, clean all the windows and mirrors, dust all the surfaces, and somehow figure out how to fix a wobbly table leg, she finally lets me off the hook.

I expected things would be quiet and awkward during dinner, but instead Abuela is talking away, telling us stories about her earlier years, which were apparently pretty rough. At least she had my grandpa back then.

"When we were younger, there was no problem my love couldn't solve by simply sitting me down and doing my two braids. It used to be that I couldn't fall asleep until those hands worked their magic on my hair." She sighs, a melancholy smile on her lips.

Her stories make me a little sad. She met my grandpa young but didn't marry him until her twenties. He passed away when my mom was only ten, and Abuela had to raise her and my tío by herself. I wonder how long it took her to be able to fall asleep without him braiding her hair.

You would think my mom would have a little more sympathy for the woman, considering it's exactly what she had to do with me and Yami ever since our dad got deported. But it seems like whatever mistakes Abuela made during my mom's childhood, she hasn't been fully forgiven for them yet. Part of me wants to know what their deal is, but the other part probably wouldn't even be bothered to listen if Abuela did try telling me.

It's a late dinner, since Moni had a surprising amount of weekend homework before she could even get to her violin, and I had all those random chores to do, so Moni and I head to bed right after.

I'm exhausted from the day, but Moni seems to be wide awake, considering how loudly she keeps rolling around and changing positions. Eventually she gives up on her poor attempt at being quiet.

"Abuela's probably asleep," Moni says out loud, not even bothering to whisper. I don't answer, but my pretending to be asleep doesn't stop her. She kicks the top bunk to wake me up.

"Fine, I'm up. *What?*"

"Abuela's probably asleep," she says again.

"Okay, and?"

"Wanna go outside and smoke?"

I scoot to the edge of the bed and let my head fall over it so I can see her. "Are you trying to get in even more trouble?"

She shrugs innocently. "Not like we have anything to lose, right?"

And I can't help but admit she's right. "You do have a point. . . ."

She then rolls out of bed and hops to the floor. "You coming or what?"

"What the hell," I say with a shrug, and climb off the bed. Not like I was about to get any sleep anyway.

We sneak over to my grandma's door, just to confirm the sound of her snoring, before quietly grabbing a utility lighter from the kitchen and heading outside.

"Let's go on the roof. I left a ladder out here from when Abuela made me fix the paint on the side of the house."

"Lead the way," I say, following her to the side of the house where the ladder rests. Luckily, it's leaning by the garage instead of by Abuela's room, so she shouldn't hear us going up.

The roof above the garage is flat, so we sit on the edge with our feet dangling over the side.

Moni pulls out a box of organic tampons from her backpack.

"Um, you're not gonna change that right here, are you?" I ask, looking away.

"No, pendejo." She laughs and unwraps one of them, revealing a blunt inside. "I call it a *Tampot.*"

"Wow." I'll give it to her, that really *is* some innovative product packaging. "I wish I had an excuse to carry those around."

"Don't lie to me. Periods fucking suck."

"I believe you." I raise my hands in surrender, and she puts the blunt to her lips and lights the end, inhaling deeply before pulling the blunt away from her mouth. She slowly lets out a breath full of smoke, then hands it over.

I take it in my mouth, and she lights it for me. On the inhale, I try my best not to cough, since we should be making as little noise as possible. Still, I can't help but let out a small one and hand it back to Moni, but the cough pulls more of them out of me, and before I know it, I'm basically hacking my lungs out. I must have inhaled too much, because with every cough, I feel my body somehow getting lighter and heavier at the same time.

"Cállate, wey," she whisper-yells, and I can't help but laugh, albeit quietly. The more I laugh, the more I cough, and I can't seem to stop the vicious cycle from repeating.

Moni doesn't seem too worried, though, because she's laughing and wheezing along with me.

"Shhh!" she whispers between quiet giggles.

"I'm sorry I'm not a weed professional like you," I say, finally catching my breath. It's not like I've never smoked weed before, but every time I do, I can't help but cough. I don't know if it's asthma or if I have weak lungs or what, but I can't help it.

"Finally, someone around here acknowledges my expertise." Moni grins proudly. "I'm basically living my dream job. When I'm old enough to open my own dispensary, people will see I know what I'm doing."

I take another puff from the blunt and blow the air out as

steadily as I can manage. "I don't have a dream job," I mumble as I pass it back to her.

"Really? You've never wanted to be something when you grew up? Even when you were little?"

"Okay, maybe when I was little." I laugh quietly. "But I'm grown now, and I'm not exactly looking forward to selling my soul to capitalism. I don't have your passion for running a business."

"Fair enough," she says, taking a long inhale before saying anything else. "I just want to make enough money for my dad to admit I can do something other than music. I don't want to let the money run my life the way he does. Like, I want my dispensary to be employee owned and shit. Let me know if you need a job after I turn twenty-one." She grins.

"I doubt I'll still be here by then," I say, my filter completely dissolved.

"You planning on moving?" she asks. I just shrug, not wanting to elaborate. Luckily, she doesn't read into it and just moves on. "Okay, subject change. I've been meaning to ask . . . What was that thing Abuela took you to on Tuesday? Was that, like, a doctor's appointment or something? Are you sick?" She hands the blunt back to me. "I can get you medical grade."

I laugh. Moni *would* use my supposed sickness as a business opportunity. "Would I get a family discount?"

She looks at me all offended. I'm in the middle of taking another whiff when she responds. "As my cousin, don't you want me to fulfill my dreams? This is one of my main income streams!"

"What do you mean, 'one of'?" I say in the midst of trying not to die from cough laughter. She pats my back until my lungs settle down.

"Seriously, though. You're not dying on me, are you?" she asks, ignoring my question.

"I'm fine," I say as I try one more inhale, coughing less this time. "It was just therapy."

"Ahh . . . ," she says it like it all makes sense now. But why would it? Do I come across as someone who needs therapy?

"My therapist thinks I have bipolar," I blurt out. It's like all my walls are melting away with this high.

She just nods, for once out of words.

"What? That doesn't surprise you?"

"Not at all," she says, plucking the blunt from between my fingers since I forgot to hand it back to her.

"Why not?" Moni barely knows me anymore, so why would she think I have bipolar?

"Because Abuela has that too. That can be genetic, right?"

For a second, I start to think that maybe this makes a lot of sense. That it explains a lot about me that I thought was just wrong. That maybe Abuela can talk me through some of this stuff. But then I remember Mami, and how she talks about her mom. How crazy she is, and how you can't trust anything she says. Mami even used to tell me not to listen to her.

Is that why she never listens to *me*? Why she always assumes she knows what's best for me, because she thinks I'm too crazy to know for myself?

No. She doesn't know I'm bipolar. Hell, *I* don't know I'm bipolar. Dr. Lee could be wrong. *Is* wrong.

"Doesn't matter," I finally say. "Dr. Lee doesn't know shit. I'm not fucking crazy."

"Don't talk about Abuela like that," Moni says, oddly defensively. "I never said either of you was crazy."

"Well good, because I'm not. Whatever Abuela has, I don't, okay?"

"Whatever you say, primo." She sucks on the blunt for a moment, then hands it back to me.

I roll my eyes and take another puff, letting the smoke fill my lungs and empty my irritation, and it works.

"I'm worried about Abuela, though," Moni admits.

"Why?" I ask.

"She's lonely, I think. Both times I got sent here, she puts on an act like I'm in trouble, but it never lasts. She likes the company, I think."

"Can you blame her? She's retired and lives here by herself. She's probably bored out of her mind when we're not here."

Moni inhales, then hums on the exhale, smoke blowing out of her nostrils. "Too bad she hates romance, or I'd be trying to set her up."

"What do you mean she hates romance?" I ask. The way she talks about how in love she used to be and how getting her hair braided helped her fall asleep, I thought she'd be pining for that kind of love again.

"She got her heart broken, you know? I'm sure that kind of thing changes you."

I nod. I guess I can understand. There was a time when I loved being in love. If someone told me then that I would willingly break up with Jamal and cut him out of my life, I would have laughed in their face.

After everything, I don't think anyone will love me like that again, and I don't want them to. If Abuela's like me, maybe that's where she's coming from, too.

The next morning, I finally get to go back to Rover, which I'm thrilled about since it means I don't have to spend the entire day doing chores anymore. Abuela drives Moni to her school first, then drops me off.

It'd be nice if Moni also went here so we could at least hang out at school and I could have a single person to call a friend, but no. She goes to Baseline, which is closer to Abuela's house. Besides, it's probably best I don't get too attached to Moni anyway. It's not like her dad disowned her like mine did, so she'll probably leave Abuela's eventually, and then I most likely won't see her again for who knows how many more years.

Once Abuela drops me off, I walk straight to the bathroom on the far end of campus where they have PE. It's best Jamal or Nick and them don't see me. Nick and his friends would probably beat the shit out of me on sight. They already hated me before, but now that I hooked up with Bianca right after she and Nick broke up? Yeah, I'm not looking forward to running into any of those guys.

I stay in the bathroom until the bell rings and I finally have to go to class.

AP Astronomy first.

It's a far-ass walk, but I don't care. What are they gonna do if I'm late, give me detention? And if they do, what then? I'm already staying with my grandma and doing every chore under the sun to keep her happy. It's not like I can get into more trouble than I'm already in.

So I take my time and walk into class a few minutes late.

And lo and behold, who else is also taking AP Astronomy? Jamal. Of *course* he is.

It's not like I can be surprised. We were in almost all the same classes sophomore year when we went here together before.

He looks at me right when I walk in, and his eyes widen. Probably because he's putting together that I must have gotten kicked out of Slayton. He's probably happy about it too. Not because I'm here with him, but because I deserve every bad thing that happens to me.

"Ahem." The teacher, Mrs. Velez, reminds me I'm just standing there staring at Jamal in front of the entire class. If this was Slayton, I'd be getting chastised for being late, but this teacher just smiles and motions for me to join her at the front of the class. "Everyone, we have a new student today. Well, a returning one. Do you want to introduce yourself for anyone who doesn't know you?" she asks.

"I'm Cesar," I say, pronouncing it the Spanish way instead of like Caesar salad, which was how I used to pronounce it at Slayton. I make sure to smile and look as friendly as possible.

"Do you want to tell us a little bit about yourself?" Mrs. Velez asks.

"Not really," I admit. What am I supposed to say? Hey, people I haven't seen in two years, I'm back because I got expelled since I went out drinking and hooked up with the girl who outed my sister, which my therapist thinks is because I'm having a bipolar manic episode!

Yeah, not doing that.

"All right then, why don't you have a seat over there?" She gestures to the single empty seat in the class, which—surprise, surprise—is right next to Jamal.

I put on a fake smile and walk over.

"Hey," Jamal says softly—without the "you," I can't help but notice. He's still looking at me like I have a second head. I can't tell if it's because he hates me or because he's worried. Either way, I look away as I take my seat, and I see from the corner of my eye that he does too.

The rest of class is monumentally awkward, and so is the entire day since I have like four classes with the dude.

I'm about to head to the abandoned PE bathroom for lunch when someone covers my eyes with their hands before I can leave the building. On instinct, I'm about to turn around swinging until I hear the voice behind me.

"Guess who?"

"Bianca?" I ask, and she lets go of my eyes and moves to stand next to me. She has two friends with her. Yami's old friend group.

"Stefani, Chachi, you remember Cesar, right?"

"Hey, Cesar. Been a minute!" Chachi says, and Stefani just smiles and waves.

Just then, Nick and his friends walk by, and I immediately tense up. Bianca notices them and takes my now nervously sweaty hand in hers.

"Well, he's my boyfriend now!" she says, loud enough for Nick to hear. I can't tell if she actually thinks we're dating or if she's just saying it to piss off Nick. Either way, she basically just sealed my fate.

They all make eye contact as they approach. I'm ready to get jumped, but that's when I notice Nick is limping slightly, and he's got a boot on his foot. But he's not the only one with unconventional footwear. I'm pretty sure Avery didn't have an ankle bracelet on at the party. Whatever happened after they left that night must have been bad news. Well, for them. It's great for me, considering Nick can't chase me with a fucked-up foot and his favorite minion won't be getting in any fights while on probation.

Nick just glares at me while they all walk past. I'm sure he's fantasizing about the revenge he'll surely get once he's healed, but it looks like I'm safe for now. It isn't until they're out of earshot that I turn back to Bianca for clarification.

My first instinct is to let go of her hand and tell her what happened at the party was a mistake and that we're definitely *not* together, but when I really think about it, this is kind of perfect.

"Boyfriend?" I ask, in case she's being serious.

Bianca glances over at Nick down the hall, then her voice is a little quieter. "Sorry, I just wanted Nick to—"

"I don't mind," I say automatically. She raises an eyebrow, and Chachi and Stefani give each other a look like my awkward comment is some kind of Hallmark movie gesture. "I mean, I can be your boyfriend, if you want."

Bianca smiles, but I can't tell if she thinks I'm being cute or if she's trying not to laugh at me. "Are you asking me out?"

"It makes sense, right?" I say without thinking twice. Me and Bianca would be a mutually beneficial relationship. She gets to make Nick jealous, and I get to piss off everyone I care about enough that they'll never fuck with me again.

Bianca chews on her lip, looking at me like I'm a walking pros and cons list. Eventually she says, "Yeah, actually, it does make a lot of sense." She smiles.

"Aw, how cute!" Stefani says, and Bianca takes my hand and pulls me toward the cafeteria.

In an unexpected twist, Bianca might just be the answer to all my prayers. This way, when I finally get the balls to leave this hell of a life, no one will feel guilty about it. Plus, I can be straight now, so I won't even go to hell after I die.

It's the perfect plan.

The next week or so goes by pretty much the same. Nick and them leave me alone. I try to like Bianca. And Jamal and I silently tolerate each other in class.

At least, until he comes up to me after school one day. It's raining pretty hard, and I'm soaked, waiting for my grandma to show up, when I hear him from behind me.

"Question," Jamal says tentatively. Suddenly the rain stops, and a shadow comes over me. Of course he has a fucking umbrella. I turn around to see him standing straight, like usual, holding the umbrella over me instead of himself, even though we can both fit. He's wearing his we-need-to-talk face.

"Yeah?" I say on reflex. For half a second, it almost feels like nothing's changed. Like he's about to ask me what I think aliens look like or what kind of creature I'd like to be reincarnated as.

"Why are you here?" If anyone else asked me that, I'd probably take it wrong, but Jamal looks more concerned than anything. He knows better than anyone how bad things were for me here before.

"Don't worry about it," I mumble, looking away. I know it

comes off cold, but I mean exactly what I say. If he's still worrying about me, this is never gonna work.

He sighs and steps closer, speaking quietly so no one besides me can hear him over the rain. "Look, Cesar, I get it. You don't want to be with me anymore. Fine. But you don't have to be a dick about it. It's not like we weren't friends, too. Just . . . talk to me?"

I turn my head to look at him. He's soaking too now, and I can't help but read into this metaphor. He's always holding out his umbrella for me and letting himself get soaked. If I wasn't here, his nice clothes and shoes he loves so much would be dry. If I wasn't here, he'd be much better off in general.

"I can't," I say, shaking my head hopelessly. "I *can't*."

"Why not?" he asks. "What changed?"

And just then, Abuela's car pulls up to the curb, and I step out from under the safety of Jamal's umbrella without pretending to have an answer.

As we're driving away, I look back at Jamal out the window, and I know that face too. I know exactly what he would say if I hadn't walked away. What he always fucking says, no matter how much I continue to hurt him.

He'd say he understands.

But it'd be a lie.

21

WHEN YOU'RE GOD'S FAVORITE SO HE INTERVENES TO HELP YOU WIN SCRABBLE

delusions of grandeur

When we get back to Abuela's house, I head straight to the bedroom.

"Ah-ah-ah, where do you think you're going?" Abuela says before I even make it to the hallway.

"Um, to the room?" I'm really not in the mood to be around people. Back home, I'd just hide myself in my room whenever I was in one of these moods. Apparently, that's not a thing you can do in this house, though.

"No, you're not. You still have homework and chores to do."

"Well, then I have to pee," I say, trying a different approach. I can't just go straight into doing my homework right now. I need *some* kind of alone time, even if it's just a few minutes in the bathroom.

She squints at me like she knows I'm lying but doesn't stop me. As I head over to the bathroom, I can hear Moni asking about game night again. She wants to play games tonight since she's going to visit her dad for the weekend. Apparently she's still in too much trouble to move back home just yet, but at least her dad still wants to see her.

I'm definitely not looking forward to being here alone, but I'll deal with that when I get there. For now, I lock myself in the bathroom. I don't have my usual eye drops to keep my eyes from looking red, so when I see myself in the mirror, I'm taken aback a little. I look like I'm either tired as hell or stoned out of my mind. I guess it makes sense since I haven't slept much the last couple of days, even in class. But apparently all the energy I've been having isn't translating to my baggy, bloodshot eyes.

I go to the end of the bathroom farthest from the door and sit on the ground with my back against the wall. My mind starts to fog a bit like it does when my body desperately needs to rest but my brain doesn't want to.

I clasp my hands together and close my eyes to focus. I got a little bit out of my after-school prayer routine when I first got here since I was in between schools, but I'm starting to get back to it.

"Thank you for answering my prayers and sending me Bianca," I whisper. And yeah, it feels gross to be thanking God for Bianca of all people after what she did to Yami, but she truly is the answer to my prayers. Besides, Father John did always say God works in mysterious ways.

Before I can finish praying, the whole room gets all wavy and reflective, like it's a mirror I could slip through at any moment.

The lights in the bathroom flood the room in white, and I can't see a thing. It's like I'm staring right at the sun. No, more like an eclipse, because there's something standing in front of the bright light. Some*one.*

It almost feels like a mirage, but I don't have to chase it anymore.

I'm right here.

He's right here.

I squint and use my hand as a visor. This can't be happening. But it *is*. ". . . God?"

"I am here, my son." His full voice bellows around the room, probably echoing throughout the entire house.

"What are you doing here?" My eyes widen despite the brightness. I'm really talking to God right now. And he's talking back!

"Hear my message," he says. "You are meant for more than this."

"What do you mean?" I ask.

"You are meant to join me. To come home."

"I know that," I say. "That's why I've been wanting to . . ." I trail off.

"When the time to act is right, I will call you to come home."

My eyes start to water. He wants me in heaven. He *wants* me there. *That's* where I'm meant to be, not this hell on earth.

I just have to wait for God to call on me.

"Cesar!" Moni calls out, banging on the bathroom door, which jolts me awake. "You okay in there?"

I have no idea how long I fell asleep for, but it must have been long enough for Moni to worry, because she's banging really hard.

"Do I need to knock down that door?" Abuela yells after not even that long of me not answering.

"Abuela, no! I'll do it!" Moni says, probably worried Abuela would break a shoulder or something.

"I'm okay," I call out groggily as I crawl up from the floor and use the toilet to help me to my feet.

When I open the door, they both stare at me with wide eyes like something's incredibly wrong, but I can't for the life of me figure out what.

"What happened to your face?" Moni asks, and Abuela grabs my cheeks with her hands, inspecting it. "Te caíste?"

I pull away and look at myself in the mirror to find tile marks from the bathroom floor on my cheeks. Shit. How long have I been in here?

"No, I didn't fall. Unless you count falling asleep, I guess."

Abuela's eyebrows furrow together, but she doesn't comment on it all concerned like Mami would have. At least, like Mami would have before she disowned me.

"What are you going to do then? Do you need to go to sleep for the night?" Abuela asks, and I'm surprised she's actually giving me a choice.

"I'll . . . go get started on my homework?" I say, both because I don't want to make the wrong choice, and because going to bed now would be the most boring move. I just saw *God*. I'm not about to waste any time sleeping.

And even though I haven't slept properly in days, I still have enough energy to speed through my homework without a hitch. Rover homework is so much easier than Slayton's, even if I'm taking the same classes.

I spend the entire time looking for some kind of sign that the conversation I had with God was real, and not just a dream, but so far there's nothing.

Once Moni and I are finished with our homework and chores, and we've all had dinner, Abuela pulls out a game of Scrabble.

"Game night?" Moni squeals.

"Game night." Abuela grins.

I feel like I'm both hypervigilant and extra out of it at the same time somehow. Like, things are happening around me, and I'm responding on autopilot, barely taking in what's going on. But at the same time, I'm noticing all the things I normally wouldn't catch. There's gotta be a sign somewhere. I find myself hyper-focusing on all the words everyone spells, thinking one of them might mean something.

I spend most of the game only finding small words with not a lot of points. I'm losing pretty bad, but I do my best to ignore Moni's trash talk. She gets a triple-letter score with her next word, which makes her laugh all evil. "HAhahaha! You both might as well just give up now! I basically already won."

Not if God has anything to do with it, I think to myself, fully confident He'll help me out.

"What are you talking about?" Moni raises an eyebrow.

Did I say that out loud? Whatever, it's the truth. Now it's my turn to laugh. "Don't be jealous. Just watch."

"Happily." She laughs back. She probably thinks I'm joking, but she'll see.

Abuela, on the other hand, isn't laughing, not that she ever does. She just looks at me like she's solving a puzzle, but *I'm* the one who's going to solve this shit.

I put my hands together and close my eyes, shooting a small prayer up to the heavens before I cross myself and pick up a new letter.

God, help me now if you really meant what you said earlier.

And, holy shit, He does.

And, the word. That word is a sign if I've ever seen one. I spell out WEEKEND on the board on a space that gives me three times the points for the entire word.

Weekend.

Sunday is on the weekend.

Church is on Sunday.

Sunday is the Lord's day.

God is definitely sending me a message right now. He chose me. I feel like the world is opening up to me to reveal heaven itself. That's where I'm headed. I can't wait for God to call me there.

I mean, I *can* wait. I can be patient. But it better not take too long. . . .

Just then, the doorbell rings. Moni's dad must be here to take her home for the weekend. I'm expecting her to jump for joy and run to the door, but she frowns.

"Do I *have* to go?" she whines. Why the hell wouldn't she want to leave? All we've been doing here is homework and chores. "You guys are so much more fun than my dad."

"At least your dad still wants to see you," I mumble, but Moni doesn't seem to hear me.

Abuela does, though, and she looks at me all sad. "I'm sorry about your papi, mijo."

"I wasn't talking about him . . . ," I say, and she just looks at me all sad like she isn't fully aware my mom hates me too now.

Before she can answer, Moni rushes into a hug with Abuela. Apparently, there are some exceptions to Moni not liking hugs. She's acting like they'll never see each other again even though it'll only be a weekend. She then comes over to me, and I almost think she'll give me a hug too, but she offers me her usual high five instead.

"Bye, Lareina!" she says as she bends down and kisses Lareina on the head before waving at us all again and heading out the door.

I start to walk to the bedroom when Abuela stops me with a soft hand on my shoulder.

"Sit with me, mijo," she says before going to sit down on the couch and patting the spot next to her. Lareina hops up into her lap.

"Okay?" I say, taking the patted spot.

"What were you saying about God earlier?" she asks.

"Nothing," I say. Suddenly I feel like I'm being interrogated. "You wouldn't get it." God chose *me*. She wouldn't understand what that's like.

"I think you'd be surprised," she says. "Do you talk to God often?"

I shrug my shoulders. "I can't blame you for being jealous."

She chuckles. "I talk to Him too, mijo."

"Really?" I ask. Did God choose her too? No, no. That wouldn't make any sense. God doesn't choose just anyone. I'm special. I have to be, otherwise none of it makes sense.

"I do, but only when I'm manic." She says the word "manic" like it's totally normal, not something crazy people experience, or something to be ashamed about. It makes me sympathize with her, even if we're not in the same situation.

"It's not like I'm manic, though," I say.

Abuela nods. "Sometimes it's hard to tell when you are. Sometimes it—"

"I'm not crazy, Abuela."

She winces at the word. "Are you calling your abuela crazy?"

"I . . . no?"

"Then you're not crazy either," she says, giving Lareina a few gentle strokes.

"I'm not . . . I'm not like you, though."

"I believe we're more alike than you think." She offers me a smile, but I don't return it.

"You don't know what you're talking about." My ears burn at the idea. She's wrong.

"I might not, but I think Dr. Lee knows enough about this to make a proper assessment."

"How do you know what Dr. Lee said?" I snap back.

"Your mami told me, mijo."

"How does *Mami* know? Why does she *care*?" I demand. She disowned me, why is she still in my business?

"Cesar, you know that your therapist has to tell your guardian about your diagnosis, right?"

That fucking bitch. "She said whatever I told her was confidential!"

"She's not going to tell anyone what you said, but she has to tell her about your diagnosis."

Anger boils all the blood in my body. How could she betray me like that? I knew I shouldn't have trusted Dr. Lee. As far as I know, Moni's dad could be personally paying Dr. Lee to prescribe something to brainwash me. But I'm not falling for it.

"My point is, mijo, it's important to recognize when you're going through these episodes so you can regulate them."

"I'm not having an episode," I say sharply.

She nods. "I see. Just know that when and if you do have one, you're not the only one, okay? This is an illness that affects a lot of people, including me."

Whatever she says, she just doesn't get it. What I'm going through is divine intervention, not mania. I would think that someone who raised my religious-ass mother might understand that much, but apparently not.

"Can I go to bed now?"

"Haven't been sleeping well, right?" she asks, and I clench my jaw. "Of course. Get some rest, mijo."

So I leave for the bedroom and crawl into bed, unable to get Abuela's words out of my head.

I believe we're more alike than you think.

22

WHEN I DIP YOU DIP WE DIP

the crash

It's a good thing it's Friday, because when my head finally meets the pillow for the night, I actually fall asleep for once. And I mean *sleep*. The next time I open my eyes, I'm not sure if it's sunrise or sunset or even how many days have passed.

I wake up to Abuela nudging my shoulder. I groan and stretch out. The rising—or setting?—sun makes the room way too bright even through the small slits between the blinds. She's carrying a tray of empanadas.

"That crash is never fun, is it?" she asks.

"What?" I ask groggily. Way too early—or late?—for thinking.

Instead of answering, she pulls the blanket from over me, which makes me squirm like a worm on hot cement.

"Abuela, whyyy?" I whine.

"Because you haven't eaten since yesterday," she says matter-of-factly.

"What time is it?" I croak.

"Las siete."

"In the morning?" Why the hell would she be waking me up 7:00 a.m. on a Saturday?

"In the evening."

"Oh . . . ," I mumble, forcing myself to sit up.

"Ten, mijo," she says, handing me the tray with three empanadas, rice, and beans on it.

"You're letting me eat in bed?" I ask.

"You need to rest," she says. "Your body and mind have been working on overdrive."

"Can't argue with that," I say, putting the tray on my lap and biting into an empanada.

She sits down on a chair that I'm just now realizing she must have pulled in from the kitchen. "Actually, I've been in the very same situation as you."

"What do you mean?" I say through a mouthful of beans.

"Don't talk with your mouth full," Abuela scolds, but her eyes aren't as firm as her voice. "During one of my worst episodes, I blew through every penny I'd saved for your mami's college tuition. When I finally crashed, I slept for *days*."

I bet that's why my mom doesn't trust her. Why would Abuela want me to know this? Doesn't she want to keep the worst mistakes to herself? "Why are you telling me this?" I finally ask.

"Because I went most of my life thinking I was alone. If I knew what I was going through was a treatable illness, it might have saved myself and the people around me a lot of grief. I'm telling you because I know what this is like. The crash after the high. It's never fun. But you get used to it eventually."

"I'm fine." I know I caused basically all the problems everyone around me has ever had. That's the whole reason I want to *leave*. If I go, I can stop causing problems for everyone. *That's* how I can save us all the grief.

She nods. "So, do you still stand by what you said last night?"

It takes awhile for my brain fog to clear up enough to realize what she must be talking about. I told her I talked to God last night. That God helped me win Scrabble. And because of what? Because of a sleep-deprived dream I had on the bathroom floor? Yesterday, and so much of the last couple of weeks, feels like one long fever dream where logic had no meaning. Suddenly, logic is back.

A flood of embarrassment rushes through me, and I sink back against the wall.

"Okay, I get it, you win. I'm crazy. Are you happy?" I say dejectedly.

She frowns. "No one here is crazy, okay? Our brains are just wired a little differently."

I feel my throat tighten. "You won't tell anyone, will you?"

She reaches forward and squeezes my knee. "When and if you're ready to tell people, that's when they'll find out. Dr. Lee, your mami, and I are the only ones who know."

I let out a sigh of relief before a familiar bubble of anger forms. My mom doesn't trust Abuela at *all*. Yet this is where she wants me, and she couldn't even drop me off herself.

"Why'd my mom even send me here if she doesn't trust you?" I ask.

She pauses for a few seconds. "You won't hear either me or your mami deny I've made more mistakes than I can count . . .

but I think she also knows I can help you. She may not be ready to forgive me herself, but she can still see that I'm different now than I was then. She's seen me lose everything and piece my life back together from rock bottom. I pushed away everyone I cared about, and I lost most of them. Sometimes there's no turning back from a soured relationship, but sometimes people will surprise you if you try to make amends."

I squint at her, not sure I buy it. "You're telling me you've tried to fix every single relationship you messed up?"

"Of course not." At first she looks confident, but after a moment, her expression drops into something a little sad. "It's not always so simple. . . ."

"That's what I thought. Most people are better off without me trying to shove my way back in their lives."

"I thought the same thing about myself once." She frowns harder. "But I was wrong. It's true that not everyone has or will forgive me, but I finally have a good relationship with Paco again, and your mami trusts me at least enough to let me care for you. We still have a long way to go, but admitting where I went wrong and apologizing was the first step."

"But you just said yourself you haven't tried to fix things with *everyone*. So obviously we both know when a relationship is too far gone, and I'm telling you now that's where I'm at."

She nods solemnly. "You know what, maybe I was wrong. You never know until you try, right? I'm going to make some calls tonight. It's going to be okay, you'll see."

Then she claps her hands together and walks out, pulling her phone from her pocket before she even reaches the door.

✦ ✦ ✦

School on Monday goes by in a blur since I sleep in every class and even in the cafeteria for lunch. With my head down on a table, no one ever bothers me here. No one cares.

Moni's still not back on Tuesday, which makes me wonder if maybe she and her dad made up, and I'll be stuck at Abuela's by myself for the foreseeable future. Having privacy again is kind of nice, but I also forgot how loud The Thoughts are when Moni isn't talking my ear off in the middle of the night. Now all I can hear is my own brain, so sleeping at night is back off the table.

If only I could catch up on sleep in therapy. But no, Dr. Snitch is expecting answers, as always. She's not getting shit from me, though. Not today. Probably not ever again. My mom can force me to see her until I shrivel up and die, but she can't force me to tell her shit. The only reason I probably listened to her before was the medication. But I'm not so easy to mind control anymore.

"I can't help but notice your energy levels are way down from last week," Dr. Lee says, and I roll my eyes.

"Maybe I'm just tired of everyone talking shit about me behind my back," I shoot back.

"You're a minor, Cesar. Your mother needs to know your diagnosis. We went over this during our first session."

I don't believe her for one second. I would have remembered if she'd mentioned that everything I tell her is fair game for my mom's ears.

She keeps asking me questions, and I keep deflecting them for most of the session.

How are your energy levels? How much sleep have you been getting? How are your eating habits?

I tell her everything is normal, and she sighs, writing something down in her notepad.

"Have you heard of rapid cycling, Cesar?"

"No," I answer shortly.

"It's when you cycle between manic and depressive episodes more quickly than usual. I think that's what you're going through currently."

Before she finishes her sentence, the second hand on the clock ticks to the fifty-minute mark, and I stand up without responding. And yes, I've been watching the clock the whole session so I don't have to go a second over. I throw my backpack over my shoulder and turn to the door.

"You're welcome to stay for group," she offers.

"I'm good."

"Before you leave, have you filled your new prescription yet? I want to make sure we monitor your reaction carefully so we can make sure to get you on the right path as soon as possible," she says, but I'm already walking out.

"Yeah, we filled it," I say as I leave. We picked up the new meds the day after she prescribed them, but I haven't taken anything. My meds weren't helping me before, and they're not going to help me now.

After I finish my homework and chores for the night, I'm about to go to bed when the doorbell rings.

"I'll get it," I say as I walk over to open it.

"I'm back!" Moni sings, bowing as soon as the door opens. And she sounds . . . happy about it?

"I thought you moved back to LA or something," I say, since she was only supposed to be gone for the weekend.

"I almost did, but then my dad figured out what a Tampot is." She shrugs like it's no big deal. Then she offers me a quick high five before rushing toward Abuela. She pulls a tub of brownies out of her bag and hands them over. "For you, Abue. Unfortunately, they don't have my special ingredient. You can blame my dad for that."

"Mija, you're going to give your father a heart attack. It's time to get your act together," Abuela scolds, but she looks like she's trying to hold back a smile.

Moni seems fully aware of Abuela's lack of anger, too. She doesn't bother hiding her own smile, and she's practically bouncing on the balls of her feet.

"You're lucky Cesar already finished all the chores for today. Tomorrow, we'll put you back to work," Abuela says sternly, and Moni gives her a military salute.

The bell rings again, and Abuela looks at both of us suspiciously. "You know you have to ask before inviting anyone over, right?"

"Wasn't me," I say, and Moni shrugs innocently.

Since I'm still right by the door, I go ahead and open it.

"It's good to see you, mijo," Doña Violeta says.

I'm about to shut the door in her face when Abuela meets me there. She just stares at Doña Violeta without saying anything.

"I got your voicemail. . . ." Doña Violeta is the first to talk.

"You invited her?" My head snaps in my grandma's direction. I won't lie, I'm a little offended. Doña Violeta tricked me into getting in her car before dumping me off here, at a house I'd never been before with a grandma I hardly knew. And now Abuela's just inviting her back like it's fine?

"I . . . didn't think you would come . . . ," Abuela finally says.

"Well, here I am." Doña Violeta shifts her weight like she's not sure if she'll be let inside. "And I think you're right, Chela. We should talk."

I almost gag at the nickname she gives my grandma. I figured they knew each other from before, but for how long? Is Doña Violeta one of the people Abuela said she'd try to make amends with? Whatever. It's none of my business, and even if it was, I wouldn't care.

"Talk as much as you want, but I'm going to bed," I say as I turn around and go straight to the room, where Moni's already lying belly down on the bottom bunk.

"Who was that lady?" she asks, propping herself up by her elbows.

"Basically, my mom's replacement for Abuela. She practically raised me and Yami."

I try not to sound bitter as I say it. Moni might not get why I'm mad, and I don't want to have to explain it, only to be told I'm overreacting.

"Huh. Seems like she and Abuela have some kind of old beef. Maybe Abuela's jealous of her relationship with your family?"

"Maybe, I don't know." I climb up to the top bunk. "Anyways, did you get caught on purpose?" I ask, desperate for a subject change.

"I didn't know if you were still here or not," Moni says as if that answers my question. "Abuela gets lonely, and it's not like she's looking for a boyfriend to keep her company. Besides, I like it here."

"Suit yourself," I say as I roll over and try to fall asleep. But Abuela and Doña Violeta aren't exactly talking quietly.

About an hour passes, and there's no sign of them shutting up. In fact, they've gone from just talking to having laughing fits every couple of minutes. I think it might be the first time I've even heard Abuela laugh. Louder than them, though, is Moni tossing and turning every time their conversation seeps through the walls.

She finally lets out an annoyed groan. "Is that lady ever gonna leave? How are we supposed to sleep in these conditions!"

"I guess they missed each other," I mumble. While I want to be mad that Doña Violeta's even here, I can't stop thinking about how much of a victory it is for Abuela.

If Doña Violeta is one of the relationships she lost forever ago, and she's able to fix it all these years later, I'm happy for her. I still don't think I want that for myself, but at least one of us can have a happy ending.

I close my eyes, and the last thing I hear before I fall asleep is my grandma's laughter.

23

WHEN YOU'RE BETTER OFF ALONE ANYWAY

isolation

Days pass, maybe weeks, no idea how many. Couldn't care less. The days are all the same, and not in the safe, predictable way they were before. There are no seven o'clock calls from Jamal and no Sunday cooking with Yami. Instead, it's lunch with Bianca, glares from Nick, and a cold shoulder from Jamal. As soon as I finish my chores and eat, I go straight to bed every day.

Surprisingly enough, Abuela hasn't made me get out of bed all weekend, but nothing wakes me up faster on a Sunday morning than hearing my own name. *Especially* if it sounds like I'm not supposed to be listening. My abuela is talking on the phone, and it doesn't take long for me to figure out it's my mom she's talking to.

"He's had enough space, what Cesar needs right now is his mother. . . . I know, mija . . . I know. . . . He thinks you don't want to see him. How do you think he feels when you—" My mom must have cut her off at that, because Abuela never finishes the thought. She's quiet for a bit before going on. "Yes, I know. . . . Okay, I'll put him on."

Then she's walking to my door, and I have to pretend I didn't just hear all that.

"Cesar, phone's for you." Abuela comes in and opens the curtains to "wake me up."

I shut my eyes and roll over. "Tell them I'm sleeping," I say, pretending I have no idea who might possibly be on the other side of the phone.

"It's your mami, mijo."

"Tell *her* I'm sleeping," I repeat myself, more firmly this time. I pull the blanket over my head.

The blanket gets yanked off, then a sharp pain in my ear pulls a yelp out of my mouth.

"Ay!" I shout, but she drags me out of bed by my ear.

"The phone is for you," she says again, and takes my hand, placing the phone in my palm. She crosses her arms and watches me intently.

I put the phone to my ear but don't say anything.

"Cesar?" Mami says, but I still don't answer. Abuela can make me hold the phone, but she can't make me talk to my mom. "Are you ready to come home?"

I look at my grandma like she's a lifeline. "Do I have to go back?" I ask quietly, not bothering to cover the phone speaker with my hand. I don't realize I'd rather stay with my grandma until I'm offered the option to go back. Going back means facing my mom . . . facing my *sister.* . . .

It's easier if I don't have to look Yami in the eye after what I did. She was right about me not having the right to wear my jaguar necklace. There's a reason I took it off.

Abuela frowns at me.

"I thought you hated all the chores I make you do," she says teasingly.

I thought I did too. But I guess it was nice to feel useful. To have some kind of sameness to my days, even when everything else has gone to shit.

Abuela's frown disappears when I don't answer, and she gives me a sad-ish smile. "As much as I love having you here, mijo, your mami needs you home."

She needs me?

What utter bullshit.

"Mijo?" Mami says through the phone.

"What?" I say, not bothering to hide my irritation.

"It's time to come home, Cesar."

"What, so I'm not in trouble anymore?" I ask.

"Oh, you're in trouble. But that doesn't mean I don't want you around."

"Then why did you send me away in the first place?" I snap.

She's quiet for a while, and when she speaks, her voice comes out as barely a whisper. "I didn't know what else to do."

I don't say shit back because what the hell am I supposed to say to *that*?

"I thought you could use someone who you could relate to—"

"—but you hate Abuela," I interrupt. Abuela's face twists for a split second before she clenches her jaw and wipes away any emotion from her expression. I immediately feel bad for saying it since I'm mad at my mom, not her.

"I don't hate your abuela," Mami says calmly.

"You called her crazy," I shoot back. "Is that what you think of me?"

"All right, that's enough." Abuela takes the phone back before I get a proper answer and puts it to her own ear.

"I know, mija. . . . Okay . . . I'll drop him off in an hour."

I can't help but notice there were no "I love you"s exchanged.

We spend the car ride home in silence. I feel like if I say anything I'll break. I know Abuela isn't abandoning me like Mami basically did. I know legally she can't keep me if my mom wants me home. Still, it feels like a betrayal somehow.

When we pull up to the curb outside my house, I don't reach for the handle, and neither does Abuela.

"You know you can always call me if you need anything, right?" she says. There's no pity in her tone, either. Just a mutual understanding. "I know kids these days prefer texting, but I'm not so tech savvy, so I dug up my old email in case you'd rather do that. Here." She hands me a piece of paper with her email on it.

Before I realize what I'm doing, I'm turned around, pulling my grandma into a tight hug. "Thank you," I say.

"Do you want me to walk in with you?" she asks.

"No," I lie. I don't want to go inside alone, but I also don't want to prolong this any longer than it needs to be. "I'll go. I . . . um . . . thank you, Abuela," I say, and she kisses my cheek before I get out of the car and make my way to the front door.

I hesitate before knocking. I look back, and Abuela hasn't driven off yet. She motions for me to knock on the door, so I finally do.

It opens almost immediately.

My mom stands there with my phone in one hand. She doesn't hesitate before moving for a hug, but I sidestep her, grabbing my phone and slipping into the house before she has a chance to touch me.

I walk straight past the kitchen, where Yami is making dinner. Has she kept up with my Sunday dinner resolution this whole time? She pointedly keeps from turning around to see me walk by. For a split second, I almost want to apologize to her before I remember this is exactly what I wanted. What I need.

"Cesar, let's talk," Mami says, but I just keep walking.

"I'm tired," I say as I try to pass her to get to the hallway.

She reaches for my arm, but I don't give her the chance to grab it.

"Don't fucking touch me!" I whirl around before she makes contact, and she pulls her hand away.

"Don't yell at her," Yami says firmly, but she doesn't raise her voice. She comes over to Mami like she's guarding her from me.

"What, so she can basically kick me out, but I can't yell? Mind your fucking business, Yami."

"I'm sorry, mijo, I just wanted to—" Mami starts, but I don't let her finish.

"I don't care!" I burst out. "And you don't either, so I don't know why you're still pretending. Just fucking leave me alone!"

"He doesn't mean that," Yami says as she touches Mami's arm. I can't help but laugh.

"Why are you even here, Yami?" She knew I was getting sent away and she didn't want to see me before I left. So why is she getting involved in my shit with Mami?

She looks like she might cry any second, so I just turn around and go straight to my room. Surprisingly enough, they both let me leave.

My bed calls to me, and I answer it, flopping down face-first. I lie limp like that for who knows how long before I even think to check my phone.

It's not like I was expecting any missed texts from Yami, or even Jamal, but it still stings when I turn my phone back on to barely any notifications. The only people who thought to text me were Hunter (who doesn't know how horrible a person I am) and Bianca (who's just as bad as me).

I lie there, staring at the ceiling, trying to will myself to respond to one of them, but I can't move. When my mom comes knocking on my door saying dinner's ready, I can't make myself get up. I want to yell at her to leave me alone, but instead I just mumble out that I'm not hungry.

When yelling does happen later that night, it's somehow not me doing it. Shouts between Yami and my mom echo from the living room. I can't exactly make out what they're saying, but I somehow just *know* they're arguing about me.

Curious, I quietly open my door and creep into the hallway, listening without making myself known.

"This will be good for you too! Why can't you see that?" Mami's voice.

"That's such bullshit—" Yami says.

"Language!"

"—you never make me do anything because it's good for *me*, and we both know it!"

"But going back to Rover *will* be good for you!" Shit. She wants Yami to follow me to Rover?

"*Why* the *hell* would I want to go back to Rover? I *hated* it there! Not that you care."

"Not everything is about you, Yamilet! Think of your brother, what if he—"

"No! No, no, no. You don't get to pull the Cesar card on me. I've done nothing but think of him first for my entire life. I'm done! I'm done putting everyone before myself! So what if I want to pay my own way and stay at Slayton? I *like* it there! I'm not going back just to babysit Cesar! And he sure as hell doesn't want me there either, trust me. He hates me!" Yami sounds like she's crying, and a lump forms in my own throat at the sound of her words. She thinks I hate her? I guess I have given her every reason to believe that. . . .

"I'm sorry, but you're going back to Rover whether you like it or not. We can't risk—"

That's when I make myself known. I can't take this anymore.

"No, she's not," I say coldly, knowing I'm about to make Yami hate me even more than she already does, but it's for her own good. "If I have to go to school with Yami, I'm dropping out. You can't force us to go to school together."

My mom and Yami both stare at me with quivering lips. I know Yami's thinking I hate her, and probably wondering why or what happened when all she's ever done is love and support me. But that's exactly why I need to keep her from coming back to Rover. I can't have her making any more sacrifices for me. She needs to live her own life.

After a long pause of all of us just staring at each other, Yami finally looks back at Mami. "Well, I guess it's settled then," she says. Suddenly the sadness in her face is completely gone, replaced by a stone and ice. Her cold tone finally mirrors mine. "I'm staying at Slayton. Take care of yourself, Cesar, because I'm done." Then she rushes past me and into her room, shutting the door surprisingly quietly.

The lack of a slam makes me even more anxious. I can't tell if she genuinely wants me to take care of myself, or if she just wants me to know she's done doing that work for me. Either way, I'm on my own now.

The next morning, I go to the bathroom to brush my teeth earlier than usual, hoping to miss Yami. I open my side of the bathroom door quietly so as not to wake her up.

I stare at the poem that's still printed out on the mirror.

In Lak'ech
Tú eres mi otro yo / You are my other me.
Si te hago daño a ti / If I do harm to you,
Me hago daño a mí mismo / I do harm to myself.
Si te amo y respeto / If I love and respect you,
Me amo y respeto yo / I love and respect myself.

As soon as I stick my toothbrush in my mouth, the other door opens and in walks Yami. She must have had the same exact idea as me.

She catches me staring at the poem for a split second before I look away from it. The look on her face says exactly what she's thinking: *hypocrite.*

I have half a mind to spit in the sink and make a run for it, leaving my dirty toothbrush on the bathroom counter, but Yami beats me to it. She turns right back around and leaves me with only my own reflection staring back at me in the mirror. We always were on the same wavelength, and it looks like us avoiding each other is no exception.

But she's wrong about one thing. I'm not a hypocrite. At least not when it comes to that poem. I know exactly what it means, and I *do* still live by it.

Hurting the people around me is the most effective way I know to sabotage myself.

So no, I'm not a hypocrite.

Just a coward.

After I finish up and then pretend to take my meds, Mami tries to guilt me into getting in the car so she can drop me off at Rover before taking Yami to Slayton.

"We're going to be late if we don't leave right now, mijo."

"Then go," I say through a mouthful of cereal. She glares at me, so I continue, if only so I don't get my head smacked. "I'll walk. Rover's close enough. You don't have to drop me off."

It's true that Rover is walking distance. Well, sort of. It's a less than thirty-minute walk, so if I leave now, I won't be late. But if I leave now with Mami and Yami, I'll be skin-crawlingly early.

"Let him walk," Yami says as she brushes past me and toward the car. "I'm not about to be late because of him."

"Fine, but if I hear you ditched school, you can kiss those walking privileges goodbye."

"'Kay," I say, to get her off my back. It wasn't like I was going to ditch. Being alone with my thoughts is a million times worse than going to school. At least there I have some kind of routine to keep me busy.

Before I know it, Yami and my mom are out the door, and I have the house to myself, which I also hate. So I scarf down the rest of my cereal, grab my backpack, and head out.

The walk isn't so bad this time of year. Yeah, it's a little chilly for March (for Arizona), but it doesn't bother me too much. I have my headphones in, so my music is louder than my brain, which helps. But even with the beat thumping in my ears, moving my feet in step with the rhythm, I hear a honk right next to me.

I almost fall on my ass at the noise, prepared to fight Nick or Avery or whoever else might be trying to mess with me, but when I whirl to the side, it's just Bianca. I didn't even know she could drive now.

"Hey, babe, need a ride?" she asks.

"Uh, sure. Why not?" I say, not able to come up with an excuse to get out of being stuck in a car with someone who is somehow both a godsend and the devil incarnate in one.

I hop in on the passenger side of her Accord, and she leans over to kiss me. I don't turn to face her, so she kisses my cheek, but it still makes me feel like an absolute piece of shit.

"So, where's Yami?" Bianca asks.

"Uh, what?" Now I turn to look at her, confused.

"I mean, I see you at school all the time, but not Yami. I would have figured you two would stick together, right?"

"I don't want to talk about Yami," I say curtly.

"So she's still at that Catholic school then?" she asks, ignoring my request completely.

"Why do you care? I thought you hated her." My voice comes out cold, but it doesn't matter.

She turns a little red at that. "I *don't* care," is all she offers.

"Good, me either," I lie, and that seems to placate her because she slithers her hand onto my knee and leaves it there the rest of the ride to school.

As soon as we get there, I run off to "class." Really, I make a beeline for the bathroom. I rush into one of the stalls, lock it behind me, kneel over the toilet, and empty my guts into it.

I don't stop when someone opens the door and walks in. I can barely hear them pissing over the sound of my own vomiting. Hopefully they ignore the awkwardness and just leave when they're done.

But of course I'm never so lucky.

"Um, you okay?"

Fuck. It had to be him.

"I'm fine," I say between coughs as I wipe my mouth with toilet paper.

"You don't sound fine, Cesar." Shit. I guess I can't be surprised he recognized my voice when I knew it was Jamal right away. A plastic water bottle rolls under the stall door.

"I said I'm fine!" I snap this time. I can't handle Jamal being kind to me right now. I can't handle it. I kick the water bottle back under the door, even though my throat is screaming for relief. "Please just leave me alone."

He hesitates, and for a moment, a small part of me hopes he'll argue back. That he'll say no. That he'd never leave me alone like this. But instead he wordlessly trails out the door without a protest.

24

WHEN STARGAZING WITH YOUR STRICTLY PLATONIC ASTRONOMY PARTNER SEEMS LIKE A GOOD PLAN

illogical reasoning

The second my end-of-therapy alarm goes off, I head straight for the door. Dr. Lee tries to invite me to group again, but I ignore her. There are a few other people around my age sitting in the lobby. Their faces are familiar since they're here every week after I get out of therapy, but we've never interacted. When I try to walk past them this time, my mom grabs my hand to stop me.

"Not so fast, mijo. You still have group to go to."

"I never agreed to go to group." I pull my hand away from her. How did she even find out about group? I sure as hell never mentioned it. I mentally curse Dr. Lee for snitching on me yet again.

"I agreed for you," she says. "It will be good for you to bond with kids your age who are going through something similar."

I can feel everyone around us staring at me, and it makes me want to make a run for it. But I don't want to make even more of a scene than I already have if I'm going to have to see the same people every single week.

None of these people care about me and my problems, so I

really don't see the point of group, but in the name of not embarrassing myself even further, I drag my feet and follow the rest of them into a larger room.

At least this will get my mom to leave me alone.

We all sit in a circle of chairs in the middle of the room, with Dr. Lee at the head of the circle. She doesn't have her usual notepad this time, which makes it feel like we're in a totally different setting, even if it's therapy all the same.

Just when she's about to start, someone else walks into the room and takes the empty chair across the circle from mine. I almost get out of my seat and walk away right then and there at seeing Avery.

He's basically Nicks' left ballsack, the way he's always hanging around him and doing literally anything Nick tells him to. When they used to jump me, Avery was the one who held me back while the rest of them wailed on me.

I clench my jaw as Avery's eyes meet mine for a split moment before he quickly looks away. The last thing I want to be doing is therapy with *him*, but if I leave now, he'll have the satisfaction of knowing it's because of him. I'll be damned if I'm giving Avery even an inch of satisfaction at seeing me here. So I refuse to let him take any information about me back to Nick and them. If there's any consolation, it's that he's still got the ankle bracelet on, so I'm relatively safe, at least from a physical fight.

"Since we have a couple of new faces today, let's go around the circle and introduce ourselves. You can start with your name, pronouns, and your diagnosis, if you're comfortable giving it. Zo, would you like to start?" Dr. Lee looks to the kid on her right, who's wearing a shirt with the Mexican flag on it, with the word DECOLONIZE written in bold over the flag.

"Sure! I'm Zo. They/them pronouns, please," they say while playing with a strand of their neon-pink hair. "I'm bipolar." Dr. Lee discreetly glances in my direction at that with a small smile, and I roll my eyes, hoping Avery didn't catch that look. Then Zo looks to the person next to them, who's also next to me. A goth Black girl with a slight facial twitch I didn't notice until now.

"I'm Nia, she/her," Nia says, blinking a little more frequently than most people. "Schizophrenia."

Then everyone looks to me, and I shift a little in my chair. "Cesar, he/him," I say, hoping to just get this over with. Dr. Lee did say we only had to give our diagnosis if we were comfortable with it, so she better not call me out on this.

Thankfully, she doesn't. Everyone's attention moves on to the guy to my right. He's a kind of plain-looking white guy in jeans and a white tee.

"I'm Aaron. He/him. Uhh . . ." He looks around the group, as if deciding what to say next. He might be even more uncomfortable here than I am. I bet he's the other new guy. "I have borderline personality disorder," he finally says, then lets out a small breath of relief and turns to the last person in the circle.

"I'm Avery. He/him. PTSD," Avery says as he shifts in his seat. Not only am I surprised he willingly gave his pronouns when that seems like something his friends would laugh at him about, but also that he volunteered his diagnosis in front of the guy he used to beat up. Part of me wonders if him saying that in front of me is some kind of peace offering.

Then again, it might have nothing to do with me. Maybe he's just comfortable in this group, even if I'm in it now. Now that I think of it, it makes sense that Jamal said he's like a different person when his friends aren't around. He even physically looks different. Like, I don't think I've ever seen him with his shoulders relaxed until now.

I still hate him, though, obviously.

"Wonderful." Dr. Lee folds her hands on her lap. "For those of you new today, I like to start our sessions by giving an opportunity for anyone to share something good that's happened in the last week."

It's quiet for a few seconds before Zo says, "Avery has some good news, right?" They mime nudging Avery with their elbow.

"I mean, kind of . . . ," he says. "Some lawyer found out about my case and wants to help me pro bono."

"That's great news!" Dr. Lee says.

"Not really." Avery shrugs and looks down. "He wants me to snitch on my friend to get off, and I'm not doing that. I don't need his charity anyway." For once, I find myself almost rooting for Avery. Him snitching on Nick would be incredible.

No one else seems to have any good news to share, so Dr. Lee goes on with the session. "This week I want to talk about medication, and all the different paths we can go on to finding the right fit for us."

She keeps talking, but I kind of zone out. I'm not really trying to get back on my medication, even if everyone around me thinks I never stopped. It isn't until Dr. Lee changes the topic that I have to pay attention again. "All right, now let's go around and talk about our journey with medication, and how we all got to where we are now. Who'd like to start us off?"

Zo raises their hand to start once again. I get a feeling Zo is Dr. Lee's favorite.

"I'm really liking the meds I'm on. I just hit six months, and I finally got my bloodwork done to see if I have any side effects." They smile widely. "Turns out every health problem my old meds caused is getting better now with these new meds, so I get to stay on them!"

"Lucky you," Avery says, crossing his arms. "When I hit the six-month mark with my meds, they stopped working. Then the next one I tried started giving me seizures because it reacted wrong to my other medication. Had to stop cold, and now I have to see a neurologist before I can get approved to switch again." Avery glances around the room but still avoids my eyes.

Yikes. Yeah, I'm definitely not going back on my meds.

"And we'll find something that works for you, Avery. It's just a matter of time," Dr. Lee says.

"That's why I'm not on meds anymore," Aaron says. "I don't want to deal with the health problems or side effects."

"And that's why we work extra hard on our coping skills, right, Aaron?" He nods. "Now that you're eighteen, that's your prerogative. What about you, Cesar? Nia?"

"I just switched meds," Nia says, saving me from having to answer the question. "I didn't think meds could make the hallucinations completely go away, but they did. Only downside is I've got this twitch now," she says with a twitch of her nose. "But I can live with a twitch if it means I'm not being told to kill myself every five seconds."

It finally comes back to me, and I have to say something so no one knows I've been lying about taking my meds this whole time. "I switched recently. Can't complain," I lie through my teeth.

Deflecting has become second nature for me now. I spend most of my time at home in my room, so no one asks me any questions. Well, so my mom doesn't. I think the Yami bridge has been thoroughly burned. It's only a matter of time before the one with my mom burns down too.

At school, I've been avoiding Bianca, and feeling like the world's biggest coward for it. Dating Bianca should be easy. I'm *into girls*. And Bianca is hot. I'm actually attracted to her, and when she went down on me at that party, I did like it. So why can't I face her?

The truth threatens to peek its head out.

Yami.

Jamal.

But I immediately brush those thoughts away. I did this on purpose. I wanted to get rid of them, and everything is going exactly according to plan. With Jamal and Yami out of my life, and my mom slowly starting to back off, there will be no one to feel guilty over whatever does or doesn't happen to me.

So I stick with the plan and make it a point to sit with Bianca and her friends at lunch the next day. For some reason, she doesn't seem to notice or care that I've been avoiding her. When I get a text from Hunter, she doesn't even seem bothered by me texting him in favor of paying any attention to her.

Hunter: Haven't seen you in a minute. What are you doing next week?

Cesar: I'm grounded, so nothing

Cesar: therapy is my only social life apparently

Hunter: I'll give you a ride home from therapy then lol

I let out a little laugh. I don't get why Hunter keeps hitting me up or why he cares to hang out with me. I'm not who he thinks I am, and hopefully he doesn't figure that out any time soon. But if Hunter driving me home from therapy gives me less time alone with my mom, I'll take it.

I send Hunter a thumbs-up before I'm pulled out of my thoughts by Bianca. She scoots sort of next to me, sort of halfway on my lap. She kisses my cheek while I eat the nasty school chicken nuggets. I don't even care that they're disgusting and probably moldy. Eating helps, if nothing else does.

I just chew silently while Bianca talks shit about her cousin or something. She's always talking shit, and if I don't say anything she usually wears herself out eventually.

"She's so annoying. I'm so glad I'm a single child. If I had to be around someone like her every day I'd jump off a bridge. How do you do it, Cesar?"

"What?" I ask, not prepared to get pulled into the conversation.

"With Yami. How do you put up with being around someone like that *all the time*?"

My face twists in disgust, but not because of the chicken nuggets. Yami might think I hate her, but I don't need Bianca jumping on board. "What do you mean, *someone like that*?"

"You know how she is," Bianca says, like she expects me to just start talking shit with her about my sister.

"I told you I don't want to talk about Yami," I say firmly. "Talk about literally anyone else."

She takes that as an invitation to turn the conversation back to her cousin, and I go back to eating and ignoring her. Eventually the chicken nuggets disappear, and Bianca puts a hand on my cheek, turning my head to face her. She kisses me in front of everyone, completely ignoring Stefani and Chachi. I can feel Nick's glare burning a hole through the back of my head from the table behind us.

At first I'm a little confused, because if Bianca likes me enough to ignore her friends, why isn't she annoyed or mad I've been avoiding her?

I push the thought down and savor the kiss, knowing how much of a privilege it is to kiss the person you're dating in public. What I would have given to be able to kiss Jamal in public when we were together . . .

The kiss grows deeper, and I turn so one of my legs is on the other side of the lunch bench. She immediately scoots closer to me and kisses me harder. But no matter how hard I kiss Bianca, she doesn't feel like Jamal. Her lips are smaller, and her breath is mintier, since she's always chewing gum. When she pulls away, she doesn't look at me the way Jamal did either. Her look is full of pride, like I'm a trophy she's showing off. Jamal never looked at me like that.

Jamal always looked at me like I was the world. His world. It didn't matter if no one else ever knew he had me. We knew, and that was enough for him. He never guilted me for not wanting to wear his promise ring in public. Never made me feel bad for taking a step away when people were watching.

"You should come over sometime," Bianca says, wrapping her arms around my neck.

"Uh, I'm busy," I say without a second thought.

Bianca's smile disappears. "I didn't even say when yet. How do you know you're busy?"

"Oh, I meant . . . I'm grounded." Okay, that part is actually true.

Bianca gives me a mischievous grin. "Sneak out then. My mom's in Mexico until next week. We'd have my house to ourselves. . . ." She winks.

Oh.

It's not that I don't want to have sex with Bianca. I do. But I hesitate for some reason.

"Come on, I know you want to," Bianca coaxes.

I swallow the uncertainty. "Okay," I say, setting my hands on her waist. "Let's do it."

In astronomy the next day, Mrs. Velez announces that we'll be partnering up to do our senior projects. She hands out a piece of paper that has everyone and their partners listed, along with a list of potential projects to do.

I scan the paper for my name, and my heart sinks into my gut when I see I'm paired with none other than Jamal. Mrs. Velez used to partner us together when we were in AP Biology freshman year and AP Chemistry sophomore year, since we got along so well and always wanted to be partners. She's obviously noticed how distant we've been lately, so my guess is that this is her way of trying to get us to make up. She may think she's doing us some kind of favor, but really, she just made it hard to breathe.

Everyone gets up and switches seats to be next to their partners, and Jamal turns to face me since we already sit by each other.

"Hi," he says tentatively.

"Hi," I say back.

Jamal smiles. It's the first time we've talked in a while, and I feel like a baby learning to walk for the first time. But when we get to talking about which project to go with, I find myself stumbling.

"I, um, what do you, uh, want to do?" I stutter, looking from Jamal to the paper listing possible projects.

Jamal scans the paper, his finger dragging down the page as he reads each prompt.

"This one looks cool," he says, ignoring the fact that I don't know how to word right now. "Create a model of starlight by developing a sensor app with your smartphone to discover the key relationship between distance and brightness."

I immediately shake my head. Creating an app together? That sounds like way too much time spent together. I want to spend the least amount of time with Jamal as possible. I can't go back on the boundary I set. And I know he has the power to make me without even trying.

"How about this one?" I ask, pointing at prompt number five. "Calculate the orbits of near-earth asteroids. This one only requires three nights of work," I say. Three nights spread out over the next few weeks, looking at the sky, barely having to talk, feels a lot less potentially romantic than spending every day together developing an app.

"Okay, we can do that one," Jamal says without protest.

"Really?" I'd expected some kind of pushback, for some reason. Maybe Jamal really is over me and isn't looking to spend a lot of extra time together. Which is a good thing.

Right?

25

WHEN A DOUBLE ANIMAL-STYLE CHEESEBURGER ISN'T ENOUGH TO FILL YOUR EMPTY SOUL

weight gain

"Okay, you can do this," I say to myself in the bathroom mirror. I pat my pockets to triple-check that I have at least two condoms in one and a mini bottle of lube in the other. I spritz myself with a few sprays of the cologne Jamal got for me. The irony is hard to ignore, both for the fact that the cologne is meant for single guys, and for the fact that it was my ex-boyfriend who got it for me, all while I'm using it to try to impress my girlfriend. I let out a slow breath. "You can do this," I repeat.

Just as I'm about to open the door to sneak out, the door leading to Yami's room opens. At first, she looks concerned, but only for a split second. Like she forgot she's supposed to hate me, and she thinks I'm just having insomnia again. But then she looks me up and down, and she must realize I'm fully dressed and ready to go out.

"Where are you going?" she asks. It's the first time she's spoken to me since the day I came home from Abuela's.

"Out," I deflect, and it's then that I realize she looks about ready to leave the house too, hoops on and everything. "Where are *you* going?" I throw the question back at her.

"To Bo's." Yami lets a small smile slip for just a moment before she glares at me again. "Where are *you* going?"

I want to laugh because Yami and I aren't new to playing this game. We deflect and keep asking the same question until one of us caves, but I'm not caving today.

Then my phone starts buzzing from its place next to the sink, and Bianca's name lights up the screen. Yami's eyes dart to the phone, and I jump into action and grab it, silencing the call, but it's too late. She saw the name.

"Are you serious?" she hisses in a loud whisper.

"You're not gonna snitch, are you?" I ask. I'm used to Yami bending over backward to protect me from my mom, not snitching. But I'm on her bad side now. Who knows what she'll do?

"I should," she threatens, hands on her hips.

"I'll tell Mom you're sneaking out too, then," I shoot back.

Then we have a glaring contest for what feels like ages before she finally turns and heads out the door. I wait as long as is reasonable before following her. Bianca's call means she's waiting for me. I thank God we're neighbors, so she doesn't have to pick me up. Seeing Yami and Bianca run into each other in the driveway would not be pretty.

I watch out the window until I see Yami get in Bo's car, and they drive off. Once they're gone, I quickly slip out the door and jog over to Bianca's. I call her instead of knocking on the door, half thinking if I knocked her mom would answer or something. But of course she's home alone. She answers the door instead of the phone.

She's wearing a mesh black robe, see-through enough that the outlines of her black lace bra and underwear are visible underneath.

"Wow . . . ," I say breathlessly, and she smiles like my reaction is exactly what she was going for.

"Get in here." She grabs my hand and pulls me inside and toward the living room.

I haven't been in Bianca's house since she and Yami were still best friends. She's clearly cleaned for me, since I remember this house being a lot messier. It's not pristine or anything, but the floors are swept and the clutter is gone.

Coming back here reminds me how much of a betrayal this is. But when Bianca drops her robe to reveal her near-naked body, the thought vanishes from my mind.

"Wow . . . ," I say again, and she grins.

"Aren't you in AP English? Could have sworn your vocabulary was a little bigger." She laughs, but it's warm.

I return the laugh, nervously, while she pulls me over to the couch and makes a show of pushing me down on it. She straddles me and leans forward, planting a few kisses on my lips, jaw, neck. Her hands travel down my chest while mine discover hers.

She scoots up so her breasts are right in front of my face, and I hope Bianca can't feel the quiver in my lips when I kiss them. All I can think about right now is how this should be easy. This should be second nature for me. It should be fun.

And to an extent, it is. I like the feeling of Bianca's lips on mine. Her breasts in my palms. Her hand between my legs.

But as fun as it is, it doesn't feel *right*.

Jamal felt right. But according to Father John, those thoughts were wrong. According to Father John, *this* is what's right. This is what I should be doing.

This should be easy.

Then Bianca kisses me harder and pulls away, looking deeply into my eyes. Usually I feel like I can read people pretty well, but I can't place her expression at all.

"I love you," she says as she unzips my pants and sticks her hand under my boxers.

My breath grows heavy, but it's not because she's got her hand wrapped around my now deflating boner. My chest gets tight, and the air gets thinner, and every breath comes out ragged and strained.

I think I'm having a panic attack.

"I have to go," I blurt out, then push her off me and make a run for the door.

When group comes around again and everyone's sharing their good news from the last week, I keep quiet like I always do. But I do pay attention this time since I'm trying not to think about all the unanswered texts I have from Bianca, who's been trying to get ahold of me since Friday.

Avery usually doesn't say much unless prompted either, but today he's the first to volunteer something. "That lawyer who's trying to help me found another angle, so I might actually be able to get this stupid thing off soon." He gestures to his ankle.

I'm not proud to admit the news deflates me. I mean, I'm not super into the U.S.'s punitive justice system, but I was kind of hoping Avery would cave and snitch on Nick to get free.

After a few others share their good news, Dr. Lee moves on to the topic of the day: relationships. So of course everyone uses that as an excuse to talk about their love lives. I know I should be talking about my girlfriend and how I've been avoiding her since she told me she loved me, but all I can think about is Jamal and how I'm going to have to spend more time with him for that fucking astronomy project that for some reason counts for half our grade.

I end up blurting out something about having to do my senior project with my ex to get Dr. Lee off my back about never participating. I'm careful not to gender Jamal, only calling him the ex, since I don't want anyone here knowing I'm bi just yet. Or ever. I push the thought down that Avery knows. When I look up at him, he doesn't look away this time.

"At least you have an ex," he says in a tone I can't quite place. "I never even had a first kiss." Is he trying to make nice with me or something? I glare at him to let him know it's not working, and he looks away.

"I just had mine yesterday!" Aaron says excitedly, grinning so hard his lips might fall off.

"Ooooh! With movie-theater girl?" Zo asks, leaning forward in amusement. Maybe I *should* pay attention in group more often, because I don't remember Aaron talking about a movie-theater girl.

Aaron blushes and nods. "Yeah. It was our fourth time going on a movie date, so I decided it was time. Apparently, she's been waiting for me to kiss her for ages." He laughs. "But don't worry, Avery, I'm sure you'll get your first kiss soon!"

"I seriously doubt it." Avery laughs humorlessly. "I did my, uh, residential treatment when I was thirteen. Kind of put me off from the whole thing."

"Wait, why would going inpatient put you off kissing?" Aaron asks what I might have, if I cared to know.

Avery stares at the ground while he answers. "Uh, I didn't go inpatient. More like, me and some other kids had to stay somewhere for a while for, um, like, a treatment program."

"You mean like sober living?" Aaron asks.

"Not really, I don't know. . . ." Avery shuffles a hand through his hair. "Can you just tell the new guys, Zo? I'm getting a little . . ." He trails off as his eyes kind of lose focus, and he doesn't finish the sentence.

"He's talking about conversion therapy," Zo says, and that finally has me interested. Avery did conversion therapy . . . and it worked? I didn't even know people still did that.

"Oh, shit. I'm sorry," Aaron says. "I didn't mean to push it."

"It's cool," Avery says, but he still doesn't look up.

"So, we were talking about relationships, right?" Zo asks, and Avery looks relieved for the subject change. "Congrats on kissing movie-theater girl!"

"Thanks," Aaron says, back to smiling.

"I'm proud of you." Dr. Lee smiles. "See, a lot of people think that people with SMIs can't be in successful relationships, but look at our diverse experiences right here!"

"Well, she doesn't know I'm borderline . . . ," Aaron says, slumping in his seat. "I don't know how to tell her. Or when. If I ever do."

"Don't feel pressured to tell her before you're ready." Zo leans over and squeezes his shoulder.

"Anyways, what about you, Zo? How are things going with you and your man?" Aaron asks. He sure has a lot of questions. I'm just glad they're not directed at me.

"Ughhh," Zo groans. "He thinks he's *straight*." They put finger quotes around "straight." "But he can't be straight if he's attracted to *me*, right? I'm *not a girl*!" They throw their hands up in frustration, and now it's Aaron's turn to squeeze Zo's shoulder.

"Have you talked to your partner about your frustration?" Dr. Lee asks, all therapist-y.

"Yeah, but he just doesn't get it!"

"You know," Dr. Lee says, "your partner thinking he's straight may have nothing to do with you at all. It can be difficult to come to terms with your own sexuality. You can't force someone to realize they're queer before they're ready. Maybe it just takes some time."

Dr. Lee glances at me for some reason, and I immediately look away.

It's not like I haven't come to terms with my sexuality. I have the opposite problem from Zo's partner. I know I'm not straight. Not yet. If Avery's experience is anything to go by, maybe I can be. Maybe it just takes some time.

I straggle a little behind everyone else after group to avoid Avery. By the time I get to the lobby, the only one in there is Hunter, waiting to pick me up like we talked about.

"Yoooo, he's alive!" Hunter stands up and yanks me into a handshake hug.

"Unfortunately, yes," I say as we start making our way outside.

"I feel that." He laughs, and I wonder if he really does or if he thinks we're joking. "So how you been, bro?"

Ah, he *is* joking. Otherwise he wouldn't be asking me that. "Fine, you?"

"Can't complain, can't complain," he says as the motion-sensored doors open for us. Unfortunately, Avery hasn't left the parking lot. Neither have Zo or Aaron, and they're all just standing there talking.

Avery spots us as we get a little closer and gives me an awkward wave. I don't want Hunter asking any questions, so I give him a nod.

"Hey, Cesar, we're gonna get food right now, want to come?" Zo asks, waving me over.

"Sorry, I got plans," I say, gesturing at Hunter.

"Oh, your friend can come too if he wants," Aaron adds. "I'm Aaron, by the way, nice to meet you." He holds his hand out for Hunter to shake, all formal. "This is Zo, and Avery."

"Hunter," Hunter says as he takes Aaron's hand awkwardly. "Is that cool with you?" he asks me. I hate being put on the spot, so I just shrug.

"Okay, then I'm down! Do you guys need a ride? I have a five-seater."

Avery looks surprised at the offer, his eyes bouncing between me and Hunter. "Uh, is that okay?"

"Of course! Any friend of Cesar's is a friend of mine."

Avery raises an eyebrow at me, and I want nothing more than to spontaneously combust right this second. If either of them remembers the other from Jamal's open mic at that Christian coffee shop, they don't show it.

"Aren't you on probation?" is all I find myself asking. I know if I say anything else now, Hunter will want to know why I don't want to hang out with Avery, and I'm not about to get into that.

"Yeah, but I can stop for food and stuff on my way home. I just can't stay out too long. But I don't have to go if—"

"It's fine, let's just go," I interrupt before he can give anyone here more information about me than I'm comfortable with.

"Oh . . . okay. Um, thanks," Avery says quickly as we all make our way to Hunter's car. I hop in the front, and everyone else files into the back.

"We were thinking about getting In-N-Out. Is that cool with you guys?" Zo asks.

"In-N-Out, got it," Hunter says as he turns on his music and pulls out of the parking lot. It's some obscure indie band I've never heard of, but Hunter's singing like no one's around to judge.

Zo and Aaron have a sort of conversation in the back while me and Avery silently pretend this is no big deal. It isn't until the song is over that Avery says anything.

"Okay, I can't not say something about this," he starts, and I hold my breath, trying to telepathically will him to shut the fuck up. "Were you just listening to Let's All Die Now?"

I let out my breath, relieved he's just talking about the music and not our old shit. I don't bother looking back at Avery when he talks, but he sounds both shocked and thrilled.

"Wait, you know them?" Hunter practically squeals. I guess they're both shocked and thrilled.

"What are they called again?" Zo asks, sounding a little concerned. I was kind of wondering the same thing, since the music doesn't sound all that emo. It sounds more hype than anything.

"Let's All Die Now," Hunter answers. "But it's not what you think! The actual name is Let's All Die N.I.A.H.W., which is short for 'naturally in a healthy way,' but everyone just says now."

Personally, I'd prefer the "now," but instead I just say, "Cool."

"Did you know they're in town this weekend?" Hunter asks Avery. It kind of feels like Hunter and Avery just transported into another reality where it's just the two of them and this music.

"Don't fuck with me, really?"

"I'm serious! I'll send you the info, here, put your number in." Hunter pulls his phone out of his pocket and hands it back to Avery without taking his eyes off the road. I actually want to puke.

If Hunter, as one of the only friends I have left, has Avery's number now, who knows what those two will say about me? Hunter could accidentally give Avery fuel for Nick, and Avery could out me being SMI, and there's nothing I can do about it.

Lovely. One more thing to add to the list of everything in my life I've lost control over.

I decide to save us a table at In-N-Out instead of waiting in line with everyone else, trying to convince myself to be less annoyed about this whole situation. All Hunter was supposed to do was give me a ride home, and now I'm stuck with people I barely know, and Avery, who I hate. The only reason I'm not insisting on getting home is because I want to be *there* even less.

Mami texts me then, asking where I am, but I ignore it. I know I'm grounded and will probably get in trouble for not going straight home, but I don't care. There's literally nothing she can do to punish me that matters anymore.

Eventually everyone else makes it to the table. Apparently, they've gone back to our therapy topic of relationships. Everyone's trying to give Zo advice about how to talk to their "straight" boyfriend.

"You should tell him how you feel," Aaron says between sips of his soda. "Like, if he knows it feels misgendering when he says he's straight, maybe he'll see it in a different way?"

I try to be nonchalant as I gauge Hunter's reaction to that. He's usually pretty cool about stuff like this, but he's also not the most informed. He looks at me like he thinks I have something valuable to add to the conversation. Which I don't. Does he think because I'm queer that I know shit about Zo's very different situation? But Zo notices Hunter looking at me, so now *they* think I have something to say.

"Uhh, maybe he's just not ready to come out?" I say almost defensively. "But I'm straight, so I wouldn't know." I punctuate that caveat with a big bite of my burger, so I don't have to say anything else. I just had to make sure Hunter knows I'm not out to this group. Well, besides Avery, but that's not by choice. Hunter and Avery both know I'm lying, but neither of them calls me out on it.

"That's a good point," Hunter says. "Maybe give him some time and let him know it's okay to question it. I mean, I've never been in a serious relationship before, so I probably don't have the best advice. But yeah, that's what I would do."

"Really?" Avery asks. I'm not sure which part he's questioning until he tacks on a "Me either."

Zo looks from Avery to Hunter and smiles a little. Avery notices and immediately looks down, blushing. Hunter's too busy typing on his phone to catch it, though.

He turns to me. "I should get you home soon. Your mom just texted me."

I sigh. She knew he was picking me up from therapy, so it was bound to happen eventually. "Is she mad?"

"Not yet," Hunter reassures me. "But we should probably head back while she's still relieved you're with your therapy friends."

"Okay, sure," I say as I start picking up my trash.

"I should probably head out too. Can't spend too much time out of the house," Avery says as he moves to stand.

"You need a ride?" Hunter asks, to my horror.

"Oh, are you sure?" Avery glances at me like it's really me he wants the answer from, but Hunter's saying yes before I can protest. Besides, I can't tell Avery no for Hunter without telling Hunter everything.

Once it's just the three of us in Hunter's car, Avery feels way more awkward. It's not the kind of tense awkward like he is around Nick, but he just seems so uncomfortable. I don't know if he feels guilty or what, but I don't care. Hunter starts playing that same indie band, and Avery's suddenly a person again. He and Hunter go off with each other about how obsessed they are with the band, and I happily ignore Avery the rest of the ride.

When I get home, I'm about to follow my new routine of heading straight to my room and staying there when I get an idea.

"I want to go to conversion therapy," I announce as I approach the living room where my mom and Yami are working.

Yami's head whips around with a disgusted look on her face before she seems to remember we aren't talking.

Mami, on the other hand, looks more sad than anything. "No, mijo. We're not doing anything like that."

"Why not?" I stand my ground, trying to keep my cool if I want to be in any way convincing.

She looks over to Yami as if for help answering me. Yami sighs and says, "It doesn't work," to Mami instead of to me.

"That's not true." I glare at Yami even though she won't look at me. "I know someone who went, and it worked for him."

"I said no, and that's final," Mami says firmly this time. "Let's not talk about this anymore. Cesar, Yami, why don't you two go check on Doña Violeta for a bit? You haven't visited in a while. She gets lonely, you know." She changes the subject, like that'll make me just forget.

And maybe it's working, because my cheeks heat up at the mention of Doña Violeta. I can't forget how she tricked me into going to my grandma's and abandoned me there. I'm not exactly in a rush to see her.

"I have homework," I start, and Yami protests too.

"But we have so much work to do, Mami. I can visit her tomorrow." I notice she says "I" and not "we." She has nothing against Doña Violeta; she just doesn't want to go with me.

"It wasn't a request," Mami says as she takes Yami and me by our wrists and ushers us out the door, practically throwing us outside before shutting the door behind us.

Yami and I stand there for a moment, her eyes catching mine for a second before they dart toward the road. She starts walking, not waiting for me to follow. Whatever.

I trudge along behind her, letting her ignore me. The least I can do for Yami right now is stay out of her way.

Doña Violeta's music grows louder the closer we get to her porch. She's talking on the phone but waves enthusiastically when she sees us approaching, and Yami waves back. I pointedly shove my hands into my pockets, so she knows I'm still pissed.

"I've got to go, Chela. Okay, I'll tell them," she says when we make it to the porch. "Your abuela says hi," she tells me and Yami as she hangs up the phone. Knowing my abuela has someone to talk to makes me just a tiny bit less bitter about Doña Violeta's existence. A *tiny* bit.

"Hola, Doña," Yami says as soon as we make it to the porch. She hugs and kisses her on her cheeks.

"Hola, mija, te quiero mucho." Doña Violeta hugs and kisses back. Then she looks at me and smiles like she didn't lie and screw me over. At least I have the decency to give Jamal and Yami some space after betraying them.

"Mijo, you've been eating too many sweets, haven't you?" she says to me, giving my stomach a playful pinch.

"Ay, ¡ya!" I say, swatting her hand away.

Usually this would be when Yami gives one of her feminist lectures she and Bo love to give about body image and how you shouldn't point out people's weight, and how gaining weight isn't necessarily indicative of health or eating habits alone, blah blah blah.

But Yami stays quiet this time, letting the backhanded comment sink into my apparently growing gut. Yes, I've gained some weight recently. No, it's none of Doña Violeta's business. So what if I've been eating more than usual? Food is one of the only things these days that makes me feel anything worth feeling. When I eat, I'm not guilty, or depressed, or angry. Eating is the only time I really get to just exist without thinking.

And now I feel like I can't even have that.

26

WHEN HE'S PERFECT FOR YOU, BUT YOU CAN'T HURT HIM AGAIN

self-sabotage

Bianca catches me between classes at school the next day. And by catches, I mean she literally corners me at the edge of the hall-way as soon as I get out of class. It's almost like she was waiting for me.

"You've been avoiding me," she says, arms crossed.

"I . . . uh . . ." I shift my weight back and forth, resisting the urge to make a run for it. I look behind Bianca at the crowds of people walking to class, and I spot Avery, who sees me looking at him. Instead of looking away this time, he gives me a small nod in acknowledgment. I glare back, and he keeps walking.

"Look," she interrupts my non-response, not that I had any-thing intelligent to say in the first place. "I know I came on a little strong the other day. Let's just pretend that didn't happen, okay? Can we just go back to before?"

Bianca's been our neighbor and was Yami's best friend long enough for me to know she's been doing this her whole life. She has this compulsive need to be liked by everyone, so whenever things get weird, she's the first to backtrack and pretend it never happened. Maybe that's why she's so hung up on the fact that Yami never forgave her.

"Hello?" Bianca waves a hand in front of my face. She might be willing to pretend she never told me she loved me, but I can't.

If Bianca loves me, that means all of this is for nothing. The whole point of dating her was to get everyone who cared about me *off* my back. But if Bianca loves me, that's just one extra person I have to feel guilty over.

"Is this about Yami?" Bianca asks when I don't respond right away.

"What? No!" It's kind of a lie. A half lie, at least. Yami was at least half of the reason I hooked up with Bianca at that party in the first place. At least half of the reason any of this spiraled so far out of control.

Then again, it is kind of weird that Bianca keeps bringing Yami up. Does she *know* I only hooked up with her to piss off Yami? It just doesn't make any sense.

I want to tell Bianca that I don't love her. That this won't work out. That loving me is nothing but bad news. But this is everything I asked for. Everything I need to get right with God.

I could love Bianca. One day. Maybe. I could end up with her. Marry her, even. Not that I plan on living long enough to do anything like that. But if I don't want to go to hell, I need to at least try, right? It's not like I'm gonna go confessing my love for her any time soon, but I can't run away at the first sign that things are actually going according to plan.

But then there's that guilt. The guilt that made me betray Yami and Jamal.

The next bell rings, and I use it as an excuse to get the hell out of there.

I want a way out. There has to be a way out.

I usually try to walk home from school fast enough that I get home before Yami so I can avoid her, but on Friday I'm too exhausted to care. I get home just as the USPS truck puts something in our mailbox.

I decide to just grab the mail since I'm right here. But before I even make it to the door with the letters, Yami is rushing out. She almost passes me on her way to the mailbox before she notices I beat her to it.

"I got it," she says as she reaches for the papers in my hand. Normally I wouldn't even care to look, but Yami's being weird. I glance down before handing her the mail . . . to find a letter to Yamilet from Whitman at the top of the pile.

"You applied out of state?" I ask, more surprised than anything. I have to resist the urge to ask more questions. What about Bo? Does she want to leave because of me? Does Mami know?

"Don't tell Mami," she says as she grabs the letters from my hand and goes back inside without another word. I guess that answers one thing.

A lump has the audacity to form in my throat, but I have no right to be upset after everything I did. Yami going out of state for school is a good thing. Getting away from me will be good for her.

Mami will probably be pissed, but I can't imagine Yami staying here forever just to take care of me and our mom. Maybe she would have if I hadn't pushed her so far in the other direction, but it's good she finally listened. She'll be way better off not having to deal with me.

It's a good thing. I tell myself that over and over again. This is what I wanted. This is what she wants. It's perfect.

But the lump in my throat stays.

Instead of going inside, I start to walk to Walmart. Tonight I'll be meeting up with Jamal for our project, so in order to spend as little time together as possible, I might as well get the telescope on my own instead of going shopping for it together. I don't have the money for it, but how hard could a little handheld telescope be to steal? At least it's better than being trapped at home alone with Yami.

My phone goes off while I'm walking, and I pull it out of my pocket to see that Moni is FaceTiming me.

"Hey, Moni, what's up?" I ask.

"So, I came up with a plan," she whispers with a grin.

"What plan? And why are you whispering?"

"Abuela fell asleep on the couch, and my phone was just sitting there under all her clothes in her drawer. I think she secretly *wanted* me to find it. Anyway, obviously I had to get my phone so I could tell you about my plan," she whispers as she looks over her shoulder, as if checking to make sure Abuela's still sleeping.

"What plan?" I ask again as I sidestep a pole. Unlike Yami, I've never been one of those people who gets so consumed with something they run into shit on the street. You never know what could happen, so I try to stay at least a little alert, even if Moni is entertaining.

"So, remember how I was talking about Abuela and how lonely she must be when we're not here? But the thing is, I only stay here when I'm in trouble, and how am I supposed to finish my secret project if I'm always grounded? Do you know how hard it is to do *anything* without that woman knowing?"

"Wait, are your plan and your secret project the same thing?" I ask. Moni really is allergic to providing context.

"No. *The* plan, which I called to tell you about, is about Abuela. The secret project is about my dad."

"Should I even ask if it's a secret?"

"Top secret. But yes, you should ask, I'm dying to tell someone." She doesn't wait for me to ask before diving in. "So I think the reason my dad *really* doesn't want to pay for my college unless it's a music program is because he's scared. Like, he paid so much money for me to do music my whole life. Maybe he thinks if I can be successful from something he had nothing to do with then I'll just abandon him. He knows I really hate his job and I think he's afraid I'll go no contact or something if I'm not relying on him.

"My secret project is the dispensary, but that's just step one. When his company inevitably goes under because of some lawsuit for malpractice or something, I'll be there to offer him a job at my dispensary. Isn't that perfect?"

I'm about to answer, but she just keeps going.

"Anyway, about *the* plan. Since I'll eventually finish earning my tuition money and leave for college to pursue my secret project, I have to find Abuela a boyfriend so she's not as lonely while I'm gone. And I think it's working! I introduced her to a guy at the dog park, and I slipped her number in a guy's pocket at the doctor's office.

"She's been on her phone a lot lately, and she gets all smiley whenever she checks her email. And that lady, her name's Violeta, right? She comes over sometimes, and remember how the first time she came they were loud as fuck?" Every time I'm about to answer one of Moni's questions, she just keeps going before I get a word in. "Well, now they get all quiet when they talk, like they don't want me to hear them. She has to be gossiping about her little crush with that lady. What was her name again?"

"Vio—"

"Gotta go!" And there's some loud scrambly noises before she hangs up on me. I guess the timing worked out, since I'm about to go inside.

Just as I'm walking in past the checkout lines by the entrance, I practically crash right into Jamal, who's walking out with a telescope in hand. I'm both relieved I don't have to steal one and annoyed that we had the same idea. Is he trying to avoid me, too?

Knowing Jamal, he's probably just here to be considerate. He almost drops the telescope at the sight of me, and I rush to catch it, our fingers overlapping as we both grip it.

"Oh, sorry," I say, letting go quickly, a blush rushing to my cheeks.

"It's okay," he says back, looking down for a moment before meeting my eyes. "I . . . I'll see you later."

And he walks off.

It's only a few short hours before the sun goes down. This time when I try sneaking out, it's to see Jamal. Only now I don't bring any lube or condoms. We're just calculating star trajectories tonight. No romance, no sex. The only reason I'm sneaking out in the first place is because I'm grounded. Even if this is for school, I doubt my mom would let me leave the house to be alone with Jamal late at night. She wouldn't get it.

Jamal picks me up down the street from my house, just to be safe. He doesn't open the passenger-side door for me, which was to be expected. He probably never will again.

I open the door myself and scoot in while Jamal nods his head along to the Saul Williams track playing. It's going to be a long drive since we have to get out of the city so there's less light pollution in order for us to actually see the stars. I don't even know if Jamal knows where we're going, but I don't want to break our unspoken code of silence by asking.

He opens his mouth a few times like he wants to say something, but stops himself every time. I clench my jaw to keep from doing the same.

We spend the ride in silence until about thirty minutes in, when Jamal seems to get comfortable and rests his hand on the center console. I glance down at it, feeling my own hand twitch in response. Our hands are supposed to be there together. That's how it's always been.

But I can't take his hand now, after everything. I've gone too far in the other direction. Besides, I doubt he's putting his hand there as an invitation anyway, like he used to. He probably just got tired of holding the wheel with both hands.

I clear my throat to shake the growing lump out of it, and that's when he seems to notice me panicking. He moves his hand back to the wheel.

We eventually take the freeway far enough that the skirt of city lights falls behind us. Jamal takes a dirt road a little farther into nowhere, then finally parks the truck.

I open the door and hop down to the ground before Jamal has a chance to not open the door for me again. It's better not to give myself the opportunity to feel any kind of way about it.

Jamal pulls the handheld telescope out of the back seat, then climbs into the bed of the truck. I follow him, making sure to sit on the opposite side of the bed so our shoulders don't touch. Jamal looks at the sky through the telescope for a while. The last time we went stargazing, Jamal probably didn't look at the sky more than two seconds. He just stared at me, insisting he was "enjoying the view." Now he doesn't even glance in my direction.

"I can't see a thing," he says as he gives up and hands me the telescope.

It isn't until he turns his head to look at me for the first time tonight that I see it.

"What's that on your neck?" I blurt out.

"It's nothing," he says, a little too fast, as his hand shoots up to cover the mark on his neck.

I pretend I don't know he has a hickey and take the telescope back, ignoring the pang in my stomach. It must be a pretty cheapy telescope because yeah, I can hardly see shit. I eventually find the moon and think for a second that maybe we can bullshit an assignment using that, but there's no way that would work.

I put the telescope down between us. I guess this is what we get for trying to get a telescope at Walmart. "We need a better—"

"Is this really what you want?" Jamal interrupts, which he never does. He finally turns back to look at me.

"What are you talking about?" I ask, feeling his eyes on me but not daring to look into them.

"To barely talk? To pretend like there's nothing between us but a bootleg telescope? Even when no one's around?" His voice catches, and I can't stand hearing him hurt, so I cave and look at him.

His eyes are soft and intense, made to look even bigger under his glasses. He's always looking at me like that. Intense. Focused. Like there's nothing else here but me.

Me.

Why would he want there to be nothing else but me?

"Who gave you that?" My voice comes out quiet, and it's anything but steady. Why would I ask him that? It's none of my business. Do I even want to know the answer?

"That's not fair," he says. "Isn't this what you wanted? To get rid of me?" My ears heat at the question, and that familiar anger rushes to the surface.

"Don't act like you know what I want!" I burst out. "You don't know me like that anymore."

I expect him get angry back, or at least hurt, but he just calmly pushes his glasses up his nose and states the obvious. "You're being mean."

I scoff. "Yeah, well if you're surprised about that, then you *really* don't know me."

"Look, I know you're trying to get a reaction out of me or something, but I'm not playing that game with you. Neither of us has a choice about being here together, and I don't expect you to pretend you're happy about it, but I can't do this if you're not gonna treat me with respect."

I swallow over the lump in my throat. He seems about as done with me as he can be, and that's a good thing. "Okay."

"So . . . question," Jamal says after a while of silence.

"Yeah?" I ask, the lump growing.

"What am I supposed to do? You act like you want nothing to do with me, and I'm trying to respect that, but you're also acting like I did something wrong. So what *do* you want, Cesar?"

"I don't know!" I blurt out. I never *wanted* to lose Jamal, but it was the only way to give him a happy ending. Me getting one has never been an option, so it doesn't matter how bad I want him. "I never *wanted* any of this, but . . ." I cover my face with my hands so he can't look at me like that anymore. "But I know what I need."

"What's that?"

"I need you to stop caring about me, okay? *You* should want nothing to do with *me*. *That's* what I need."

He's quiet again for way too long. I don't have to see him to know those big eyes are still trained on me.

"I understand," he finally says. And when I move my hands from my face, he's looking at the stars.

27

WHEN EVERYONE WOULD BE BETTER OFF WITHOUT YOU

unwanted thoughts

I spend all of Saturday in bed being depressed. Hunter texts me wanting to hang out again, and I ignore it. He calls me. I ignore it.

I can't bring myself to get my poetry notebook out of my desk, but I find myself really wanting to get out my pent-up shit about Jamal. So, I type it in my notes app instead.

J is for just a friend. Just a test from God, or the devil. Just the reason I'm going to hell. Just the reason I'm still here.

A is for attempt. I tried to be good enough for him, but I'm not. So I tried to forget instead.

M is for magic. Enchanting and bewitching in the best way, until I disappeared in a puff of smoke. Maybe I was the illusion all along.

A is for always. Always understanding. Always on my mind. Always without him.

L is for lost. L is for light. L is for laugh. Love. Lost. Lucky. Lost. Lost.

An email notification finally pulls me out of my brooding. I haven't checked my email since I got that message from my dad, but I doubt I've missed much other than spam. This subject line and preview, while still Bible related, feels a lot less earth-shattering.

Subject: horoverse of the day
Moni and I had a nice talk about . . .

When I open up the Gmail app on my phone to read Abuela's message, the email from my dad taunts me. It takes all my willpower not to click and fixate on that instead. I haven't been able to bring myself to delete his message, but I know if I open it, I'll go spiraling again. I finally force myself to click on the one from my grandma instead.

Subject: horoverse of the day
Moni and I had a nice talk about the horoverse from today, and I thought you might like to hear about it. I got your email address from your mami since I haven't heard from you yet. I'm sure you're busy so I won't keep you long, but I wanted to share today's scripture as it made me think of you.

Can a fig tree, my brothers, bear olives, or a grapevine produce figs? Neither can a salt pond yield fresh water.

Ha! Maybe we're just a couple of fig trees trying to make grapes. Silly, isn't it? We beat ourselves up over not being able to make grapes when we could be enjoying the free figs! Your mami actually told me something like this when she was younger, and I brushed it off.

For years, your mami was stuck on milk and wouldn't drink anything else. She absolutely loved oranges, so I thought if I tricked her into trying orange juice by saying it was milk, she'd realize how much she loves it and be able to branch out.

I should have known that was a mistake. Not only did she lose trust in me, but she was repulsed by orange juice for another decade. She may love orange juice now, but it took her so long to warm back up to it. She later told me she would have loved orange juice if I hadn't pretended it was something it wasn't. That it was the expectation, not the taste that ruined it for her.

I want you to remember this when you feel pressured to be anything other than your natural self. We may not be able to control what others expect from us, but we can start by accepting ourselves for who we are, and enjoying whatever fruit we happen to bear (however forbidden it may be).

At first I can't help but wonder if Abuela knows I'm bi. If that's yet another thing Dr. Lee or even my mom snitched on me about. Is she trying to encourage me to accept my sexuality? Does she know about Jamal? But then logic resurfaces, and I realize she's talking about bipolar. Which would be much more relevant for me and Abuela.

Before I can read too much into it, there's a thump on my bedroom window, like a small bird flew into it or something. I'm too depressed to get up and check it out, so I just roll over in bed.

Another thump.

The hell?

After a third thump, I finally get up and go to my window, opening the blinds to see Hunter standing outside with a few pebbles in hand. I open it.

"Hunter? What are you doing here?" I ask, my manners completely missing in my depression haze.

"I'm gonna break you out of here," he says with a determined look.

"What are you talking about?"

"You're grounded, right? What kind of friend would I be if I let you stay cooped up in your house with no contact with the outside world for *months*?"

Guilt swirls around in my chest again. He thinks that's why I haven't been answering his calls or texts. And yeah, I am kind of grounded, but I have my phone. I have access to the outside world. I just don't have the energy to enter it.

"You don't have to do that. I'm okay, really," I say.

"The world hasn't stopped turning, bro. I'm not gonna let you waste away stuck in here alone when I could be taking you to your first-ever college party. I'm officially kidnapping you." He smirks and puffs out his chest.

I laugh, and Hunter steps toward me, grabbing my wrist and practically yanking me out the window.

"I'm not ready!" I protest, but he doesn't stop.

"You look fine. And I'm kidnapping you, remember? You don't have to be ready."

I let out an actual giggle as he pulls me out the window. You know what, why the hell not? I could use a drink or four.

We rush into Hunter's car and drive. I expect us to be heading to downtown Tempe near ASU, hence the whole college-party label, but we end up going closer to where I have therapy.

"This is your first college party, right?" Hunter asks.

"Yup," I say, a small amount of excitement admittedly coming out in my voice.

"Glad I get to be the one to pop your cherry." Hunter grins as we pull up to a neighborhood I recognize from the last time I was in his car. "So, I have a surprise for you."

The excitement vanishes.

"You invited Avery?" I ask as we watch Avery sneak out his own bedroom window.

"Yeah, I invited your whole group! I thought you'd have a better time if I wasn't the only person you knew at the party." He grins earnestly, and I do my best to keep the dread from showing on my face. "Besides, I really like Avery! We went to that concert last night."

"Oh, that's cool," I say in the most this-is-incredibly-uncool way, but Hunter doesn't notice. I don't *think* he's the type to go running his mouth about me, but you can't trust anyone these days.

Avery climbs into the back seat, and I do my best not to show how annoyed I am that he's even here.

"Aren't you supposed to be on house arrest or something? Pretty sure a party doesn't count as stopping for food," I say, hoping maybe Avery just hasn't realized how stupid an idea this is and backs out last minute.

Instead of answering, Avery grabs his leg by the ankle and raises it in the air above the center console. It's somehow bracelet free.

"Got moved to unsupervised probation, so I'm not on house arrest anymore. As long as I keep meeting with my PO and stay out of trouble, I can go wherever I want."

"Any chance you took your lawyer's advice about Nick?" I ask, hoping Avery grew the balls to snitch, but he just scoffs.

"Do I look like I have a death wish? No."

"Who's Nick?" Hunter asks.

"Oh, Avery didn't tell you about Nick? Huh, wonder why?" I know I shouldn't be antagonizing Avery now that he's got a little more freedom, but I can't help it. For a second, Avery almost looks nervous. Like he's afraid I'll tell Hunter I'm his best friend's favorite punching bag. For some reason, I end up choosing peace. "He's Avery's friend."

Luckily Hunter's phone buzzes, which distracts him from talking about Nick. He glances down at his phone, then back at the road.

"So, uh, heads up," he says in that weird voice that feels both super serious but also pretends to be nonchalant.

"What?" I ask when he takes too long to finish his thought.

"Um, Sasha just told me he brought Jamal to the party."

"Cool," I say, trying not to sound tense at the insinuation I'd have a problem with Jamal going to the party with Sasha. Not because I *don't* have a problem, but because Avery's literally right here. I don't want Avery to put together that Jamal was the one I wrote that note to back in sophomore year—the whole reason Nick decided to put a target on my back. He doesn't say anything, though, so hopefully it's safe.

I reach forward and turn up the music so I don't have to pretend not to feel weird about any of this. Sasha brought Jamal to the party. Which means they've been hanging out, probably ever since that open mic. Was *Sasha* the one who gave Jamal that hickey? Are they together now? Not that it's any of my business. . . .

I spend the rest of the ride trying so hard not to think about it that it's all I can think about. Soon enough, we're pulling up to a street with cars parked along the sidewalk. We hop out of the car, and Avery and I awkwardly follow Hunter inside.

It looks like the rest of my group-therapy friends haven't made it yet, so Hunter introduces us to a few of his friends. But before long, he turns to Avery and me to say, "I'm gonna see what they have to drink. Be right back," and then walks away, completely unaware of the tension he's left behind.

And then my stomach tightens even more when Hunter's heads-up warning comes straight toward us.

Sasha comes up first, with Jamal stumbling right behind him. Sasha waves at me, and I nod back.

"Anyone seen the money shot? I promised this one I'd find it for him," Sasha says, gesturing at Jamal like he's about to win him a giant teddy bear at a fair.

"Money shot?" Avery asks.

"Every time Ethan throws a party, he hides a *money shot* somewhere. I don't think anyone's ever actually tried to find it, but I'm here to break generational curses," Sasha says before looking from Jamal to me, like he can smell the tension. "It's Cesar, right?"

I nod, fully at a loss for words. Jamal seems to be too.

"I don't think we've met," Sasha says to Avery next, like he's trying to diffuse the awkwardness. Does he know about me and

Jamal? Thankfully, it seems like I'm the only one who remembers Avery was at that open mic.

Avery introduces himself, and Jamal sways a little as he looks between me and Avery. He looks way too drunk to even try piecing together why we might possibly be hanging out. He'd probably tip over if you tapped his shoulder at this point.

Avery and Sasha make small talk for a bit while I try not to stare at Jamal and pretend not to notice him staring too. He's probably too drunk to realize how awkward this is, but I'm not.

He's never been one to look away when I catch him looking, but I guess things are different now. Now, he practically flinches when I look at him and immediately looks the other way. He's not exactly slick with the staring, but I don't know if it's because he's too drunk to pretend, or if he's just not used to pretending with me at all.

Eventually Sasha seems to catch on that Jamal doesn't want to be talking to us, so they go somewhere else.

Hunter comes back just as Sasha and Jamal are walking away, precariously balancing three red cups in his hands. "Got us some drinks!"

"Oh, sorry, I shouldn't," Avery says. "I may not have that bootleg Rolex anymore, but I'm still on probation."

"Bootleg Rolex!" Hunter lets out the biggest belly laugh I've heard from him at Avery's not-even-that-funny joke. "All right, I'll get you something else."

And he turns around and leaves us alone once again. He could have at least given me *my* drink before walking off. That way I'd have something to distract myself from being stuck at a party with only Avery.

"So, I didn't know you were coming . . . ," Avery says without looking at me.

"Do you have a problem?" I snap back, not even trying to hide my irritation.

"I'm trying to say, you probably didn't know I was coming either. So . . . I guess, sorry if I caught you off guard."

"Oh, that's what you're sorry about?" I roll my eyes.

"Well, yeah. And . . . the other stuff."

I narrow my eyes on him. What the hell is his angle here? Does he think I'll lower my guard from some fuck-ass non-apology?

"Could you, uh . . . not tell Nick you saw me here?" Avery sounds a little on edge.

I want to ask why he'd think I would have any desire to talk to Nick in the first place, but Hunter's back before I have to answer.

He hands one cup to Avery and the other to me, and I eagerly start chugging mine. Anything to make tonight less awkward. But the disappointment just keeps coming.

"Is this just . . . regular Coke?" I ask.

"Yeah!" Hunter smiles like this is somehow a *good* thing. "I thought Avery might feel pressured if we drink in front of him, you know?"

I almost spit out my regular Coke. Why the fuck would I care how Avery feels about me drinking? I. Do. Not. Care. About. Avery.

"Oh, um, that's really nice, but y'all can drink if you want," Avery says.

"I'm gonna get a real drink." I walk off at that and head to the kitchen.

The counter is littered with red cups, even though whoever

threw this party clearly put out a bunch of trash bins to keep people from doing just that.

I scan the room while I pour my drink, looking for something to distract myself with. Jamal and Sasha are the opposite of a distraction, so I quickly look back down and decide it's better to focus on my drink.

Someone taps me on the shoulder, and I turn to see Zo. It looks like Aaron stayed behind to say hi to Avery and Hunter first.

"Everything okay?" Zo asks.

"Everything's great why wouldn't it be I'm obviously fine," I say in one cramped stream of words.

"Right," Zo says with an awkward laugh. "So, wanna pour an extra shot for me?"

I nod and pour one more, but when I look up to hand it to Zo, I catch a glimpse of the back of Jamal's head from across the room, and my stomach twists. He and Sasha are grinding on each other like they're the only ones here.

Zo glances in the direction I'm looking and turns back to me. "Friend of yours?" they ask.

"Yeah, we're friends," I say, hating how sad the word sounds out loud. "I'm gonna go to the bathroom."

I slip out of the kitchen and make my way across the living room without giving them a chance to ask questions. I weave my way through a sea of drunk college students until I make it to the bathroom. Once again, it seems like no one here has heard of a trash can. A few red cups line the sink, some precariously stacked on top of each other. I sigh and start pushing them into the trash, which is *right fucking there*. One of the cups unstacks and misses the bin, rolling onto the floor, a condom falling right on my shoe.

I pinch the bridge of my nose, trying to keep my irritation tempered. But when I go to bite the bullet and throw the condom away, I realize it's . . . off. Whatever's inside it isn't any kind of liquid. It's almost like there's a crumpled-up piece of paper in there. I pick it up, doing my best to convince myself it's not gross if it's not actually used.

I turn it inside out, and fifty bucks pops out.

Maybe I get to have one thing Sasha can't tonight. Looks like I found the money shot.

I shove the cash in my pocket and make my way back to the party. My satisfaction is almost immediately interrupted when I find Jamal and Sasha full-on making out. I'm not even upset that he's making out with someone, but at how *not him* he seems. Jamal doesn't party. He doesn't do PDA. He barely drinks. I know I've been pushing him away for a while now, but has he really changed that much?

How many open mics have I missed by now? How many accomplishments or failures has he had without me? How many drunken kisses? All this time, someone else has been there through all those things with him, and I've been nowhere to be found.

I want to slap myself in the face for feeling jealous. I have no right to feel any kind of way about who Jamal kisses. He has *every* right to kiss other boys. He *should* kiss other boys. I want him to. Want him to be happy. To find someone who can love him back out in the open. To be loved by someone who feels no shame.

But I still want to throw up.

I can still see Jamal from across the room as I get closer to the hallway, even though I'm trying not to look. He pulls away from Sasha, and right when I feel like I could throw up, puke shoots out of Jamal's mouth instead. Right onto Sasha's shirt.

From the distance I'm at, I can't hear what Sasha says, but he looks disgusted, and he runs away to the bathroom.

Without thinking, I quickly grab one of the trash bins near the wall and rush over to Jamal.

He doesn't see that it's me holding the trash can in front of his face as he vomits into it. Doesn't see that it's me who's rubbing his back and telling him to let it out.

I've never seen Jamal actually get drunk before. He was always the one who took care of me while I blacked out. But if it's going to be the other way around tonight, at least it's good that he won't remember this in the morning.

"Did you drive here?" I ask, and Jamal wipes his mouth with his sleeve.

"Cesar?" he asks instead of answering my question, like he somehow already forgot I was here. "What are you . . ." Then he throws up again into the bin a few more times.

"Let's get you some fresh air," I say when he finally seems to be done. Not only because fresh air would do him good right now, but because he'll be less embarrassed if he's throwing up outside with no one to watch.

"M'kay . . . ," he slurs as I pull one of his arms over my shoulder and lead him out to the front yard so we can be alone without judging eyes.

We sit on the grass in front of the curb. Well, I sit. Jamal flops down in my lap. He must be too drunk to remember he hates me right now.

"I'm so drunk . . ." He states the obvious, and I chuckle to myself.

"Did you drive here?" I ask again. He should probably get home, but there's no way he can drive in his condition.

"Mmhm . . ."

Then Hunter comes out looking for us. "Jamal, you okay, bro?" he asks.

"He's shit-faced," I say. "I think I'm gonna take him home."

"Damn," Hunter says, disappointed. "Do you want me to drive so I can take you back here after?" he asks.

"Thanks, but nah, I'll take Jamal's car. Otherwise, he'll have to figure out how to get here tomorrow to pick it up." And I'm not really in a partying mood after seeing Jamal puke his guts out just now. Besides, my house is walking distance from Jamal's, so I won't need to drive home. I feel a little bad since Hunter invited everyone from group here just for me, but I'm sure they'll have a better time without my sulking anyways.

"All right, I'm glad you still have his back. He's lucky." Hunter smiles a little for some reason. "Next time we'll show up before anyone has a chance to get shit-faced, promise." He laughs, then goes back inside.

Do I have Jamal's back? I fucked him over so many times. It's more *un*lucky than anything that he had to meet me. I look back down at Jamal, whose eyes are half open as he stares off into the distance. He groans, eyes still closed.

"Let's get you home, all right?"

"I'm fine, I swearrrr. . . . ," he says slowly. "Party's not over till I sayyy soooo. . . ."

"You just emptied your guts on a hot college guy. The party is over." I laugh and try to help him up, but he doesn't budge. "Come on, we need to get you home."

Jamal looks up at me with a pouty lip. "But I'm hungry."

I laugh again. "Okay, we'll get you some food, then get you home."

At that, he lights up with a huge grin and finally lets me help him to his feet. I try putting his arm around my shoulder again, but he just stumble runs toward his truck. I race after him, surprised by how fast his drunken steps are. We make it to his truck at the same time, and he hands me his keys. I open the passenger door for him and help him climb inside before going around to the driver's side and taking the wheel. Jamal leans the seat all the way back so he's practically lying down in the car.

"Does Sasha make you happy?" I ask. Not out of jealousy this time, but because if Jamal tells me he's happy, it'll all be worth it.

"What?" is all he says in response.

"Sasha, the guy you were making out with? Are you guys together now?"

"Oh . . ." Jamal frowns. "No, we've been hooking up. He probably blocked my number now, though. Too much baggage, and also puke."

I can't help but feel like I'm responsible for at least a good chunk of said baggage. Instead of delving deeper into the issue, though, I change the subject.

"Taco Bell or Jack in the Box?" I ask, since those are the two main late-night drunk eateries I know of.

"Jack in my crack," Jamal mumbles, smiling to himself like he's never said anything funnier. I spit out an unexpected laugh. He must really not realize who he's talking to if he's making that kind of joke.

"All right, what do you want?" I ask as we pull up to the drive-through.

"A hundred tacos," he says, dead serious.

"You are not eating a hundred tacos." I laugh again.

"You're no fun. Fifty tacos."

"I'll get twenty," I compromise, knowing if I suggest anything less, he'll never let us leave the drive-through. Besides, with tax, my newly acquired condom treasure is barely enough to cover twenty.

"Fine."

Jamal hums his eagerness when I pass him the giant bag of tacos. He eats them without unreclining his seat on the drive to his house.

"Question," he says thoughtfully.

"Yeah?" I ask, trying to ignore the aching in my heart at how normal this feels. He takes awhile to ask his question, so I figure it must be extra ridiculous. I turn to look at him after another few moments of silence, only to see him fully asleep with a half-eaten taco on his chest.

I don't know why, but it makes me want to cry. What if that was the last chance I had at hearing one of his random questions?

I pull up to his cousin's driveway and look at the sleeping boy next to me, letting a small smile tug at my lips despite everything.

The truck rumbles to a stop, and I quietly get out and go around to Jamal's side and unbuckle him. I pull out the keys, then scoop one hand under his knees and the other under his back.

I've carried Jamal before, but he's a little taller now than when we were dating, so he's a bit heavier than he was then. Still, I manage to get him out of the car and slowly stalk over to his house, where I somehow manage to get the door unlocked and open without letting him fall. I carry him into his room as quietly as possible before laying him gently down on the bed, pulling the blanket over him.

"Mmmmlove you," he mumbles, eyes still closed.

My heart breaks.

"I love you too," I whisper only after he starts snoring again.

The only comfort I have is that he'll forget all of this in the morning. I wish he could just forget that he loved me altogether.

28

WHEN YOUR MEDS ARE DEFINITELY BEING USED TO BRAINWASH YOU

psychosis

My chest is heavy on the walk home, and my breath comes out shallow. I start jogging, and then running, like I can outrun the pain. If my breath is ragged from running, at least that's a reason.

I sneak back into my room through my open window and close it before toppling down clumsily on the floor. Even though I'm not running anymore, I still can't breathe. I scramble up and rush into the bathroom with an urge to follow Jamal's lead and puke my guts out. I hyperventilate over the toilet for a few minutes before the door leading to the bathroom from Yami's room opens.

"Are . . . you okay?" she asks hesitantly.

Instead of answering, I grip the sides of the toilet with my hands and dry heave.

She walks over and sits down next to me. Her hand touches my back, but I shrug her off.

"Go. Away," I say, voice icy even though my lungs are filled with heat instead of air.

Her next words come out soft, defeated. "I'm just trying to help," she whispers.

"Don't!" I shout, not caring about my volume anymore.

She stands up and takes a step back, her pity turning to a desperate kind of anger. "Why do you hate me so much? All I've done is support you. I've tried *so hard* to help you with your shit! I did everything for you! *What* is your problem with me?"

"*That's* the problem! I need you to stop!" I shout again. "Please just stop!"

Hot tears spill down my face as I continue struggling to breathe. Then I can't help it, I throw up into the toilet.

"Okay," Yami whispers as she finally walks away, but leaves her bedroom door open. A few seconds later, she walks back in the bathroom, sets a water bottle down on the sink, and walks out again. She closes her door this time, leaving me to puke my guilt out into the toilet.

When Tuesday comes around, I stare off into space while Dr. Lee drones on about who knows what in therapy. I answer her questions on autopilot, and she gives some bullshit advice I don't bother absorbing. It's not like she can help me, anyway. The only one who can help me is God at this point.

He has to see how hard I've been trying, right? How I've stuck it out with Bianca all this time to get over Jamal. To fulfill my penance from junior year.

I think back to that confession. I felt even more guilty back then than I do now, especially since my shame and guilt over being with Jamal was no doubt starting to rub off on him and how he viewed himself. I didn't want that. Even if it was right. Even if we *were* sinners. Even if we *were* going to hell. I wanted

Jamal to live a happy life, blissfully unaware of the eternal damnation that awaited him.

Me, though? I couldn't get that fear out of my head to save my life. Not that I wanted to save my own life. Life was already hell, so it didn't matter if I was headed there after death, too. But all Jamal had was this life, and I was ruining it for him.

Somehow, I doubt God is proud of me, even after all the lengths I went through to fulfill my penance. Bianca loves me, but I'm only hurting her. She's better off without me too. They all are.

The session is almost over when Dr. Lee finally unfolds her legs and sighs. "You know, Cesar, I can't help you if you don't want to help yourself."

"You can't make me want help," I snap back at her, a little harsher than I'd meant it to come out. But it's more than true.

I *don't* want help. I want out.

After therapy, I say I have to go to the bathroom, so my mom doesn't notice I have no intention of going to group today. There's a second exit from the office building near the bathrooms, and I quickly go out that way the second the coast is clear.

It's not like I have anywhere else to go, so I just walk behind the office, where only the employees are parked, and sit down against the curb.

"Hey, that's my spot," Nia says playfully. I've only ever seen her in a couple of group sessions before since she's not usually there. Apparently, my idea to ditch out here wasn't original.

"You too?" I ask as I scoot over, and she sits down next to me.

She chuckles. "Yup. Been coming out here almost every week since my mom started making me come."

"Smart," I say, looking at the graffiti on the wall on the other side of the employee parking lot. "It's all bullshit. I don't know why they make us go there."

"Agreed." She nods. "You don't care about my problems, and I don't care about yours. Don't see why we're supposed to pretend."

"Ouch," I tease, and she shrugs.

"Hey, we all know it's true."

I think on that. It's true that I don't care about anyone in group like that, and they don't care about me. But I'm not so sure *none* of them care about each other. Like, Zo, Aaron, and Avery seem to like each other just fine. In fact, I'd be surprised if they didn't hang out outside of group on the regular.

Then, because I love to contradict myself, I ask a question I didn't realize I wanted the answer to until it leaves my mouth. "So are you really doing better after switching medication?"

Nia raises an eyebrow. "Yeah. My meds literally saved my life."

I laugh, then stop when I realize she's not joking. "I don't trust meds anymore."

"Why not?" she asks.

I just shrug. I don't know how to explain to her that I'm pretty sure the powers that be are trying to brainwash all of us. For what, I don't know yet. But why else would Dr. Lee, and everyone else for that matter, be so insistent I pop pills every day? Either everyone else is right and I'm wrong, or they're all trying to make me feel crazy, just so I'll do what they say. Seeing as I'm no longer being actively mind controlled, the second option feels more logical. I don't know what their end goal is with that, but it can't be good.

But then again, if Nia's being brainwashed, she should know, right? There's no way she hasn't at least considered it by now.

"Do you ever wonder if, like, your meds are . . . I don't know, brainwashing you?"

"What, like making me a mindless zombie or something? I mean, some meds do that, but that's why you have to switch until you find the right ones."

"No, not like a zombie, I mean more like . . . I don't know. Never mind."

"Ohhh . . . I see what you're saying."

Now she's getting it.

"You know, it's actually a really common psychotic symptom to believe your meds are being used for mind control."

"That sounds exactly like something someone who was mind controlled would say," I scoff. I can't believe I said that out loud.

I expect Nia to burst out laughing at me, but she doesn't. "Did you tell anyone you want to go off your meds?" she asks.

My head snaps in her direction. How would she even know that? "What are you talking about? I'm not off my meds."

"Didn't say you were. But chill, I'm not gonna narc on you if you are. It's just . . . if I don't take my meds for a while I start believing shit like that too, and it goes down a vicious cycle until I hit rock bottom. It's really hard to get out of that mindset."

"Again. You sound seriously brainwashed," I say. Of course she gets in the mindset of thinking she's brainwashed when she stops taking the meds that are doing the brainwashing.

"You're not gonna convince me to go off my meds, if that's what you're trying to do." She scowls at me.

"That's your prerogative, I guess," I say, trying not to judge, but I super am. How can anyone be okay with being brainwashed like that after having been confronted with the truth?

"Look, I know you don't get it, but when I go off my meds, I go full crazy."

"Well, I'm not crazy," I say defensively.

Now she laughs. "Sorry to break it to you, but you wouldn't be here if you weren't at least a little crazy. We all are. Embrace it."

"If you're all about embracing it, then why are you trying to avoid going crazy?" I ask, fully aware I'm doing the asshole devil's advocate thing everyone hates. She knows I have a point, though.

"No one wants to see me full crazy," she says. "Look, I won't tell anyone, but you really shouldn't go advertising that you're off your meds. Especially since you're clearly not working on coping skills or anything like that to substitute them."

"I'm not advertising shit."

"Right, but you're obvious. If anyone finds out you're off your meds, you'll probably get institutionalized."

"Yeah, that's not happening." No one's noticed I'm off my meds so far, and it's been months.

But I do know one thing for sure. It has to stay that way. I *just* got everyone to stop babying me. No way in hell am I going back to the hospital and starting all over. I'd rather go full crazy.

29

WHEN ALL YOU WANT IS A HUG AND ALSO FOR NO ONE TO EVER TOUCH YOU AGAIN

self-contradiction

"I think the plan is failing," Moni whispers over FaceTime while I walk to school and she's putting on her makeup. Who knows how she managed to sneak her phone away this time. It takes me a second to remember about her multiple plans.

Right. The secret project is about her dad. *The* plan is about Abuela.

"What happened? I thought you said she found someone?"

"I know! And how long has it been since then? How long since she got all smiley every time she looked at her phone?" She doesn't wait for me to answer. "And yet she hasn't gone on a single date! I thought maybe things didn't work out with that guy, so I tried to set her up with someone else, but every single time, she flakes! Are you thinking what I'm thinking?" I'm about to ask what that is, but I don't know why I expected anything other than for her to answer herself. "Exactly. She must be gay." Moni somehow got out that entire whispered monologue without stopping for air even once.

"Isn't she, like, extremely religious, though?" I ask. For someone so into Bible horoscopes, I have a hard time believing my grandma is anything but straight.

"Hmm . . . maybe she's one of those repressed gays who hates themselves."

I ignore the sting those words carry.

"I think she just needs a little push in the right direction," Moni says with a thoughtful look in her eye.

"What do you mean, 'the right direction'?" Does she mean trying to push Abuela to be straight?

"I mean, we just need to give her a little hint that we'd accept her no matter what, you know?" she says. "Maybe mention to her you have a gay sister or something."

"Yeah, I'm not doing that." Not only do I not want to talk about Yami, but I doubt Moni is right about this little hunch. Just because Abuela doesn't want to go on a date with a stranger her grandkid set her up with doesn't mean she's gay.

"Maybe we could have a Xena watch party. Xena's a lesbian, right?" she asks. "Oh! I gotta g—" She hangs up before finishing her sentence.

I can't even laugh about Moni's antics right now, because only one part of what she said is sticking with me.

. . . *one of those repressed gays who hates themselves* . . .

The words bounce around in my brain all morning. By the time astronomy starts, my throat is tight and my palms are sweaty and my ears are hot and I can't fucking do this.

"I have to pee!" I blurt out as I literally run away, the sounds of laughter behind me only serving to heat my reddened ears as I rush out the door and make a run for the staircase.

The stairwell door closes behind me with a thud, but I only make it down a few steps before I have to grab the banister to keep from falling all the way down. I sit on the steps, gasping for air. What the fuck is happening to me?

The door below me opens, but I can't get myself together before whoever it is will see me, so I just hide my face in my knees and keep desperately trying to breathe.

I can't fucking breathe!

"Cesar?" someone asks, and my head whips up at the voice. Avery.

Seeing him only makes the hyperventilating stronger. I can't even bring myself to speak to tell him to go away. Tears prick my eyelashes, and anger heats my blood. I'm fucking crying in front of Avery. If this had happened two years ago, he would have told his friends and I'd have gotten a good beating.

But instead he just reaches inside his backpack and pulls out an icy water bottle. I expect him to hand it to me, but he unscrews it and splashes it right in my fucking face.

For a second, I'm too stunned to move.

"What the hell is your problem?" I manage to get out as I shake the water from my hair like a wet dog.

Avery sits down next to me and lets a smile crack. "You're breathing again, aren't you?"

And I hate that his weird trick worked, but I am in fact breathing again.

"How did you know to do that?" I ask incredulously.

He just shrugs. "Learned it by accident. Cold water kind of resets you. You should carry around some ice water, and next time it happens just pour some on your hands and splash your face. Works like magic."

"Oh," I say, not knowing what else to say. With all the panic attacks I've been having lately, it might actually be a good idea to take his advice. "Thanks . . ."

"Take it," he says, handing me the water bottle. "I think you need it more than me. Anyways, gotta get back to class."

Then he's gone.

I refill the water bottle before I start sneaking out of the house for the second astronomy night with Jamal. I have a feeling I might need it. But when I leave the bathroom and pass through the living room, the light turns on.

"Where do you think you're going?" Mami sits on the recliner with her arms crossed, staring at me like she's a movie mastermind and I've just fallen into her trap. Which I kind of have.

"Were you just sitting there waiting this whole time?"

"Where are you going?" she asks again.

I groan. There's no use lying to her now. The truth is probably way less incriminating than whatever she has in mind.

"It's for my senior project. I have to observe the stars with Jamal. He's my astronomy partner." I can hear that it sounds like a lie coming from my mouth. Especially after the hell of a year I've given my mom. Still, she doesn't accuse me.

"Bring Yamilet with you, then," Mami says, as if it's completely normal to make your daughter wake up late at night to go watch her brother and his ex do homework.

"What? I'm not doing that." I cross my arms like this is a game of chicken, waiting to see which one of us will back down first.

"Yamilet goes with you, or you're not going."

"But it's for school!" I protest, but Mami doesn't unfold her arms or un-Mom her expression.

"Yamilet!" Mami calls out, and I rush over to her.

"Mami, stop!" I whisper-yell. Partly because I really don't want Yami coming with us. It would make our awkward situation even worse. But also because I've been enough of a burden to Yami already. I'm supposed to be moving past that stage in my life.

But it's too late. Luckily, Yami doesn't seem like she was asleep yet, so when she opens her door and walks into the living room, she doesn't look quite as angry as she could or should be.

"What's going on?" Yami asks, eyes flip-flopping between me and our mom.

"Your brother needs you to go with him on a trip. For school."

"But—" Yami and I both start to protest, but Mami shushes us with a raised finger.

"I'm not letting him go out alone right now." She says that part like it's code for something else. Like Yami should know exactly what she's talking about, even if I don't.

"But I'll be with Jamal!" I say, but neither of them listens.

"Okay, I'll go with him," Yami says, ignoring me like I'm not even there.

"Seriously?" I ask, but she ignores me again.

"But only if I can bring Bo." She grins.

Mami sighs and pinches the bridge of her nose. "Fine. Bring whoever you need to. But don't leave him alone."

Yami nods and gets out her phone to call Bo.

"She'll meet us there," Yami says after telling Bo she'll text her the location, then hangs up. "Jamal's here waiting already, no?"

she asks as she makes her way for the front door like she expects me to follow. And, because I basically have no other choice, I do.

"Make sure he gets home safe," Mami says before we shut the door behind us.

Yami rolls her eyes, and I know what Mami just said got to her. Mami loves both of us, sure, but I'm the problem child. I'm the one who needs protecting. I'm sure it makes Yami feel like our mom doesn't care about her. Like I'm the only one who needs to be brought home safe.

Yami takes the front seat of Jamal's car, and for a second, I forget she hates me. For a second, I think this is her messing with me, making fun of how I always used to get shotgun in Bo's car even though Yami was her girlfriend. But Yami's not laughing. And Jamal's not my boyfriend.

The car ride this time isn't spent in tension-filled silence. Yami and Jamal catch up the entire time, laughing and telling stories and joking around like I'm not even here. I can't help thinking how much better off they'll be when I'm not.

I like them like this.

But at the same time, I hate it.

By the time we get to our viewpoint and stop the truck, Bo's car is already waiting on the empty dirt road.

Before I know it, Yami, Bo, and Jamal are all living it up outside. They lean on the hood of Bo's car and talk for what feels like ages. It's like they haven't even noticed I'm still in the truck.

They finally turn their heads when I get out and shut the door hard behind me. Then I stomp off past them, not knowing where I'm going, or why I'm mad, but also not really caring.

I walk off the road through some tallish grass and bushes before sitting down in the middle of nowhere and hugging my knees to my chest, resting my head between my legs.

I can hear the grass moving in the distance as someone gets closer and closer, but I don't look up.

"I thought this was what you wanted," Jamal says.

Of course it's Jamal. And thank God he doesn't seem to remember Saturday night.

I feel the earth shift next to me as he sits down by my side, waiting for an answer I don't give.

"You can't do everything in your power to make sure you have nothing to do with any of us, then get mad when we respect your boundaries." Jamal doesn't sound mad. He never does. His voice is calm as ever, despite the words coming out of his mouth.

I finally look up to find his ever-intense eyes trained on me. "Shit, Jamal . . . ," I say, feeling a lump forming in my throat. This *is* what I wanted. So why the hell am I so unhappy? "I know I've been an asshole. If we lived in a different world, maybe . . . maybe things would have turned out different."

Jamal's lips quirk into a small smile. "Is this your way of trying to apologize?"

"What? No. I'm not apologizing," I say. I know it sounds harsh, but I'm not going to apologize for something I would do again if given the chance. I did what I had to do, and no matter how much I hate it, no matter how much it hurts, I would do it again.

If I needed to hurt Jamal to get him to stop loving me, then that's what I had to do. There's no use apologizing. In fact, that would only make it worse. Still, I wish there was something I could say to make him feel better about all of this. "I never wanted to hurt you," I admit.

"I know," Jamal says, but I don't buy it. How could he be so sure, after everything I did, that my intentions were good? "But you did," he adds.

"I know," I say. "This is why you're better off without me."

Jamal lets out a little breath of a laugh through his nose at that. "And you're better off without me."

I meet his eyes again to check if he's serious. Like always, he is. "How?" I ask. How am I possibly better off without Jamal?

He just looks at me for a moment like the answer is obvious. "You hate yourself when you're with me. And as much as I love you, I can't love you out of hating yourself."

I open my mouth to answer, but nothing escapes. I do hate myself, but how can he possibly think that's because of him?

"I mean . . . I'm sorry. I shouldn't have said I love you. I didn't mean to cross a boundary. I just—"

"I love you too," I blurt out. "But you're right. I hate myself. Not because of you, but I do and you should too, so we can't be together. I want what's best for you, and that's not me."

Jamal's quiet again for a while. I expect him to give me his usual "I understand," but he doesn't. "You're wrong." He shakes his head. "You're so wrong."

"*You're* wrong," I shoot back. "I'm a fucking mess. All I've done is hurt you. I don't deserve you. I never did, and you know it."

Jamal lets out a measured breath. "I won't say what I want to say right now because I don't want to make you feel uncomfortable."

"Just say it," I challenge him.

"You don't want to hear it."

"Or you don't really want to say it."

Jamal sighs, caving. "Cesar." He shifts so his whole body is facing me. "You deserve to be happy. I *want* you to be happy. And if I don't make you happy anymore, then fine. I can live with that. But don't go fooling yourself into thinking you're doing this for me. Because you *did* hurt me, Cesar. But you also loved me harder than anyone else ever has.

"You were there for me when no one else was. You showed me how to be brave. How to be myself. And whether you like it or not, you made my life so, so much better. So I don't know why you're doing any of this, but you're not doing it for my sake. You can tell yourself that all you want, but we both know it's not true. The best thing you can do for me now, Cesar, is let yourself be happy."

A lump forms in my throat again, and when I speak it weighs down my words. I want to ask him how? How the hell am I supposed to just *be happy*? I don't know how to do that. Not for him or for anyone else. So instead, I just say the only thing that makes sense right now.

"I understand." I lie back down on the ground and close my eyes so Jamal can't see the tears forming in them.

"As much as I want to be here for you right now, I think you need someone else," Jamal says, and I hear him get up and walk away. That's when I let the tears fall down the sides of my face.

Be happy.

Is that really all he wants from me? And what if I can't give him that? What if I can never give him that?

Then the grass shifts next to me again.

I want so badly to open my eyes and throw myself into Jamal's arms and cry into them. To kiss him out here under the stars, where no one can see but God. I want to not care about any of it. But I do.

"Hey . . ." I jolt upright when I realize it's Yami's voice, not Jamal's that greets me. We haven't had a real conversation in ages, so I have no idea what to expect.

"Do you really like Bianca?" she finally asks.

"What?" I ask. Not what I was expecting.

"Because if you do . . ." She sighs. "You don't need my permission to be with who you want to be with—and I really do just want you to be happy. But don't expect me to go playing nice with her."

I let out a laugh-cry at that. Is she really saying she's okay with me dating Bianca?

"If you really like her—"

"I don't," I interrupt.

She looks taken aback for a moment. A brief pained expression etches onto her features before they shift into something softer. Before she can ask my why I'm such a horrible person, I change the subject. "So did you get in?"

"What are you talking about?"

"To Whitman. The letter you didn't want Mami to see?" I remind her, and she lets out a little laugh.

"No. But you should probably know . . . I did get accepted somewhere else."

"That's good," I say with a nod, even though it feels awful.

She squints her eyes like she's skeptical. "That's good? Is that it?"

I just shrug. "You'll be better off."

"Yeah, but . . . what about you, though? What about Mami?" she asks as she nervously starts plucking grass from the ground.

"What about us?" I say, but I don't actually want her to answer that by justifying why her needs are less important, so I keep going. "We'll be fine. You should do what's best for you."

She's quiet for a while. Eventually she stops picking grass and lets out a breath. "Thanks for understanding."

I want to tell her I'm happy for her and that she deserves to be happy for herself. But I'm a coward who doesn't know how to say nice things, so I just nod. We sit there awkwardly for a while before she breaks the silence again.

"So you don't like Bianca. . . ." She trails off. Great. I almost thought we wouldn't have to talk about this.

"I don't," I admit again.

"Then why . . . ?" she asks quietly. "Do you really hate me that much?"

"I don't hate you, Yami," I say just as quiet. Then, loud enough to make sure she hears me, "I could never hate you."

"Then why did you do it?"

"Because I'm a bad person!" I find myself shouting. "Why is that so hard for everyone to understand? I'm a bad person, I hurt people, I fuck everything up, I ruin lives! That's why you're better off leaving!" I don't realize I'm crying again until she yanks me into a hug.

It's the first time we've hugged since before I hooked up with Bianca at that party. I sink into her embrace and cry harder, and I can feel from the movement of her chest and shoulders that she's crying too.

"You're not a bad person, Cesar," she says through sniffles as she pulls herself away to look me in the eye, hands firmly grasping my shaking shoulders as her shiny pupils bore into mine. "You can hurt everyone around you as much as you want, but you can't make us stop caring about you, okay? It's just not gonna happen. Tú eres mi otro yo."

I can't hold myself together at that phrase. *You are my other me.* Yami has always been that for me. It's always been the two of us, no matter what. I think back to the last time she said that to me. It was when I was inpatient at Horizon.

I ask her the same question now that I asked her then, still somehow completely at a loss for the answer. "Why did God make me like this if I'm not supposed to be like this?" My voice cracks, and she pulls me close to her again, this time letting me cry into her lap. "I hate being like this . . . I hate it so fucking much."

She strokes my hair while I sob. She doesn't bother telling me what she told me back then. That there's nothing wrong with me. Nothing to fix. That God made us exactly how we're supposed to be. She knows I wouldn't buy it. Instead, she just says, "I love you. I love you. I love you."

30

WHEN YOU'RE ITCHING FOR ANOTHER FIGHT

antagonizing others

I'm about to ditch group again the next week, but this time Mami is actually paying attention when I get out of therapy. She'll notice if I make a run for it instead of going to the bathroom. I sigh and end up trudging along to group instead of following Nia to freedom.

I pretend not to listen, but everyone's giving updates from last week that I'm definitely not curious about because I definitely don't care about these people.

Zo's boyfriend finally came around and had a pansexual awakening and no longer identifies as straight. Don't care.

Aaron finally told his girlfriend he has borderline personality disorder, and she dumped him. Don't care.

Avery thinks he might actually like someone now. Don't. Care.

I definitely don't care.

Then it gets to me, and I already regret mentioning having to do my senior project with The Ex because everyone wants to know how that's going. I try to keep it short, but as soon as I start talking, it all just kind of slips out. I tell them about the other night, and how my sister and her girlfriend had to babysit me and the ex. I mention the talk I had with Jamal without gendering him, and the one I had with Yami, and how I feel guilty that they both just want me to be happy, even after everything I've done to hurt them.

"You sure you're over your ex, bro?" Aaron asks, and I shake my head.

"I'm not," I admit.

"Being able to realize you still love someone, but also to admit that you're not ready to commit to the relationship just yet, shows some real maturity," Dr. Lee says. And for once, I don't despise the words coming out of her mouth. It's the first time I've felt validated in all of this.

Of course I want to be with Jamal. But what I want doesn't matter when I'm this fucked up.

But then I realize I *did* commit to a relationship. With Bianca.

And dammit, I feel fucking trapped.

"So, would you get back with your ex after you get better?" Zo asks.

"No," I say immediately. "I have a girlfriend."

Aaron frowns. "Isn't that kind of messed up if you still love your ex?"

"Yeah, well, I do a lot of messed-up shit," I say. I'm not proud of it, but it's true. It is kind of fucked up.

"Do you want to break things off with your girlfriend?" Zo asks, leaning forward like they're really interested.

"Well, yeah," I finally admit, and I know it makes me a horrible person. I wonder if God will be disappointed in me if I break up with Bianca. "But I feel like I'm supposed to be with her."

"Why?" Aaron asks. "Why draw it out when your heart's not in it?"

"God wants me to be with a girl," I find myself saying. I feel like my filter is completely gone today.

I expect everyone to react to the news that I'm queer, but the only reaction I get is that Dr. Lee gives a little micro frown, and Zo looks like they just ate a bitter lemon.

"That's bullshit," they say.

"Agreed," echoes Avery.

I snap my head toward him. "Don't be a fucking hypocrite, aren't you straight now too for the same exact reason?"

Avery opens his mouth like he has something to say but only croaks a little.

"God isn't even real," Aaron adds. "Who cares what sky daddy thinks?"

I glare at him next. "He's real."

"Okay," Dr. Lee interjects. "We're not here to invalidate anyone's belief system or sexuality. Why don't we use 'I' statements instead of blanket statements?"

"Fine, *I* don't believe in God," Aaron says.

"Well, *I* do," I shoot back, my hand automatically reaching for the cross necklace that's no longer around my neck. Right. I took it off a long time ago. I shake my head. "I *know* He's real. I've talked to Him."

Zo puts a hand on my shoulder, and I flinch. They're so touchy with everyone, but this is the first time they've tried it with me.

"What?" I snap at them.

"Sorry, it's just . . . I can relate. I believe in God too, but when

I'm manic, sometimes I have delusions about Him. It's a complicated relationship since I can't always trust my feelings, you know?"

"I'm not delusional," I say quickly, though I can't help but remember Abuela telling me that exact same thing. But they're both wrong. "I'm not fucking crazy. I'm chosen," I say, ignoring the fact that, yeah, I *sound* kind of crazy. But who cares? None of them would get it.

I have a special relationship with God now. I messed up by blaming it on "mania" or whatever before. Just because I had a crash doesn't mean I can't believe what I saw and heard before that.

That conversation I had in Abuela's bathroom with God was *real.* And now I've done the work. I can be patient. I'll wait for His sign, and then I'll get to go straight to heaven.

"I just have to walk the path God laid out for me, and everything will be fine," I say.

Just then, Avery stands up abruptly and speed-walks out of the room.

I stop talking then, watching him leave. Was it something I said?

I look down at my feet, where Avery's water bottle is sitting, since he gave it to me. Maybe he needs it right now. I let out a sigh since I might have been a little harsh on him. "I'll go check on him."

I follow Avery out to the hallway, but since I don't see him there, I go to check the bathroom next.

As soon as I open the door, I can hear him hyperventilating in one of the stalls. I walk in front of the stall and roll the water bottle underneath, just like Jamal did for me all those weeks ago.

Avery doesn't reject it like I did, though. I just hear him opening the bottle and splashing some water on his face.

"Thanks," he croaks.

"What happened?" I ask.

He's quiet for a while. "Um, religion is kind of a trigger topic for me, I guess."

"Oh . . ." For a second, I almost apologize, but instead I just ask, "You okay?"

"Yeah." Then after a moment, the stall door opens, and he comes out to meet me. "You know, we have to stop meeting like this." He grins.

Is he . . . flirting with me?

At that, I can't help the burst of anger that rushes through me. I almost forgot who Avery was to me. "Don't fucking do that," I snap.

His smile drops. "I was just joking."

"Yeah, well, it's not funny. You used to beat the shit out of me for being queer and now you think you can just casually make jokes about it? Fuck you."

"I never actually hit you," he says, as if that makes it any better.

"Oh, thank you *so much* for holding me down while your friends beat the shit out of me, my mistake." I turn to walk out, but he puts a hand on my shoulder.

"Look, I'm sorry, okay?" he says softly. "I know that doesn't fix what I did, but I'm still sorry. You don't have to forgive me."

I let out a heavy breath. If I hadn't already forgiven him, I doubt I'd be here trying to help him out of a panic attack. My feelings about Avery are complicated. I guess I don't know who he is anymore. He used to be a bully for sure, but now? We're both in treatment, and he's got PTSD from religious trauma, and he knows how to help me out of a panic attack. . . .

"Why'd you do it?" I finally ask. It still doesn't make any sense. Avery doesn't even act like he likes Nick, but he still follows him around and does everything the guy says.

Avery lets out an unsteady breath. "I guess you do deserve to know . . . but you can't tell anyone," he says, crossing his arms like he's giving himself a hug.

"Okay," I say tentatively, no idea what to expect.

He leans his back against the bathroom wall and slides to the floor. I sit across from him with my own back leaning against the divider between two stalls.

"I've known Nick since we were little because our parents go to the same church. It didn't used to be as bad before, but he's always kind of been . . . well, you know how he is."

I nod, but don't say anything.

"I didn't even realize I was gay yet when Nick figured it out. He knew my parents would lose their shit so he promised he wouldn't say anything. But after that he just kind of held it over my head whenever he wanted something. We were twelve then."

"So he blackmailed you?"

Avery nods. "I basically became Nick's fall guy. At first it wasn't so bad, I'd just do his homework for him and stuff, but every time I did something for him, he'd test the limits even more."

"Like how?" I don't really know why I'm asking. I guess I want to know what kind of stuff Nick needs people to do for him. Maybe it's something to use against him later, I don't know.

"Like shoplifting, slashing people's tires he didn't like, stuff that's like, against the law. I did whatever he wanted for almost a year before I got sick of it. I went to confession and told the priest everything. I don't know why I thought he'd be able to fix any of it."

I have a hard time responding. Maybe I should tell him I did the same thing. That this all started for me with a similar confession to a priest. But instead I just nod so he knows I'm still listening, and he keeps going.

"Anyway, the priest told my parents, and they sent me to conversion therapy. It, uh . . . didn't work. In case you haven't figured that out. But I pretended like it did."

That part has me a little annoyed. Avery said he went to conversion therapy when he was thirteen, but he still follows Nick around everywhere. I bet if Nick asked him to hold me down while he kicked my ass today, Avery would do it. "If Nick thought you were straight after that, why do you still do what he says? Why are you still scared of him?"

Avery leans his head back against the wall and closes his eyes, his Adam's apple bobbing as he prepares for whatever he's about to say. "Like I said, I did a lot of illegal shit for him. He can basically get me sent to jail any time he wants. And after that party, he almost did."

I glance down at Avery's ankle, now free from the monitor, and remember Nick's injury. Ever since the party where Nick and Bianca broke up, he's been wearing that boot.

"What happened?"

"It was so stupid." Avery runs a frustrated hand through his hair. "Nick was pissed off after the breakup, so we all went to some construction site and he just started smashing shit, letting off steam or whatever. The cops showed up from a neighbor's noise complaint, I guess, so we ran. Nick landed on his foot wrong when he jumped the fence, so he told me if he got caught, he'd snitch on me about all of it. It was either take the fall for it so the rest of them could help Nick get out of there, or let Nick get caught and end up in way more trouble."

"Shit . . ." This whole time, I'd known that whatever happened after that party got Nick his injury and Avery on probation, but I didn't realize it was *my fault*. Nick and Bianca basically broke up because of me. And I'm sure me dating Bianca after the fact didn't help Avery's situation either.

"So, yeah . . . like I said, I am sorry, but I don't exactly have a way out at the moment. I get it if you can't forgive me."

I can't lie, it really sucks to get confirmation that Avery would, in fact, still hold me down while his friends beat me if Nick asked him to. But I guess I can't really blame him. Especially when I'm the reason he got put on probation in the first place. If I was in his position, I don't know if I could promise to be any different. For all the people I've hurt who still willingly put up with me, it just feels unfair if I get forgiven and he doesn't.

"Okay," I finally say. "I forgive you."

"Guess who!" Bianca says as she covers my eyes from behind me before lunch.

I have to resist the urge not to swing when someone sneaks up on me like that, even if I know it's a safe interaction. I force my muscles to relax.

"Hey," I say, turning around to face her. She takes my hand and walks with me to the cafeteria. I follow her on autopilot.

"So, are you done avoiding me?" she asks.

"I'm not avoiding you," I lie.

"You are," she says. "Does avoidance run in the family? Because Yami stopped talking to me after an 'I love you' too." Bianca laughs, and my face heats. It was Yami's "I love you," not Bianca's, that separated those two. The "I love you" that Bianca used against Yami before outing her. *That* is my girlfriend.

"Why are you so obsessed with my sister? It's like you like her or something," I snap. I know I'm probably out of line, but I can't help it. It's almost like I'm just looking for a reason to be miserable. Like getting a reaction out of Bianca will fix some broken part of me somehow.

"It's not like that," Bianca says, without letting go of my hand. She's not even mad. "Yami and I used to be best friends, and then she just ran away to Catholic school and dropped me after one fight."

"Because you outed her," I say plainly. Does Bianca really not get it?

"Yeah, well, people can change, right? She hasn't even given me the chance."

We get to the lunch table before I can answer, and I'm distracted by Nick and them sitting where we usually sit. My stomach drops into my gut. Avery's there too, and we make eye contact for just a second while I try to gauge why they're all here, but his eyes are kind of glazed over like he's dissociated or something. I can't see under the table to check if Nick still has the boot on, so I don't know what to expect. Is Nick here for a fight?

Because that's fine with me. . . .

I march over to the table. "What do you want?" I ask them.

Nick ignores me, looking at Bianca instead. "So, I'm having a party this weekend. You should come," he says, licking his bottom lip.

Bianca glances at Nick's friends, then at me, like she's surprised he's talking to her in front of us. "You're not mad?"

Is she actually thinking about it? I guess I can't be surprised, considering how she needs everyone to love her at all times.

"Nah, how can I stay mad at *all that*?" He looks Bianca up and down like she's a three-course meal. Obviously, I know what he's trying to imply, but I also know he's just doing it to get under my skin, and I'm not giving him the satisfaction.

Bianca doesn't seem offended at the objectification. She just giggles and looks to me as if for approval.

"Yeah, I'm not doing that." There's no way I'm going to a Nick party with Bianca.

"You don't want to go?" she asks with a pouty lip.

"The invite was for Bianca," Nick says before I can answer, rolling his eyes.

I let go of Bianca's hand and put both of mine on the table, leaning forward. "You're not her boyfriend anymore, Nick. Are you jealous?" I smirk.

Nick stands up, puffing out his chest, "That's funny, could have sworn I'm the one she was fucking last night." I just roll my eyes since he's obviously lying.

"Nick, what the fuck?" Bianca's eyes widen and her face turns red.

Wait, *is* he lying?

"You got a problem?" Nick says to me, ignoring her completely, but she throws herself between us before I can react.

"What the hell, guys?" Bianca looks at me, then at him, holding her arms out to separate us. "I'll go to your party and Cesar won't. Is that what you want?"

"Whatever, do what you want," I say as I storm off in the other direction, which takes literally all of my will power. I don't know if Nick is lying about fucking Bianca or not, but for some reason, I can't find a fuck to give.

Even if Nick is still injured, I know if I pick a fight with him, all his friends would back him up, including Avery, and I'd get my ass kicked to hell and back. Then again, a fight sounds like exactly what I need. I turn my head to see a snarling Nick and Co. glaring in my direction. "I'll see you," I say, as if a threat from me has any kind of power when it comes to them.

Still, it makes me feel good.

"Just fucking wait till I get this thing off. You won't be so cocky then!" Nick yells back.

And no matter how little sense it makes, I look forward to it.

31

WHEN YOU GET A LITTLE GLIMPSE OF HEAVEN

rapid cycling

When Friday rolls around, Bianca drives me home from school like she normally does, but this time we're tense. She's going to Nick's party tonight, and I know I'm the one who said I didn't want to go, but a party seems like the perfect place to be right now. Especially if I get to confront Nick.

"Will you do me a favor?" she asks shyly. At first I'm surprised she's not trying to address Nick's claims about them having sex, but then again, why would she? She can clearly tell I'm not pressed about it either way, so bringing it up would just shed light on how little I care. That would kind of fuck with her whole needing-to-be-liked complex. Somehow, it's a relief that we're so deep in these mind games that she won't call me out about it.

"Uh, depends what kind of favor," I say without looking up from my phone.

"Can you tell Yami to unblock my number? I wanna talk to her."

"I've told you that I'm not getting in the middle of that."

"You're already in the middle of it. You're my boyfriend and her brother. You couldn't stay out of it if you tried."

"If you miss her so bad, why'd you out her?" I accuse.

"I only told Chachi and Stefani!" Bianca looks taken aback, like she's surprised I'm standing up for my sister. I guess no one's ever called her out on her shit before.

"It wasn't your secret to tell. You shouldn't have told anyone!" I say, feeling that familiar twinge of anger bubbling up in my chest again.

"They deserved to know! What if she never told them? Friends aren't supposed to keep secrets from each other, but she lied to us for *years*!"

Angry, manic laughter spills out of me. "Oh my god, you are not fucking serious right now!" I laugh harder, and she just stares at me.

"You're acting crazy," she says.

"And you're acting like a bitch. Have fun at Nick's party," I say as I grab the door handle and see myself out of her car, shutting it behind me before she can respond.

She rolls down her window. "I will! Maybe I'll sleep with him again!"

I turn around and flip her off. I mean, I never succeeded at having feelings for her, so I don't really care that she slept with Nick, but it does surprise me. "Why are you even dating me then? What's the point?" I ask, stepping closer to her driver's side window.

She's quiet for a moment before answering. "Don't act like you don't already know. I'm doing the same thing as you," she finally says.

"I'm not acting like anything. What are we doing here exactly? What is the point?"

"I wanted to hurt Yami back, okay? I wanted to make her feel the way she made me feel when she dropped me out of her life!" She's yelling now, face red and eyes welling up.

"Fuck you!" I say, hypocritically. She's right that I'm no better, since we both did this to hurt my sister. Yami doesn't deserve that, from either of us. "We're done."

"Yeah, no shit," Bianca says, backing the car away and driving off. I flip her off again before storming inside, and she returns the favor.

Mami's working overtime today, and Yami's staying the night at Bo's, so I'm home alone for a few hours. I'm itching to do something with myself, but I have no idea what. Despite just having a fight with Bianca, I'm starting to get that euphoric feeling I got a while back, where everything feels just a little better than usual. Like I'm getting a glimpse of what heaven might be like. I lie back in my bed and smile, thanking God for giving me this little teaser.

His signal is coming tonight, I can feel it.

I jump out of bed and rush over to my desk, pulling out my notebook and a pen and getting to work right away. It's been so long since I've written in here, and I don't know where the urge comes from, but I need to write this down. Need to show the world what this calling from God looks like and how I plan on answering it when He tells me it's time.

I write about this little glimpse of heaven. About how before God gave me this glimpse, everything was uninteresting. Life before being chosen was boring and miserable. The colors were dull, the food bland. Even my bed feels more comfortable than before, the blankets silkier and the pillows softer.

I write about how I'm finally going to give everyone what they want from me.

I'm going to end it, and then I'll finally go home. I can finally be happy.

After I've filled pages upon pages of my notebook, I rip them out and lay the papers face up on the kitchen table. This is the world's most beautiful suicide note. It's the perfect gift to leave behind. They'll all have to realize this is what's best.

Now all that's left to do is wait for God's signal.

I leave my note for Yami and Mami to find, then rummage through the recycling bin, grabbing an empty water bottle. I take it to my mom's room and raid her secret liquor cabinet. If Bianca gets to have fun and get drunk tonight, so do I.

I grab a bottle of vodka and fill the water bottle to its brim before putting the glass bottle back in the cabinet. I don't even care if Mami notices the missing liquor. What's she going to do? Ground me? Send me to Abuela's? I'll be long gone before she has a chance.

I smile down at my phone. Nick posted the party's address on his Instagram stories like a dumbass. I pull up the address on my GPS and start walking. The sun's already been down for who knows how long. I must have lost track of time writing. It's a miracle I got out before Mami got home from working overtime.

It's only about a fifteen-minute walk, and when I get into the neighborhood, I realize I've been here before, many times.

It's a neighborhood surrounding a man-made lake. The lake right at the edge of Jamal's street. How could I forget they lived on the same block?

Resist temptation, I hear God say in my ear.

I almost fall on my ass when a truck honks loudly as it passes way too fast and way too close. I recognize the truck as one of Nick's friends', since it's not the first time I've almost been run over by it.

Bummer. That could have been a relatively easy way to go, but I guess I have to wait a little longer.

I make my way to the lake, and the water glistens against the moonlight so beautifully I completely forget about the truck and the party. I walk toward the lake and sit down at the edge, sticking my feet in the murky water.

Eventually my phone rings, and I look at it to see Mami's calling. I ignore it. She probably just got home way too late and saw my suicide note. I'm sure she's confused and wants to know where I am, but if I tell her, she'll just make me come back. I can't do that. Tonight is too special to waste at home.

About ten minutes and a few more missed calls later, it's Jamal who's calling me.

Him, I answer right away.

"Jamal, I'm gonna do it," I say.

"Do what?" He sounds worried. "Cesar, tell me you're safe."

"Be happy," I answer. "For you. I'm gonna do it for you."

"Where are you?" he asks, but my attention is drawn away by the sound of a few loud drunks who I'd *love* to get my fists on.

"You looking for a fight, Flores, you got one!" Nick calls out as he and his friends march up to me. Nick's friend must have told him he saw me here. Good.

"Cesar? Who's that?" Jamal asks frantically. "Are you okay?"

"I gotta go." I hang up, then stand to face them.

"Nick, calm down," Avery says, catching his breath as he jogs up behind the rest of the guys.

"Nah, he needs an ass whooping to set him straight," Nick says with a grin as he takes a step closer, but Avery runs in between me and Nick and holds his arms out to separate us. Why is he defending me? Maybe he just doesn't want to get in a fight since it would break his probation.

"It's not worth it, bro. Let's just go back," Avery says.

"No, let him come," I say as I take another step closer.

"Get out of my way or I'll beat your ass too," Nick threatens. Avery looks back and forth from me to Nick with fear in his eyes. He knows Nick is serious.

For the first time in all the fights I've had with Nick, Avery doesn't hold me down. This time, he runs away.

I look down at Nick's foot to see he's finally free of the boot. There's nothing holding him back anymore.

That's my signal.

I look the guys up and down. Five of them, and one of me. They could kill me if they wanted to.

I think about all the saints who were stoned or beaten to death. It's a noble way to go. A godly departure from this world.

I smile, and rush toward them.

32

WHEN EVEN DEATH WON'T KILL YOUR VIBE

mania

I don't even try going for a punch this time, I just full-on tackle Nick. As soon as we thud against the ground, I'm yanked back by my arms and dragged away from him. It takes four of them to pin me down, one for each arm and leg, and then Nick starts kicking me over and over.

I shut my eyes, waiting for him to kick me in just the right spot in my head and take me out, but he keeps his fists and feet on my stomach for the most part. I find myself gasping for air as the wind gets knocked out of me again and again.

"What's the matter? Can't breathe?" Nick asks as he raises his foot and brings it crashing down against my sternum.

"Fuck!" I wheeze, unable to hold back the outburst. "I'm . . . breathing just . . . fine . . . ," I taunt through coughs.

Nick motions his friends toward the lake. "How 'bout now?" he asks, and before I know it, I'm being dragged to the edge of the water. Two of them pull my arms behind my back, and Nick grabs the back of my neck firmly before shoving my head under.

I gasp at the shock of the water engulfing my face, filling my lungs. On instinct, I cough and try to inhale violently under the surface. My body convulses with each cough, lungs desperate for air and mind desperate for release. No matter how bad I want this, my body fights it, thrashing and struggling hard against the hands holding me down.

But it doesn't matter. Combined, they're all much stronger than I am, especially when I have no air in my lungs. Finally the edges of my blurry vision go dark and my lungs stop fighting to breathe.

Just when I'm about to give in to the pull of the darkness, the hands clumsily pull me out and throw me on the dry ground.

The coughing and hacking come back, and water spurts out of my mouth in waves. My vision is still spotty from almost succumbing to it, so it takes awhile for me to realize what's going on.

When my lungs are finally emptied of water, I look up to see Jamal and Avery standing in front of all five guys. I guess that explains why Avery ran off before. Jamal is talking to them with his hands up.

"Look, if you leave him alone now, I won't call the cops," he says calmly.

I'm anything but calm. If any of them puts a fucking finger on Jamal, I'll kill them. I see red as I push myself off the ground and rush forward, swinging at whoever's closest in the back of the head.

Then all hell breaks loose. Through the commotion, all I can see are fists flying. I can't even tell whose they are anymore. My vision goes white when someone punches my nose, stomach, chin, nose again. But the fists don't stop flying. Mine, I decide. They make contact more than they should be able to with how weak I am right now.

I can't see Jamal or Avery through the chaos. All I can see are fists and flashes of white.

Then something hard hits me in the back of my head, and white turns to black as I finally crumple to the ground.

33

WHEN IT ALL CATCHES UP TO YOU

guilt

"Cesar! Cesar, wake up! No, no, no, no, wake up!" Jamal's voice sounds distant and out of focus, but the five sets of running footsteps sound even farther away until they're gone. I don't know how long it is before Jamal's calls feels closer and closer, like I'm slowly coming out of a dream.

I groan, and shut my eyes harder than they already were, as if that will make the pounding in the back of my head go away.

"Cesar, can you hear me?" he asks, and it's weird hearing his voice sound so uncalm. "Look at me, Cesar."

"Mmm," I grumble as I finally open my eyes to see Jamal's and Avery's concerned forms hovering over me.

"I'm calling 911," Avery says.

"No, I'm fine," I say.

"Dammit, Cesar, I just woke you up in a puddle of your own blood! You're not fine! You need a hospital, we're calling 911," Jamal says, more firmly than I've ever heard him speak.

"We can't afford that," I protest weakly as Jamal scrambles to fish his phone out of his pocket.

"That doesn't matter right now!"

"Avery will get in trouble . . . ," I protest again. He broke probation fighting because of me.

"Don't worry about me," Avery says.

"Call my abuela instead, okay?" I insist. "She'll take me to the hospital. Please?"

There's a moment of hesitation before Jamal answers. "Fine. What's her number?"

My answer must not be coherent, because Jamal just digs right into my pocket and pulls out my phone, saying something I can't make out before I close my eyes again.

The next thing I know, I find myself lying soaking wet in the back of Abuela's car with my head in Jamal's lap and Avery looking back at me all concerned from the front seat. I look up at Jamal drowsily and notice for the first time that he's all bruised up, too. His lip is fat, and his eye is swollen with a cut splitting his brow.

This is not what I wanted. This could not possibly be what God wanted. Not only did I fail at ending things, but I pulled Jamal and Avery into it. This can't be right. Did I misunderstand the signal? Nothing makes sense. . . .

"I'm sorry," I croak. "I'm really sorry. . . ."

Then the world fades to black.

Someone wakes me up every thirty minutes or so in the hospital to make sure I'm okay since I apparently have a concussion. I don't know how long I'm lying on the cot before I finally wake up on my own. I don't open my eyes just yet.

Mami and Abuela are actually in the same room. And they're . . . talking?

"I'll come home with him. I can take care of him this week while you work, mija," Abuela says.

"That won't be necessary." Mami's voice.

"Why? Do you have another mother who can take care of him for you?"

"As a matter of fact, I do," Mami says coldly. She must be talking about Doña Violeta.

Okay, maybe them talking isn't the best thing right now. I open my eyes and groan, which gets their attention off each other.

"He's awake," Abuela says quietly.

Within seconds, Yami, my mom, Jamal, Avery, and my abuela are all surrounding the hospital bed.

"What happened?" I ask, trying to sit up, but Yami puts a hand on my chest and softly pushes me back down. I'm too weak to protest. I barely remember how I got here. All I remember is water filling my lungs.

"Your friends here filed a police report," Abuela says. "Those boys have already been arrested. They won't be hurting you any-more."

"What about Avery?"

"Worry about yourself," Avery says. He sounds on edge, but course corrects pretty quick. "I didn't get arrested or anything, and I still have that lawyer helping me. I'll be fine."

"You need to tell *us* what happened, mijo. What is going on with you? Are you self-harming?" Mami's voice quivers, and tears fill my eyes.

No one ever stopped caring about me, no matter what I did. I hurt all of them. But most of all, she's right. I hurt myself.

I nod, unable to deny it or admit it out loud.

I might not have been self-harming in the traditional sense, but everything I've done this year has been purposely self-destructive. I tried to get myself killed less than an hour ago.

I look at the worried faces around me, and the reality hits harder than any gut punch from Nick. If I died, they would all blame themselves. None of them would recover.

Despite my best efforts, I am loved.

"Do I have to go away again?" I ask as tears cling to my lashes, already knowing the answer.

"We found your note, mijo. You really need to get help," Mami says.

I let out a resigned sigh. I tried to end it tonight. Of course they're going to send me away. I don't know what else I could have expected.

I move to get up, but Yami puts a hand on my shoulder.

"You should rest. There's no rush to get up right now," she says.

Then I just burst out crying. I don't know if I have it in me to ask for help. But I can ask for one thing. "I just want a fucking hug," I whimper, and Jamal takes one of my hands while Abuela takes the other, and they help me to stand.

As soon as I'm out of the bed, all four of them gently wrap their arms around me, while Avery awkwardly pats my back. Then I can't help it. I start sobbing uncontrollably, held on my own two feet only by the strength of the embrace.

34

WHEN GOD IS GOD AND THE UNIVERSE AND SCIENCE AND ME AND HIM

questioning

It isn't until the next night that I'm cleared to leave the regular hospital and go to the mental one. I walk like a zombie as I'm led down the hall by a staff member, trying my best to ignore the pain brought on by the movement. It's only around ten, but everyone besides the staff is already asleep or pretending to be.

"Here's your bed," the lady says as she leads me into a room, gesturing to one of two uncomfortable-looking cots. The other one has a big blanket lump on it, which may or may not have a human underneath. Whoever's bed that is must have brought their own blanket or had someone else bring it, because the one on *my* cot is abysmally thin in comparison.

Another staff member walks past the door, and the lady helping me leans out to talk to him. "One of the phones is missing. Keep an eye out on your rounds."

I kind of surprise myself at how annoyed I am by that. If someone's hogging one of the phones, it'll be that much harder to get a call in. I didn't realize I even wanted to talk to anyone until the option was harder to grasp.

The woman turns back to me and starts giving me the rundown of what to expect, but I'm in way too much pain right now to be bothered to listen. Besides, I've been here before, so I don't really need to be briefed. The pain in my ribs reminds me why I'm here in the first place. God gave me the sign I'd been waiting for this whole time. I was supposed to end things, and I failed. Not only that, but I brought Jamal and Avery into it.

When I finally get left alone, I make my way to the cot and ease myself to sit at the edge. I'm about to brace myself to lie down when I notice something peeking out from the edge of my room-mate's blanket lump.

Looks like the phone hoarder is in the room.

When the staff inevitably finds it or it gets returned, I just know they're gonna start cracking down on phone use because of this. So I decide to seize the opportunity while it's here. I creep toward the other bed and gently ease the phone out from under the blankets.

Not even a stir.

Relieved, I go back to my own bed and dial the first number that comes to mind. My stomach sinks further down with every ring. All two of them.

"Hello?" Jamal finally answers, but it takes me a few seconds before I can bring myself to say anything back.

". . . Aren't you scared?" I finally whisper, gripping the phone tight.

"Cesar? What are you talking about?"

"It's me, yeah. . . ." For some reason, hearing Jamal's voice makes my own words that much harder to get out. I try to bring myself to speak, but all that leaves my mouth is one shaky breath after another.

"Nick and his friends already got arrested. They can't hurt you anymore. You're safe now." Jamal's voice is comforting, even if the words make no difference.

"No, not that," I say. "I mean, I'm pretty sure we're both going to hell . . . aren't you scared?"

"I don't think that's true," Jamal answers. I don't know how he manages to disagree without ever sounding argumentative.

"Why?" I ask.

"Okay, so . . ." He pauses for a moment, and I can so clearly picture him adjusting his glasses as he tries to figure out how to say what he's thinking. "From what I've heard, God is everywhere, all the time, right? Like, an intrinsic part of every aspect of life as we know it. There's no beginning and no end to his existence? So, if you think about it, isn't God just . . . the universe? Is the universe really that rigid about who we happen to fuck or fall in love with?"

"No," I say, almost defensively. "God is God. He *created* the universe. There are rules."

"Like the rules of science, right?" Jamal asks.

"I meant more like sins and virtues. Rules we have to choose to follow. Science is just the observation of things, so everything is science. It wasn't created, science is just . . . there."

"So, no beginning and no end . . . ?" I can almost hear his little smile in his tone, and I know what he's getting at before he says it. "Just an intrinsic part of existence as we know it. It's in everything, everywhere, all the time, kind of like the universe, right? Kind of like God?"

"No, not like that." I find myself laughing, despite my frustration. I miss talking with him like this. "You can't just go around saying random things are God. God is different."

"I don't know, I feel like everything is holy in a way. Aren't we all just an extension of the universe, or God, or whatever created us?"

My frustration dwindles to nothing as I realize how much sense it makes that Jamal would think like that. He's a really sentimental guy, and he appreciates everything in life, even when the good things are damn near impossible to find behind all the utter shit. Even if Jamal did believe in God, I doubt he'd worship out of fear the way I do.

It makes me think of the two necklaces I used to wear. If the jaguar represents facing fears, then does the cross represent everything I'm afraid of?

"My point is, we're both sinners," I say, trying to bring it back to my original question. "Aren't you afraid of going to hell after we die?"

Jamal's quiet again for a bit. "Well, however it happened, you and I both exist now. Whether that's because of the universe, or science, or God, or something else, it doesn't matter. We're here. *You're* here. . . ." His voice catches at that part, and I can hear him trying to rein himself in. "Maybe God exists, and maybe he doesn't, and no one will ever know with absolute certainty. But what I do know is that *you* exist, Cesar. I thought we were going to lose you, but you're still here. And I need you to know that your life is just as holy and precious as any god."

Even though I can't agree, I know he's not telling me he

worships me like a god. He's saying he sees me as an integral part of his universe. And I can't help but feel the same way about him. Maybe he is right, in a way. Maybe there is something holy about being completely intertwined with everything and everyone surrounding you.

Maybe there is something holy about loving every part of someone else, even, and especially, the parts made just like you.

35

WHEN YOU'RE FINALLY READY TO ASK FOR HELP. MAYBE? NO, PROBABLY NOT. NO, YES. DEFINITELY.

racing thoughts

HORIZON BEHAVIORAL HEALTH

Day One: Visiting Hours

"You look tired, mijo. Did you get any sleep last night?" Mami asks with a pained expression. Even though she and Yami probably came here together, it's just my mom sitting across the table from me. I don't know if it's because they're fighting like the last time I was in here or if both of them just want to have a private conversation, but I don't ask.

"Not really," I answer honestly. I know she's pretending the bruises around my eyes are dark circles to keep from bringing up the fight, and I'm okay with that. I find myself remembering the stories Abuela told me and Moni about Abuelo's trick to solve all her problems and help her sleep. "Maybe I need to grow my hair out so someone can braid it like Abuelo used to do for Abuela."

Her brows crease. "What are you talking about?"

"You know how Abuela said she couldn't sleep unless he braided her hair for her?"

She shakes her head, looking confused. "Your abuelo never did that. He tried to braid my hair once in my life and accidentally gave me a fat bald spot."

"That's what Abuela told me," I say with a shrug. I doubt she would lie about that, but maybe Mami just doesn't remember.

"Well, maybe we can find something similar for you, to help you sleep."

"I don't need you to help me figure out how to sleep." I sigh. These kinds of conversations never end well. It's just a bunch of suggestions that don't work from someone who's never had to even try counting sheep. If she did, she'd know that shit is pointless.

Mami frowns. "Well, what *do* you need my help with? I want to help, mijo. Just, tell me how, and I'll try my best."

"Well . . ." I hesitate for a second before saying anything, unsure if I should answer honestly or not. While thinking of things I want her to do for me is kind of impossible right now, there are a whole bunch of things I'd gladly have her *stop* doing. "I don't exactly love all the babying," I finally admit.

"Babying?" she asks, almost sounding offended.

"Yeah, like treating me like a helpless baby who needs constant protection and can do no wrong. I'm basically an adult!"

"Mijo, look where we are!" She gestures around the room wildly. "If I don't cradle you like a baby bird, you're going to fall out of the nest and break your neck!"

"But I'm not a baby bird!" I didn't realize how touchy this subject was going to be when it came up, but I'm already heated, and I can't stop myself from saying what I've been holding back since getting sent to Abuela's. "You're only involved in my life when I'm your perfect golden child, but when I'm here? When

I'm doing bad, you're always walking on eggshells! You look like just the sight of me makes you want to cry, like I'm that much of a disappointment. You act like I'm just a bomb you don't want to set off. . . ." My voice cracks when I realize that's kind of what I was.

Her lip quivers, but instead of arguing, she just sits there waiting for me to get it all out. But I don't know if I can. Being the grenade I was, I always thought my mom would be the type of parent who'd hold me to her chest and die with me as I exploded. Instead, she threw me across enemy lines and let me go off somewhere she didn't have to watch.

"You know what, Mami, I do need something from you."

"Anything, mijo." She reaches across the table with her palm up like an invitation for me to hold on. I don't take it yet. I need to hear her answer first.

"I can't be a gifted prodigy kid my whole life. When everyone acts like I'm perfect, like I have so much limitless potential, all it does is make it that much worse when I can't pretend anymore. I need to feel like you're my mom, *all* the time. If you're only happy around me when I'm pretending to be perfect, how am I supposed to feel? It's like you're scared of me being anything real! Just because I can't be your golden child doesn't mean I'm not still your son."

She wipes her eyes, but then puts her hands back on the table, palms up so I can still reach for them if I want to. "I'm so sorry, mijo. I love you no matter what. You're my son, you're always my son, okay?"

And I know it feels counterintuitive, but I grab her hand for comfort, even though I'm still so angry. "Then why did you leave me? Why couldn't *you* be the one to take care of me when I started spiraling?" Despite how frustrated I am, it feels good to get the words out, and when she squeezes my hand, it does calm the shaking.

"I . . . I really tried to be the one to take care of you, but it was like I could feel my influence on you fading. I wanted to help, but I thought you couldn't hear me. Like whatever I said just kept making things worse."

"Because you don't understand me!" I blurt out, trying not to yell and lose my visiting privileges before getting to see Yami.

"I know I don't understand you, that's why I sent you to your abuela's! Even if I have a hard time with her, she at least knows what you're going through. I thought maybe her experience could help you more than I could."

"If you need help, Mami, then ask for help! You could have had Abuela come and help without completely abandoning me without any warning. It's no wonder you didn't even know she needed her hair braided to fall asleep. You don't pay attention or listen to her either! You said it yourself, she's like me. If you hate her so much, how do you think that makes me feel?"

She's quiet for a while, still holding tight to my hand. "My relationship with my mother is . . . complicated. And I'll admit I may have let some of my grievances against her affect how much pressure I put on you. But I do love both of you. I can see how my problems with my mother have affected you, and I'm so sorry for that. I'll . . ." She lets out a breath like she needs to hype herself up. "I'll talk to her. But on one condition, okay?"

I squint at her, but answer. "What?"

"You ask for help when you need it, too. We can both work on that, together."

I take a deep breath of my own. Asking for help has never been my strong suit. Luckily, before I have a chance to answer her, the alarm on her phone goes off.

"Yami's turn," she tells me, then gives my hand another squeeze since we're not allowed to hug. I don't let go of her hand, though.

"Yami needs you too, you know," I say before she can leave. I expect her to ask for clarification so I can tell her to stop being so hard on Yami and pay attention to her too. Instead, she just nods solemnly. She already knows.

"You're right." Tears fill her eyes again. "I could spend a lifetime apologizing and it wouldn't be enough."

"Yeah, same . . . ," I admit. I wish I didn't relate to that so much. Of course it's easy to give advice like "Just apologize, what's the worst that could happen?" But that would make me a hypocrite. Once again, Mami seems to know where I'm coming from without me having to explain.

She's quiet for a while, biting her cheek in contemplation. Eventually she says, "Maybe I've been doing this all wrong. Asking for forgiveness from God instead of talking to the people I've hurt. I'll work on that, too."

She gives my hand a final squeeze, then rushes out to give Yami some time with me. I was barely able to hold it together for my mom, but for some reason seeing Yami doubles the size of the lump in my throat. She sits down across from me, setting a bag of Takis on the table as a peace offering just like she did when I was in here last year.

The simple gesture makes me choke on an unexpected sob.

I cover my face with my hands and whimper into them. "I don't deserve this," I say, the words muffled behind my palms.

"Everyone deserves Takis," Yami jokes, but when I don't laugh, she gently coaxes my hands away from my face to hold them on the table and squeezes.

Even after she literally held me while I sobbed in her arms the week before, I just can't wrap my head around why she's still here, holding my hands. I don't even care that the other patients can see me breaking down right now. It doesn't matter. All that matters is that I say what I need to say to Yami. What I should have said ages ago.

"I'm sorry," I choke out. The words don't come easy, but they still don't feel like they could ever be enough. "I'm sorry, I'm sorry. . . ."

"Hey, it's okay. It's okay."

"It's not, though," I say. "I did the worst possible thing I could think to do to you, and you're still here. You're still giving me Takis like you're the one who needs to apologize. Everyone's still trying to give me whatever I need. I might not always have the best grip on reality, but I did that shit. I know that much was real, and I don't want to brush it off because you're worried about me." I pull my hands away from hers and hug myself.

"It was real," Yami admits. "I still don't know why you did all that, but you did. I thought things were getting better after we talked, but now you're here, and clearly, I missed something, or—"

"Yami, it's not your fault I'm here," I interrupt. After everything, she needs to know that much. Maybe she needs to know all of it. I stare at the table while I tell her since I know I can't handle looking in her eyes right now. "When I was in that space, like, wanting to make it all stop, I thought the only way to end things without ruining everyone's lives was if I made you all hate me first.

When I get like that, I want to push you all away so you're not sad when I die."

From the corner of my eye, I see Yami wiping her tears before I look back up at her. But I'm not done yet. She needs to know one more thing.

"I need you, Yami. But I don't want my life to dictate yours. You should get what *you* want in life, too." I finally look up at her, so she really gets it. "I know I don't act like it, but when life is good, you're one of the reasons why. I feel like I'm the opposite for you."

"You're not! How do you not get that I need you too? I need you just as bad, okay? Please, don't leave. . . ."

I blink away the tears welling up in my eyes. This whole time, she needed me too, and I abandoned her, just like I was so mad at my mom for doing to me. "I'll try not to," I manage to calm myself enough to get out.

"Cesar, I need you to really hear me right now, okay?" she looks at me almost as intensely as Jamal usually does. "You deserve to be loved."

"Bullshit," I say, feeling my lips shrug like I'm gonna cry again. "You should hate me. You should fucking yell at me or something. Hit me or throw something! Get yourself kicked out, *that's* what I deserve!"

She just shakes her head. "I couldn't possibly punish you any worse than you're punishing yourself—and why would I want to? I love you. If you don't believe me, I'll tell you again."

"I believe you," I say with a hand up so she doesn't keep saying it and make me cry again. "But I want to fix it, Yami. Just tell me what to do to make it up to you and I'll do it."

"If staying alive is all you can do, it's enough. It's like I said before, I need you too. You make my life better when you're in it." She smiles and nudges the bag of Takis toward me. "I just want you to be okay."

"I can't promise you that," I say. After everything, I don't want to put a Band-Aid over it by making a promise I can't be 100 percent sure I'll keep.

"Then I want you to tell someone when you need support. If it's not me, that's fine, just tell someone. I want you to stop shutting everyone out. I want you to stop trying to brave all of this alone."

"Okay." I swallow the lump in my throat. That, I can at least try. "I promise."

Day Two: Visiting Hours

Since they actually check to make sure you take your meds here, I don't really have the option to fake it like I've been doing. I don't really know what that means for me. I mean, I'm at least at a place now where I can admit I was a mess without the meds, but was I any better with them? I'm not so sure. Besides, Moni's anecdote about her dad paying off doctors gets to me. What if I just go right back to being brainwashed?

Luckily, I don't have to wait long to ask her about it, since the next person to visit is Moni.

She starts talking before she's done pulling out her chair. "Abuela wanted to get you some snacks, so she's at the vending machine."

I'm actually kind of relieved to have a minute with just Moni so I can ask what I want. We probably don't have a ton of time, so I start talking before she has a chance to ask her own questions. I'd rather steer the conversation my own way than have to answer any "How are you feeling?" types of questions.

"How's your dispensary fundraising going?" I ask, trying to find a segue to talking about the meds.

Moni shrugs, looking confused about the question. I guess I can't blame her, considering where we are. Luckily, she humors me. "My Tampots are selling faster than I can make them, so that's a good sign! I've been thinking of hiring some help so I don't have to be as selective about who to sell to, but expanding a business like mine comes with risks, you know?"

She goes on to tell me all the details of said risks and I'm already regretting my choice of segue. Abuela's quickly making her way toward me, so my window is basically over. I clear my throat to try and signal to Moni that she should stop talking about anything that could get her in trouble before Abuela reaches us, but she doesn't seem to get the hint.

"Moni—" I try to interrupt, but she doesn't even seem to hear me. By the time she realizes I'm trying to help her, Abuela's already sitting in the chair next to her with a bag of chips in her hand.

"Surprise! Abuela brought snacks!" Moni grabs the chips and sets them in front of me as if Abuela didn't hear a thing.

"I would be thanking the Lord we're in this hospital right now if I were you," Abuela says firmly.

"What do you expect me to do?" Moni tilts her head innocently. "How else am I supposed to raise the funds to open my own dispensary? To even go to college?" I know Moni has no shame about what she does, but she apparently has the same amount of self-preservation instincts.

Abuela pinches the bridge of her nose. "If you get caught, there's no way you would be allowed to open a dispensary. You know that, right?"

"Then I won't get caught." She shrugs, and a little laugh escapes from me.

"You already got caught, though," I jump in. I might be a little cynical, but it's not like it's outside the realm of possibilities. She said so herself, he's desperate. "If your dad really wants you to stop, what makes you think he won't report you himself?"

Moni opens her mouth to answer, but all that comes out is a little croak.

"We'll talk about this later, Monica," Abuela says, then turns to me, and I just know she's about to ask how I'm feeling or something, so I go first.

"Anyways." I decide to just ask outright since the segue was a bust and I got Moni in trouble for nothing. "Are the doctors at places like this fair game for your dad too?"

"Huh?" Moni asks, and Abuela raises an eyebrow.

"You said your dad pays doctors off to brainwash their patients. Is that a thing here too?"

Her eyes widen a bit. "Shit, did you go off your meds because of me?"

"I was already off them," I admit, making a point not to look at Abuela's probably disappointed face. "But why would I go back on them if they're brainwashing me?"

"I never said they were for brainwashing!" Moni sounds a little frantic. Not really used to her like that. "It's true that some drug companies pay some doctors to prescribe their preferred medication, but I wasn't trying to imply *your* doctor was being paid off or anything."

"Well, how can I trust *any* doctor if that's a thing? Don't act like I'm being paranoid if that's something that actually happens!" I ball my fists to stop my hands from shaking in anger. This isn't me being crazy. She *told* me that happens!

Abuela nods, and I almost think she's about to agree with me, until she doesn't. "Mijo, there's nothing wrong with having these kinds of worries, but it's good to voice them out loud instead of holding them in. That way you can take a step toward finding the truth instead of just being afraid."

Moni nods quickly. "We can find out right now actually! It's publicly accessible information which doctors are taking money from drug companies." She pulls out her phone and starts typing. "What's your therapist's name again?"

"Uh, Dr. Lee . . . I think her first name's Jen."

She types for a second before showing me her screen with Dr. Lee's name and the office address. "Is this the right place?"

I nod, scanning the page. There are different types of payments listed, like research payments and investment interest. I don't know what any of them mean, but I can relax knowing there's a big N/A next to each and every type.

Somehow, I'm both relieved and incredibly embarrassed. "I guess I really am crazy, huh?"

Abuela frowns. "Mijo, there's nothing crazy about asking questions. It's almost impossible to find the truth without speaking your fears out loud. Sometimes being perceived as 'crazy' is the scariest thing, so saying what you're afraid of feels harder than giving in to the paranoia. But I promise it's worth it."

"And tell me next time I say something that freaks you out like that, okay? I can't help you logic out of it unless I know what you're thinking," Moni says. "Sometimes I forget people can't see everything in my brain, so I don't always explain myself like I should."

"Okay," I say tentatively. I guess I can try saying things out loud. Maybe not to everyone, but at least I know Abuela will understand. I don't know if every fear I have can just be logic-ed away, but at least this one could. Maybe that's a start.

Day Three: Activity Time

Instead of getting to go outside with the other patients, I'm escorted to an activity room during free time. When the door opens, I'm met with my usual group therapy crowd, including Dr. Lee and even Nia.

"What are you guys doing here?" I ask.

"Avery told us you were in here, so we asked Dr. Lee if we could get special permission to have group here instead of at the office today," Zo says with a smile.

"Oh . . ." I don't know what else to say. If this had happened a week ago, I would have turned around and run away. I would have been pissed at Avery for telling anyone about where I am. Today is different, though. Today, I walk over to the empty seat in the circle and sit down. Maybe I am making progress.

I can't help but notice everyone's staring at me when I sit down, though. I wish I could hide the fact that I'm struggling so hard, but the bruises are literally all over my face, not to mention where we are.

"You guys were on the news," Nia says bluntly, looking back and forth from me to Avery, who is also sporting a pretty gnarly black eye. "Apparently those guys are waiting for their hearing in juvie, so you should be safe from them now."

"And if they try to fuck with you again, we'll handle 'em," Aaron adds, puffing out his chin like he's trying to look tough.

"You okay, though?" Zo asks, and I bite my lip, resisting the urge to brush it off and say I'm fine. How hard could it be to admit I'm not okay? When I'm here, of all places? "It's okay to ask for help," they say, like they're reading my mind.

"We're here for you, bro," Avery adds with a reassuring nod.

But when I try to speak, I get all choked up. They know I'm not okay. I just need to admit it out loud. That's the first step, right? I lean forward and cover my face with my hands again. Maybe if I can't see them staring at me it'll be easier?

"I need help!" I whimper through my hands.

"Asking for help is an important first step," Dr. Lee confirms. "I'm proud of you."

Zo starts rubbing my back from their seat next to me. "How can we help you?" they ask.

"I think . . . ," I start, mulling it over. "I think I need to switch medication. I've been back on my meds since I got in here, but I don't feel like it's doing anything." After I say it, I feel a huge weight off my chest. "But I'm afraid to switch and have bad side effects or go on meds that make me like a zombie." I figure now is as good a time as any to implement the say-your-fears-out-loud advice.

"It's a process," Nia says. "Sometimes it takes a while for them to really kick in, and sometimes you have to try a few to find the right ones, but once you do, it's like magic."

"Mine took a couple weeks before I started noticing a change," Avery adds. "Like, I know I'm still mentally ill, but I can deal a lot better now."

"It's all about communication," Dr. Lee adds. "As long as you let me know when you have any side effects or if a few weeks pass and you still feel like your meds aren't working, we can go from there."

"Okay," I say.

Maybe Dr. Lee isn't as bad as I thought. I don't know if I fully trust her yet, but at least I know she doesn't have any ulterior motives about my medication.

Could medication actually make me feel better? I don't know. But for the first time in a long time, I let myself feel a tiny bit hopeful.

Day Four: Phone Call

Jamal has managed to call me every night since I've been in the hospital, but I've always been in group or the line has been busy, so aside from the first night, we've missed each other until now. When the staff tells me the phone's for me, I recognize his number immediately.

"Hey, you," I find myself saying.

"Hey, you," he says back.

And even though we can't talk long, even though it's just a "hey, you," I still feel like it's a sign that things might just be salvageable between us. Maybe Abuela was right. Maybe it's possible to fix things. Maybe I even want to.

Day Five: Visiting Hours

When I get called to the visiting room the next day, I'm surprised when it's not my mom or Yami, but Doña Violeta who wants to talk to me. We both sit at the table staring at each other for a bit before either of us says anything.

It's weird seeing her without her music blasting on her porch. She's usually so enveloped in the melody that she sways as she speaks and talks rhythmically with the beat, but today she seems to be choosing her words more carefully.

At first I want to stay mad at her. She did lie to me about that doctor's appointment before dropping me off at Abuela's. Then again, I know it was my mom who put her up to it. I know everyone was just scrambling trying to figure out what to do with me. It sucks, and it still stings to think about, but if Yami and Jamal can forgive me after everything I've done, maybe there's a little extra grace to go around.

"Do you want to play a song on your phone or something?" I ask after we're both just quiet for a while, but Doña just shakes her head.

"You are my music today, mijo." She smiles sweetly, rocking back and forth in her chair as if there was a melody playing. She still doesn't say much, and I can't bear to just stare at each other like this.

"How did you get better?" I blurt out. Doña Violeta was practically inconsolable for over a year after her husband died. She didn't take care of herself, barely ate, and spent all her time crying on her porch.

"That's a good question." She smiles again. "I guess I let the people around me help me. I allowed myself to lean on my loved ones. On you, and your mami, and Yamilet. And when you went to the hospital last year, I realized I needed to take care of you back. Loving you was loving myself."

I think back to the poem on my bathroom mirror.

Si te amo y respeto, me amo y respeto yo.
If I love and respect you, I love and respect myself.

And I do love, hard. I love Doña Violeta. I love my abuela. I love Moni. I love my mom. I love Yami. I love Jamal.

I'm *in love* with Jamal. Still.

And I've treated everyone like absolute shit. Hurting them to hurt myself. And it worked, for a while. But I don't want to hurt them anymore. Maybe I don't want to hurt myself either. I don't feel like the solution is to push everyone away anymore. I want to fix my relationships. I want to deserve their love. I know it'll take work, and time, and a lot of healing, but I want to do it.

It's like Jamal said. They're all an integral part of my universe, and I can't even begin to unravel who I am without the community standing beside me, the community whose roots I'm growing and blooming from. And maybe spring isn't as far off as I thought.

36

WHEN TALKING ABOUT FEELINGS MIGHT ACTUALLY GET US SOMEWHERE JUST THIS ONE TIME

acceptance

When we get home from the hospital the next morning, both Abuela's and Doña Violeta's cars are parked on the curb. I try to gauge my mom's reaction without being too obvious, but she doesn't seem fazed. Did she plan this?

When we come inside, Abuela and Doña Violeta stand from their spots on the couch, but my mom stops them.

"No, no, we'll all sit," she says as she ushers us all into the living room. It almost feels like an intervention. Part of me is bummed that Moni's not here to ease the tension, since apparently she's spending another weekend trip with her dad and won't be back until tomorrow. Then again, something tells me this is an immediate-family kind of conversation, whatever that means for us.

I sit next to Abuela, with the rest on the other couch. "We need to clear the air. Life is too precious to hold it all in and live with regrets, and I know I'm not the only one who needs to get something off my chest. I want us to be able to hash things out as a family. I'll go first."

Mami closes her eyes as her mouth moves like she's saying a quick prayer to herself. We all just kind of sit there in silent anticipation with no idea what's about to happen. Eventually she gives herself the sign of the cross and continues.

"I have some apologies I need to share. First of all, to you, Mami."

"To me?" Abuela looks at my mom like she's trying to solve an impossible math equation in her head. "Mija, you don't have to—"

"No, I do. Just let me say this, okay, Mami? I can't pretend to understand everything that's happened, but I know it's not as simple as I used to think. I know you're trying now, and I know calling you crazy instead of trying to understand didn't help our situation." She turns to me at that. "And, Cesar, I'm so sorry for anything I might have said about your abuela that you ended up internalizing. I don't think either of you are crazy, okay?"

My heart gets heavy. It's true that every time I heard my mom call my grandma crazy, it made it a little harder to breathe. Like if she hated her mom so much for being crazy, was that how she felt about me?

"I am crazy, though," I admit.

"Okay, then I'll say this." Mami looks at me with tears in her eyes. "I'm not ashamed of you. Not for being bisexual, and not for being bipolar. Either of you."

Abuela smiles, her eyes also getting a bit misty. "Thank you, mija."

I want to say something too, but my words are stuck in my throat. Mami doesn't seem to be done yet, though, so maybe that's all right.

"And, Yami." She turns to face Yami, who's sitting next to her. Both of them are already getting choked up. "I love you more than I can put into words, and I'm so, so sorry for everything I've said or done to make you feel otherwise. You've carried so much on your shoulders over the years, and I need you to know that it's enough. *You* are enough."

By the time Mami's done with all her apologies, at least half the room is in tears, and she and Yami are holding hands like their lives depend on it. Then Mami starts looking around at the rest of us, as if to say "Who's next?"

I won't lie, the idea of apologizing for everything I've done to all these people right now scares the shit out of me, so I'm relieved when Abuela volunteers herself next.

"I need to apologize too, mija," she says to my mom. "I know I didn't make things easy on you growing up. Now that you've given me the chance to be in your life again, I promise to be a better mother and grandmother for the rest of mine. I don't take this gift for granted. And . . . I also want to apologize to you, Viva." She shifts her gaze to Doña Violeta, who smiles, not at all fazed by the play on her name. "I made a choice, all those years ago, and I can admit now that it was the wrong one. Even if I suffered more for it, I'm sorry."

"I'm sorry too," Doña Violeta says. "I should have kept in touch then. I was so glad to hear you've been doing better recently, but I regret that I wasn't a part of that journey." Doña Violeta's apology makes me think about how I've felt about Jamal lately. About how much I've missed.

Not being a part of his journey with coming out and all his

performances was one of the hardest parts about pushing him away. I need to fix that.

"And I'm sorry to you too, Cesar." Doña Violeta turns to me now. "I shouldn't have lied to you."

"I wouldn't have gone with you to Abuela's if you told the truth," I admit. "But don't do it again."

"Promise, mijo," she says with a smile.

"Okay, I'll go next," Yami says with a shaky breath, and I know what she's about to say before she gets it out. Even though she has nothing to apologize for, it must be scary bringing this up to our mom. I give her an encouraging nod so she knows I have her back. "I've been keeping a secret from you, Mami. I didn't say anything because I haven't really decided yet, but . . ." She pauses, running her hands over her braid nervously. "I didn't just get into ASU. Bo and I both got into the art program at NAU." She avoids my mom's gaze.

I can't help but smile. She said it out loud, which tells me how bad she wants this. She's never been super sure of what she wanted to do after high school, so this is clearly a bigger deal than she's letting on.

The few seconds of silence waiting to see Mami's reaction feels like forever. She eventually wipes a tear and clears her throat. "I'm so proud of you, mija. That's really great news."

"Really?" Yami looks more confused than relieved. "If you need me to stay to help with the business, I can. And, Cesar, literally, if you tell me you need me here, I'll go to ASU instead. I don't want to abandon you guys."

"Yami, stop," I say, my voice coming out softer than she's used to from me lately. "You want to go to NAU, right? When have you ever considered your own needs before mine? For once in your life, do what *you* want to do."

"But are you gonna be okay if I leave?"

I hate that I can't confidently say I will. But if I'm not, it's not on her. "I don't know," I answer honestly. "But I definitely won't be okay if you don't go to the college you want because of me. You should go."

Yami opens her mouth like she's about to protest, but Mami stops her. "Mija, I want you to do what is best for you and your future. I'll be here with your brother, and so will Violeta and your abuela. We've got plenty of support to go around. You've done more than enough for all of us. It's time you do something for yourself."

Mami's barely finished her sentence before Yami throws herself into a hug. "Thank you, Mami. I'll call all the time, and we can all visit whenever." She pulls away. "I love you guys so much, but . . . I do really want to go."

"Then it's settled," Mami says, squeezing Yami's hand.

It's quiet for a bit before I realize I'm the only one who hasn't apologized yet. And probably the one who has the most apologizing to do, even if they probably don't expect me to say anything.

I feel almost like I'm going to confession, but this time it's not God I need forgiveness from. Instead of waiting for someone to change the subject and let me off the hook, I just start blurting out all of it.

I apologize for everything I can remember doing. Hooking up with Bianca, lashing out at everyone, yelling at Yami and my mom, being so mean to everyone else and myself, and even not following through with making Sunday dinners. I basically get it all out without stopping for air, but I'm still holding my breath when I'm done.

I still can't breathe until Yami gets up and pulls me into a hug. Then everyone else joins in, and before I know it, I'm wrapped up like a cinnamon roll, and I can't tell if I'm laughing or crying. Maybe both.

After the emotional roller coaster that was that whole conversation, I'm probably exhausted enough to sleep for several days. Doña Violeta and Abuela promise to come back for dinner tomorrow, but they all keep hanging out for a bit while I let myself go take a nap. For the first time in a long time, sleep comes easily and peacefully.

When I wake up again, I check my phone to see it's already eleven at night. My throat is dry as hell—I might be dehydrated from the crying—so I get up for some water. When I get to the end of the hallway, I'm surprised to hear Abuela and Doña Violeta still awake and having a quiet conversation.

It feels intimate, so I try to be discreet as I sneak past them and into the kitchen to give them some privacy. It isn't until I turn back around with my water that it all makes sense.

Doña Violeta is sitting on the couch with Abuela on the floor, head between Violeta's knees. There's a relaxed smile on Abuela's lips as she closes her eyes while Doña Violeta gently braids her hair. They must have just started, because the braid is still only a few inches off Abuela's scalp. Doña Violeta hums softly as her hands weave effortlessly through my abuela's hair like she's done it a million times before.

Because she has.

It wasn't my abuelo who braided Abuela's hair all those years ago, but Doña Violeta. *She's* the one Abuela called "her love" in all the stories she told me and Moni. The person she had to learn how to sleep without. Was my grandpa the "choice" Abuela was talking about when she apologized? It doesn't take long to get my confirmation in the form of a snore.

She's already asleep.

It may have been years since this was normal for them, but right now it looks like the most natural thing in the world. If I'm right—and I know I am—it's been ages since they've been able to be intimate like this.

But looking at them now, if I didn't know any better, I'd think they never stopped.

37

WHEN YOU DON'T WANT TO BE A BOMB ANYMORE

progress

Despite the hours-long nap I took yesterday, I guess I was emotionally exhausted enough to sleep through the entire night and half the day. When I eventually crawl out of bed and into the living room, I realize it's already almost time to start getting dinner ready.

I know no one expects me to keep up with the Sunday cooking promise I made months ago, especially not right now, but I don't know. It feels like a good gesture to help Yami and my mom with dinner. Like if I can do this one thing, even if it's just for today, even if it's not how I originally planned, maybe that means things can get better.

I head to the kitchen, where Yami's already digging in the fridge and my mom's filling a pot with water to boil.

"Need some help?" I ask, and they both turn around like I jump scared them.

I expect them to keep babying me and insist I rest up instead, but Mami smiles and gestures toward the vegetables on the chopping board. "I'd love that."

With the three of us working together, we end up spending

more time just talking than we do cooking. Not about anything important, but it still feels good. I don't remember the last time I laughed about nothing.

Before long, there's a knock on the door before the lock turns, and Doña Violeta, Abuela, and Moni all come in. I almost go in for a hug with Moni before I remember she doesn't do those. Usually I'm not a huge hugger for no reason either, but I kind of thought maybe she wouldn't be coming back from visiting her dad this time. It's been a really long punishment.

After we all say hi, Mami shoos me, Yami, and Moni away to the living room so she can talk with Abuela and Doña Violeta. I guess we're off dinner duty for now. Instead of following us to the living room, though, Yami goes to the bathroom. I know she and Moni aren't exactly close anymore, but I can't tell if she's purposely avoiding her or not.

"So, you still not going back to L.A.?" I ask when we're out of earshot of everyone else.

"It's okay, I like it here way better," Moni says as she plops down on the couch. "My dad thought I'd cave by now and go to the school he wants, but that's not gonna happen."

"That sucks," I say. I can't help but feel bad that I was able to start repairing things with my mom, but Moni is still going through the same shit. She knows better than anyone else how I felt being the family disappointment. Somehow, though, Moni never seems to feel guilty or bothered in the least by what her dad thinks of her. "You okay?"

"Yeah, why wouldn't I be?" she asks. "I did think about what you and Abuela said about the dispensary. I don't want to sabotage my business before it even starts, so I decided to put a pause on things. For now."

"It'll be okay," I say, trying to make her feel better, because Moni actually seems pretty bummed. Honestly, I'm surprised; Moni's not usually one to change her mind about something, so it feels like a big deal.

"Don't worry about me. Abuela said we could find another way to fund it together," Moni says with a smile. "And I'm an entrepreneur. I'll definitely figure it out. At least Abuela doesn't act like I'm a failure for wanting to do anything besides play the violin for the rest of my life. But, um, you're the one who went there, so . . . are *you* okay?"

Dammit. I did go there first, I guess . . . I'm done lying about it, but I also don't really know how to respond. I decide to answer with another question. "Don't you feel guilty? Everyone expects us to be the next big thing, but we're just always getting in trouble."

She looks at me like I'm speaking gibberish. "Why would *I* feel guilty about other people being wrong? Sounds like a them problem to me."

I laugh. Her answer reminds me of the email Abuela sent me a while back about us being fig trees trying to make grapes. Maybe they're both right. If I didn't worry about what anyone expected out of me, would I still feel like a disappointment? I definitely still did a lot of shitty things, but maybe I wouldn't have been so set on acting that way if I wasn't trying to prove something.

Before we get too into it, Yami comes out from the bathroom. She stands there awkwardly for a second before saying, "Um, hey, Moni."

"Hey, Yami."

I don't know why they're being weird, but it doesn't last long since Abuela comes calling us over to the table just then. Besides Yami and Moni's awkwardness, it's nice to be hanging out and eating dinner with everyone. I've aired out all my shit, and they're all still here.

Yami stays quiet most of dinner, and I almost think I'm the only one who notices until Moni calls it out.

"So, Yami, do you have a problem with me or something?" The words feel confrontational, but her tone isn't. Knowing Moni, she's just genuinely curious.

If this happened another time, Yami might have gotten defensive and denied it, but maybe our group apology intervention changed things.

"I don't have a problem with *you*. I just . . ." She trails off. "I just kind of feel like I got replaced, you know? You and Cesar got so close lately, and I didn't get to hang out with either of you. Like, me and Cesar are good now, but I feel like everyone here knows you except for me."

Doña Violeta, my mom, and my abuela exchange a quick telepathic message I can't decipher before they all stand up at the same time.

"I'll help your mami with cleanup, all right?" Doña Violeta says, and Abuela's adding on almost immediately after. "Cesar, mijo, what do you say we go for a ride?" she asks, not bothering with subtlety. "I think your prima and your sister could use some quality time."

Moni looks at Yami expectantly, like she's afraid of what her reaction might be. Yami just smiles. It's a nervous smile, but she doesn't seem upset.

"That sounds like a good idea, actually," Yami says.

"Really?" Moni asks, lighting up a bit.

"Yeah. I miss you," Yami admits.

"I miss you too," Moni says before my mom practically shoves them into the living room so they can have some semblance of privacy.

Normally I'd be suspicious of an offer to go for a ride alone right after getting out of the hospital. It just screams "Let's have an emotional heart-to-heart!" But this time it's not about me. Moni and Yami should really talk. Besides, maybe a heart-to-heart with my grandma isn't the worst thing in the world.

"Okay, let's go," I say as I hop up from the table and follow my abuela to the door, leaving Yami and Moni to talk it out.

When we get in the car, I'm expecting Abuela to start with some small talk like people usually do before they get into what they really want to say, but she doesn't.

"I'm sure you have questions," she says instead.

"Huh?" Not exactly the question she was probably expecting, but I have no idea what she's talking about, so I got nothing.

"Violeta told me you saw us last night." She says it like I caught them doing something way more scandalous than braiding hair. I didn't even realize Doña Violeta knew I was watching, but I guess there's no use lying if they both know I saw them.

"Doña Violeta was your first love, wasn't she? The one you told me and Moni about?"

Abuela just nods.

"Does anyone else know?" I ask.

She shakes her head. "Not yet, at least. I wanted to tell you first, but you beat me to the punch." She laughs.

"Why me?" That makes no sense. Why would she want to tell me, of all people?

"Because I want you to learn from my mistakes, mijo."

"What are you talking about?" My face gets hotter. Does she know about Jamal? Who would have told her? And *why*?

"I saw the way you and that boy looked at each other at the hospital," she says with a smile. "I know that look. I've lived the life you're trying to make for yourself. It's heartbreaking to see you following in my footsteps without even knowing it."

I want to ask what made her choose my grandpa over Doña Violeta, but I feel like I already know the answer. Abuela's just as religious as I am, if not more. It's not why she made the choice she did that confuses me, but why she'd choose differently now.

"What changed?" I end up asking.

"I used to fear God more than anything, but I've changed." She pauses for a moment as the car slows at a stoplight. "I use the Bible to understand things better, but the original version was written by men doing their best interpretation of the word of God. Never mind that the current version has been translated and edited into something completely different."

It takes me a second to let that sink in. I guess I knew it was true, but I never really considered what that meant. "So how do you know which parts to live by and what some random guy forever ago decided to change?"

"Nothing is set in stone, but I will take any opportunity to learn more about the context behind the scriptures I read. I have to be open to being wrong and diving into the meaning. But I think the people who hate us read the Bible differently than I do. They cherry-pick the verses that confirm their worldview and shut their eyes to everything else. But I think those people believe in a different God than I do."

For some reason, hearing her say that makes me want to cry. Maybe I'm just so off emotionally from all the ups and downs lately, but it seems like everything I lived by (and almost died by) is just falling apart right in front of me. What if I was wrong about all of it? I'm scared of what the answer might be, but I already promised I'd voice my fears instead of letting them build.

"What if they're right, though?"

With one hand on the wheel, she reaches the other over to squeeze my shoulder. "No one can know for sure until they die, right? But if I can be sure about one thing *now*, it's that I still love my Violeta." Her voice softens at Doña Violeta's name, and she smiles. "If I'm right, then I'll die and spend an eternity with my loved ones in heaven. But if I'm wrong, then I won't have the afterlife to spend with my Violeta. If I'm wrong, then all we have is now, and I've wasted too much of this life without her already. I want you to spend yours with someone who makes you happy."

It takes me awhile to respond to that. She's right that Jamal makes me happy. I've always felt safe around him. He makes me laugh and doesn't expect me to be anything I'm not. But . . . what if he's not happy with me? After everything I did, what if I can't make him happy anymore?

"But what if it's too late?" I ask, barely above a whisper. She pulls into our driveway and parks, but neither of us moves to get out.

"You won't know unless you ask, right?"

I nod hesitantly. Maybe there is a chance. And if there's any way I can make things up to Jamal, I have to at least try.

It isn't until after everyone goes to their rooms for the night that I realize I might have one more sentimental conversation left in me. That talk with Abuela has me questioning everything. I've been wrong about so much, but I finally feel like I'm starting to understand the people around me. I used to think *I* was the one nobody understood. I thought no matter how hard people tried, they wouldn't really get me. But looking back on everything that led me here, it's me who hasn't made much of an effort to figure out anyone else.

I haven't exactly been the most consistent person in the world. It didn't matter what I thought I wanted. No matter what my mom did, I was mad about it. I'm still not really sure why, but everyone keeps telling me I have to talk about things instead of letting them stew. So, instead of going to bed confused, I get up and head straight for my mom's room.

She sleeps with the door open, so I peep inside to check if she's still awake before going in. She's up, sitting in bed just scrolling on her phone.

"Everything okay?" she asks, putting her phone down on the nightstand.

"Can I come in?" I say instead of answering her question. I know I don't have to ask—she leaves her door open for a reason—but maybe hearing her specifically tell me it's okay will make this conversation easier.

"Of course, mijo." She scoots over and pats the spot beside her.

A weight I didn't realize I was carrying floats away as I go to sit on her bed. "Everything's okay, but . . ." I shift, wanting to move closer but not feeling ready. Maybe if I was leaning on her or something it'd be easier to get the words out. "I want to get better about saying stuff," I say, but the "stuff" remains in my throat.

"What's on your mind?" she asks. I thought me coming in here late would worry her, but she looks more relieved than anything.

"So, um . . . I think I get why you didn't know what to do with me. I was kind of out of control," I say as I dig my fingers into the comforter to ground me.

"I still should have told you before sending you with your abuela," she says with a sad look on her face. "I'll always be sorry for the way all that happened."

"I mean, yeah. I wish you had told me, but that's not what I was even mad about."

She tilts her head in a question mark but gives me the space to go on without pushing.

"I would have been mad anyway. It didn't matter what you did," I admit, adjusting my grip on the comforter. "You did exactly what I wanted you to do. I *wanted* to get disowned and mean nothing to anyone anymore. But when I thought it happened, I was pissed anyway." I feel myself choking up, but I have to keep going or I'll never say it. "Maybe I was just mad at myself, and I blamed everyone else so I wouldn't have to face it."

I finally move my hand from the comforter to wipe my eyes, which are now apparently leaking. My mom offers her hand when I pull mine away from my face, and I take it. She must know I still have more to say, because she just squeezes my hand as a silent encouragement. I let out a shaky breath, trying to will myself to say what I'm thinking, no matter how shameful it feels.

"I saw how you stopped sleeping when you noticed I did. You were always so protective of me, to the point where it was hurting you. I didn't want that, but it was what I was used to. You walked on eggshells like I was a land mine. And I always thought that was the reason everyone was so afraid of me going off. Like we all knew I was gonna take everyone out with me." My voice cracks as my mom starts rubbing her thumb along the back of my hand. "I didn't want that, but I . . . kind of expected it? Like if I died, I thought you'd never recover. And when you sent me to Abuela's, I thought it meant I was wrong, and that I could just go out alone. Which is what I wanted! But . . ."

I can't finish my sentence anymore since we're both crying now. She doesn't seem to have the words either, so she starts stroking my hair while I try to catch my breath.

"I want to unhurt everyone. I want to fix it. I just . . . ," I manage to get out between broken sniffles. "I don't want to be like a bomb anymore!"

"You were never a bomb, mijo." She pulls me to her chest and rubs my back. "You're the sun," she whispers, holding me closer still. "My beautiful son."

And in this moment, she's not holding me like a grenade she'd sacrifice herself to protect the world from. Right now, she's holding me like I'm the sunrise she wouldn't miss for anything. She's holding me like the world could end any second and she'd still hold on. Like we're protecting each other.

We just hold on like that for a while before we're finally ready to say goodnight. Eventually she kisses the top of my head and gives a final squeeze before I go to let her sleep.

When I get back to my room, I find myself heading straight for the drawer that's been hiding my poetry notebook, the promise ring, cross necklace, and jaguar necklace.

I take out the jaguar necklace and wrap my fist around it.

I don't know if I'm ready to face my fears yet, but maybe putting this back on will help me get there.

38

WHEN YOU'RE DONE HIDING

boldness

I don't know what I was expecting coming to school the next week, but I could really do without the stares and sympathetic looks. With what happened at the lake being all over the news, I don't think there's a single person in the halls who doesn't whisper about it when I pass them.

I get some acknowledging nods, and one person I never interacted with even congratulated me on Nick's arrest. For the most part, though, it's just inaudible murmurs. I'm kind of wishing I had showed up to school late, just so I wouldn't have to deal with the excruciating downtime before class.

Relief washes over me when it's finally a familiar face approaching.

"You're back!" Avery says with a smile. Despite his friendly tone, the dark circles under his eyes and the way he's shifting his weight say he's seriously stressed out.

"You good?" I ask, not bothering with the awkward small talk.

"I mean, we don't have to go there. You're probably more stressed about it than I am."

"About what?" Honestly, I've been too busy having emotional breakthroughs left and right to remember what I'm supposed to be stressed about.

"The trial? Are you not freaking out?"

Oh. That. "Not really," I say. I hadn't really thought about it, but I don't think I can handle putting myself through something like that right now. "I'm probably not gonna testify."

"I get it." Avery nods his understanding. Knowing how against snitching Avery is, I would have expected him to say the same thing, but instead he says, "Don't worry, though. I got you."

"What do you mean?" Is Avery actually planning on testifying against Nick?

"I still have that lawyer helping me. He thinks I might be able to clear my record if I tell my story now that Nick's on trial for attempted murder." He shifts his weight again. "I get why you don't want to testify, but maybe think about it?"

On instinct, I want to get defensive about the insinuation I haven't thought about it, even though it's true. I've definitely been avoiding thinking about Nick after what happened. If I don't see him for the rest of my life it'd be too soon. So testifying against him in a courtroom he's physically in isn't exactly on my to do list.

"I won't do it." This time, it's more than a vague "probably not." I'm sure.

"Yeah, I mean, that's fair." Avery doesn't try to convince me, which I appreciate. I think he gets it, since it's taken him this long to decide to speak out against Nick himself.

The bell rings then, and we both go our separate ways to class. In astronomy, Jamal and I get to partner up to work on our senior projects. When I go to sit next to him, his eyes immediately find the jaguar necklace around my neck. He smiles, cracking his swollen lip even more.

"You haven't worn that in a while," he points out.

"Yeah, well, I think I'm ready to face my fears," I say, looking up at him, taking in his bruised face. I did that. Maybe not directly, but it was my fault.

All I want to do is lean forward and touch his swollen cheek with the tips of my fingers. I want to kiss his bruised eye and busted lips until they heal. I want to do this, in front of everyone.

"So, I'm having another stupid thing next weekend. Want to come?" he asks.

My ears burn at the memory of me ditching the first open mic Jamal was hosting. "It's not a stupid thing. I shouldn't have said that. I'm really sorry." Shit, apologizing never gets easier, does it?

"I forgive you," he says, and I know he's not just talking about me calling his open mic a stupid thing. He's talking about all of it. Somehow, he forgives me for all of it.

Whether I deserve his love or not, I have it. And no matter how much I hate myself, I love Jamal more.

"I'll be there," I say. "Wouldn't miss it for the world."

Unfortunately, people haven't seemed to get the gossiping out of their systems by the end of the day. I guess several students attempting to murder another student is more interesting a topic than the usual who's hooking up or fighting with who.

I just ignore the stares and start looking for Bianca. While I'm still on my apology spree, I might as well give one more. I find her in the courtyard. She folds her arms and frowns at me.

"I owe you an apology," I say, determined to bang them all out.

"Damn right you do," she starts, but when I get closer, her eyes widen when she sees the bruises on my face. "Nick really did that?" she asks, the steam from her anger evaporating into thin air.

I just get on with it, ignoring the question. "I owe you an apology because you were right. I used you too."

"Well, yeah, I thought we were both kind of doing that." I figured Bianca knew we were using each other after our last conversation, but I didn't realize how little it seemed to matter to her. "Why are you bringing it up now?"

"I just thought you should know I didn't love you like that. I know you probably didn't love me either, but I'm in love with someone else," I say, and I see Jamal from across the courtyard heading in our direction. He looks at me like he knows what I'm about to say. I touch the jaguar necklace for strength. "I'm in love with a guy," I say, not caring who might hear. "And I'm learning to love myself, and that means taking accountability. I hope you can get there someday too."

Her face scrunches like she's offended. "Don't talk like you know me like that."

"No, but Yami did. You act like she's the one in the wrong for walking away, without asking yourself why she'd want to do that. I might not know you like that, but Yami knew you better than anyone, and she left. Maybe ask yourself why."

She opens her mouth like she's about to go off, but nothing

comes out. Instead she just turns around and quickly walks away. I can admit that wasn't the most successful apology, but at least I said something.

Jamal's still walking toward me, close enough now to have heard all of that. I turn toward him to meet him halfway.

"Need a ride?" he asks with a smile.

"I'd like that."

39

WHEN YOU JUST HAVE TO TAKE IT ONE DAY AT A TIME

maintenance

"I told you, I'm not gonna testify," I say for what feels like the millionth time. Yami found out Nick's trial is coming up, and Jamal must have mentioned to her that I'm not planning on going.

"He tried to kill you!" Yami says as she paces my room. "Don't you want him to face consequences?"

I just shrug. I may be ready to face *some* of my fears, but my jaguar necklace has no bearing on how I never want to see Nick's face again. "Why should I have to if there were witnesses? Jamal and Avery are gonna testify. That should be enough."

"What if it's not?" She throws up her arms. "What if they get away with it and do the same thing to someone else? What if they come after *you* again?"

"Maybe Jamal and Avery's testimonies will be enough, maybe they won't. But I just want to enjoy whatever time I don't have to think about Nick while I have it, okay? Can we just drop it?"

Yami stops pacing, then reaches for her phone in her pocket and lets out a breath, like she's trying to make a decision. "Okay," she finally says, then pulls out her phone and leaves the room.

That was easier than expected.

I feel like I have to move, so I leave my room too. I know Yami was trying to help, but I'm just anxious now. When I go to the kitchen to fill up my bottle with ice water, there's a knock on the door. I expect it to be mail or something, so I take my time filling up my water instead of answering it.

I guess I take too long, because Yami comes out of her room to get it before I even leave the kitchen. Before either of us make it to the door, though, there's another, louder, knock.

I'm not proud to say I recognize the knock. Bianca's been our neighbor and Yami's best friend basically our whole lives, and her "You're taking too long to answer the door!" knock is distinctive.

"You invited Bianca?"

Instead of answering, Yami stands in front of the door and takes a deep breath before opening it. I follow behind her, more curious than anything.

"I unblocked your number so you could text me back, not show up at my house," Yami says as she opens the door.

Bianca just stands there, staring at Yami like she's a ghost or something.

"What are you doing here?" I ask.

"I don't know . . . taking your advice, I guess," she says hesitantly, then turns to Yami. "I, um, I got your text. I'll do it."

"Do what?" I ask, feeling completely out of the loop. Then again, I guess this is the first time they're interacting on purpose since Yami came out.

Finally Bianca looks at me. "I'm gonna testify against Nick. I think I have some shit on him that'll help."

"Oh, um . . . thanks," I say. No matter how bad I want to avoid thinking about Nick, it's comforting to know there's someone else who can vouch for me.

"So, Yami . . . can we talk?" Bianca asks, nervously shifting her weight between her feet. I wasn't really trying to give Bianca advice before, but maybe she really does want to take accountability now.

Yami hesitates for a second before opening the door wider. "Okay."

Then she goes to her room, and Bianca follows.

I'm almost too shocked to move. I can think of several ways that conversation could go sideways, but I figure I should mind my own business. I resist the urge to eavesdrop and head to my room, getting out my poetry notebook as a distraction.

Jamal's open mic is coming up, and I think it'd be a good time for me to branch out. I wrap my fist around my jaguar necklace. I might not be good at poetry, but I want to practice being more honest. I want to share something I like doing without worrying about it being perfect. Just poetry for the sake of expression.

I write and write, not bothering to edit as I go, just getting it all out. When I'm done, I feel proud of what I've made. Not because it's perfect, but because it's true.

The door to Yami's room opens just as I'm finishing, so I head over to check on her. Bianca's on her way out, and she gives me a little nod that feels almost like a thank you. Then she's gone.

When I go in Yami's room, her body language is hard to read. She doesn't look angry or happy. Maybe just relaxed.

"How did that go?" I ask.

"Good," she says, looking thoughtful. "I mean, I don't think we're ever gonna be friends again, but . . . I guess I don't have to waste energy hating her anymore."

A heavy weight lifts from my shoulders at that. Not because I particularly care about Bianca's redemption arc, but because Yami's not hurting about what happened anymore. Maybe that means there's hope for everyone I've hurt. Maybe they'll all be okay, even with me still in the picture.

I refuse to repeat my mistake from last time, so I make sure to invite everyone I know and their mother to Jamal's open mic next weekend. It's just one of many ways I plan to start making things up to him. The other plan involves me walking to the mall after school to get Jamal a gift as a peace offering. I'll give it to him tonight for our second-to-last astronomy viewing. We still have another one to do since we didn't exactly get a lot of work done last time.

This time, Mami actually lets me go without a chaperone. I think she trusts Jamal enough to know he'll keep me safe, which I appreciate.

Once we get to the viewpoint, we climb into the bed of the truck together, this time with a nicer telescope. We sit closer to each other this time, our shoulders barely touching while we take turns looking at the sky and writing down our trajectories.

It only takes so long before we're finished, but when we are, neither of us moves to go back in the truck.

Jamal looks at me intensely. "Are you in pain?" he finally asks.

"A little," I admit, though it's an understatement. My head still hurts where the rock hit me, and even though the bruises are heal-ing, my whole body is still sore. "Are you?"

"A little . . . ," he says as his eyes trail tenderly across different parts of my face, probably from one bruise to the other.

I don't know how long we've just been staring at each other when he breaks the silence.

"Who were you talking about earlier, when you were talking to Bianca? The guy you're . . . in love with," he asks, his eyes hold-ing an equal amount of fear and hope.

I pause before answering as I reach into my backpack for what I brought him.

Jamal smiles as I pull out a bottle of the "couples" cologne that the mall kiosk lady had originally offered Jamal.

"Took me forever to find this scent, but I figured . . . if we're gonna have matching cologne, we might as well use the right kind, right?"

"Is this your way of asking me out?" Jamal laughs.

"Yeah," I say with a nervous smile. This was so much smoother in my head. "I still love you, Jamal."

"I still love you, too," Jamal says, but his smile fades, and I can't read his expression anymore. "But I don't know. I have a lot of questions."

"Like what?"

"Are you asking because you're manic? You just got out of the hospital, so I don't want to move too fast. I don't know if we're ready yet."

I think on that for a second. It's hard to tell if I'm manic or not sometimes, but if Jamal thinks I am, then I don't want to seem like I'm being impulsive. "I can be patient," I finally say. "I don't always have the right answers, but I want to prove myself to you. We can wait until we're both sure."

Jamal brings a tender hand toward a bruise on my cheek. I almost think he's gonna pull me in for a kiss when he just says, "Question."

"Yeah?" I answer breathlessly.

"Why did you do that?" he asks, sad eyes moving from the bruise on my cheek to a cut on my chin.

"Do what?" He could be talking about anything. Why did I write a manic manifesto about suicide? Why did I show up in his neighborhood that night? Why did I just ask him out?

"Why did you keep antagonizing Nick? Avery and I had it handled. They were going to leave you alone before you hit him."

Oh. That. "They tried to kill me!" I say defensively, even though that part was exactly what I wanted. "They could have tried to kill you, too. I wasn't about to let that happen."

"They *could* have killed you!" Jamal's frustrated tone confuses me.

"I would do anything to protect you, Jamal. That's why I hurt you in the first place. I know I was misguided, and it was wrong, but I was trying to protect you. And I wanted to protect you from them, too. It didn't matter if they'd kill me for it. I would die for you," I say, and I mean it.

Jamal touches my cheek again, gently rubbing his thumb along the bruise. "I'd rather you live for me."

I put my hand over his and close my eyes. That would be easier said than done. But if I want to prove myself to Jamal, I can't exactly go dying on him. And as long as Jamal's there to call me at seven o'clock, I can take it one day at a time. "I can do that," I finally say.

"Promise?" He holds out his pinky.

I nod, and I really mean it. "You're worth living for, Jamal. I promise."

I take his pinky in mine.

40

WHEN YOU CHIP AWAY THE WORST PARTS TO MAKE SOMETHING BEAUTIFUL

rehabilitation

I haven't had one-on-one therapy with Dr. Lee since before going to the hospital, but I'm actually kind of eager for it. She gives me a surprisingly regular-sized smile when I sit on the couch across from her. Since I actually know what I want to talk about today, I just jump into it.

"Do you think I'm capable of being in a healthy relationship?" I almost don't want to hear the answer, but I'm also desperate for professional confirmation.

"Are you capable of it? Of course," she says as she writes something in her notepad. "Whether you're ready for it is another question entirely, and one only you can answer."

I sigh, trying my best not to roll my eyes. "I get that you're trying to be all cryptic and therapist-y, but can you at least tell me *how* to answer the question for myself?"

Micro smile. "Healthy relationships take a lot of work, both on yourself and with your partner. If you're willing to work on the things that have hurt you and your partner in the past, I think that's a great sign."

"I am," I reassure her. "I know it's not gonna be a quick fix, but I want to try at least. I promised Jamal I'd live for him. That's something, right?"

Even after knowing her all this time, the expression Dr. Lee gives at that is too micro for me to decipher. "For now, if that's what you need to make it to the next day, that's a good thing."

"What do you mean for now?" I ask. I kind of thought I had hacked the whole suicidal ideation thing with that promise. As long as I have Jamal, I can make it another day. Why would that be only good for now?

"Well, it's a promising first step," she says. "I'd love to see you get to a point where it doesn't take an external force to give you the will to live. But like I said, for now, anything to keep you going another day is a good sign in my book."

I frown. "You're telling me you don't live for any external reasons? You just live . . . because you *want* to?"

She nods. "I'm not saying life doesn't get hard for all of us, but having to search for an external reason to live isn't something your average person struggles with."

"I don't know, that sounds fake."

Micro smile. "What I mean to say is that life is a lot less painful when you live for the things that make you happy, instead of living to keep someone else from grieving. When you live only to avoid the grief of people you love, you end up shouldering all that grief on your own, mourning yourself while you're still here."

I can't even respond to that. I never thought of it like that, but maybe that's exactly what I've been doing. I've been grieving the person I thought everyone wanted me to be. But when they thought I was going to die, it wasn't that person they wanted to save, it was *me*.

Just me.

When I get home, I finally gather up the courage to pull up my email to delete the message that kick-started my spiraling. I don't mean to, but I can't help but read it one last time.

> **Subject: Re: been a long time . . .**
>
> I know it's taken me a long time to explain my thoughts here, and I apologize for that. I thought maybe if I gave it some time, things would work themselves out on their own, but I guess I can't make you change. I got your email and thought, it better be good. But you're both still doing what you're doing.
>
> I can't lie to you. I'm very disappointed.
>
> You and your sister have been brainwashed, and I can acknowledge that my absence in the last few years has made this harder on all of us. But I can't pretend to support what I know in my heart is not right.
>
> If you only take one thing I say to heart, let it be this: It doesn't matter what anyone has tried to convince you until now. What you're doing is a choice. And you're making the wrong one. I can't just sit around and enable my kids to choose this lifestyle over family, and over God. You're both throwing away my legacy and your own futures.
>
> I won't force you, but whatever you choose, you get to live with the consequences.

I want to delete it not just from my email but from my memory. But for some reason, I can't bring myself to erase the evidence. Honestly, my dad is basically dead to me, but that doesn't mean the influence he left isn't still there.

He's the one who showed me the poem I keep taped up in my and Yami's bathroom. He's the reason I'm so attached to my jaguar necklace. The reason I feel such a strong connection to my heritage.

And even though he's the reason those things came into my life, he doesn't get to sour them for me now. So, instead of deleting the email, I grab a marker, print it out, and start blacking out the words I don't want to see.

If he can pick and choose Bible verses to live by, I can pick and choose which of his words I take to heart. I don't have to erase all of him, but he doesn't get to dictate how I feel about what he left behind.

By the time I'm done, I have a new poem to go alongside the code of the heart in the bathroom. I tape it to the mirror next to my other motto.

I can't pretend

my heart is not right.

If you   let it be   It

is a choice. And

I

choose this   family, and

my   future.

I   choose   to

live

41

WHEN YOU JUST WANT TO PUNCH HIM IN THE MOUTH . . . WITH YOUR MOUTH . . . FOR A LONG TIME

heightened sexuality

Before leaving to meet Jamal for our final astronomy night, I grab what used to be the Jamal section of my poetry notebook, all the pages now held together in a binder just for him. I put the binder in my bag and head out. This time, it's not an impulsive decision, but something I've wanted to share with him as long as I've had the notebook.

When we get to the dirt road and climb into the bed of his truck, I can't help but stare at him while he watches the sky. Jamal always made me feel loved. More than that, he made me feel *worthy* of love. Looking back on everything, it hurts knowing that I didn't do the same for him, at least not intentionally.

"I'm sorry," I eventually say. The phrase gets slightly less painful, but no more comfortable every time.

"For what?" Jamal asks as he puts the telescope down to look at me.

My fingers twitch, since our hands are so close to touching, but I don't know if he'd want me to hold his hand. Jamal looks down, always noticing the tiny ways he affects me. Apparently, he's okay with it, because he turns his palm up, and I slip my fingers through his. He squeezes as if to encourage me to go on.

"You always wanted me to know I deserved to be loved. Even when I was awful to you, you made sure I knew I was loved. Maybe I never told you because it just seems like the most obvious thing, but you deserve to be loved, too. I'm sorry I didn't show you how much I loved you. I'm sorry I didn't tell you how important you are to me."

Jamal smiles. "You didn't have to say that."

"But I *should* have. I loved you the whole time I was treating you like shit, and if you ever felt like you weren't loved, or didn't deserve to be loved because of how I treated you, I want to fix that. So . . . I have something I want to show you."

I reach into my backpack and hand him the binder.

"What's this?" he asks, eyeing the binder before opening it like it's booby-trapped or something.

"Proof," I say tentatively. "You were always everything to me, Jamal. There was never a day you weren't an integral part of my universe." I smile at the words Jamal himself gave me. "These are all poems I wrote about you. Some of them are really old, like from before we even started dating. This isn't me trying to convince you that we're ready to get back together or anything. It's just me trying to be more honest. This is how I really felt, and I'm not interested in hiding anymore. Not from you, or anyone else."

"I didn't know you wrote poetry," Jamal says softly as he opens the binder.

"I haven't told anyone else," I say, cheeks still warm, but not from nerves. "So I thought about what you said before. If we ever do get back together, I want it to be healthy. But I don't know if there's ever gonna be a time we can be 100 percent sure it won't go wrong, you know? There won't be any clear-cut signal to tell us I'm officially 'better' enough to be capable of a relationship. But I'm done running away when things get real. I'm done keeping my fears to myself. No matter what happens with us, I want to work on that."

He's quiet for a bit, his fingers tracing the pages of the binder, but his eyes still on me.

"Can I read these?" he finally asks.

I laugh. "That's why I'm giving them to you. You don't have to read them right now, but they're yours. They're all for you."

Jamal starts reading one of the poems right in front of me and smiles. "You're my universe too, Cesar," he says with zero hesitation. "I know you have a lot to work out. I'm ready to get back together, but if you're not—"

"I'm ready," I say as I bring his hand my lips and kiss the healing scabs on his knuckles, one by one.

He leans forward and presses his forehead against mine, taking both my hands in his. I hold my breath, praying he wants this as bad as I do. He kisses me, softly since we're both still healing, but fully.

We open our eyes at the same time in between kisses, just to look at each other. To make sure we're both still here. I can feel the "I love you" lingering in his eyes. I tell him I love him too, with my lips. I cup his face in my hands and tenderly kiss the faded bruises on his cheek, his swollen eye, his busted lip, as if my mouth can heal all of it. My mouth moves to his neck, and I kiss there too, leaving a mark of my own.

He lets out a sigh of pleasure, and I keep going. My hands softly travel to his chest and stomach, feeling the slight dips of muscle but not pressing too hard. I lift his shirt and kiss those bruises too. I kiss everywhere that looks like it hurts, wishing my lips would magically right my wrongs. I pull away again to look at him. Sometimes I can't decide if I'd rather touch him or kiss him or just stare, he's that beautiful. He stares back.

Shoulders relaxed, lips parted slightly, eyes doting as he looks into mine.

"I want to be with you," I say breathlessly. I've never been more sure of anything.

"Are you still manic?" Jamal asks.

"I don't know, maybe?" I say honestly. I think I'm coming down from it, but it's a little hard to tell.

"Do you want to be with me when you're not manic?" he asks.

"Of course I do." I always want to be with Jamal. Even when I fooled myself into thinking that leaving him in the dust was good for him. I still wanted him.

Jamal brings the back of my hand to his lips and kisses it. "I want to be with you too."

I kiss him again, longer this time, letting myself fully sink into it. He brings a hand behind my neck, and I lean in to him, trying my best not to kiss too hard and hurt his lip. When we pull away, I lean my head on his shoulder.

"So I changed my mind about something," I say after a long moment of pause.

"About what?"

"I told you I'd live for you. I wanted to prove to you I'd do anything for you. That I wanted you back badly enough to stay alive."

"What are you saying?" he asks, and his pained expression hurts more than the bruises.

"I'll live. But not for you," I say, snuggling closer to him. "I want to live for me."

42

WHEN YOU'RE LOVED ANYWAY

euphoria

Since I've kind of been neglecting Hunter as a friend, I offer to meet up with him before the open mic. I'm half expecting him to ignore me since I've been a shitty friend, but he texts back right away saying he'll meet me at the coffee shop an hour early.

Before heading out, I stare at the promise ring and the cross necklace still left in my drawer. I take a deep breath before grabbing the promise ring and putting it on.

Then I look at the necklace.

I decide I'll put this one on when I'm sure I'm no longer manic. For now, I can accept a complicated relationship with God, like Zo said.

When I arrive at the coffee shop, it's clear why Jamal picked it to host his queer-friendly open mics as soon as I walk in. There are flags everywhere, and not the American kind. The progress flag, rainbow flag, and trans flag are plastered all over the shop. Jamal told me that even the name, Brick Road, is a nod to an old euphemism people used to find other LGBTQ+ folk. I guess being a "friend of Dorothy" meant you were gay. So the whole coffee shop is Wizard of Oz themed.

A quick scan of the area shows me Hunter isn't here yet. I get to the front of the line and order a cinnamon roll latte, then wait at one of the tables. It's only a couple minutes before he shows up. The barista greets him enthusiastically, and they chat for a bit before he orders his drink. It's not until after he orders that he notices I'm already here.

"What is *up*, Flores! How've you been?" he says enthusiastically. I don't know if he's just excited to see me after a while, or if it's the open mic or something else, but he definitely seems a little more cheery than usual, if that's possible. I instinctually go for the bro hug I'm used to from him, but then he extends his arms and pulls me into a full-on bear hug, squeezing hard and almost picking me up off the floor.

"I've been . . . ," I start as we both sit down. I'm not sure if I should wreck the mood by being honest or not. But I'm done pretending everything is fine when it's not. Hunter is good people. He'll understand. "Not great, honestly. I'm getting better, though."

"Good to hear you're getting better," he says. "Do you want to talk about it?"

"Maybe another time. Uh, what about you?" I ask awkwardly. Small talk is a little weird with anyone but Jamal for me. But I do want to know how he's been.

"I'm great, I'm great. So, hey, I have a question for you."

"What's up?" I ask, already feeling nervous.

"You know your friend Avery? Uh, do you happen to know if he's, like . . . um, straight?"

I tense up a bit at the question. "Why does it matter?"

"This is a little awkward, but . . ." Hunter's ears and cheeks go completely red. "I might have, like, a little crush. . . ."

"Wait, *you're* not straight?" I feel like I just took a pie to the face.

"I mean, I don't know. I guess not? I'm just as shocked as you are, believe me." He laughs all nervous.

"So you like Avery? Since when?"

"Well, we went to that concert together, you know? And we just kind of hit it off, and . . . I don't know, man. I'm just kind of figuring all this out. I guess I'm bi?"

I can't hold back my smile, which makes him blush harder and retract his neck like a startled turtle. Why does he seem so nervous to tell me? "I'm bi too, remember?" I remind him.

"Wait, you don't like Avery too, do you?"

It hits me then that my defensiveness over being asked if Avery was straight probably didn't give Hunter the best impression. "Don't worry, he's all yours."

"Oh, thank God." Hunter holds a hand to his heart like he's having chest pain.

"You must really like him, then, huh?" I ask.

"Yeah." His face gets even more red, and he smiles so big I'm surprised his lips don't crack.

The rest of the time until the open mic passes before we know it. Jamal is one of the first to show up, then Avery, Moni and Abuela, Mami, Doña Violeta, Yami, Bo, and our friends from Slayton.

Hunter and I had saved some seats for everyone, so we can all sit together. Jamal doesn't notice the ring on my finger until after he sits down next to me. I swear his sudden smile could light up the bottom of the Pacific. I let the ring be the proof that I'm done hiding him away. He takes my hand in his, right in front of everyone, and kisses the ring, then the back of my hand.

Maybe my PDA with Jamal gives Hunter some confidence, because he turns to Avery and asks if he wants to hang out again. I'm not sure if Avery realizes Hunter is trying to ask him out or not, but he agrees nonetheless.

Then I notice Abuela and Doña Violeta go to sit together, and since I still don't think they've told anyone else about their situation, I pretend not to notice that they're holding hands under the table.

But then I catch Moni's eyes and see she's also noticing Abuela and Violeta holding hands. Her mouth is dropped open in a huge smile and she gives me a thumbs-up, mouthing the words "I did it!" even though she had nothing to do with this pairing.

A sign-up sheet for the open mic gets passed around, and with Jamal's encouragement, I gather the courage to put my own name on the list.

Jamal stands at the mic when the event starts, introducing the mission of the open mic, which is to amplify queer voices and create a safe space for LGBTQ+ creatives to share their hearts on stage. He leads off the open mic with a queer love poem about falling in love a second time with your first love.

A musician follows his act with a few gay love songs, inviting people to get up and dance. Yami and Bo giggle as they slow dance together. Doña Violeta takes Abuela's hand, hips swaying to the music, and Abuela reluctantly steps into rhythm with her.

If you had told me a month ago that Abuela would be dancing and laughing like this for everyone to see, I would have said you're crazier than me.

Eventually Jamal calls *my* name, and the crowd looks around expectantly for someone named Cesar to come to the stage. I take a deep breath and force my feet to move one by one until I'm in front of the crowd.

I let out my breath and pull the spoken-word piece I've written out of my pocket, unfolding the paper in my shaking hands. I can do this.

> The first thing I learned after my bipolar diagnosis was to keep my mouth shut.
>
> You don't tell anyone when you're manic that you can talk to God.
>
> You don't tell anyone when you're depressed that you haven't showered in a week.
>
> You don't tell anyone that you think your meds are being used to mind control you, because it's better to be dead than crazy.
>
> You don't ask your mom for the day off school because God told you to kill yourself, and you're afraid if you get out of bed for class you just might. You don't ask for the day off, because it's better to be dead than crazy.
>
> And most importantly, you can't ask for help. They'll think you're crazy.
>
> Crazy, according to Google: adjective. Mentally deranged in a wild or aggressive manner. Used in a sentence: 'She went crazy and assaulted a visitor.'
>
> Noun. Mentally deranged. Used in a sentence: 'Keep that crazy away from me.'

Deranged: Adjective: mad, insane. Used in a
sentence: 'The gunman was deranged.'

So, for a long time, I kept my mouth shut. I don't
bother telling them I feel guilty killing mosquitos, or
that I can't hurt the monsters playing Undertale. It
wouldn't matter if they knew I was crazy. So, for a
long time, I kept my mouth shut.

No one needs to be reminded I'm crazy. No one
needs to know how, even though I can talk to God and
he talks back, I still feel alone.

I don't tell anyone, even when God tells me to kill
myself, because I learned it's better to be dead than to
be crazy.

It was never the voices in my head telling me that,
though. It's my peers, movies, TV, comics, video games,
Google, even myself.

But I'm not better dead.

I won't stay silent anymore, so go ahead and call
me crazy.

Maybe I am crazy.

Crazy . . . and alive.

Everyone snaps supportively, and I go back to my seat feeling lighter than I've felt in a long time. It's not a "good" poem necessarily. It's unedited and rough, but it's a big step for me. Jamal kisses me again, and I can't tell if I'm still manic, or if this euphoric feeling is real. The coffee tastes divine, the music has us all dancing, and the love is warm.

It isn't until I hear God's familiar voice in my ear, repeating the signal he had for me before, that I'm sure.

It is time to come home, my son.

So I am still manic. But it's okay. No one here will let me hurt myself, and I don't want to anymore. I squeeze Jamal's hand tighter and look around the room at everyone I love. Who loves me.

Maybe I'll have a complicated relationship with God for the rest of my life. Maybe I don't know what to call God anymore. I don't know what's holy and what isn't. Maybe God really is just the universe, or science, or all of it, including Jamal and me and my family and friends and everyone and everything in existence. Maybe we're all a little bit sacred.

Until now, I thought the thing I was most afraid of was going to hell, but I'm done pretending to be something I'm not to find my way to heaven.

The world, God, and the entire universe can disapprove of what I have with Jamal, but my entire universe *is* Jamal. It's Yami. It's all of them. If there's a heaven without them, I don't want it.

I look around at all the people sacred to me. I know being loved doesn't mean I'm magically fixed. It doesn't mean my life will be easy, or that I won't one day hit another rock bottom and do all of this over again. But there will also be moments like this. There will always be little glimpses of heaven I don't have to die for.

And that's enough to keep me going until I find the next one. I even look forward to it.

EPILOGUE

"Okay, you go first," Yami says over the phone as I lie in bed in my Barrett dorm room. She had this idea for a game she wants to try. Since she moved to Flagstaff with Bo to go to NAU, our sibling telepathy doesn't work over long distances. So the game is to take turns saying the usually unspoken thing out loud.

"Umm . . . I don't think I've ever been more sore in my life," I admit. I can hardly move from my spot in bed, completely exhausted from a long day of helping Abuela move in with Doña Violeta. She says she wanted to move there to be closer to Mami without them having to get on each other's last nerve, but I happen to know better.

I think back to the time I accidentally saw Doña Violeta braiding Abuela's hair. The time they held hands under the table at Jamal's open mic. I smile to myself and roll over in bed. I'll keep their secret as long as they want me to.

"That doesn't count." I can almost hear Yami's eye roll. "You have to say something you normally wouldn't. Like, imagine I can read your mind, but it's the stuff you wouldn't say out loud."

"Okay. I miss you." I don't hesitate to admit it.

"I miss you, too."

"You can't steal my thing," I scold with a finger raised even though she can't see. "You have to say something different."

She laughs before sighing and saying, "I wonder if I made the right choice by coming here."

"Do you like it there?" I ask.

"I really, really love it," she says.

"What's the problem then?"

"I just worry about you and Mami, you know?"

"We're doing all right. This is the first time I think you've *ever* done something for you. You definitely made the right choice. But if you miss us so much, maybe we should do a weekend trip up there," I say, as if it's only her missing us and not the other way around.

We spend the next few minutes planning a trip before saying our goodbyes. My alarm goes off a few minutes later to take my meds. It's been a new development, trying to take them in the evening instead of the morning. Dr. Lee thinks this might make me less tired during the day, and it seems to be working out well so far.

I get out of bed and pop my meds in my mouth, swallowing them with a swig of my water bottle. I know now I'll probably have to be on medication for the rest of my life, but that doesn't mean I'm broken or bad. Some people's brains make mental stability for free, and I just so happen to have to get mine at the pharmacy, and fuck anyone who tries to make me feel any kind of way about it.

I check my phone to see a text from Moni with a link to her new online store, which she rebranded into the Tampossibilities. Now she sells discreet packages disguised as period products. She's not officially selling anything illegal, but she fully hints that you can hide weed in there. I'm not surprised she's already figured something else out that seems to be taking off, but it's still a relief to see it working out for her.

My phone buzzes again with a text from Jamal, and I can't help but smile as I read it.

Jamal: Stars are beautiful tonight. Meet me at the secret garden?

He doesn't have to ask me twice. I'm already throwing on my sweater and hopping into some jeans, and I'm out the door before my roommate can ask where I'm headed.

I make my way into the secret garden, fully ignoring the flowers, roses, and fountain in favor of the beautiful man waiting for me. He's sitting on a bench looking up at the sky, so mesmerized by the stars he barely notices me until I sit right next to him and kiss his cheek. He smiles and turns his head to return my kiss, our lips softly colliding like we haven't seen each other all day, which we haven't.

He takes my hand in his, and the love in his gaze rushes over me.

"I love you." I answer his unspoken declaration as I kiss the back of his hand, letting the warmth of his adoration envelop me like a blanket. We stare into each other's eyes instead of at the stars. He's beautiful, and he's here, and I'm alive. I'm alive. I'm alive.

RESOURCES

If you or someone you know is struggling with mental health, here are some resources that may help:

The Trevor Project:

www.thetrevorproject.org

National Alliance on Mental Illness:

www.nami.org

988 Suicide and Crisis Lifeline:

www.988lifeline.org

ACKNOWLEDGMENTS

This book has been, by far, the most difficult to finish. I'm used to writing personal books with some heavy topics, but this one was the first I worked on while still actively going through those hardships. I wasn't fully healed when I wrote it, and I'm still not, but this book helped me in ways I hadn't imagined possible. I really hope it can do the same for others. So, thank you, me, for doing the thing! That was so hard. Good job!

With that out of the way, I want to thank everyone who helped make this book possible. Thank you to my agent, Alexandra Levick, for being such an incredible advocate from the very beginning. To Alessandra Balzer, who took a chance on *The Lesbiana's Guide to Catholic School* and believed in Cesar's story enough to take a chance on him, too. To Carolina Mancheno Ortiz, for helping me bring this story to its full potential and being so patient with all the revision delays—this book was a difficult one to write, but the patience from my publishing team allowed me to take the time I needed to care for myself while working on it.

I also want to thank the rest of the team at HarperCollins, especially Meghan Pettit, Shona McCarthy, Samantha Brown, and Shannon Cox for all the work that went into bringing this book to life and into the hands of readers. Thank you to Jessie S. Gang for yet another incredible cover design and to Be Fernández for bringing it to life! This book is everything I could have hoped for thanks to you all!

Thank you to Stray Kids for giving me some much-needed serotonin while I was at my lowest. As a treat, there are two Stray Kids references in this book, so I also have to thank everyone who found the more obscure one. You get a cookie!

I couldn't have done this alone, so thank you to all the family and friends who have supported me. Thank you to all my beta readers for encouraging me before this book was any good. Thank you especially to Lee Call for the hours upon hours of metaphorical blood and literal sweat and tears we've shared through this whole journey.

And, finally, thank you, Lalo, for being the first one to show me I wasn't alone. This book exists so others will know it, too. Rest well, primo.